WHERE
LOST
GIRLS
GO

BOOKS BY B.R. SPANGLER

WHERE LOST GIRLS GO

B.R. SPANGLER

Bookouture

Published by Bookouture in 2020

An imprint of Storyfire Ltd.
Carmelite House
50 Victoria Embankment
London EC4Y 0DZ

www.bookouture.com

ISBN: 978-1-80019-068-9
eBook ISBN: 978-1-83888-255-6

Previously published as *Taken from Home* (978-1-83888-256-3)

To my friends and family for their love, support and patience.

PROLOGUE

I imagined you riding your bike today. You would have been five years old. Given the date, if I tried really hard, I could say your age to the minute too. I know. Mothers always do.

In my story, your hair has grown to your shoulders like mine, and you look a lot like your father. But sometimes, I can see my mother's face as well. Your dimples are like charms that everyone enjoys, along with your light-blue eyes, full of joy and bright like starlight. So, yes, you are five and we've just put your first bicycle together.

"Training wheels," I'd insisted.

"No thank you," you answered politely enough. But I could hear the uncertainty, the hesitation, and offered you a helmet and an *are-you-sure* look. You took the helmet, adding, "I'll be fine, Momma."

It doesn't take you long to get the hang of riding—just a few tries, your father holding the seat as you pedal and steer. Before I can even finish my coffee, I know you're on your way, riding a bike for the first time in your life.

"Hold on. Not so fast," your father yelled. You laughed giddily and then cycled faster. He let go. He let you ride on your own, and shouted after you, "Go, Hannah! Yeah!"

"I got it Daddy," you'd said, circling him, the front tire shakily guiding you forward. And then you turned too tight, the wheel going sideways, causing you to fall. You didn't complain though, didn't even cry. Instead, you picked yourself up, brushed off the street dirt, and asked your father to help you get back onto your bike.

"That's right, Hannah," I called from the front porch, steam rising from my coffee. "That's it. When you fall you get back up and try again."

"I know, Momma," you told me. And then you were on your bike and riding without any help from us.

I imagined you loved it. I imagined you felt like a bird venturing from the nest, daring to ride faster and further each time. I imagined you took flight from the safety of our home, just a short one, not too far, nothing out of sight, just enough to spread your wings for a stretch.

I imagined all these things. And despite the crushing reality, I imagined they were real.

CHAPTER 1

The taste of earth. The taste of grit and blood. Soil held her eyelids shut. A sharp jolt brushed a memory and woke her with frightful urgency.

"Bab—," she whispered, choking on dust. The blindness terrified her. Her pulse boomed in her ears, and every muscle twitched and became alert. Muck held her arms, sticking like thick tar. Her legs were frozen too, locked in the same muddy shackles.

Only these weren't the leather and metal restraints she'd worn before. Confusion invaded her thoughts like the earth seeping into her pores, slipping into her mouth and her nose and her ears. Suffocating. She squirmed, moving against its force, but helplessly slid deeper.

This can't be the place he'd promised me. He'd never allow it.

Cleanliness is a virtue, he'd always said. *It's next to godliness.*

She was clean for him. Not like some of the others. Since the earliest days, she'd always been clean.

A vicious bite of pain jabbed her side, rippling outward like a stone punching the surface of a still pond. The spasm caused her to push unexpectedly, the pressure forcing her to bear down.

No. Not here!

She could feel another memory, of bearing down before, of the small fist in her belly and the unrelenting sensation of being split into two.

He did this to me. An image flashed like the flick of a spark, fleeting and deadly.

It's a sinister evil! He'd shouted at the top of his lungs.

He struck her abruptly, bloodying her nose, lights exploding with pain behind her eyelids. She fought him, but his hands were fast and the labor pain overpowering. His fingers clutched her neck, the father of her child choking her to death.

But I am alive, she thought to herself, coughing and spitting the gritty loam. She struggled to touch her belly. *We're alive.*

But there was no movement.

"Baby?" she moaned softly, speaking to her stomach, torment scratching her mind, insisting an impossible truth. "Come on, baby."

They needed help. She wriggled until the ground loosened, her shoulders moving. A bird shouted from somewhere, it's call muffled by the cushion of earth around her head.

He choked me. And then he buried me? she thought with immense hurt and terror.

The ground shifted, the grave collapsing onto her tiny frame, crushing her as her lungs emptied. Panic eclipsed all other senses. She scooped handfuls of soil, shoving and hurrying to stay ahead of the cave-in. Her chest ached; stars streaked her sight. She clawed at the grave's abrasive face, a wall of sand and rock, her nails chipping and peeling until they were gone. Razor pain burned the joints of her fingers as exhaustion urged her to quit.

Air. She reached fresh air, fingers first, her lips touching next, her face emerging. The daylight pierced her sight, her hair matted against her skin. A contraction ravaged her abdomen and tightened like a vice. She bit through her lip and filled her mouth with the taste of iron.

"God!" she screamed, sweeping the grave's blanket from her middle. There were tears, but not for the labor. They were for the hurtful pain of abandonment. Deeper than any surface pain imaginable, she came to understand what he'd done. He'd buried her alive, believing she was dead, believing they were dead. Another jolt knifed her gut, wringing her insides like a damp towel. She cried out, her insides on fire.

A bird replied, telling her life was here, encouraging her to come up out of the ground like a flower in springtime. She did, the grave's depth proving he'd considered her no threat, considered her a corpse. The earthy walls were packed with stone, enough to grip, and to pull herself up and out until she was over the grave's lip and able to roll onto her back.

A heavy scent of pine trees mixed with the dank smell of the burial ground. Blue sifted through the treetops, the sky filled with cotton-ball clouds, and the woods she'd emerged in were thick with shades of green, brown, and yellow. The sting of dewy summer coated her head and neck, but the rest of her had gone cold with a chill. Her eyelids heavy, the dusky blue turned gray and threatened to go black.

A warm gush between her bare legs roused her. The baleful sign filled her with fear.

"No," she cried, daring to check. Even in the forest's shadow, the wet color on her fingers was unmistakable. Blood pooled around her—too much. "Oh please, no."

Somewhere distant there were tires crunching stone, a car passing over gravel. She got to her knees with a heinous scream, her mind a mess of dizzying and random thoughts. Cramps came like tidal waves, lifting her enough to chance a few steps, but then taking her to her knees. She was terrified for her baby's life, terrified for the both of them.

When she stood, blood dripped onto her feet and ran down her legs. She staggered weakly then doubled over and collapsed with a thud. The bird cawed as she managed to stand again and search for the road. She found a mound piled next to the grave, his work incomplete. There was a trail following her, shimmering in the streaky sunlight.

She faded in and out, the woods spinning sideways. When she focused, the first bird had become three. They wore feathered over-coats, their eyes like black beads, their heads bobbing up and down as they watched like spectators sitting in the front row of a prize fight.

This was a fight; her and her baby's life in the balance. She leaned on a tree, shivering and panting. The tree's gnarled bark was sticky with sap, the details unfocused and fuzzy. The car she'd heard became three more, like the birds.

I can make it, was the sole thought in her head. *I have to.*

The road. She could see it. A yellow blur passed with a plume of dust and smoke; the car unlike any she'd seen before. How long had it been? How long since she'd been outside, since she was his?

She whimpered when a contraction began to build, the pain mounting like an ocean swell. She hugged her body, belting out a harsh scream that echoed across the woods. Birds fanned the air, taking flight in a launch from a shrub.

"Help me," she sobbed, her small frame sitting squat between the trees, unmoving, a ghost in the forest, blood drying on her nightgown and legs. "Please."

Her heart stuttered and she fell over and took to her hands and knees, finding it the easiest path. The silence broke, her gaze chasing a red car this time, music gaining, a woman singing, her voice warbling as it approached, and disappeared in a puff of road-dust.

One hill, she considered, crawling to the edge of the forest, peering up the steep embankment. She'd have to climb. She was naked beneath her gown. His burying her the way he did, leaving her in the ground like that: it broke her heart. Her mind wandered aimlessly with dark questions asking why. *Why our baby?*

There was distant music, the song familiar, one of the few he'd allowed her to listen to. It was a gift from him—an hour of music for having been good and clean. And she was good for him, cleaning with the scrub brush twice a day, keeping herself fresh. When he wasn't with her, she heard the song like a secret, the hour he'd given her staying with her long after.

The music was gone, but she cautiously hummed the tune, distracting herself from the pain. He wasn't here, wouldn't hear her anyway. She hummed louder, more defiantly. She rose from the forest, her head peering above the gravel as another car passed, the aftermath pelting her skin and filling her eyes, mouth, and nose with road-dust and exhaust. She batted at the fumes, covering herself until they were gone.

Ignoring the demands of her body to collapse, to give up, she mustered a will and strength from the same place she was humming her song, her secret helping her to stand. She took a step, dragging herself, her sight fading.

CHAPTER 2

FOURTEEN YEARS EARLIER

The roar of a car engine rushed through our home, and beneath it, I heard my baby girl's laughter. I flipped the radio, turning it off. There was a second rumble, powerful, breaking with a sharp clap. I heard her laugh again, harder this time, the sound coming from outside the front door. She was the only child I knew who liked noises. The louder the better.

As I realized what I was hearing I shook my head, confused by what shouldn't be. Surely Hannah was still in front of the television, a cartoon singing in the background, her tiny body pressed against the carpet and her eyes alive with colorful reflections. I told myself I had to have heard something else, something different, the raucous cry of a crow, or a blue jay outside the window.

The air felt still, unnerving, and I could smell car exhaust—its noxious breath filling my nose. Another roar broke the stillness and the deep tones shook our wedding china and rattled my insides. Hannah shrieked as the motor howled over her voice.

A child-proof safety guard for the screen door, I'd told Ronald. *It needs to be high enough so Hannah can't reach it.*

My husband, Ronald, had side-eyed the idea and said the small latch on the handle was fine enough. What if he was wrong? I took my finger from the cookbook, the pages fanning the air as it collapsed, like my reasoning. Concerned, I wiped my hands, an unease coming over me like a sickly chill.

"Ms. Hannah White," I announced in a comical voice and entered the room where I'd put her. I wanted to see her upturned face, her bright smile and her baby-blue eyes. But the carpet in front of the television was bare, save for her sippy cup laying on its side next to a plate of half-chewed apple slices. Nervously, I added, "Hannah, are you playing hide and seek again?"

No answer.

The motor muscled the air once more, and in the quiet that followed, I heard Hannah scream with delight. A dark notion ticked in my gut and I knew to trust it, to trust my first thoughts of the unlocked porch door and Hannah wandering into the front yard.

I ran to the front of the house, calling out, "Hannah? Baby! Hannah?"

My voice caught in my throat when I reached the porch door and saw the car on the street and my little girl standing next to it. The dish towel fell as my bare feet struck the patio's hot pavement, a seeming mile of lawn ahead of me. *A home should have a big yard*, Ronald had insisted. A brief thought of my gun and radio came to me, but could I get to them in time? I chanced it, going back inside, the porch door slamming behind me. It was a single moment I'd never recover.

When I heard the mechanical clacks of a car door, I knew the mistake made, knew I was losing precious steps and moments. I forgot about being a cop then—my police training instantly eclipsed by a powerful instinct to protect my child. I swiveled back toward the porch.

"Momma!" Hannah said to me, seeing me across the yard, laughing and pointing at the candy-red car. The front end heaved up and the passenger door eased open like the jaws of a monster.

A woman's voice inside spoke, garnering my girl's trust. "Momma, ride! Going for a ride!"

"Hannah! Get away from there!" I yelled sternly, jumping onto the lawn in a run, the distance taking my breath.

Hannah's face changed, her tiny mouth turning into a pout, frightened by my tone, her dimpled cheeks fading.

"Momma?" she asked. "Momma car?"

"Come here now!" I shouted frantically.

"Momma?"

"Hannah, baby," I said gently, too far to reach her, shoving my hand into the air, gaining on her but not soon enough, the seconds passing too quickly, beckoning. "Momma needs you to come inside!"

The connection was brief and Hannah stepped to me, her toy charm bracelet throwing a glint of sunlight caught in one of the plastic shapes.

The motor growled.

"Ride?" she asked, her brow furrowing with indecision.

"Hannah!" I shouted again. "Come here!"

The red classic car growled like an animal, suffocating my words. Hannah wasn't afraid though, her laugh returning. Hannah's attention was drawn inside the car. From the dark interior, a furry shape appeared. It was enough to steal Hannah entirely. The gnawing panic in my gut turned vicious then, biting my insides like a rabid dog, urging the screams and tears to surface. I had to keep it together, had to keep control, keep my composure.

"No! Hannah!" I scolded, becoming breathless in my run. "Hannah, you come to Momma!"

But Hannah's face had already exploded with excited enchantment, her pudgy arms rising, her pink fingers clutching the air, begging to take hold of the cuddly prize. Mesmerized by the stuffed animal, Hannah crawled into the mouth of the red car, her short legs hanging over the lip of the passenger seat. For the briefest of moments, I froze, the sight of my girl entering the strange car seeming freakishly unreal.

My run became a dive, my body in flight, arms stretching, leaping in desperation. It was enough to grab hold of my girl's foot, wrapping my fingers around her ankle until I heard her scream. The pain in Hannah's voice killed me inside, but I tightened my grip even more, knowing it hurt, but knowing it was my only chance. The red car barked at me and lurched forward. The abrupt motion was enough, and Hannah's foot leapt out of my grasp, leaving behind her tiny shoe.

The passenger door slammed shut. The taillights winked and the rear tires spun into a blur of white smoke, spitting loose asphalt. I screamed as the car sped from the house, screamed until my throat closed, razors stabbing deep inside my middle.

As if hearing my pleas, the car slowed, coming to a stop with traffic entering the intersection at the bottom of our street. I opened into a run, my bare feet slapping against the blacktop. I'd become hysterical, my shrieks filled with nonsensical words while waving fiercely. I was distantly aware of the neighbors who'd collected on their porches and front doors, their eyes filled with morbid curiosity, some with their phones to their ears. The red car was too far though, and I collapsed on the road, my lungs on fire, my chest pounding, and my brain a dizzying mess of emotion.

"Hannah!" I cried. "Someone took my daughter!"

I saw eyes. Starry blue.

Composure had surfaced in my raging mind; the cop I'd been trained to be appearing long enough for me to record what I was seeing. The driver had glared at me through the rearview mirror. There was more. Her brow had been stretched as though she were smiling—a vicious smile.

A car screeched to a sudden stop behind me. Doors opened, and voices came from all directions, asking if I'd been hurt, if I'd been in an accident. The voices were irrelevant, barely noticed, like a wind rustling leaves. I clutched Hannah's empty shoe and waved toward the red car, locking my gaze on the woman's blue eyes. I clenched my jaw until it hurt and memorized the details before shifting my focus to the bumper and license plate.

My heart seized, filling my soul with darkness. There was a cover hiding the tags, hiding the numbers and letters. The car's turn signal gave a final wink—the taillights fading, dousing my hope, taking my child, disappearing with my little girl and vanishing from my life. Nothing would ever be the same.

CHAPTER 3

It was the smell of sea air that told me I was close to the Outer Banks. I slid down my car window and perched my elbow on the sill. A summer breeze rushed through my fingers and blew the city out of my hair. The islands making up the Outer Banks would be new to me, but the briny tang had the same feel on my skin and taste in my mouth I remembered from being a child vacationing along the Jersey coast.

Ahead of me lay the expectations of squishing hot sand between my toes, wading in the cool surf, the cloudless skies an endless blanket of blue. The walks on slanted wood planks, the boardwalk beneath my sandaled feet, the punches of sea air with every breath. And the dazzle of neon signs baiting me to play games and eat pizza delights and fries swimming in cheese. It all awaited me, but none of it was planned.

My drive to the Outer Banks wasn't exactly a vacation—not any vacation I'd selected to take. The time away from my home in Philadelphia, from my work, was a reprimand. It was forced time off for a mistake I'd made. An almost tragic mistake. When you're a cop, a detective, an almost tragic mistake is life changing. It can also be a career killer too.

An image of Detective Steve Sholes hit me like a thunder's rumble, my beachside memories and expectations ditched mercilessly at mile marker one-eighty-two or so. I entered the final stretches of highway with a heavy sentiment for the detective, his terror-struck expression, his life in the balance, all caused by a haunting certainty tricking every part of me into believing something that wasn't.

My phone interrupted my self-torture, the tinny sound abrupt. "At the next intersection, make a U-turn, and proceed to the route." I strained my eyes with a squint, trying to find the intersection. There was none.

Annoyed, I drove on, and put the miles behind me, distancing myself from what I'd done as if it would help somehow. I'd left the station with resentment, the bitterness gnawing. Maybe the captain was right. Maybe time away was what I needed. I glanced at my daughter's case folder, the corner of it sticking out of my bag, more than fourteen years of clues stuffed inside it. With a sigh, I reminded myself that a forced vacation gave me time to work on what was important.

At some point during the drive, I'd made a left when I should have made a right, but the map application was insisting my destination was in front of me, insisting I had arrived. But this wasn't the garage I'd been heading to. I was in the middle of a forest, on a gravel-filled dirt road with nothing but trees in every direction.

I snagged the index card clipped to the front of the case folder, one of the many old, unpromising and unlikely leads in Hannah's kidnapping case. On it, there was a name and address, Fitz's Garage. The map application displayed the same information, the two addresses a match. But there was nothing here. It left me wondering if the clue had been wrong all along. It was old. Maybe too old. The index card was one of the earliest belonging to my daughter's case and had fallen to the bottom of my priority list, a hundred other more promising notes and pictures surpassing it and slowly covering it in the file.

Back at my place, I maintained a record of my investigations on a wall, the entirety of it covered with leads. It started with a single picture of Hannah, with her chubby dimpled cheeks, at the center, alone, and always in my sight from anywhere in the one-bedroom apartment I called home. Over time, countless other photos and notes were added, joining my daughter's image. From the newly tacked pictures, I strung yarn, tightly wrapping the dyed wool around every thumbtack, each leading to another clue or case, the colored thread spanning lives lost, lives found, connecting them.

I worked my wall every night like a mother spider tending to her web. Most of the cases, their leads, went cold, went nowhere—dead ends, the yarn thready and frayed, like the broken hopes of those who'd lost a child. There were also the leads I could never follow up, the impossible leads that frustrated me, each rich with suspicion, but lacking the vital clues I'd needed to continue. How many were there? Dozens? Hundreds?

In my haste to leave for my forced vacation, I'd started to pack blindly, and I'd brushed the wall, spilling an index card from beneath one of the other notes. The card, having yellowed with age, falling to my feet like an autumn leaf. Fitz's Garage was owned by Tommy Fitzgerald. Their specialty was restoring classic cars. There was the smallest, thinnest chance that they could lead me to the classic car that had taken Hannah. It was that card that led me to select the Outer Banks as my vacation destination. It was also the address that got me lost in the woods.

It took everything I had not to throw my phone out of the window. For miles around, there was nothing but heavy woods, the tops of evergreen trees climbing the hilly roadside. I should have heeded the warning signs—the smooth asphalt becoming gravel, the road narrowing to two lanes and then becoming one when I crossed a small creek.

Frustrated, I hit the gas. Stones ticked beneath the tires, striking the car's underside and feeding my irritation with technology. Sharp sunlight jutted through the high branches, the light flicking in and out of my eyes, causing me to squint until the landscape turned into a washed-out tapestry. It was pretty, but it wasn't what I was looking for. I checked the time, checked my case folder on the passenger seat, anxious to get to where I was going.

The road climbed upward, convincing me I was on a mountain, the elevation high enough to punch air into my ears and make them pop. The forest seemed endless, my car laboring with the steep road. I rolled the radio tuner until I found a song, but even with the music playing, I sensed I'd driven too far off course.

Nervous about the time, I slowed again and stopped. A red car buzzed past while I checked the map, tracing the roads and the turns, my finger crossing the highway and bridge where I should have been. Then I saw it was in the opposite direction. I looked over my shoulder. I'd have to turn the car around, the width of the lanes making it a challenge. The last thing I wanted to do was dump the rear tires off the road's embankment and get myself stuck in the middle of nowhere.

I chanced a look and peered through the passenger window, where I found a twenty-foot drop from the edge of the road down onto the forest floor. My stomach jumped into my throat as I braced against the car door. I let out a nervous laugh, which ended abruptly when a figure in the woods caught my eye.

I wasn't alone.

CHAPTER 4

I felt for the outline of my gun, found it in my bag and fished it out, the metal cold, the gun loaded. I was a woman alone in the woods and uncertain of who it was climbing the embankment. A hiker climbing the hills and trekking through the wooded trails? There was something off about their gait though, maybe an injury.

I gripped the door's handle, uncertain of what to expect as a girl climbed over the embankment's lip like something out of a movie. She got to her feet, her silhouette brightly lit by the sunshine behind her.

"Hello?" I said as a face appeared. "Oh, my—" I began, but was too choked up, alarmed as more of her came into view.

She had no backpack, no hat, no pants. Not even a pair of shoes. She was tiny, like a spring sapling, straining to stand, her shoulders slumped and her long black hair hanging flat in front of her face. The girl wore nothing but a white nightgown, her frame showing through the fabric, her legs and arms telling me she was underweight, but her middle showing she was pregnant, maybe six or seven months. Every inch of her gown was covered in dirt and stained red, most of it dry and dark. It was the bright, fresh blood on the inside of her thighs that had me opening the door's handle.

I jumped out of the driver's seat, waving my hand, my muscles tensed as the road's gravel teased my legs and threatened to turn my ankles. The smell of her was pungent, like earth or sod or mulch, the loam heavily mixed with body odor and blood. I shaded my face from the sunlight and moved her, placing the sun behind me so I could assess what had happened. I glanced over the road and searched for a steeple of smoke, and then tried to listen for a motor running or anything to indicate if she'd been involved in a car accident, if maybe she'd gone into labor and tried to drive herself to the hospital. There was nothing. The road was clean too, absent of any skid marks or tire tracks rutted into the gravel.

"My name's Detective Casey White. Can you tell me where you came from?" I asked, my voice shaky and loud. The girl winced and shied away. I'd scared her, but it was a good sign. She was aware of me. I feared she was in shock though, the color of her skin pale like a gray sky.

"Are you having contractions?" I asked, lowering my voice to a whisper.

"Ba—" she tried, grunting, and lifted her face enough for me to see her eyes, round and large and blotted with pooling tears. The color gave me a moment's pause, golden like honey. Her lips quivered, her expression showing desperation and exhaustion.

My pulse pounded in my brain as I assessed the situation, putting into order everything I'd learned to do. I glanced up and down the road convinced there had to be a car, convinced she couldn't be alone out here and that someone else might be hurt.

"My baby?"

Baby, I thought, questioning the girl's age in my mind. I couldn't stop the thought that she was no older than my Hannah would be, no more than sixteen or so.

A rush of panic, of terrible hope filled me, my mind taking me where it always wanted to go—the case of my girl's kidnapping. Since that day, I'd believed every child crossing my path could be my girl. I'd believed the possibility, anyway. It was torture. Instinctively, I checked my list, but thought of the girl's eye color, and the unique-ness of them. I dismissed the notion as fast as it came, my training taking over again, the girl's care and welfare a priority.

I asked, "How far along are you?"

No answer. The woman's nightgown was the type I'd seen in old movies and on television, the style set long before my time. The cloth was deeply soiled in the same dirt she'd climbed up, the sooty black and brown ground into the threads, littered throughout her hair and covering her skin in a fine dust. I searched for bruising and scratch marks but found nothing to indicate a fall, but I did see the injuries circling the woman's throat—purple-and-black bruising the size and shape of a man's hands. I'd seen the same before, every cop has, countless times.

"Did someone do that to you?" I asked, raising my voice.

She winced again, pulling back.

I shifted, digging my shoes into the road's gravel and noticed her bare feet, blood oozing, her heels and the end of her toes bruised and cut to shreds as though she'd run barefoot through a room of broken glass. She must have trudged through the rough terrain, but for how long? How many miles does it take to do that to your feet? I held up one of her hands, finding the tips of her fingers were bruised and cut too, her fingernails torn away, some of them completely gone. She'd been digging. But why?

Her size told me she was a child, a young teenager, but she was pregnant. And she was asking about her baby. I was careful around her belly, but touched her arm, holding her. I tried to lead her to my car, but she was stuck, her gaze falling over her shoulder toward the woods where she'd emerged. Behind her I saw a trail of blood, spilled onto the road like a painter having tipped his paint can. I'd have to pick her up if I was going to get her to the hospital.

"Can you tell me your name?" I asked, holding her hand, trying to reassure her I was there to help. "Are you having contractions?"

The girl lifted her head, a low moan coming from her mouth, her motions slow, the effort immense. She found me again, her gold eyes staring into my soul as fresh tears cut streaks into the filth on her cheeks. I gently lifted the girl's hair, nuggets of soil falling, pushing a lock behind her ears, checking the extent of the bruises around her neck. There was no doubt she'd been strangled. And then I saw more evidence of what had happened—a hundred scattered blood splatters, each appearing like a tiny explosion, a swarm of petechia speckling her face and orbiting in the whites of her eyes.

"Who did this to you?" I asked, my voice cracking.

"Baby," she cried, falling forward, her frail body collapsing into my arms. Her weight barely moved me. I wrapped my arms around her, sleeving one beneath her legs, and the other behind her shoulders. I held her a moment and checked what vitals I could, concerned she might have died. I felt a weak pulse and hoisted her into the air, carrying her to my car.

I was breathing hard, panting, the panic rising like a turbulent wind as I laid her down in the rear seat, shoving my suitcase full of clothes to one side. I'd been trained for emergencies like this one, but when the shit actually happened, the training became a stranded memory, an afterthought mixed with instinct and gut reactions.

In the back of my mind, I was already questioning everything about this girl, my other training taking on the position of investigation. Where did she come from? Who strangled her? Why was she digging? But more than any other question, how far along were her contractions?

I did my best to get her comfortable, not that it mattered. She was completely out, every ounce of her was dead weight. I took her wrist, searching for a pulse again. I found the faintest rhythm and shifted to place my hand on her belly, hoping to feel the baby move, hoping the child was still alive.

I wondered about a miscarriage, my focus on the blood, the amount of it, the concentration around her middle and legs. When the seat belts were in place, I changed the map application's destination to the closest hospital, finding it was just over the bridge in the other direction to which I'd been travelling. As I drove, the girl let out a hopeful groan and moved, telling me she was still alive.

Miles passed. The gravel road becoming asphalt again, leading us back to the highway, to the bridge and to civilization. And in the miles, there was silence. I heard my tires on the road, and air whistling through a window I'd opened. There was the girl's shallow breathing too, her short breaths, the time between them growing apart. Every few minutes, I checked on her, her touch cold, but still alive.

"Please, no traffic," I said, my focus on the road, my hand on her belly, waiting for movement. I spoke soft, encouraging words. "Come on, baby, tell me you're okay."

When I reached the apex of the bridge and saw the morning traffic piling over the bay, I dialed 9-1-1. I told them I was a detective from out of town, offering my captain's name and my badge number. I explained to them I had an emergency, the life of a pregnant woman in dire need of a hospital. The operator didn't question me, didn't delay, and agreed to my request of providing a patrol-car escort to clear the last miles. I found my badge on its lanyard and took it from my bag, stringing it around my neck.

Within minutes of the call, a patrol car was in front of me, the red-and-blue lights flashing, its siren whaling, cars and trucks leaning onto the road's shoulders. Hospital-emergency signs seemed to pop up from out of nowhere—their pale-blue color with the large white H on the face, and an arrow beneath, pointing the way.

With the patrol-car escort, we made it to the hospital where there was a team of white-coats and paisley-scrubs waiting. The hospital staff carried the girl inside. She'd said nothing more after the last groan, and I never felt movement from her baby. Her skin had become grayer than I imagined possible.

As the emergency-room staff surrounded us, a flood of voices came with a chaotic blur of hands and arms flying in and out of my view, the girl being moved to a gurney and to a doctor's full attention. The doctor raised a hand and called for silence from the group as she placed her stethoscope on the girl's chest and then onto her belly. The doctor barked orders to the team as they wheeled her toward another set of mechanical double-doors, a gurney wheel rattling out of unison with the others. In the last glimpse before the doors closed, I saw the doctor holding the girl's shoulder, comforting in a way that gave me hope.

Suddenly, after all the action and energy, I was alone. I looked around the hospital's emergency room, to the rows of empty seats on my left, a television near the ceiling, and to the desk and the hospital staff on my right. The entrance doors behind me shut with a whoosh, and crisp air poured from a vent in the drop ceiling. I dared to glance down at my front, my body covered in blood and dirt and sweat, my legs trembling, my arms outstretched and my hands shaking.

The tears came without warning. A hard cry ravaged my insides like a bright day suddenly turning stormy. I knew it was the adrenaline and the emotional rocket suddenly crashing, along with everything else that comes when there's a traumatic event. I swiped errantly at the tears and tried to stop, but it was a girl's life, a child in her own right, a mother and a baby, both of them on the verge of dying or dead already. It was tragic and sad, and it touched me.

CHAPTER 5

HIM

He had to do it. Had to. It was time. The need consumed his mind like she had consumed him. The relenting need to clean was over. She was clean. *Forever.* The thought came with a satisfying tug, the same fate for the others nearing. *She was clean forever.*

He lit the end of a cigarette, the hot cherry bobbing, the words in his mind a jumble as he searched for the television's remote control. He found it and smashed the buttons. The old TV buzzed with energy, the screen filling with snow, a static discharge racing across the heavy glass. He punched the buttons again, finding the news—the channel-seven news with the reporter he'd almost gotten.

"There you are."

She was nine when he found her walking alone, the boardwalk hot beneath their feet. A lollipop in his right hand. A cigarette in the other. He'd offered her the lollipop, and when she shook her head, he offered her both. She was wise to him though, refusing to talk with strangers, walking away, her chin in the air. But she was afraid. He felt the fear on her like dirt on his skin and fed on it.

His mouth watered, like it had that day. "Now look at you." He wiped his chin. "A woman."

He liked to watch her. He liked to watch her lips move, the television's volume turned down, her eyes looking straight into his. He waited to see if there was a news story, to see if he was still safe.

Ten minutes, and there was nothing of his evening's efforts, nothing of the girl he'd buried, nothing of his secrets with her.

He took to the floor, content, and kicked aside the children's toys scattered about, the room absent of furniture. There were eyes feeding on the television along with his, their ghostly faces peering from behind bars.

"Scrub!" he demanded. A murmur. He growled and turned to stand. A scurry. Then came stout bristles rubbing against skin. The rawness of it pleasing. "That's good. I'll play some music for us."

He faced the television again; their time was coming. He'd bury them too. He'd bury all of them. Just like he'd buried many before. It was time to do it again. Nothing lasts forever.

CHAPTER 6

A half hour had passed, giving me time to change my clothes, to wash the blood from my hands, arms, and neck. Time marched forward, driving the hands of the clock on the wall, my hope of the doctor returning soon fading quickly. I thought to stay longer, to wait and hear some news, but the cold air-conditioning and antiseptic smell of the hospital's waiting area urged me to move on, to leave. I could call the next day asking for updates. And the local force would want my statement soon enough.

"One second," a woman from the reception desk said as I headed to the doors. "If you're leaving, can we get your contact information?"

"Detective Casey White," I answered her, approaching the counter and offering my badge. A look of surprise showed on her round face, the kind I'd often seen when telling someone I was a cop. I gave her my phone next, showing my contact information on the screen. As she grabbed a paper form and pen, I saw an alert pop open on the phone, and held the temptation to read it.

"Thank you," the woman said, swiping the alert clear and returning to my contact information.

I was addicted to the alerts. They were my lifeblood. With the reprimand, the sudden vacation in the Outer Banks, I'd take the time off, but the alerts would continue. I made sure of it. There was no knowing when an alert might be a clue. My daughter would be sixteen now, and I carry her case wherever I go. It's a part of me.

"Is that it?" I asked, taking my phone.

"Will you be in town for long?" she asked, her finger on my address, smudging the ink on the paper.

"I don't know," I answered. "I'm here for short break, but also have some work to do. A few days, maybe longer."

"This certainly is not the best way to start a vacation, is it?"

"No. No it isn't," I agreed.

I really had no idea how long I'd stay. I'd left my home with hardly any plans, not even a hotel-room reservation. I'd thrown some clothes into a suitcase that lay in the back seat of my car, and had managed to call in a favor, asking my coworker Clive to forward any alerts, extending the usual range to include the Outer Banks.

As I walked away from the desk, I flipped through the alert, and read the report of a dead girl found on an abandoned yacht.

Abandoned yacht? I questioned, going to a large window, warming myself in the sunny heat. *Was that a common thing around here?*

I read some more. The case didn't quite fit what I'd normally investigate. My first thought was the girl's death could be accidental—a late summer outing, topless yachting, drugs, alcohol, a tight group of rich kids borrowing their parent's expensive boat—that sort of thing. This probably wasn't a case of kidnapping or murder.

"Description?" I texted back to Clive, not wanting to dismiss it entirely. If there was more detail, I'd consider swinging by the yacht and take a look for myself. I had my badge and had brought a stack of drawings of Hannah, her image advanced in years to match how old she'd be today. With those, I could talk my way onto the investigation's scene and nose around, hopefully get a look at the girl.

He texted a reply, *Approximate age: 15 or 16. Light-brown hair.*

It wasn't much to go on, but of my top five must-haves, those were two from my checklist.

Thanks, I texted back, continuing to debate what to do, but feeling the usual urge, the need to look for myself and confirm if it was or wasn't a match to my case. "Anything else? How about the yacht's location?" I flipped over to my map app, finding the coast, finding where the land met the ocean, believing that's where I'd go. Where else would you park a yacht?

Clive answered, "Possible trauma." I shook my head, his description vague. My phone buzzed again with the coordinates to where the yacht was docked. "I'll send more when it comes in."

"Thank you," I texted again, a sense of obligation tugging my insides, driving me to go. The dead girl's age and hair color was a close enough match to my case, and that was all I needed to give the crime scene a look before settling into my vacation.

A stir of impatience left me unsettled, leading me to change my plans. Before I left, I needed to know about the girl and her baby. Also, my legs were like rubber from the rush of the events, and they led me back to a chair, to sit with a few others and to wait to hear from the doctor. I leaned into the thin cushions, air wheezing, the last of my energy draining with it.

Careful, I thought, closing my eyes, letting myself rest.

Hospitals have a voice: the bells, doors, emergencies over the speaker. Hospitals have many voices, and one by one, they began to fade and then altogether disappear. The moment of rest stretched, and before I knew it, I was falling asleep. I let it happen, needed it to happen.

When there was silence, I found the mystical place before sleep. I'd hoped to see Hannah there like I sometimes did. Instead, I heard the steady thrum of rain on my car's roof, heard it hitting my windshield with massive drops. It was a memory, the Burgess case. It was when I'd almost killed a cop.

CHAPTER 7

BEFORE

Raindrops pelted the windshield with thick watery blooms. A blade scratching the glass made me cringe with every swipe. My husband had always taken care of the cars—changing the oil, filling the radiator, replacing the wiper blades, all the nuisance chores I never considered when we were together. Another pass, another scrape of metal on glass, and I shook, goosebumps rising on my arms. I flipped the switch, stopping the blades mid wipe, the torn rubber in a sad dangle, a reminder of something to fix later.

"You miss him?" I asked my car, turning the wipers back on briefly, thinking of my ex-husband, and wondering where he was these days. With nothing left between us, it had been years since I saw Ronald last.

The rainfall quickened to a steady pour. Flashes of blue and red came into view, a swarm of police officers garbed in dingy rain parkas, their patrol cars staged around a suspect's car—a friend of the family in the Burgess kidnapping case.

I squinted through the blurred glass and saw abrupt motions in the front seat. But it was the car that took my attention—it looked like the same make and model Hannah had crawled into.

Chevy Nova, I confirmed and jumped to the edge of my seat. *Mid-seventies,* I also confirmed, my heart thumping. *And a license-plate cover!*

Another motion erupted inside the red car. The figure of a woman.

I threw my car door open. My shoes hit the gravelly road, kicking stones as I sprinted. I shoved through the crime scene like a bulldozer clearing a field, screaming, "It's the red car!"

Officers parted to make room for me, their expressions fixed with empty stares like something out of a dream.

My gaze went straight to the rearview mirror—and there they were: the starry blue eyes of the woman who'd stolen my little girl.

"Freeze!" I yelled at the top of my voice. I pulled my gun and cocked the hammer.

"Whoa!" a man hollered.

"Step out of the vehicle!" I demanded as rainwater dripped from my brow. I could feel the surrounding officers approach, questioning my actions. *Why didn't they have their guns drawn?*

"Detective White!" I heard from the car as a pair of hands emerged, pale skin glowing in the dank weather. "Casey! Would you mind holstering your gun?"

I recognized the voice as I blinked away raindrops. The woman's eyes vanished from the rearview mirror. And the license plate had changed too. There was no dark cover. I could clearly see the numbers and letters—the embossed text of a Pennsylvania tag.

Detective Steve Sholes exited the vehicle, his hands raised, his detective's badge catching my attention like a slap across the face. He pointed cautiously, and I realized my gun was still drawn and pointing at him. My fingers tingled suddenly, as drops of rain formed on the tip of the gun's barrel. My arms bent like a frown, the gun feeling oddly heavy and enormously uncomfortable. How many times had I drawn my weapon since I'd been promoted to a detective? I couldn't think of a single incident. A flash of brilliant embarrassment burned on my neck and face and swelled my insides with dread. This was bad. I holstered my gun and raised my hands.

"I saw something," I tried to offer, my voice wavering with uncertainty, my excuse shameful.

Detective Sholes approached. A damp gust caught his sandy hair, his face grim with disappointment. "You could have shot me," he said.

"I—" I began, but stopped when he waved his hand, cutting me off.

He took me by the arm to lead me away from the scene so we couldn't be heard.

"Not in front of them," he started, guarding, leaning in and lowering his voice so only I could hear him.

"I saw something," I repeated. "I did. I'm so sorry."

"Well, at least you didn't pull the trigger," he offered, pressing against his chest. No vest. He wasn't wearing his bullet-proof vest. His eyes met mine, and I could see there was no ill-will, but he looked shaken.

"Eyes, rearview mirror," I managed to get out. "They—they were blue, same as the kidnapper's."

Sholes patted my shoulder and faced the car. "It *is* a red car. And if it were my little girl? Well, I might've thought the same. Or maybe not. It's been a long time, Casey."

"I'm so sorry," I said again.

"Nothing fatal—this time. There are a few I put away who'd probably wish it was," he assured me with a smile, hoping humor would help. I tried smiling with him but couldn't. He glanced around at the other officers, adding, "Listen, I'm not sure this won't get back to the captain."

My heart sank, realizing how many had seen me, seen my behavior and pulling my gun.

"Hey, detective," one of the officers called out. I craned my neck, seeking to find the voice behind Steve's shoulder. "I found something between the seat cushions. You might want to take a look at this."

Steve stepped away, revealing the officer on the passenger side of the car. My hand went to my mouth as I held in a scream, my mind filling with images of the morning my daughter was taken. I recalled every detail: what Hannah wore, how her hair was combed, food stains on the front of her shirt, everything. And when Steve had stepped back from the car, the steady rain turning the image of him blue, one of those memories came rushing back. Trapped between the officer's slender fingers was a pencil and dangling from its end was a plastic charm bracelet.

CHAPTER 8

I woke with a start, sitting up with a jump that nearly took me out of the chair. I had my phone in my hand, a list of new alerts about the yacht and the dead girl. It was Clive sending more details. I'd been asleep thirty minutes, and there was still no word from the doctor. The waiting room looked about the same, the attendant behind the counter seeming to have remained unmoved, fixed, possibly asleep too for all I knew. I stood to give my legs a stretch.

"Your appointment is set, Sheriff," I heard from behind me. The voice was from another receptionist, a few years out of college, her big eyes fixed on an older man, her slender fingers on his arm. "We'll see you soon, and I hope you consider running again. You'd have my vote."

"Thank you," he told her.

Sheriff? I asked myself as the receptionist left the man alone. He was tall and dressed for crabbing or fishing, with one of his arms in a black sling, his fingers badly bruised and matching the colors of a storm cloud. At first glance, I assumed the man was at the hospital as a patient, an accident while fishing perhaps. The condition of his arm wasn't new though. He had a radio on his hip and around his neck he wore a chain lanyard with a badge and identification. *Marine Patrol.*

Beneath the unshaven days on his face and the fishing outfit, he was a ruggedly handsome man, but did well to hide it. He caught me looking and gave me a nod, his hair in a tangle of brown highlights as he fished out his phone and gave it a cursory glance before stuffing it away.

I went to him, holding my badge and identification, "Sheriff?" I asked.

"Ma'am," he said, leading with his good hand and taking mine. Tired pouches carried his blue-green eyes, but they were soft, warm, and welcoming. "My name is Jericho Flynn, Marine Patrol. 'Sheriff' is an old title that… well, never mind, it doesn't matter. What can I do for you?"

"I'm in town working a kidnapping case and received an alert about a dead girl found on a yacht—"

"The super yacht. I'm familiar with the case. I called it in." He looked briefly at the reception desk, adding, "This is the hospital though, are you looking for the morgue?"

"Maybe you can help answer that," I said. "I was traveling here when I came across a pregnant girl wandering along the road. She was in bad shape."

"That was you?" he asked, gripping the radio handset on his belt. "I heard the request called in for a police escort. Is she okay?"

I shook my head, answering, "I haven't heard anything, yet. Regarding the girl on the yacht… could I get her description?"

He gave me a nod, answering, "You want to check for a possible match?" He motioned to my bag and the case folder. "She's already been moved to the medical examiner's office."

"Do you have a name or an identification?"

He shook his head. "Nothing. We don't even have numbers on the yacht yet."

"Maybe I could check with the medical examiner?"

"Her office is near here," he agreed, his tone half-hearted. "But Dr. Swales isn't keen on interruptions. She has a process. I can have her notify me. And I'm headed to the yacht to give the chief a brief now."

"I have the location," I said, understanding what he was suggesting.

"You're welcome to join."

"Hi Sheriff," a man said, greeting him with a clap on his shoulder.

"Mr. Jonathan, was the fishing good?"

"Great!" he answered. "Thanks for the tip."

"You're quite popular," I noted, growing curious about the man everyone called Sheriff.

"Oh, I've been around a while," he said. "I'll see you at the yacht?"

"Here's my number," I offered, deciding to trust him. I showed him my screen as he used one hand to type into his phone.

He eyed my chest, reading my identification. "From the Philadelphia area. You came a long way for one case."

"I'm planning to take some time off too."

His gaze went to the case file next. "A vacation?"

"Yeah, something like that."

"The invite to the yacht is open, and if I hear from Dr. Swales, I'll let you know."

"Thank you," I told him, turning to leave, trying to decide if I wanted to go to the yacht and inspect the scene. The lure of sand and sun was tempting too. I could find a cheap hotel, ditch the clothes, shake off the day and lay in the sun. But curiosity about the girl on the yacht, and the circumstance surrounding her death sparked an interest. And being in touch with Jericho Flynn meant I could get updates on the girl found in the woods, too—and her baby. I spun around, holding up my phone. "Sheriff, I'll see you over there."

"Call me Jericho," he said and nudged his chin. "I'll see you there."

CHAPTER 9

Unlike my earlier attempt to find my destination, the map application took me directly to the yacht. And, to my surprise, the entire boat ramp was packed—a flood of bodies moving slowly through it like debris choking a swollen stream. Some were there on purpose, hands extended, phones recording. Others were coming or going, their beach or vacation homes foremost on their minds. The inlet was stopped too, patrol boats blocking the traffic to the pier and their slips, leaving a litter of boats anchored in waiting, peppering the ocean's surface like seashells scattered across the beach. Scores of patrol cars and crime-scene vans were parked along the water's edge, pockets of technicians and patrol officers huddling in conference. I opened my window and heard the familiar sound of coastal summer, of trilling cicadas and crashing waves as the wind pushed foamy water onto the bank. It may have been late summer, but the Outer Banks was full today.

It wasn't quite afternoon, but the air had already become hot, the sky turning a hazy yellow, giving the patrol car's flashing lights an eerie glow. The electric blue shined on the face of the yacht; a black-and-white luxury boat, expensive, like something in a magazine. It wasn't just any boat, and not one that would have been abandoned. The yacht was nearly pristine, with a beautifully clean deck and tall panes of black glass glinting in the daylight as the sun slipped in and out of the clouds. The front held a silver railing, short and winding around until it came to a point. The idea of this boat being discarded at sea was as suspect as the discovery of a body on it.

There were dozens of other boats moored near the yacht—some for fishing, some for partying, most with full decks, drinks in hand and curious eyes gazing as the scene unfolded. I didn't envy the investigating officers. There were far too many people to count, too many to question if needed. None of the other boats were quite the size nor had the grandeur of the super yacht, which told me it didn't come from here. But where exactly was here? Having blindly plugged in the coordinates from Clive into my GPS, I didn't know where in the Outer Banks I'd actually landed.

The investigation seemed heaviest on the deck. I focused there, wondering if that had been where the girl was found. From the looks of the crime-scene technicians, the processing was well underway. They were easy to spot. Dressed in dark-blue khakis and taupe polos, they covered the yacht like worker bees on a hive. It was studious work—bodies hunched over, eyes cast down, faces cramped with focused attention, taking samples and lifting prints, swabbing for blood and saliva, and maybe even semen, all the while tagging and bagging anything they believed to be evidence.

Stark flashes struck the yacht like lightning. I stayed fixed on the camera activities, finding a crime-scene photographer centering on one location. I followed two more camera flashes until I found a thick crimson patch streaked along the deck's edge. A patrol car moved beyond the heavy foot traffic and cleared my view to reveal the rest of the blood—runs of burgundy and dark red along the side, nearly touching the water as though the yacht had been struck mortally, like a whale having been harpooned and towed to port.

The amount of blood was a surprise and had me dismissing my initial thoughts about the girl's death. It was a lot. Far more than expected.

Crime-scene tape was strung up, but that didn't stop the gawking crowd from hovering. There were the older folks, the ones who looked like they never left the island, maybe lived here year-round. They shook their heads, chatted amongst themselves, sharing looks of disappointment and grave concern. And then there was the younger crowd—the vacationers— taking pictures of themselves with the crime scene behind them. I'm sure if I knew what to search for, I'd find posts online of the girl's body as the bloodied yacht was boarded. Nothing was sacred anymore. Not even death.

More technicians and photographers worked along the yacht's side, carefully balancing on the lip of the floating dock, their camera flashes stinging the air, capturing the streaky evidence. The inlet's gusty wind pushed the yacht back and forth, rocking it up and down. I noticed the men and women struggling to keep their balance and realized I'd need my sea legs if I got the chance to go on board. I couldn't remember the last time I was on a boat.

You're just here for permission to look at the girl, I reminded myself, feeling the investigative itch set in my gut. Beyond the technicians and patrol officers, I had spotted a few suits who might be the investigating officers. *This is their case. Just get permission and be on your way.* I searched for Jericho but didn't see him around yet.

I took hold of my badge, straightening it nervously and slipping the lanyard beneath my collar. In my bag, I found an old, thin jacket. I brushed it clean and put it on, folding the lapel and tucking in my shirt, which helped with the look. I checked my reflection in the mirror, pushed my hair around until it looked as if I'd come from an office and not a lengthy drive with the windows rolled down. Jericho had mentioned meeting with the chief. I felt it best to look as official as I could when asking permission to visit the morgue and to poke around.

"You can't stop here, ma'am," a patrol officer yelled with a rap of her knuckles on the top of my car.

Instinctively, I lifted my badge to the window. Her expression remained unchanged, but she swung her arm in the other direction.

"For official business, you'll park over there along with the others." Before I could thank her, she went on to the next car and followed the same script, working to drive the congestion past the crime scene.

I drove to the end of the road and parked the car beyond a parade of fresh onlookers—tanned bodies, dressed for the sand and surf, the slap of flip flops and low mumblings about the police, the crime scene, and the shame of it all.

There were uniforms and officials milling around the site, but I easily picked out who was in charge. Like the yacht, he was the center of attention—tall, burly, wearing a suit, a mop of gray hair swaying errantly, driven by a salty breeze. A line of officials came and went as he pointed and waved and managed the scene like a conductor working an orchestra. He was this town's version of my captain from back home. I overheard a reference to him as "Chief" which was enough for me. The marine-patrol officer, Flynn, was with him too.

As I exited my car and gave my legs and back a stretch, the smell of sunblock and insect repellent came to me as a young family waded through the crowd and then slowed in front of me, their eyes fixed on my badge, a murmur passing between the mother and father, questions likely. They were summer-tanned and fit, and carried bags filled with beach towels and toys. Two children kept close to them, a boy and a girl, twins maybe, their noses white with gobs of sunblock, and their shiny eyes wide and alive with the patrol car's blue flashes.

"Did someone die?" the small boy asked me, his face pensive with concern. The father took another look at my badge and then glanced over to the yacht.

"I bet someone got murdered," the girl told the boy. She made choking sounds and a gruesome face as if telling a ghost story, adding, "And I bet the killer is still on the loose."

"Carol," her mother scolded. "Don't tease your brother."

"Well… did they?" the father asked, repeating the boy's question as he gently gripped his children's shoulders, bringing them closer.

"It's an ongoing investigation," I said, sounding rehearsed. I didn't want to draw attention or invite additional questions.

"It would be such a shame," the mother concluded. "Such a nice place—a family place, you know."

"If you'll excuse me," I said to them casually and made my way to the chief.

"Sir?" I asked, trying to get the chief's attention. He put his hand up between us as he instructed a patrol officer. I was familiar with the move and stepped back, giving him space.

"I see you decided to stop by," the marine-patrol officer said.

"I did, Mr. Flynn," I answered.

"Call me Jericho, please," he corrected with a warm gleam in his eyes.

"Jericho," I agreed.

Next to them was a short man, his head shaved bald. He wore round, wiry glasses and a full suit with his arms folded. In the heat, and the layers of clothes, he should have been sweating, but I couldn't find a single drop on his head. And he wasn't shy about studying me as I spoke with Jericho, his dull eyes wandering up and down as he swept the pier's gravel with his foot. With his curiosity satisfied, he unfolded his hands, extending one to me, and said, "The name is Ashtole."

I took his hand—small, clammy—answering, "Detective Casey White."

"District Attorney Daniel Ashtole," he clarified. And then asked, "I take it you are our new detective? If so, you've got great timing."

New? I thought, seeing the chief's ears perk up as he looked briefly over his shoulder. I shook my head, "No, not me. I'm just passing through."

"We've got more patrol officers and technicians than we have sand on the beach," Ashtole answered without looking at me. The district attorney folded his arms again, his gaze traveling to the yacht and around to the crime scene. "What we don't have is a detective to process the scene. Isn't that right?" His comments and question were directed toward Jericho.

"Unfortunate circumstances, Daniel," Jericho answered him.

"Unfortunate indeed," Ashtole grumbled. "Left us in a real pickle."

"I assist with investigations some of the time," Jericho said, turning to me. He raised his arm, the Velcro on his sling peeling. "I have a surgery coming up and we're short on staff, particularly detectives."

"So you have a new detective joining?" I asked, continuing the small talk while I waited for the chief.

"Given the recent events, I would've opened a requisition for a replacement immediately," Ashtole answered flatly. "But I'm not even sure the chief gave it a thought."

"We're a small community," Jericho said, offering an explanation. "And we recently lost a detective."

"Oh, I'm sorry for your loss," I told him. "Line of duty?"

Ashtole gave Jericho a hard look, his focus shifting to the man's arm. The District Attorney said without looking up, "Yeah. Something like that."

"So, what did I miss?" the chief asked, turning to face us.

"Afternoon, sir, Detective Casey White," I said, taking the chief's hand. "I was just getting an update on your recent loss. A Detective?"

"Chief Peter Pryce, nice to make your acquaintance." The chief fixed a look on Jericho and sighed. I sensed there was history here but didn't want to pry.

Chief Pryce answered, "About the detective, that's a bit of a story. For another time, perhaps."

"Well, I am sorry for your town's loss," I repeated.

"White?" the chief asked. "You're the one who found the girl on the road? The hospital didn't mention you were on the job."

"Yes, sir," I answered, wondering if he'd been informed of any news. I lifted my phone, adding, "Have you heard anything?"

He shook his head. "The girl is in surgery, that's all I know. There are some questions about how you found her, and where. We'll need some of your time to get a report."

"Of course, sir. And there's something else I wanted to talk to you about," I told him. "I'm on a vacation, but I'm working an open investigation. If possible, I'd like a minute with the girl's body from the yacht. Maybe some time on board too?"

The chief said nothing but searched the face of my badge and plugged my numbers into his phone. When he was ready, he asked, "Do you always bring your work with you on vacation?"

"Just the open ones," I told him. "I'd already spoken with Patrol Officer Flynn."

Chief Pryce offered a nod, with a smile on his round face. "Nice. Always working. I like that." He tapped on his phone again, adding, "Okay, Detective Casey White, badge number 1134."

"Thank you, sir," I said. "I'll just take a look and then I'll be on my way."

"Whoa, not so fast," he said, his voice lifting. "Seems you have a need. And, as you are aware, we have a need too."

"Sir?" I asked, confused.

"While you're here, maybe you could help us out. We could use a detective's perspective on the scene. If there's a murder, that means there's a murderer at large in our town. That adds some urgency to the help we'll need."

"Sir," Ashtole objected.

"Wait," I said, wanting to clarify. "What I said earlier... I didn't mean—"

The chief rolled his eyes. "Listen, it's temporary. Plus you're already involved with the girl you picked up along the road. We'll need a report from you, anyway. Add the yacht, tack on a few hours, write another report—I'm not asking for much. A day, or two at most."

"I generally work missing persons and kidnapping," I began, agreeing with the district attorney's objection.

"We're in a bind," the chief said, gently taking my arm, urging me to turn toward the yacht. "The tide is going to surge. It's a time-crunch."

"This is highly unusual," Ashtole continued, speaking quietly. "There's jurisdiction. And there's—"

"Shut it!" the chief demanded. "I'll take care of all the logistics, it's what I do. Right now, we've got rising water and evidence being lost—"

"Sir, with all due respect," I interrupted, shaking my head, but wondering if his request might work in my favor.

The chief closed the distance between us, blocking the district attorney. He was a large man and carried the smell of aftershave and liniment. "Look, it's not like we're asking you to cheat off of your friend's test," he said. "We just want a report, or even a copy of your notes. Like I said, the tide is coming in, the pier is busy with tourists, and it's windy. In another few hours, we won't have much of anything to process."

As he stepped back, his hair rose to a point in the middle of his head, driven by the wind, before flopping to the other side. I took a look at the yacht, the surface whitecaps, and the blood along the side of the hull. He was right. Before long, the elements would make it all disappear. And whoever was behind the death of a young girl could be long gone.

"Few hours to a day?" I asked, negotiating the terms, a rise of disbelief stirring in my gut. It was a simple enough trade. I'd help them if they helped me. My afternoon plans already had me back at the hospital to check on the girl and her baby anyway. I could work with them. "I'll help."

Ashtole let out a guffaw, Jericho and the chief ignoring him. I got the sense they often did. He seemed the type who reacted to everything just for the sake of hearing himself react to something.

"Listen, sweetie," Ashtole began, stepping between me and the chief. "Have you ever worked a crime scene like this? This isn't like the city or wherever you're from."

His words struck me hot, and a rush of anger roiled inside. I didn't know this man. And I didn't care to know this man. But damn. A young girl was dead, a potential murder victim. Now I wanted to help with the case just to piss him off.

I took a long breath, and stood over him, and said, "The last person to call me sweetie spoke with a lisp for a month."

"Excuse me!" Ashtole replied, his voice rising with a crack, his eyes round and white as though he'd just seen the dead rise. "Do you know who—?"

"Yes," the chief said, cutting him off. I could see he was trying not to laugh, which was more than could be said for the man folks liked to call 'Sheriff'. "We all know who you are, and as chief, I'll tell you to mind your choice of words, political correctness and all."

"What?" Ashtole went on. "What'd I say?"

"So, a few hours?" I repeated, setting a timeline as I focused on the yacht. "A day at most. I'll do what I can for you, process what's there, hand over my findings. Agreed?"

"Agreed. Thank you. So that's one less problem—just three dozen to go."

I wasn't prepared to process a scene and immediately questioned my decision. I'd no idea why I agreed to it. Maybe it was the blood or the sight of the yacht... or maybe it was my ego screaming. *Show them how good you are. Solve the case in under twenty-four hours.* I studied the blood, finding less definition since I'd arrived. The chief was right—the ocean's spray had already taken some evidence, stealing a drop at a time. Before long, it'd be gone.

"I'll get started," I told them, sounding urgent and confident. The urgency was rehearsed, knowing how to manage expectations. As for the confidence, I was lying through my teeth. I shifted to go back to my car, get a notepad, a pencil, anything I could find to use.

"Jericho will work with you," the chief said abruptly, surprising me. "He knows the lay of the land and can squeeze in the time before getting sidelined by the surgeons."

"Are you kidding?" Ashtole objected. "With a bad arm? He's not even supposed to be on duty."

"Would you take a pill!" the chief yelled, his chest bloating, his tolerance for the man waning. Ashtole cowered and stepped back. "None of this is ideal. We got the shitty end of piss-poor timing and have gotta make do with the cards dealt."

"I don't mind helping," Jericho said calmly as he unraveled the sling around his arm. "I'll meet you over there."

"Give me a few minutes," I told him.

The walk back to my car seemed to take forever—each step came with a crunch of stone beneath my feet, my breathing was deep, nerves tickling my belly, while my mind raced with ideas of where to begin. Was this a kidnapping case, as well as a murder?

As I rummaged through my car, searching for whatever would be useful for the task ahead, I couldn't help but also wonder what the story was with the police department here. What happened to the man's arm I was going to spend the afternoon with? And what happened to their detective? It wasn't my place to ask, or pry. I'd help process the scene before it was gone and then take a look at the dead girl's body.

I stopped a moment and thought about the girl I found on the road, thought about her baby; a flutter in my chest, a wish for them to be okay. I checked my phone hopeful of seeing alerts or missed text messages or a phone call. Nothing. I didn't know if that was a good thing or not.

CHAPTER 10

The first news vans rolled onto the crime scene as we began to approach the boat. By now, I was sure the online coverage had made its rounds with all the social-media sites. The van slowed to a crawl and then stopped, a giant satellite dish on the roof pitching upward in a spin and making a whirring sound as the crew emptied onto the pavement. There was a stout man, a camera on his broad shoulders, a woman near him carrying a microphone. And from the van's side, another man emerged, tall and lanky, college maybe or recently graduated, his hair a fiery red and his face smooth. He was sharply dressed, wearing only half a suit—the top half—his legs bare, save for the plaid beach pants and sandals.

"Took them longer than I thought," Jericho said, his eyes following the scene as he scratched the stubble on his chin.

Buttoning his suit jacket, the man waved in our direction, eager to get a word with us before we boarded the yacht. But from Jericho's gait, I could tell he wanted to avoid the press.

"He won't report anything," I answered flatly. "We have to process the scene first."

"Just a warning, but there isn't much more here than when I found the girl."

"Beyond boarding, was there any other activity?"

"None. Just to see if there was anyone else." Pointing, he continued, "I was out for a test run on that boat when we came across the yacht."

He raised his bad arm toward the pier, and a man who looked as old as the deck on which he stood. The fisherman leaned his broad shoulders against the wheelhouse, a puff of white smoke circling his head.

From the grime-stained rubber coveralls, and the boat's open front with the piles of traps, I made a guess, "Crab boat?"

"Peterson's crab boat," Jericho answered. "Hate to admit it, but Ashtole was right back there. With this arm, I'm supposed to be on desk duty… I'm even considering retirement."

"So, you were here, how exactly?" I asked, turning our exchange into an interview, realizing the officer escorting me could have been the first witness in the case. I needed clarification, needed to see if the crab fisherman would be the second.

Jericho gave me a subtle smile, an understanding in his eyes, knowing why I asked.

"I was with Peterson and Shawn Rogers, his first mate. Peterson is selling his crab boat along with his crabbing lease. He took me out to fish a string of pots, and to work with Rogers, to get a feel for the business before I made any commitments."

"And that's when you saw the yacht?"

"Correct," he answered.

"I'll want to talk with Peterson and Rogers too."

"They'll corroborate. Peterson will chew a little on the subject, he wasn't too happy about my cutting the trip short."

"I'm sure, but still, for completeness, processing the scene and initial investigation."

He gave a nod. "Peterson was with me in the wheelhouse. And Rogers was behind, on the deck."

"Did you two see the body before or after you boarded?"

"Before. I saw both at the same time. The woman's arm hung over the lip of the upper deck, port side," he answered as he used his teeth to dig out a cigarette from a crumpled pack, gave it a second look, and then put it back. "Open water, early sunlight, it wasn't hard to miss."

"Port side?" I asked, looking left and tight, uncertain which side was which. "And that would be?"

"Port is left, and starboard is the right," he answered.

"Has anyone ordered divers?" I asked, thinking there could be more to the scene beneath the water.

"Marine patrol," he answered, taking a drag. Smoke slipped from the corner of his mouth and drifted into nothing. He shook his head, adding, "My divers are scouring the bottom. The yacht wasn't in deep water, but she was loose, adrift. I insisted on grabbing her because she was nearing a line of shallow rocks and would've sunk by day's end."

"And the young woman?"

I continued my questioning but was interrupted as Jericho faced the fisherman.

"For now, stay docked," he yelled toward the crab boat. The old man raised his hands. "We'll need to interview the both of you." The old man dropped his hands, his face pinched in a frown. Peterson's first mate appeared alongside and mirrored his boss's reaction.

"Yeah, they're not happy at all," I said, familiar with the look, and with inconveniencing a witness.

Jericho let out a quiet laugh. "Peterson? That old man is never happy."

We approached the yacht. The blood on the side was dark maroon, dried like paint, a day old, possibly more. The edges of the stain were soft, brighter and weeping, the tide's spray taking hold. I followed an outline, assumed it to be of the dead girl's arm.

"Tell me about the wounds."

"At first glance I saw most of the blood around her head. Blunt force trauma would be my call."

As I climbed the ladder, a technician photographed the lip of the bow and the side of the yacht. A bloody puddle had dried along the edge, thick and almost black, like the stain on the side. I stopped my climb and questioned, "All that from a head wound?"

"That was my first thought too, but there were no other wounds. Maybe more will show at autopsy. My thinking is, with the boat adrift, listing, pitching back and forth, any amount of blood can spread, making it appear to be more than it is."

"I suppose," I said, unconvinced. I finished my climb and stood atop the yacht's deck. I turned to look at the crowd, seeing it had begun to thin, the gawkers moving on, their morbid hunger satiated.

There was one man who stood out from the crowd, catching my attention. I almost missed him on my first look but found him again. I'd learned early on in my career to watch the crowds around a crime scene. I learned to look at anyone who stands out—no reason needed, just trusting your gut. The man's eyes were fixed on the yacht, on us. Alone, standing in front of an old pickup truck, he focused on me and then on Jericho. I could tell he wasn't a vacationer. He seemed smarmy, he chewed on a toothpick, shuffling it from one corner of his mouth to the other. He was balding, portly, wearing soiled dungarees, his shirt heavily stained with sweat and motor grease. He kept his hands in his pockets as if waiting for someone or something to happen.

"Officer Jericho?" I said.

"Jericho, please," he insisted, catching his breath as he finished his climb to the deck. "Did you find something?"

I tilted my chin, trying to do so without being obvious. "That guy look familiar to you?"

"Harlan?"

"A local?"

He nodded and made his way around me, adding, "Harlan Jacobs owns a local marina. He's probably here to tow the yacht in, to help us with the investigation. We can't leave a yacht this size here."

When I looked again, Harlan was already on the move, sitting behind the wheel of his truck and revving the motor.

"Walk me through the scene," I said, dismissing the man and my reaction to him. "Show me where the body was found. What did you see first?"

Jericho struggled to work the sling around his broken arm, his bruised fingers poking through, dead, unmoving. Without thinking, I tugged on the gauzy wrap, helping him. "Thank you," he said, his eyes appreciative. "At first, I thought the girl was naked, but once we secured the yacht, I could she was wearing a bathing suit."

"What kind?" I asked.

Jericho shook his head. "Maybe a two piece?"

"Two piece. Thin," a technician confirmed, snapping her gum in my ear as she held up her camera. "We have pictures."

"Show me."

The technician popped her gum again, adding, "I'll flip through the images, just say when."

I cupped my hands around the camera's small display and saw the dead girl, her face turned away, wearing a white, spaghetti-strap bikini. Her body lay flat, her skin a deadly pallor, her legs spread apart, and her head askew at an awkward angle with one arm hanging over the yacht's left side. Immediately I centered on what I could see of the girl's face—some of her hair was a platinum blonde, but most of it was light brown, matching Hannah's, a tick for my kidnapping case. What little I saw of her face was caked in dried blood and mixed with her hair. It'd take the medical examiner's washing before I could see enough to identify anyone. I'd have to go to the morgue and see the body. With disappointment, I realized this wasn't going to be the quick stopover I'd hoped for.

"Head is at an awkward angle, and covered," I noted, my words catching Jericho's attention. He made his way to my side, peering over my shoulder as the technician advanced to the next photograph. "I think we're looking at a broken neck."

"We can confirm with Dr. Swales," he offered. And then added, "But from the photo, from the amount of blood, she might have been alive for some time."

A hard thump vibrated through my feet as if the yacht had suddenly been bumped. Instinctively, the technician pulled her camera close to her chest, and I braced myself, waiting for another hit. The air broke then with a blood-curdling scream.

CHAPTER 11

The screams set my hair on end. They were followed by a deep bellowing voice, "Sheriff!"

Jericho ran from my side, disappearing into the belly of the yacht in a single swift motion. I followed, trying to keep up, my fingers sliding along the handrail, my body shooting through the narrow stairwell.

When I came through to the lower deck, I found myself in luxurious living quarters—a wrap-around couch, a large-screen television, two paintings on opposite walls like prized bookends. The room was dimly lit in a wash of golden color.

Beyond the swanky room was the yacht's kitchen, the galley, and the source of the screams. The kitchen's lighting was better; it was brighter, fluorescent white. Like the first room, everything was made for luxury—earthy-colored granite, brushed-steel appliances, a densely filled wine rack, a chef's sink, all the amenities imaginable for living on the water. There was money here—"lifestyles of the rich and famous" kind of money. And again, the idea of the yacht being abandoned struck me as odd. Someone had got scared and took off, maybe afraid of being blamed for the death of the girl. And maybe they should be.

Another blood-curdling scream came. Jericho raised his hand in a wave to calm the girl standing at the center of the galley, her eyes glazed with fright and focused on something hidden behind a counter. She was in her early twenties, her blond hair bundled and tucked beneath a navy-blue baseball cap I'd seen all the technicians wearing, her round face an ash white, and her camera dangling from a strap around her neck. She held her hands over her mouth, cupped, as she stifled another scream. Behind her a tall pantry cabinet, its door swinging in a soft rocking motion, back and forth like a baby's cradle.

"What is it?" Jericho yelled.

The technician saw us, her eyes seeming to register and acknowledge who we were. She pointed to the floor behind her, her screams having turned into a whimpered cry.

"She just fell out," the technician said, her breath muffled and shaky. "The boat rocked as I opened the door, and she fell on me."

"Who?" Jericho asked, reaching the technician, his attention immediately directed to what was on the galley floor.

I reached them and leaned over the counter, the touch of granite cold on my arms. Beneath a kneeling technician, a pair of legs stuck out, a woman's feet bound with a thin rope, her toenails painted electric red, her skin a creamy tan—not a summer tan, not Latino or Caucasian, possibly Asian.

"Status?" Jericho asked.

The technician on the floor moved enough for me to see a pair of hands next, the woman's wrists bound as well, the same electric red painted on her fingernails. "Sheriff, I need some help here!" The technician's upturned face was pinched, frowning. Confusion blazed in his glassy eyes.

"Everyone take it easy," Jericho answered, trying to calm the two technicians. "Tell us what happened."

"She just fell out of the closet," the female technician repeated in a rapid breath. She clapped her hands to her damp forehead. She gestured toward the body, the bound legs, and shrieked, "She just fell out!"

"Pull yourself together," the male technician barked. He glanced at me and then Jericho, and confirmed, "Sheriff, ma'am, we have a second body."

He stood and moved out of the kitchen, revealing a pretty woman, her face covered in heavy makeup, lips matching the painted nails, and her hair combed neatly straight, shiny brown and covering most of her face. Her body was dressed in the same spaghetti-strap bikini as the first victim, with one side of her top having shifted, revealing her breast. Her hands and feet were a pale blue, the binding wraps around her wrists and ankles having slowed the blood flow. There was no sign of immediate trauma that I could see. However, there were track marks, pin-hole bruises draped atop both feet like a delicate string of pearls. And while the cosmetics, the painted nails, and the hair style said she was in her mid-twenties, the rest of her body told me she was younger—late teens at the most.

"Sheriff, I'm going to call this into the medical examiner, get another wagon out here," the technician said as he passed me.

"Give Dr. Swales a heads-up. Tell her there's a second body en route," Jericho answered, his voice tense.

I wanted a closer look at the dead girl and slipped on a pair of latex gloves, snapping the ends to free the trapped air. Unlike the girl on the upper deck, this girl's face told me all I needed to know—it wasn't a match to my case, a match to Hannah. The sight of her body on the galley floor struck me then, the sadness of it, half-naked, wrists and ankles bound, drugs and possible signs of abuse. This was someone's child. Like Hannah's kidnapping, this was someone's daughter; her parents would be crushed and heartbroken by the sight of her. I dropped to my knees then to cover the girl's exposed breast, carefully holding the padded bikini between my fingers, lightly brushing against her nipple as I pulled the top across. But something wasn't right. The girl's skin wasn't cold or stiff and didn't have that dry and papery dead feel. Her skin was supple and warm. Responsive.

"Hold on a minute!" I yelled to the technician and pressed my fingers against the girl's neck to check for a pulse. Nothing. I put my cheek above her mouth, raising my hand for everyone to be quiet. And there it was—subtle and almost mistakable. What I felt was warm and moist, a breath on my skin. My heart jumped, and I lifted one of the girl's eyelids, expecting to find it gray and lifeless, but her pupil sprang to life, shrinking against the sudden rush of light.

"This girl is alive!"

CHAPTER 12

We cut the ropes from the girl's ankles and wrists, color returning to them immediately as we bagged the braided nylon as evidence. Jericho mentioned the knots were amateur, and the girl likely unconscious when they'd been tied. He also recognized the rope's type, saying it was common as an anchor line for a dinghy. I was only vaguely familiar with the term, enough to know that he was referring to a smaller boat, a type of inflatable life-raft. I jotted down notes on my phone, underlining the part about the rope.

Soon after our radio call to the dispatcher, two paramedics came through the lower deck's opening like a whirlwind, their bodies wet with sweat, red medical bags slung over their shoulders like bloated pillows, their gloved hands moving a mile a minute, their lips moving even faster. They'd left the gurney outside, grumbling about the stairwell's tight fit and then hoisted the girl into the air, whisking her away in what felt like a single heartbeat.

I wasn't sure the girl would live. She was unresponsive, her pulse thready, and her breathing almost non-existent. In my career, I'd seen my share of overdose cases, and from the bruising around her toes, the track marks, I was certain drugs were the cause. But there was a mystery to how she'd ended up in the closet, her hands and feet bound, alone, and adrift at sea. We were no longer investigating one person's cause of death, but a possible kidnapping as well. In my head, I heard the stir of reminders, the warnings, words telling me not to dig too deep, not to get involved—*just get the notes and pass them on and be on your way.* There was the detective in me too—eager to know more, curious to the outcome, needing to see it resolved.

"I thought she was dead," the technician said, sounding humbled as the ambulance's sirens warbled and then quieted.

I assured him, "You did everything right."

He tucked the straps of nylon rope into a larger cardboard evidence bin. By now, the bin was nearly overflowing with bagged champagne glasses, a few wine bottles, hair samples, blood swabs, and manila envelopes containing the collected fingerprint cards along with their evidence sheets. There'd been a party, the kind I'd suspected when Clive forwarded the initial alert.

The technician lowered his head as I spoke. "Anyone looking at her would have thought the same."

"But you knew better," he said.

"I've seen it before," I told him. "I've seen more drug overdoses than I can count."

"Do you think she'll live?"

I shrugged, pausing to think about his question, finding it impossible for me to answer. "The important thing is you guys found her and gave her a chance she didn't have."

"Quite the party for only two girls," Jericho interrupted. He took a moment to look at the cabinet walls and plush furnishing and then opened the galley's refrigerator. We gathered around him, the cold spilling in a frosty tumble and nipping at my legs. The shelves were filled with more champagne bottles, exotic cheeses, fruit platters, seafood, and tins with writing I didn't recognize.

"Good thing you discovered the yacht before it got hung up in the shallows and broke apart," the technician said.

Jericho gave a nod and asked, "Electronics? Anyone been in the wheelhouse yet?"

The technician shook his head as I asked, "How will the electronics help?"

"The GPS unit. A yacht like this doesn't just appear," Jericho answered. He carefully picked up a food tin, pinching it with a latex glove between his fingers. His brow raised, he held the tin to show us the label and foreign writing. "My guess, whoever they are, they're not from around here."

"The yacht's identification? A registration? A VIN number like on a car?" I asked, rattling off questions as I took hold of the tin, snapping a picture of the food's label. I opened a translator app for a quick deciphering of the foreign words. My phone's signal was bad, but the words came back to identify the language.

"Mett-wurst," the technician said in a slow voice, pronouncing the name on the label.

"It's German. The food is *Mettwurst*. And according to my search, it's a meat spread," I said.

"Yum. Meat in a can. Might be their version of Spam," Jericho joked. "Now we've got an idea of who was onboard. But I doubt they abandoned ship and took the dinghy across the Atlantic."

"The yacht could be corporate owned," the technician said. "There's a lot of these super yachts filling the harbors and marinas for service, stowage, getting them prepped at the last minute. They're a company perk, a frill for the executives."

"Some frill."

"We could be looking for a German corporation with offices in the area," I suggested, making a note.

"Or someone from the marina deciding to borrow the yacht for a party," Jericho added. "Like joyriding. Take the yacht out and return it before anyone notices."

"Let's start with the local marina," I offered.

"Harlan Jacobs," Jericho answered. "We saw him earlier. He might be able to help. As for the hull's identification numbers, it could help, but might take longer if it's international."

"I'll get on it," the technician said. "Send the numbers to you."

"Loop in PK too. We'll go check the wheelhouse," Jericho added. "How about the dinghy? Any sign of it?"

"Gone," the technician answered, shaking his head. "And not just the dinghy. There's a place to stow a jet ski and a small fishing boat too. The storage is empty."

"PK?" I asked. I was an outsider but wanted to keep up with the names. The more I knew, the better for me.

"Our resident IT genius," the technician explained, as he dusted a champagne bottle, throwing black powder and then lightly spinning a fiber brush above it. A fingerprint began to emerge.

"So. Why the name wheelhouse?" I asked, wondering if there might be a literal wheel used to steer the yacht.

"Old term," Jericho answered. "The control room. While there's a wheel, there are more computers and instrumentation than anything else."

We made our way back to the yacht's upper deck and then fished through a sea of technicians until we found a second flight of narrow stairs. Jericho was careful with his bad arm, guarding it, using his body to shield it when passing the technicians. With the DA's comments, and the way he looked at Jericho, I was curious about what had caused his injury, curious whether it was related to their recent loss. We climbed the narrow pass, leading us to the wheelhouse.

From this height, I could see the bay side of the Outer Banks—the seawater's calm surface crowded with boats, some of them swimming along the tall grass while others were anchored for hand-crabbing or drifting with drag nets. A few of the boats trolled the open water, easing through the backwater canals, their fishing tackle draped like lacy curtains from the stern. A flash of glassy light came from a pontoon boat, the sharp glare catching my eyes. The boat's deck was filled with bird photographers, their camera lenses perched like cannon barrels, pointing toward a massive twiggy nest, a mother standing guard, her white breast swelled, her yellow beak darting from one chick to the next in a frenzy to keep up with the feeding. From behind the mother, another bird rose into the sky effortlessly, fanning the air as it lumbered over the open water, the group of photographers sounding a collective gasp, their camera shutters firing rapidly.

The ocean side was equally busy, the edge of the beach thick with beach grass, opening to blooming umbrellas and giant blankets, turning the sand into a colorful checkerboard littered with oily bodies, their skin glistening, bronzed and red, breaking waves rolling toward their feet in a crash of white foam. There were children dancing in the sand and playing in the tidal surf—tumbling, splashing, and flying kites. I watched the fun as a group of teen boys glided on the ocean's lip, whooping and hollering, trying to race the tide only to have it slip from beneath their wakeboards.

Beyond the boat ramp, I could see the local boardwalk, the planked walkway bordering the beach, separating the vacation homes and hotels with stores, amusements, and restaurants. I typed a list of a few of the names as a reminder to visit during my stay. All were busy with patrons filing in and out like a family of bumblebees working a flowerbed during a seasonal bloom. I closed my eyes, listening—the ocean's roar, kids playing, amusement rides clamoring. And for a moment, for just an instant, I'd forgotten why I was here. I'd forgotten about the case file in my bag and the girl on the road, her baby, and the yacht.

"You okay?" Jericho asked.

I opened my eyes, the unexpected respite fading. "Sorry, it's been a long time," I told him.

He cocked his head, confused.

"Growing up, I used to spend my summers along the Jersey shore and forgot what it felt like to be near the ocean."

"Well, welcome home," he offered with a grin, his gaze staying until I returned the smile. "Outer Banks is definitely the type of place that settles in your soul. You know what I mean?"

"I do," I told him, understanding and envying him. A gust from the ocean pushed my hair into my eyes. I added, "Maybe I'll stay long enough to let that happen."

"Oh, it won't take long," he said, producing a kerchief from his pocket and covering the door's handle. Before entering, he turned back to me, sunlight flashing from the blue and green in his eyes as he said, "Listen, I know it's an unusual circumstance we're in, and I appreciate your stepping up. Let me make it up to you and show you the sights while you're in town. A professional courtesy."

His offer was innocent enough, but a strange flutter stirred in my belly, the kind that made me feel shy. Being in a strange town with new people, an unplanned vacation—I suppose it was apt to experience more than my day to day. And I suppose that could include getting to know someone. Feelings for anyone had languished over the years. I'd all but forgotten what it was like to be with another person.

"I'd like that," I told him, surprising myself. I gave a shrug, adding, "I mean, my trip was a last-minute thing, and I didn't make any plans."

"That's good, your schedule is open," he said, glancing at his watch. "We may hear from Dr. Swales soon, and by the time we're done at the morgue, I'm sure we'll both be hungry."

"Yes." I nodded with a cringe, wondering if he was trying to make a joke. The sharp smell of embalming fluid could kill anyone's appetite.

He moved to open the door, making room for us both. The wheelhouse was filled with electronics and nautical equipment and looked like something out of a science-fiction movie. Jericho seemed to know exactly where to go.

"Smell that?" he asked, his face cramped. I followed him inside, slowing when the odor hit me. The burnt smell of ozone and charred electronics filled my nose. "If the yacht was abandoned, I think I know why."

I waved my hand in front of my face, asking, "Was it a fire?" I scanned the room, feeling frantic, searching for the obvious signs. The air was dense, thick with the pungent smell, but I couldn't find a source.

"Not a fire," Jericho answered, flipping switches to the off position and pushing buttons to disable the remaining electronics. "It's a bad short, some fried relays, but oddly, not enough to trip all the breakers."

"Some of those are already dead," I said, pointing to the far bay of electronics stacked from floor to ceiling—the displays empty, the screens dark, the pixels lifeless. A few of the nautical instruments were alive though, showing the weather and tidal charts.

"The one I need is up," he said, pointing to the front, toward a screen resembling the map application on my phone.

"Shit," he said, raising his good hand in a mock surrender. I could see his mind working, thinking, and he rushed, ducking beneath the equipment to open a cabinet's panel door next to the yacht's wheel. "That one is gone too! I guess I shouldn't be surprised."

"What?" I asked, kneeling next to him, searching the wires, following them as they snaked along the cabinet's insides, leading into a computer mounted to the floor. "Maybe now is a good time to tell you, I know almost nothing about a boat's electronics."

"That's not a problem. Anything you don't know, I'll be able to help with."

"You can start with telling me what you're looking for," I said, curious. "The yacht's coordinates, right? Or where it had been?"

He nodded. "The GPS unit's memory card. It would show us the navigation history, the path, telling us the origination point and how it ended up at the inlet's mouth."

"It's been taken?"

"No SIM card, and no memory card. See those slots?" I leaned onto his shoulder, finding the empty space. "That's where the cards should be. And the backup is gone too."

"A girl dies on the deck. It could be accidental. Or murder. She has no identification. And then there's a failure in the wheelhouse, a short in the control panel's electronics, killing the motors and the navigation. So, they decide to abandon ship, taking with them any evidence of where they'd come from," I said, trying to summarize. His eyes told me he agreed. "But we don't know who the girl in the galley is, or why they didn't take her with them."

"Or why she was bound," he added. "My guess would be drugs and sex games, partying? They left in a hurry and decided she was dead too."

"Perhaps, but something tells me this wasn't some off-site office get-together."

"How do you mean?" he asked.

I mulled over the idea I had, recalling a case I'd worked that was similar—young girls, initially thought to be guests. It turned out they'd been hired. All of them were juveniles. Most of them runaways. The case was handled by the vice squad, but a station tip led me there, a picture of Hannah in hand, what she would look like at their age. It was another dead end for my case, but the vice squad broke up a small ring, made the evening news and received commendations.

"I have a strong suspicion the girls aren't exactly guests. At least not the kind we'd consider," I answered. "If I'm right, the girls *were* the party, if you know what I mean."

"You mean, escorts?" he asked, shaking his head, disgusted by the idea. "They're children."

"I've seen this before."

"If you're right, the case is much bigger."

I gave him a nod, exclaiming, "If they are minors, that'd make this a case of trafficking."

"Correct," he said, as we helped each other back to our feet. "How long did you say you were in town for?"

"Not sure yet," I answered, sensing why he was asking. I glanced at my phone. A message had me eager to leave.

"Hospital?"

"It is. The girl is still in surgery, and there's no mention of the baby's status yet either."

"I know the staff," he told me. "They're in great hands."

"I'm hoping the non-medical staff are on the case too."

"Identification?"

"Fingerprints, rape kit, all of it. There's no knowing how she ended up in the woods. Abducted? Raped? Buried alive? And what about the father? We're stuck without an identification." From the look on Jericho's face, I realized I was rambling, something I tended to do when faced with more questions than answers. "Sorry. I want to be there when the doctor has news."

"There're a lot of unknowns," he said, his tone understanding. "I'll join you, if that's okay?"

"Yes," I agreed. "You know the lay of the land, and I could use a hand in navigating."

"The morgue is near the hospital. If Dr. Swales is ready, we can swing by."

"Let's hope so."

As we made our way to the door, he motioned to my bag, to the corner of the case folder poking through. "The case you're working. Swales should be able to help with an identification too."

Clutching my bag, my drawings, we left the wheelhouse. The sea air blew through my hair and beach noises reached my ears. I couldn't decide how far I wanted to go with the investigation. There was a case here. I sensed it was big, too. The kind that could easily steal my days if I let it. I could help them, but once we were finished at the morgue, my question would be answered, and I'd know to stay or move on. I hurried down the narrow steps, my feet clanking against the metal, eager to get to the hospital and see how the girl and her baby were doing.

CHAPTER 13

We'd lost time working the crime scene, answering questions as the technicians searched for any clues as to who was onboard with the girls. By now, I had my notes, the technicians had their work, and we had the hospital firmly set in mind as our next stop. As of our last radio call, the girl discovered in the galley was still alive, but had to be placed on a ventilator. Her kidneys and liver were shutting down as well—a course of dialysis needed, we were told. Maybe two. And as I'd suspected, it was an overdose—probably heroin or maybe a speedball, a powerful mix of cocaine and heroin.

"Can you drive?" Jericho asked.

"Sure," I answered, stealing a look at his bad arm and trying to recall the dirty details of my car's interior—fast-food wrappers, foldable maps in case the GPS app sent me down some unnamed road, the battered old case full of clothes I'd thrown in the back when I left my apartment. I was sure I'd overpacked but hadn't thought about how long I'd stay. "Have to shuffle some stuff into the back."

"Appreciate it," he answered solemnly while picking at his arm's bandaging.

"Mind if I ask?" I said, questioning, motioning to the sling.

"It was a boating accident," he said without hesitation.

"Line of duty?" I asked, continuing to pry. His gaze went to the yacht and then to the ocean, his voice silent. I felt awkward, but then heard footfall coming from behind us.

"Sheriff? A minute, please!" We turned to face the crab fisherman Jericho had been with when the yacht was discovered. He approached with a spry gait, his rubber boots scraping the stony landing. "Sheriff. I can't stay docked forever."

"Peterson," Jericho said, turning to face me. "This is Detective Casey White. She'll be leading the investigation."

Before I could say a word, the old crab fisherman took hold of my fingers, cupping them in his hands. He was tall, lean and stood inches from me, presenting himself like an old-world gentleman, a seasoned maître d'. If not for his sea-smelling coveralls and the wiry grays sprouting from beneath his shabby fisherman's cap, I could easily imagine him in a tuxedo. The fisherman's hands were warm, and though his grip was gentle, I felt the touch of his long days—strong and calloused, and years in the making.

He shook my hand in a slow manner, his eyes centered on mine as he spoke with a toothless whistle, "Ma'am, it is my pleasure to meet you," he began, his voice tired and worn by the cigarettes he smoked. "But I'm afraid I cannot stay docked. We have gear to haul, and the crab just won't keep."

"I understand," I told him, slipping my hand from his, and searching Jericho's face for his opinion. Jericho gave a short nod, which was all I needed. "Can I count on you to answer some additional questions if they come up?"

"Certainly," he said, relief brightening his face. His smile broadening, he added, "The sheriff, he'll know how to reach me."

"At a moment's notice?" I insisted, raising my brow, knowing how easily a potential witness can become impossible to get a hold of.

He crossed his chest as if blessing himself and then held a few fingers in the air in what might have been a Boy-Scout pledge. "My promise to you," he said, his voice firm. "Ma'am, you have a fine day." And as fast as he'd appeared, the crab fisherman returned to his boat.

"He's a pleasant fellow," I said.

"He has his moments," Jericho said one brow raised. "But catch him on a day when a boater ruins a string of his gear."

"I have to ask," I began, my curiosity getting to me. "*Sheriff?* Everyone still refers to you by the title."

Jericho sighed, answering, "That's one name I can't shake. Even after joining the marine patrol."

"It is an elected position. Correct?"

"It is," Jericho answered. We reached my car, and I opened the passenger door for him. Before he could enter, I jumped inside to clear the seat, tossing everything I could get my hands on into the back. "And?"

"It seems like a lifetime ago now that I think about it," he said, easing himself inside. "Elected twice. And would have continued too, but… life can get in the way." His words faded as his gaze went back to the yacht.

I sensed there was disappointment and didn't press. I gave him a way out of the conversation, prompting with an innocent enough question, "So you still want me to call you Jericho?"

His sly smile made me stop and take notice. He was handsome. There was a bashful redness in his cheeks too, warming his face. "Yes. Please. Jericho is preferred," he said, closing the car door, and pulling his phone from his pocket. His smile faded as he showed me the text message on the screen. "It's Swales. Unfortunately, she won't be ready for us today."

"The Medical Examiner?"

"Correct," he answered. "The mayor has her in a conference call. The press on this is going to be heavy. They're doing prep for a press release and news conference. She might be ready to see you tomorrow morning."

"The morning?" I asked, disappointed. This was going to take longer than I'd wanted. "Any chance you can have them send a photo of the girl's face?"

"For comparison?" he asked, his eyes shifting to my case folder. I gave a nod and started the car.

"I'll ask, but if I know Swales, we won't hear from her again until she is ready for us. She has—"

"A process," I finished for him. "Yeah, you mentioned it."

"When we get to the hospital, let's get a picture of our girl from the yacht. I have an idea."

I'd never been a fan of hospitals, the unforgiving smell, the lights a blinding constant. I uncapped my bottle of water and drank down a gulp, trying to settle the tightness in my chest. It wasn't just the smell and the brightness, I think hospitals in general just made me uncomfortable.

This visit was part of an official investigation and involved my checking on the girl we'd found alive on the yacht. While I kept that at the forefront of my mind, I couldn't help but think of my morning and my first visit to the hospital. As we took to the halls, I spied every open door, every window and curtained bed, hoping to see the young woman I'd found in the woods. This visit was official business, but my heart was still with the girl and with her baby too.

We found the victim from the yacht, her appearance changing entirely from when she was bound and lying on the galley floor. Her expression was empty, a thick breathing tube protruding from between her lips with white hospital tape cinched in a crisscross on her cheeks and chin. Other tubes, skinny, snaked down her arms, and appeared from beneath gauzy wraps, the needle tips buried beneath her skin. A few hung slack between the bed and a machine, the insides filled with blood, the shade a deep burgundy—kidney dialysis, filtering the toxins from her blood.

A good-looking doctor greeted us as he prepared to exit the room. Before leaving, he took hold of Jericho's shoulder with a shake, his gaze falling to Jericho's bandaged arm.

"Sheriff, how are you coming along?" he asked. There was sincerity in his voice. "Big day coming up?"

Jericho offered a hesitant smile, answering nervously, "Yeah. I hope it's the last one. I'm tired of seeing you guys."

"Fingers crossed. Call if you need anything." Huge dimples appeared on the doctor's cheeks, showing a smile reserved for patients.

"How is she?" I asked.

A buzz came from his hip, a small phone that reminded me of an old-school pager.

"I understand she was discovered on an abandoned super yacht?" the doctor answered with a question, and a shake of his head.

"The victim was found in the yacht's galley." I pointed to the black-and-blue creases around her wrists and ankles. "She was discovered bound and unconscious. We also suspect drugs may have been involved."

The doctor checked the display and nodded. "Drugs could be involved. We'll know more when we get her bloodwork. Unfortunately, she's lapsed into a coma." His hip buzzed again, stealing his attention. He glanced down and added apologetically, "If you'll excuse me." Before I could say another word, the doctor was gone, leaving us alone.

"Let's try to get a picture of her," Jericho said, approaching the girl's bed while my focus shifted to the television in the corner, the tuned station displaying a news conference. Pictures of the yacht flashed onto the screen, along with a picture of Jericho and me standing on the deck, our investigation of the blood patterns being played back to the viewing audience. "Yup. And that'd be the press conference I mentioned."

If I'd been trying to keep a low profile, my cover was blown. "It looks that way," I answered.

The screen flashed to the press conference, a podium and microphone, the front of it adorned with the Outer Banks name. An older man stood behind the microphone, his hand in the air, motioning, calling on reporters.

"Who's that?"

"Mr. Jonathon Miller, our mayor."

"And that's the district attorney next to him?" I asked, referring to the shorter, white-haired man. "I thought he kind of gave you a hard time earlier."

Jericho chuckled, answering, "Yeah, that's Ashtole. He gives everyone a hard time. You certainly put him in his place."

A warm flash rose on my neck. "I'm not much for terms of endearment from strangers."

"Well, the look on his face was absolutely camera worthy. And he'll probably be our next mayor. Miller's been grooming him to take over. I guess he's giving Ashtole time in front of the camera, some public exposure."

Jericho held his phone at an angle above the hospital bed. Using his one hand to do all the work, he struggled to get the picture.

"I can do that," I offered, holding my phone. The girl's eyes were shut, and her hair pulled back, tucked behind her head. As I snapped a picture, I saw the makeup had been completely removed. Even her fingernails had been cleaned. To look at her now, she was younger than I'd initially guessed—maybe thirteen or fourteen, her age striking close, as if personal, visceral even. "Got it."

"Might work. Might not," Jericho said, taking his phone, swapping it with mine. I snapped the photo and handed his back to him.

"What's your idea with the pictures?"

"I mentioned PK, our resident IT guy," he began as he pocketed his phone and went to the door. I nodded. "Kids do everything online. If there is someone who can find out who the girls are, it'll be PK."

I lifted the girl's hand, showing the inky residue from a fingerprint pad. "What about these?" I asked. "Most elementary schools should have some records. If she's young enough, she might have been registered in the event of having to raise an Amber Alert."

"True," he agreed, urging me to follow. I lifted the girl's sheet, tucking her in as though she were my own. "But with her photo, and with the dead girl's photo, our IT expert may find exactly how it is the two ended up together on the same yacht."

"We need some concentration on the trafficking possibility. Is your IT expert open to taking direction?"

Jericho slowed. "Certainly. Where do you want him to start?"

"My suggestion, let's begin with social media." We continued to walk, his gait matching mine as I clarified, "If we get a hit, let's find the circles the victim ran with. Check all the regulars too—Facebook, Instagram, Snapchat. And also research some of the lesser-known platforms, then check them as well."

"That's a good place to start," he agreed, passing the nurses station, nodding a hello to a pretty brunette who'd called out his name. "I'll give PK the instructions."

"Just my hunch, but there's probably one person, maybe two, who are actually responsible for the girls being on the yacht. In my experience, it's very unlikely they ended up there on their own."

"Exactly," he agreed. "We need to find what's in common and focus on it. Then we'll know what's what."

"Whatever the findings, I'll note them and pass it along," I reminded him.

"What's that?"

"You said *we*," I answered. "When I leave, I'll transfer the case, along with my notes."

His grin returned, inviting, his body swaying subtly as he asked, "Are you sure you don't want to hang around and help us solve a mystery?"

"I'll admit, this one is intriguing, but I've got my own case," I said, lifting my bag, my hand on Hannah's case folder.

He continued to smile, his grin contagious.

My phone buzzed with the message I'd been waiting for. I read the screen and searched the signs on the hospital's walls, finding I was completely turned around.

"What is it?"

"The girl I picked up along the road this morning. She's out of surgery," I told him.

"This way," he said, leading me to the stairs. "The waiting room is one level below us."

CHAPTER 14

Jericho brought us to the waiting area where I'd given the receptionist my contact information earlier. There was no doctor present when we arrived, no staff at the door like the first time. A different person was at the desk now—an older, balding man, tufts of gray hair sprouting from his ears, his thick glasses endlessly slipping toward the end of his nose. His face was without expression, a computer terminal, binary, on or off.

"I'm sorry?" he said. "Who did you say contacted you?"

"Someone at this ward," I answered, trying to keep my tone even. "I brought in a pregnant girl. It was an emergency. She'd been found in the woods."

"Her name?"

"I don't know her name," I said, my voice rising with my frustration.

"Sir," Jericho began. "If you could send a message to the emergency-room staff from this morning's shift. Mention it is with regard to the police escort that had been requested, I'm sure it will help."

"Right, the hospital was notified," I added. "I'd called 9-1-1, and there was a team already waiting for us."

"I'll get on it."

"I can get us something to drink. A coffee, water, or a soda pop?" Jericho offered as we moved to the seating area. Cold air poured from the overhead vents, making me shiver. "Or a jacket?"

"No, but thank you," I said, shaking my head. I was nervous, more than I expected, and tried not to show it.

"Are you okay?"

"I'm scared for her," I answered, my head filling with images of the woods, the roadside, the girl's blood-soaked nightgown, her pregnancy, and her hands and toes, the skin shredded. "And I'm scared for her baby too."

"That's understandable," he said. "I'd heard she was in rough shape. But just know you did everything you could. Like you said earlier, you gave her a chance."

He was using my words, the same I'd used with the technician. He meant well, and I appreciated it, but it didn't stave off the nervousness eating my insides. There was something about the way the girl looked at me that I couldn't shake.

"Someone did that to her." I turned to face him, a dark notion I wanted him to understand, to make sure it got investigated after I was gone. "She had bruising on her neck, the shape of fingers, hands. This was a crime. Attempted murder."

"The chief mentioned it. He also mentioned it's already a new case, opening with your report."

"It'll definitely require my accounts of the morning," I said as footsteps approached. I motioned to the doors, asking, "Have you heard if the techs found anything at the scene? Were they told she came from the woods?"

"I'm not sure what they've been told," he shrugged. "And I asked. The technicians haven't gotten to the site yet."

I stared at him, incredulous, my head filled with the morning again. "What? The site should have been secured the moment I provided a location. And the search needs to expand deep into the woods adjacent to the road. You should have seen her feet—"

"With all the attention on the yacht… but yes. You're right," he said, a look of embarrassment on his face.

His expression made me feel bad, made me feel uncomfortable for having questioned their officers. But a girl and her unborn child had been attacked.

"Listen, I didn't mean to snap."

"We're better than this," he said. "Between my team, and the sheriff's office, we're facing some resourcing challenges."

Before I knew what I was saying, I offered, "I'll take a ride back to the site, and try to bring a technician with me. Who knows what we might find."

And then it was time. The doctor found us. She looked no older than the girl I'd brought in, her scrubs a marbled purple-turquoise, and her shoes the same. Her expression told me nothing. It was plain, absent of emotion, like a poker player.

"How is she?" I asked.

"I understand you found her?" she asked me.

Without hesitation I brought out my badge, hanging it around my neck, answering, "Yes. I came across her on the road in the woods."

The doctor's eyes darted from me to Jericho. She shifted, seeming uncomfortable, apprehensive, her expression changing. My heart dropped. She was going to deliver bad news.

"Well," she began, and tried to swallow.

"It's okay," Jericho told her. "Go on."

"I'm afraid there was too much blood loss. In fact, I'm surprised she was standing at all."

"She died?" I asked, my voice weak.

"I'm sorry," the doctor said. Then added, "We did everything we could."

My legs trembled, but I didn't show it. I didn't know this girl, but strangely, I felt for her loss, felt connected. She could have been

Hannah—the same age, similar features. My mind began digging through scenarios of how I could have made a difference. *What if I'd left my apartment a few minutes earlier? Would I have saved her then?* My mind quickly snapped back defensively: *If you'd made a right instead of a left turn, nobody would have ever found her.*

"Of course you did," I said, shaking her hand. "Thank you."

"I have to mention, we found significant injuries we believe require further investigation."

"The marks around her neck?" I asked.

"Yes," she answered. "There are other injuries too. Older. The X-rays showed broken ribs that had healed, an arm—"

"Doc," I interrupted, "what about her baby?"

"The delivery?" she asked. "We should know more after the autopsy, but the cause of death is likely due to complications from birth."

"No, I don't think that's the question," Jericho said, shaking his head.

"Was the girl miscarrying?" I asked, confused. "Is that what caused all the bleeding?"

The doctor's composure turned instantly, alarm showing on her face as she shifted. "I'm sorry. Now I'm confused. The girl brought in had already delivered her baby. The delivery caused the complications, the excessive bleeding. Wasn't the baby brought in too?"

"What do you mean, *already* delivered?" Jericho asked, looking to me. "You said she was pregnant when you found her?"

An unsettling panic filled me. My mind raced, retracing the morning, the girl, my hand on her belly, searching for life, for a baby's kick or anything. But was her baby there?

"Oh God!" I exclaimed, believing I understood. "The woods. We have to go back!"

As I spun around, I heard the doctor's voice calling after me, "Where's the baby?"

CHAPTER 15

A baby was missing. My pulse raced as I weaved through traffic and blew through a stop sign. I saw disapproval in Jericho's expression and eased up on the gas pedal. My slowing the car only lasted a moment as the urgency to get to the woods hit me like a fever. We had no way of knowing where the girl gave birth. It could have been in the woods, or somewhere else. We couldn't chance it.

"I was certain she was in labor," I shouted over the traffic.

"She could have just given birth," he offered. "Contractions continue afterward."

"Is that right?" I asked, recalling my experience but curious how he would know.

He caught my expression, adding, "My son. He's older now, but I remember."

Jericho called out the directions, having taken the GPS coordinates from my phone. I remembered most of the turns and followed the paved roads over Wright Memorial Bridge, then skidded onto backroads that turned to dirt and gravel. My old car kept up with the demand, the motor revving and the temperature light flashing on and off during the longer runs. Jericho kept busy with phone call after phone call, demanding support, pulling whatever resources he could find to form a search party.

"Over there," Jericho said, stealing my attention as a flash of red and blue bounced in my mirrors. A parade of patrol cars had formed behind us. I took the lead, driving to the exact section of road where the pregnant girl had appeared. There were others following too—civilians, each of them parking with us. They had come to help. Jericho saw that I was watching and said, "Told you I'd make a few calls."

"Yeah, you sure did." We exited the car with no idea in mind of where to begin. The sun had dipped into the afternoon, giving the sky a cloudy light. In the hilly elevation, with the height of the trees, shadows awoke with a stretch, touching hands across the road as the western sky turned into a patch of faded denim.

I scanned the forest, noting the deeper recesses hidden from the sun. I yelled over the growing crowd, "Folks, it will be dark in some areas. Flashlights if you have them! Two if you have the room!"

"Who's leading this?" someone called. I heard a dog's bark. Then two. An eruption of them joining the request. "I brought my hounds."

"Wow, you really did make some calls," I said to Jericho, impressed.

"Clyde! Bring them here!" Jericho yelled.

A shorter man approached. Older, with pale-brown skin and freckles covering every inch of his face and neck. He wore green overalls, the seams frayed and tattered, his arm straining as he was led by two large bloodhounds. I recognized the breed, their ears long, skin loose on their faces, their mouths glistening wet and hanging in droopy folds.

"Where do you want us, Sheriff?" the man asked, shoving his fingers through his stringy beard.

"Clyde, this is Detective White."

"Ma'am," he said, taking my hand before yanking a twig from between his teeth. Without warning, the larger dog shoved his nose into my leg and then lurched forward, diving into my crotch. I jumped back, startled and embarrassed, spinning around and shoving the dog's face. Drool covered my hands. "Sorry about that, ma'am. He's just greeting you."

"Hope he doesn't mind if I choose not to reciprocate," I answered. "What do they need to help to pick up a scent?"

"They good if you got something with her scent on it?"

"Will blood work?" I asked, the words sounding morbid.

"That'd work," he answered.

I sifted through the rear of my car and found the shirt I'd worn earlier, the girl's blood already drying in tie-dye patches, some of it maroon, almost unrecognizable, and some of it still bright and tacky. I knelt down next to the dogs and was immediately met with a wet nose on my chin and a tongue on my cheek.

"Down boy!" Clyde yelled, jerking a leash and taking hold of the scruff behind their necks, his grip harsh, squeezing until one of the dogs cried out.

"I got this!" I said sternly, finding Clyde's eyes and urging him to ease his hold.

"I'm still training them, ma'am," he remarked sheepishly. "They getting better though."

Behind us, men and women entered the woods, flashlights beaming in the shadows, the search already starting. I was eager to get moving too and waved the shirt in front of the dogs. Instantly they reacted. I waved it again, closer to their noses this time. Their front legs straightened, and their posture went stiff. Their bodies became zombie-like as the girl's scent seemed to register some deep, primal instinct. The hounds jerked their heads back, and in their rich-brown eyes, I saw their ancestral programming flick into overdrive.

"I think they've got it," I said, my voice registered with surprise.

Clyde saw it too and shouted excitedly, "Yup, they on it! Here we go!"

*

We could barely keep up with the hounds—their strength overpowering Clyde as he did his best to follow the dogs. At times, the short man stumbled, or got the leashes caught up around a tree. He held on though, never letting go of the leather straps, the dogs dragging him free and bouncing him along the ground.

"Never seen anything like this," I said, my breathing heavy.

"Yeah, me neither," Jericho said, his words raspy as we tried to keep the pace. He let out a hearty chuckle, "Clyde's been talking about training those dogs for years."

"Over here," someone yelled. We'd heard the same declaration a few times already, each bringing more clues, more traces of blood, but no baby. We stayed the course with the dogs, the search party flashlights shining like laser pointers. In the light beams, I caught glimpses of every tree and leaf the hounds inspected. There was blood on all of them.

The ground was a graveyard of autumn-colored leaves and dead branches spat by the trees. With one misstep, the snap of a stick twisted my ankle, sending me off balance. Jericho caught hold of me, gripping my arm until I was standing on my own again. The woods grew denser as we descended further, a forest made up of thick foliage and high trees, a canopy the color of black coffee, the entire search party hidden in gray light. For a brief moment, I thought I heard kids playing. I stopped, the sound reminding me of a park, afternoon visits to a playground near our home, Hannah in my arms. But then the sound was gone.

"Do you see a trail?" I asked, ditching the memory.

"Not around here," Jericho answered. "I can't be sure, but I think this might be private property."

"Is that right?" I asked with an idea coming to my mind.

Jericho must have shared the same, adding, "But it doesn't mean the girl didn't come from the road—a car—and then brought into the woods."

"Sheriff!" Clyde yelled, his voice breaking.

We'd missed the commotion as we talked. Rather, we'd missed the lack of commotion. The dogs had stopped barking entirely.

"I got something here!"

CHAPTER 16

I jumped over a log and then another, wincing at the pain in my ankle as I raced to catch up to Clyde and his dogs. Jericho followed closely, the two of us finding the short man and his hounds. When we reached him, he looked like something out of an old painting—rural America, a hundred years before our time. Clyde stood with each dog next to him, the hounds upright and at attention, their postures fixed on the sight in front of them. I stepped softly, aware of the search party forming around us. It was a grave. A shallow, bloody grave.

The ground had been hollowed out, just enough to hold the body of the girl. It wasn't deep though, three feet, maybe four in parts, the bottom turning stony which might have slowed or stopped the digging altogether. There were mounds of loose earth and rock piled errantly on each side, and bright-white tree roots around the soil like stiff twine. There was no mistaking what it was. And there was no question the girl had come from this place, her claw marks and scratches where she'd dug herself free easy to see. Beams of lights shined on the walls of the grave, the morbid details met with hushed gasps.

"She was buried alive," I said.

Red puddles covered the ground, the leaves and shrubbery leading away from the hole stained with the same. At once I understood what the doctor meant when she'd said the girl shouldn't have been able to stand at all. I'd seen my share of crime scenes, but I'd never seen this amount of blood from one person at any time. It was as if her entire body had emptied.

Before we touched anything, I turned to a patrol officer, ordering, "We need to preserve the scene. Can you place a barricade? Put an eight- to ten-foot perimeter line around it."

He gave a firm nod, a roll of shiny yellow crime-scene tape at the ready. As the patrol officer began his work, he told us, "There are two crime-scene technicians on their way."

"My God!" someone said, turning away in a run. The smell of earth and clay and blood was thunderously potent. "That can't all be from one person. Can it?"

"The baby," I said quietly, searching the loose dirt, turning the stones, hoping to see movement. There was dead silence. Abruptly, a second person ran from the grave. I sleeved a pair of latex gloves onto my hands and covered my mouth, preparing to dig. I had to know.

"I'll check," Jericho said, daring to kneel, touching the ground first and testing if it was wet. His fingers came up dry. He eased onto one knee, taking a stout branch to sift through the grave's remains, easing the pointed end into the soil and probing for a body. The group fell silent as the tension grew thick like the humid air. Jericho slipped the end of the stick into the earth with dirt and stone grating the wood. After a few minutes of repeating the same, he concluded, "There's no baby. Not here."

"But her mother was," I said, shining a light on a fingernail jutting from the soil. I opened an evidence bag and carefully retrieved it.

"She was here. At least there is that to investigate," Jericho said. He stood as the crowd moved on, their search for the baby continuing. "This is a grave. Any thoughts?"

"This early into the investigation, my best guess, the victim was strangled and then she was buried. Only, she was alive and in labor. The killer may have assumed both of them were dead," I answered, anxious to continue searching. Laughter drifted through the trees again. I stopped to listen, recognizing the playful sounds from before. "Jericho, tell me you heard that?"

"I did," he answered. "It came from over there."

As the patrol officer continued stringing the crime-scene barricade around trees, we followed the sounds, the high-pitched voices unmistakable. With each step, each broken branch, relief set in me. I hadn't been hearing things. It was laughter, my memories of visiting the park with my daughter preserved and authentic, and not my imagination gone rogue.

The laughter became loud with distinct voices separated by pitch and tone as I continued flashing the surrounding ground with my phone's light, hoping and praying for a miracle—a baby's arm, pudgy fingers clutching the air, anything. A rabbit froze as I approached, its black marble eye glinting in my phone's light. If not for its nose, and the whiskers moving, I would have thought the animal was stuffed. In a blink, it was gone.

"Careful," Jericho said. "That next step is a doozie." I braced his good arm, stopping when the woods opened up to a ledge, a steep hill cresting a magnificent valley. The sight was clear for miles. We were at the wood's edge, out of its shadows and facing the west and the brightness. Sunlight hung high above the horizon, the edge of the earth burning daylight. I followed the laughter and found the source.

"I'd no idea this patch of woods led to this place," Jericho said.

To one side of the valley I saw what looked like a prison—high fences with spiraling razor wire strung around the perimeter. Behind the fenced barriers, girls, teenagers, all of them wearing jumpsuits, typical inmate issue. They carried on with playground games like hopscotch and basketball and wall-ball. A few girls huddled into corners, tending to each other's hair, while others leaned against the fence, their stares fixed on the hillside as guards roamed around in a slow stroll.

On the other side of the valley, there was an old estate that went on for acres. The buildings were steeped in beautiful riches, adorned with grand patios and walkways lined with statues like something out of ancient Greece. Nestled inside the estate grounds, there were tennis courts and swimming pools with lavish fountains and ponds, and every corner had a perfectly manicured lawn.

"A prison?" I asked, my interest tuned to the girls, to their ages and the likeness of our pregnant victim. My mind immediately raced with speculations and a possible conspiracy, a story forming that told the tale of the girl's pregnancy, the possibility of a prison official's involvement, of sexual misconduct, their ultimate disgrace and a potential cover-up. I knew I was reaching and jumping to a conclusion, but that's how my brain works, it's how I'm wired. And most of the time, I'm right.

"That's the detention center."

"Is it an all-girl's detention center?"

"It is," he answered, spying my gaze and catching my tone. "Are you cooking up a theory?"

"Maybe," I answered, confident we had our first lead. A strong lead. "What do you think the chances are we'll find a baby inside those fences and walls?"

"I'd say it's possible. I'd also say it's just a theory. And I have one too. But in mine, I believe the victim was strangled and brought here."

"And the baby?"

"Nowhere around here," he said glumly, facing the valley again, the sun gleaming in his eyes. "She was buried alive, gave birth, wandered off, confused, near death when you came across her on the road."

"So the baby…?' I repeated, but afraid to hear him say what we were both thinking.

He dug his toe into the ground, pebbles and dirt skittered off the side of the cliff. "There's a lot of wildlife out here."

"Oh, Jericho," I whispered, shaking my head.

"Yeah. I know. It's not the ending anyone wants."

"We'll know more when we get an identification," I said, hoping my idea was right. I turned to the estate, asking, "What about their neighbor?"

"Oh, there's a lot of history in there. It's also how the detention center came to be," he said. "That is the home of our mayor."

"All that?"

"It's his family's estate. I think it was his great, great grandfather's or something like that. At one time the family owned all of this land. Then about fifteen years ago, after the last of his relatives died, the mayor donated the whole south side to the county. That estate is what's left now, but at one time the mayor's family *was* the Outer Banks."

"And they built a detention center?"

"Uh-huh. It's been there ever since," he explained.

Even though the girls were fenced in, their laughter was a welcome change. I closed my eyes to listen a moment, but quickly found, more than anything, I wanted to hear the cries of a baby.

CHAPTER 17

Jericho and I left the woods; the other officers would coordinate the search for the baby. There was talk of the search party becoming a recovery team, and the belief in what Jericho mentioned—an animal could have taken the baby, a coyote or possibly a bobcat. I hated the thought of it, the idea of it. I hated the truth of nature intervening. It was another gruesome detail of the job to accept.

By the third road, I was completely lost. I'd made my way out of the woods, driving us back to the land of asphalt and streetlights, and even got us across the bridge. When I saw the ocean, I'd kept the beach and waves to my left, but had lost sight of them again after we entered the center of town. Jericho assured me we were on track, promising to get us to a place where there was hot food and cold drinks. While there was plenty of daylight remaining, we'd slipped well into the afternoon and the need for food was getting strong.

When we were stopped in traffic, I contacted my station back home, checking in with my captain. There was hesitation, but I'd made him a promise when the reprimand was given. I'd tell him where I landed and when I planned my return. I also texted details about staying in the Outer Banks and that I'd been volunteered into helping with a case. His reply let me know the chief had already reached out to him, paving the way for me by removing all administrative and logistical obstacles. I showed my phone to Jericho. It was official. I was cleared to work as a temporary transfer.

Jericho joked, "There's nothing more permanent than something temporary."

I laughed. "Is that right?" But deep down, I worried it was true. I had my own case to follow up on, to keep as a priority. As if agreeing, my stomach let out a hungry growl. I rolled the window down to mask the sound, the breeze filled the car. The smell of sea air helped erase some of the odor from the morning, which had permeated the rear seats.

Maybe the Outer Banks and "permanent" was a good idea, I thought, glancing at Jericho, his eyes closed, sunshine on his face. I didn't know him that well yet, but sensed I'd like to. I already knew I wanted to get to know the Outer Banks much more.

Eventually we arrived in front of a small diner, its steely shell and neon colors very typical of the kind I used to visit when my family vacationed along the Jersey shore. A woman and her two boys held the door as we approached, the scent of coffee and toast and pancakes hitting me in a warm rush, bringing more memories of childhood summers.

"Thank you," I said to the small boys, their upturned faces greeting me.

"Get the waffles," one of them instructed.

"With the whipped cream," the other followed, his front baby teeth missing, the word whipped sounding like *whip-ped*.

"Maybe I will," I said. "Maybe I'll make it a double."

"Whoa," one said to the other, shaking his head comically.

"Sheriff," the woman said, greeting us, a grin on her round face. "Come on you two."

Jericho took the lead as I held the inner door for him. He was met by one of the diner's staff, the owner maybe, bowing respectfully, whispering soft words in a private conversation. I heard Jericho thank him as the gentleman led us to a table against the window in a booth meant for two. We sat and were promptly given a basket of bread and glasses of water. My stomach rumbled again.

"Excuse me," I said, embarrassed, and tried to think back to my last meal and realized it might have been the day before—not counting the cereal bar and the coffee from the drive.

"I guess we came to the right place." Jericho laughed.

"Sheriff," a portly waitress said, approaching our table. Breathless and ruddy cheeks, she walked with a slight limp, wincing and favoring one side. She wrapped her thick fingers on Jericho's shoulder and leaned in to give him a hug. "It's so good to see you, hun."

"And you, Gladys," he answered, meeting her halfway. "Still got troubles with the knee?"

She leaned away from him, balancing herself against the table. "Knee... back, hip, it's all the same," she chuckled with a snort. She patted her face with a dish towel, drying the sweat on her upper lip and forehead, and motioned to Jericho's bandage. "And how is the arm, dear? On the mend?"

"Afraid not. It's coming off this Tuesday," he answered. Her eyes opened wide, their whites like saucers. Jericho grinned, his lips curling from ear to ear. "Gladys, I'm kidding."

"Oh you! Always fooling!" she said, rapping the towel against him. She got serious then. "But they'll be able to fix it?"

"About ninety percent," he answered, sounding confident. "Gladys, this is my colleague, Detective Casey White."

"Nice to meet you, ma'am," the waitress said, taking hold of my hand, squeezing my fingers with an alarming amount of strength.

"And you," I said, picking up the menu.

"I heard that you'll be the replacement?" she said, her tone asking, and leaving me to wonder if everyone in town was familiar with the chief's staffing issues. I began to shake my head, but was cut off, the waitress turning to Jericho. "What a terrible business, you and that Paige. I feel so bad. And your boy. I mean, what an ordeal, the poor soul."

Jericho shifted, and at once I could sense his discomfort, his expression emptying with a dour look. "Thank you," he said, trying to interrupt and followed my lead by taking hold of a menu.

"And your wife," the waitress continued. "What a tragedy. It's just so awful—"

"How's Robert doing?" Jericho asked, talking over her. The woman shifted her weight, plunking her other hand onto the table, steadying herself. A fresh rush of deep red filled her cheeks in blotches, her skin shining. "Is he still working at the detention center? We were near there earlier this afternoon, but I didn't see him on duty."

"I'm sure he's there. And thank you for helping my Robert, Sheriff, it meant the world to us. It truly did."

"So he's good?" Jericho asked.

"Has been. He's working full-time, going on six months or so now. Your putting in a word for him was a blessing," the waitress answered. A frown came over her face then.

"But?" Jericho asked, urging her to continue.

"I don't want to bother you with it," she said, making herself busy, wiping the table.

"Gladys?" he asked, stretching her name in a long breath.

The waitress dipped her head and said, "Robert didn't come home last night." She shook her face as she spoke, adding, "With his shift tonight, it's not like him. Not like him at all."

"Robert is a young man. Handsome. Maybe he has a girlfriend," Jericho began, trying to calm the woman's concerns. "I'm sure he's fine."

"Well, there is a girl. I don't really know her," she said, nodding her head, agreeing. "And they've been together a lot."

"See," he exclaimed reassuringly. "Robert has a girlfriend."

"I'm sure you're right. It's probably nothing." She wiped her face again, and with an order pad and pencil at the ready, she asked, "What can I get for you kids?"

I'd forgotten how wonderfully delicious diner food was. Compared to my usual fare of microwavable dinners, a cooked meal was like coming home. Jericho did well for working with just the one hand. He'd ordered breakfast for his meal, keeping to scrambled eggs, topping them with melted cheese, and added two strips of bacon, rye toast, and black coffee. I kept it traditional—a cheeseburger, french-fries and a dill pickle. I could taste the memory of a milkshake, a craving settling in, but wasn't sure I had the room for it.

Three times we were interrupted by supporters from when Jericho had been sheriff, strange faces stopping at our table, wishing him well in his recovery, offering apologetic words about his family. And more than once, they'd asked him to run again, telling him he'd have their vote, a few chanting, "Vote Flynn to win."

I said nothing, keeping to myself, keeping to my food, my case file in my bag next to me. But from the sounds of it, the man across from me had been through something terribly tragic, a living nightmare.

"Paige?" I asked eventually, tactfully I hoped, having picked up on the name a few times now. From the conversation he'd had with the waitress, I'd gathered this was the name of their previous detective, the one being replaced. "Was she fired for insubordination? Or was it a performance issue?"

He put his fork down, freeing his hand to take a sip of coffee, steam rolling above the cup. "Fired, yes. But nothing quite like you'd expect."

"On the job, it takes a lot to get fired where I come from," I said. "There are review boards and hearings, probation periods, and peer reviews, all kinds of catches and remediation efforts before a termination is made final."

"Breaking the law?" he asked. "How about a prison sentence?"

I nodded, sipping my cola. "Yup, that'd do it for sure," I answered. "She broke the law? Stole evidence or something?"

"How about you?" he asked, leaning over the lip of the table, tipping his head toward my bag. "Why are you here?

"Like I said. Vacation."

"I don't think so," he answered, his tone sly. "What's the case you're working? From the looks of that folder, it's been with you a while."

I glanced at the folder, the edges worn, the corners frayed. Nerves ticked the hairs on the back of my neck. You'd think by now I would be accustomed to the questions. But nerves were funny that way—defensive and primal, preparing us. "The case is a missing girl."

"You already mentioned that. She's the same age as the victim on the yacht, the woods too?"

"Correct," I answered formally. I opened up a little, adding, "She would be in her teens now. Sixteen."

He eased up onto his chair, closing the distance between us. "I'm guessing you are related to her."

His comment took my breath like the sting of cold air in winter. I didn't expect his insightfulness, which left me feeling disarmed and vulnerable. I cocked my head, asking, "Why would you say that?"

"I know a lot of cops. I've known a lot of cops," he said, motioning to my bag again. "But I've never met any that brought a case with them on vacation. It's kinda like breaking a cardinal rule. Time off the job is sacred."

I took my bag and put it in my lap, crossing my arms in front of it as though protecting a secret. I couldn't relax. It wasn't intentional, just protective. I was afraid if he knew why I was here then it would jeopardize any chance of my going to the morgue.

"Listen, I made a deal with your boss. I'll help with a few investigations, and you grant me access to the body."

Jericho gave me a look, unconcerned with the arrangement. "I'm just asking," he said. "If we're going to spend time together, I thought it best to know about your case. Maybe I can help."

The air felt thick, an awkward silence falling between us. I mulled over the idea of letting him see my world, see me. "You're right. It's a good idea," I told him.

The tension eased, and I tried to relax, but the emotion hung around. Telling him the truth could help. A tear pricked my eye as I tried to make myself busy, shoving my bag onto the floor, cutting my food with my knife and fork. When Jericho put his hand on mine, I realized I was trembling.

"Anyway, you were right. She is related," I said.

"Casey, I'm sorry if I made you uncomfortable."

"Sorry," I said as well, unsure of why I was apologizing. Maybe it was the embarrassment, my showing emotion to someone I'd just met. "I never talk about it."

"Casey, I understand."

He let go and put his phone on the table, swiping the screen until he found the picture he wanted. With a soft sigh, Jericho pushed the phone toward me.

"Beautiful," I said. "Who is she?"

"My wife," he replied. "She's been gone a little over a year now."

A shiver ran through me. "I'm sorry for your loss," I said, wishing I could have said something better, something more meaningful.

"And you?" The sting came back then, tears standing. I did my best to stop them, swiping. "It's okay, Casey," he said, tilting his head. "We're just sharing."

"I lost my baby," I said, my words choked. The scar of an old wound opened, the dull ache a rift in my heart.

"What do you mean?"

"I lost my baby, and I've been looking for her ever since."

I'd revealed the truth to someone and the earth hadn't opened and swallowed me whole. I couldn't breathe.

Jericho took my hand again, inviting me to tell my story. My tears went dry, and so did my mouth. Nervous, I grabbed for my drink to wet my lips. When I looked up, the diner was gone, the clamoring dishes and flatware, the waitresses, the table and food. It was just him and me. I began by telling him monsters were real. His eyes told me he already knew. He'd seen them too. I told him it had all started with a sound. One sound. Everything changed after that.

For the next ten minutes, maybe longer, I told him about the car, and the passenger door opening, a stuffed toy appearing from the blackest depths of black I'd ever seen, and I told him how my baby daughter crawled inside and disappeared from my life.

When I finished, I felt an urgent need to run, to pick up my bag and escape his sad stare. But amidst the return of clanking dishes and orders being called, Jericho held my hand, telling me he understood. There was no judging or opinions or questions. He just understood.

"And you think the girl on the yacht could be—?"

"No," I said, shaking my head but sounding uncertain. "I don't know. It's just what I do. My daughter's name is Hannah, and I carry her pictures wherever I go. I was on my way to the Outer Banks when I got an alert about a body on the yacht."

"And your husband?"

I blurted an ugly laugh, but composed myself with a sip of my drink, and answered, "Gone. We tried to stay together the year after the kidnapping, but we couldn't make it work."

"I'm sorry, Casey."

I shrugged. "It was for the best," I said, hoping I sounded confident. "He said he loved me, but he just didn't love *us* anymore."

There was silence as Jericho gave me a moment.

"I'll help as much as I can," he said. "The morgue, the yacht, Dr. Swales. Whatever you need."

"Thank you," I said, feeling comfortable, feeling as though he got it, he got me. After all, he'd lost someone too. "Mind if I ask how you lost your wife?"

Jericho sat straight up in his chair and cleared his throat, "She was murdered."

CHAPTER 18

Murder. Jericho said his wife had been murdered. There was a sorrow in his eyes that told me not to press. Not to pry. Instead, we made small talk as we finished our meals, leaving me to keep the years since Hannah to myself. Maybe in time, I'd share more. For now, what was said opened the door for me. It wasn't much, just a crack, but I felt better, felt as though we had a kinship.

"You kids have a terrific afternoon," the waitress told us when we stood to leave.

"Gladys," Jericho began. "If you haven't heard from Robert in the next day or so, give me a call. You still have my number?"

"I do, thank you," she said, wrapping her arms around him with a squeeze.

"Gladys!" he yelled. "My arm!"

"Oh, Lord!" she said, jumping back with a jiggle and a look of horror on her face.

"Kidding," he joked.

"Always fooling," she said, swinging her dish towel again.

"I'm sure Robert is fine," he assured her.

"I know, it's just good to have someone's help."

We left the diner, my belly full, my mind stirring with the revelation about his wife.

"Anything from Dr. Swales?" I asked.

Jericho checked his phone, his head shaking. "Nothing yet." He checked the time, adding, "I know her, there'll be silence today, but we'll be busy tomorrow."

I reached into my bag, taking hold of an index card with *Fitz's Garage* in my handwriting across the top. "You said you'd help," I said, offering it to him, thinking he might know of the garage. "This is the lead I was following that got me lost this morning."

Jericho read the card, the sunlight making him squint. He motioned for me to hold it as he entered the name into his phone. A moment later, he answered, "I don't remember the garage, but we have another address. It looks like a residential address."

"Is it near the search party in the woods?" I asked, thinking we could check in with the team. There'd been no news about the baby, but the crime-scene technicians had arrived on site and could supply a report.

"Not far from the original address," he answered. "What's the interest?"

"Muscle cars," I told him.

He cocked his head. "You mean the souped-up kind? As in supercharged, decked out?"

"Yeah. Those cars," I said, trying not to smile at his reaction. "The owner of the car that took my daughter probably belonged to a club."

He nodded with understanding. "And you researched all the muscle-car clubs?" he asked.

"All, but those on the shores of North Carolina."

He peered at his phone, swiping the display. "From what I found, the garage closed eleven years ago, but the residential address isn't far from that location. We could swing by?"

"We?" I asked, not wanting to impose on his time. His presence would help though, his having been sheriff. "I mean, if you're not busy."

"I'm waiting on Dr. Swales too," he answered, his hand on the car's door.

"You're sure you don't mind?"

"I don't mind. Onward to Tommy Fitzgerald's place," he answered firmly.

"Are we close enough to the search?" I asked, repeating, hoping to swing by.

He studied the sun, its position, and checked his watch. "Once we cross the Wright Memorial Bridge, off route 158, we'll go in the other direction. I don't think we'll be able to get back before dark."

An image of a newborn baby alone in the woods after dark appeared in my mind. I was beginning to believe survival was impossible.

"The search is going to become a recovery."

"It is," Jericho answered without looking up. "Even then... there's a lot of ground left to cover."

"Thanks for the company, and the help," I told him, changing the topic, knowing there was nothing more any of us could do.

"Well, I did promise to show you some Outer Banks sights, remember?"

"Yes, you did," I answered. "I didn't think this was what you had in mind."

"Neither did I," he added. "Let's call it a warm-up."

We exited the diner's parking lot, and drove into heavy traffic, stopping at every crosswalk, a parade of families passing in packs, along with cruiser bicycles and riders on long skateboards and Segways, the vacationers settling into their afternoons. One right turn became three more, the beaches and ocean behind us as we traveled toward the bay. I bit down on my lip, chewing the corner as an old hope stirred. I wanted to feel it, wanted to get excited about the clue, but held it, swallowing dryly. Having an address and a possible connection to Hannah was enormous. I'd felt this way before though. I'd felt it too many times to count.

*

We crossed the bridge, making good time. The sky turned hazy, the sun tipping toward the west. The winds had picked up too, stirring the bay's calm surface into a weave of breaking swells. The smooth asphalt turned pebbly, reminding me of the early morning, the road's pavement replaced with gravel. The road's four lanes had been whittled to two, and even then, I had to hug the shoulder to let an oncoming car pass. Overgrown shrubs scraped the windows before I eased back onto the road while Jericho called out mailbox numbers, searching for Fitzgerald's last known address. We drove an extra ten minutes, ascending a hill, the woods looking familiar before we found the correct road and turned into a driveway.

"Man, we are in the sticks now," he said as low-hanging branches stretched across the driveway, touching, entwined, an arch forming. I glanced at Jericho, his eyes big like a curious child on safari. "I thought I'd been just about everywhere when I campaigned for sheriff, but not here."

"Appreciate the help. Just hope you don't regret it."

"Not at all," he said. He nudged toward an opening at the end of a driveway, adding, "Over there."

The road had leveled. I slowed the car as the trees parted and the gravel road turned to dirt. "What the hell is that?"

We opened the car and stood, taking in the sight, the stench of burnt lumber hitting me—pungent, sharp—the house on the property a mere shell of what it once was. The wood frame was charred beyond use, the rafters caved on one side and crumbled on top of the other. There was nothing else, all of it having been destroyed in what must have been a magnificent fire. At first glance, I thought the fire had been recent, expecting the house to be smoldering. But grass and shrubs and ivy had made a home along the brick foundation, climbing, growing, taking over the dwelling. The tin roof had fallen in also, and large sections of it were missing. Recovered or reclaimed, was my guess. Behind the home there was a large barn, the kind with the swinging doors on the second level for a hayloft. At some point there must have been horses, but from the looks of the surrounding fences—dilapidated, unkempt and leaning—that had been a long time ago.

"There," Jericho said, motioning toward a trailer—a silver airstream tucked in behind the burnt shell.

A woman came around the side, carrying a bag of gardening tools and wearing an apron, the front soiled. She was dressed for the sun, a large white hat covering her head and shoulders while sunglasses covered much of her face. In her other hand, she held a patch of green, blue and yellow flowers, maybe for a centerpiece or a vase. She found us and squeezed her hand tight, crushing the blossoms before dropping them to the ground.

I gave her a wave, saying, "Hello, ma'am."

"What do you want?" she asked, her voice terse, lowering her bag, and then also dropping it. We approached but stopped when she raised her hand. "Nope! I'm not interested. I'm not buying anything from nobody. You might as well turn yourselves around and be gone."

"Ma'am, we're not selling anything," I explained. "I'm looking for Mr. Fitzgerald—"

"Tommy?" she asked, kicking at the ground, pitching her toe into the flowery remains, pulverizing one of them like a spent cigarette. She put a hand on her hip. "Who's asking?"

I took another step as a blade of sunlight cut through the trees and found my face. I raised my hand to cover my eyes and answered, "My name is Detective Casey White, ma'am. I understand he knows about classic cars." She shook her head vigorously, aggravated and disagreeing. "I could use his help—"

"No!" she said, raising her voice. "No. No. No. That can't be!"

"I don't understand," I said, confused by her reaction.

"Why would you need to speak with him?" she asked, carrying on, waving her hands. "Why you?"

"I think we might want to leave," I heard Jericho say. "She's not open to answering your questions."

"Let me try again."

"I wouldn't advise—" he began to warn.

"Ma'am, we're just here to ask about classic cars." My patience was thinning. I approached closer, but the woman reacted suddenly, guarding herself with a spade she swept from her bag. I knew at once it was time to end this trip, the clue a dead end.

"He's not answering any questions," she yelled, waving the spade. "Not a one!"

"I understand, ma'am," I told her, turning around, recognizing there were possible issues. I'd dealt with the likes of it before and knew when to leave well enough alone. It was the unknown that'd get you killed, especially when unprepared. In my career, I'd learned to steer clear, call for a backup, treat it like a third rail. Her picking up the spade was a warning. Who knew what else was in her gardening bag or in the airstream? We returned to my car.

"You shouldn't be here!" she screamed nonsensically.

"I understand, ma'am. Our apologies!" I said, remaining professional, a stew of annoyance and disappointment rising in my throat.

Jericho turned and said, "Maybe we can find Tommy Fitzgerald another way."

I shrugged, feeling slammed by another dead end in a line of dead ends that had spanned fourteen years deep. I faced the woods, hiding my face, cringing, bracing, holding it in. Real thoughts of giving up emerged, tempting me to quit rather than face the sadness.

"A moment," I said, waving my hand. Jericho took a step toward me, his shoes scraping against the dirt road. "Please!"

"Why you?!" the woman continued to yell.

"Apologies, ma'am," Jericho answered. "We'll be on our way."

The emotions passed enough for me to turn around. And as usual my mind pondered and considered legal documents, court filings, anything that'd trace back to a bankruptcy or the sale of a property.

"Yes, we should be able to find him another way," I told Jericho, warming to the idea. "If Fitz's Garage was incorporated, there'd be a paper trail when it was dissolved. There's the property too. Someone owned the land at one time. Someone owns it now."

"I know a few people at the courthouse and township building. If there were any documents filed, they'd be able to dig around and find an address or phone number."

When we were back at my car, Jericho offered to drive.

"You can drive?" I asked him, lifting my arm, having thought he was unable.

"Oh, I can drive," he assured me. He lifted his bad arm and added, "I still have one good arm. I just didn't feel like driving earlier."

I let out a laugh, a much-needed laugh. I copied the woman's address, adding it to my phone, creating a new note.

"Why? Why would you be here?" the woman went on rambling, her irrational yells and screams reaching a fevered pitch. "Tommy won't answer anything. He won't help you!"

It was safest for us to ignore the confrontation and walk away. I didn't give in to her rants, didn't offer a parting wave or even a second look, other than to glimpse the barn, give it a hard look.

"By the way, I don't think she's interested in helping you," Jericho teased, settling into the driver's seat, rocking his hips up and back to give himself some leg room.

"Makes me wonder what she's hiding," I said.

"Hiding? The thought never crossed my mind," he said, surprised by the idea. He twirled his fingers around his head, adding, "A few other things did though. She's a touch sensitive!"

I spied the woman through the side mirror, her arms flailing. "I know mental illness, worked a lot of cases involving it. I suspect this isn't that."

"What makes you think she's hiding something?"

"Carrying on the way she is, she's trying too hard," I answered. "Did you take a look at that house? Arson. The place was torched on purpose."

"You're an arson investigator too?" he asked, intentionally sounding sarcastic.

"Not an investigator, just observant. Check it out." I pointed toward the shell of a gas grill next to the wood frame. "Now take a look at what's next to the gas grill."

He squinted, trying to decipher what I was showing him. "Okay, what am I looking for?"

"It's a pile of wood," I told him. I swung my finger to an old cord of wood stacked in the far corner of the yard. "Someone took logs from the wood pile and stashed them between the house and the gas grill. They probably hit the wood with an accelerant like fuel or propane, maybe even fertilizer from the garden."

"The grill's propane tank. They wanted an explosion?" Jericho asked.

"Correct. This wasn't an arson for insurance either," I answered. "They wanted to make a statement, make sure the home burned to the ground."

"The way she's acting," he said, brow lifting with curiosity, "maybe she burned her own house down, thinking it was infested with invisible rabbits or chickens roosting in the walls."

I shook my head. "You can joke, but there's more here than just some loner pissed off at us."

"Sorry this wasn't more productive," he said, snapping the index card between his fingers and handing it to me.

"Yeah, it's not the first time one of these led to nowhere."

"Like you said, tracing the paperwork, it shouldn't take much to find Tommy Fitzgerald."

The car's roof dinged like a broken bell, our eyes darting upward.

"What was that?" I asked, turning around in time to see the woman wind up her arm like a baseball player. She threw a stone, hitting my car's rear window and chipping the glass.

"And that'd be our signal. It's time for us to go!" Jericho said, raising his voice and hitting the gas. The car lurched forward, the sudden motion throwing my body against the passenger seat.

"I think it best if we go faster," I yelled over the motor.

"Trying!" he answered as another rock hit, cracking the glass, a sharp spider web forming.

"Oh damn!" I began to yell, furious and sad at the sight of my rear window.

"Jesus! She's still coming!" Jericho shouted, disbelief on his face. He floored the gas pedal, spinning the tires against the road's gravel. But my car was old and in desperate need of a tune-up and struggled to get out of its own way. Sadly, the acceleration was no match for the woman's throwing arm. The next rock was bigger and broke through, landing in the back seat. My rear window opened with a single hole in the middle—a gap-toothed smile I could see through—the woman at the center, shaking a clenched fist at us.

"Well that's just great," I said as the car finally picked up speed, leaving the woman's figure in a cloud of dust. I didn't have it in me to report the damage to my property, to take it any further.

We raced to the end of the drive, turning sharply, the tires skipping over loose stones. We said nothing for a mile or more, the road crumpling beneath us, the wind whistling through the rear window. The quiet was deafening.

"I have a guy," Jericho finally said, sensing I was upset. "He can fix up the window for you."

"Just drive," I told him, uncertain if I wanted to laugh or cry.

I wasn't sure if I was more upset about my car's window or the possible end to another lead in Hannah's case. I glanced at my phone, looking at Tommy's address and the notes I'd jotted. I opened another note, adding to the extension of my virtual wall, and jotted a few more lines about the woman, the burnt-out shell of a home, the pile of charred wood next to the gas grill, the trailer, and the barn.

When my temper simmered, I said, "One hell of an act she put on back there."

"I'm not so sure you're right. I've seen crazy before too, and it looked a lot like that."

"Crazy?" I questioned, cringing at the word. I shook my head, and continued, "I'm sure it was an act, completely rehearsed. She's hiding something."

CHAPTER 19

The drive was quiet, Jericho's comments about the lady acting crazy stayed fixed on my mind as I worked the mobile version of my wall. *Hiding.* Maybe Tommy Fitzgerald was there all along? Maybe she was hiding him on the property? I decided I'd go back. I'd check the barn and her trailer too. But I'd go by myself, saving Jericho from tipping the line of doing anything illegal or unethical. When it came to Hannah's case, for me, the line was a blur.

When we reached the road with the steep embankment, a streetlight flicked on, its dome atop a wooden pole glowing pink. As if by some sleight of hand, the evening had snuck in and stolen the daylight. There were no city lights to guide us; it was almost complete darkness. Jericho ticked the car lights as I rolled down my window and sought the sky through the trees. The early stars caught me, surprised me, their brightness appearing close enough to pluck from the inky black like fruit from a tree.

"It's something to see, isn't it?" Jericho said, catching my wonderment.

"It is," I enthused. "I think I've been living in the city too long."

He slowed at a stop sign, the crossroads empty, a breeze swaying the treetops. The woods came alive, voices from within, an orchestra singing a melody as if it were a concert hall.

"Tree frogs," Jericho told me.

"I've definitely been living in the city too long." The cool air brought on an unexpected shiver, reminding me that I'd never booked a room. "Any chance you have a motel you can recommend?"

Jericho's eyes grew and he shook his head, taking his hand from the wheel briefly to wipe his brow. "Afraid not. Especially not this time of year. Most places are house rentals—they book in advance and usually from Sunday to Sunday."

"None?" I said, imploring, wanting the day to be over. "A hotel, motel, trailer park?"

"It's the time of year, and unless you booked early, then everything is going to be full."

Unbuckling my seat, I turned around. Smashed glass littered the backseat, and blood had seeped into the cloth and the floor. "I suppose, I can try to sleep in the car."

"In here? Tell you what, you can come home with me," Jericho offered, his voice lifting with the invitation.

"I'm not that kind of girl," I joked, ripping open a paper bag to cover the bloodstain as a whistle sounded through the broken window.

"Well, it's not that type of invitation," he answered with a smile from the corner of his mouth. For a brief moment, I think I would have considered that type of invitation. It had been a long time and while our partnership had been thrown together—there was something about this guy I really liked. He was sexy without trying. And he was also genuine. "I have a guest room. It has its own bathroom too. It's not much, but you're welcome to it."

"Really?" I asked, returning to my seat, buckling the safety belt. "I don't want to impose."

"I'd say we were the ones who imposed," he answered. "Plus, it's a big house, and it's just my son and me. Most nights he's out with friends or at a study group."

"High school?"

"College," Jericho answered, sounding proud. "His first year."

"Well, I do appreciate the help," I said, my eyelids feeling heavy as I eagerly accepted his invitation.

*

I've always held a strange fascination, a curiosity really, about seeing a person's life outside of work—where they call home, how they dressed off the clock, their taste in furniture, that kind of thing. There was a time before Hannah, a time when my husband and I were quite the couple—a pair of social butterflies, visiting anyone who'd have us. We were always the first to arrive and the last to leave. After Hannah though, I tried, but sadly, the few times I'd gone out, it was always the same: introductions, then drinks, followed by small talk, and then the unveiling of sympathetic eyes and the pity dripping from them. I could feel the caring burn on my skin like heat from an oven. I hated it. Loathed it. After a while, I decided that being alone was easier.

As Jericho told me about his small neighborhood, the canals running behind the houses and linking to the bay, I found I wanted to know more, and couldn't help but feel a connection with him. I couldn't remember the last time that happened. It might have been because I was tired, my mind making something out of nothing. Or maybe there was something. I caught his eye more than once during the drive. Maybe I wasn't alone in my thinking after all.

Right now, what I needed was a bed. I wanted to review the day before sleeping, go over the cases I'd been volunteered to manage. What of the girl on the yacht? Or the teenager I picked up along the road? My chest hurt as I thought of the way she'd looked at me, her eyes pleading. Had I failed her? Failed her baby?

I let my thoughts wander but felt myself shutting down. I was ready to crash. As we pulled up to Jericho's home, it was the tail end of dusk, the moon peering brightly over the shoulder of his house—full, the color reminding me of autumn nights. In the dim light, I could tell the old Victorian house had seen better days. Compared to his neighbors, his home stood out like a sore thumb. A few shutters hung askew, and paint had peeled and flaked from the steep roof's gingerbread trim. A mold or algae had also taken over some of the foundation, staining the bricks with a drab green and gray.

The sight told me a lot about his last year. Following his wife's death, and the injuries to his arm, working on the home's upkeep had probably fallen low on his list of things to do. At once, I felt sorry for him. Watching him as we parked the car, I realized I was guilty of the same pity I'd cursed my coworkers for. I told myself there was a difference to my sympathy, though—I'd been through something too.

I thought of my home and what it was before Hannah. I saw the images of the year after, the shambles our house had become, and the burden of it when I no longer cared. We'd finally sold the house for pennies on the dollar when we divorced. I'd found my way to a single-room apartment, a kitchenette and a mattress on the floor, and a pet goldfish I named Howie as my only company. But even in its simplicity, its efficiency, my apartment fared no better, which only proved the problem was with me and had nothing to do with the house.

"Ain't much to look at, but she's got a roof and windows," Jericho said as we exited the car. He groaned, adding, "It was my wife's project. I was finally getting around to working on the upkeep when the accident happened."

"It's beautiful," I told him, trying to make him feel better. I had no sense of where we'd ended up, and asked, "Where are we exactly?"

"My hometown, just above Kill Devil Hills," he answered. "It's basically the armpit of Kitty Hawk Bay."

"Armpit?"

"I say that entirely in a geographic way. Look at a map and you'll get what I mean."

"Kitty Hawk?" I began to ask. "As in the first flight?"

"The same," he said. "The Wright brothers put this place on the map. Their actual flights were in Kill Devil, which has the best beaches for kite flying in all the Outer Banks."

"I'll add that to our list for some sightseeing," I said, admiring the history. "And tell me if you think of some other places I might want to see."

"Sure thing. That's your room up there," he said, pointing toward the corner room on the second floor. "The bathroom has fresh towels, everything you need."

"Mints on the pillows?" I joked and grabbed my travel bag, relieved it was intact. I took hold of the leather strap and hoisted it onto my shoulder. "I really appreciate the help."

"My pleasure. The room isn't used. And the house is big enough, so we won't get under each other's feet." The front door opened, and an older teen or early twenties appeared, filling the frame. Jericho had mentioned having a son in college. "Hey, Ryan. I want you to meet Detective Casey White. She'll be staying with us while helping with a case."

"Ma'am. You guys working the yacht?" Ryan asked, and quickly followed up with, "I just had a pizza delivered if you're hungry."

"You heard about the yacht?" Jericho asked.

"I saw a news conference with your buddy, Ashtole. Word of a yacht like that gets around quick."

"It was odd to have a news conference so soon," I commented.

"I suspect it has more to do with getting Ashtole some press time. Elections are coming up and the mayor's seat will be vacant," Jericho said.

"Can't escape politics," I said. "Not even here."

"Nope."

As we entered, the cozy smell of pizza made me feel nostalgic. While the outside of the house was in dire need of some love and care, Jericho kept a very nice home. Everything was in place—clean, comforting, homey. I wondered if it might have been his son helping. Ryan was taller than his father, broad like a football player, and had a cleaning towel hanging over his shoulder, a spray bottle of blue window cleaner in his hand.

I took in the surroundings, quickly focusing on pictures of the family, and what I took to be a photo of the boy's mother on a table nearby. Of all the framed pictures, hers was the largest. She was beautiful, and I could see her resemblance in Jericho's son.

We went into the kitchen, which had been renovated, turning the century-old place into a modern chef's dream. Through the patio doors, I saw the bay side of the island, the moon's reflection rippling on the surface, the night becoming lively again with the tune of tree frogs and loons.

"Drink?" Jericho asked, opening the pizza box. The doughy smell hit me and I was suddenly ravenous.

"Water is fine," I answered. I was sure we'd have a long day tomorrow, and I wanted to be fresh. "Food, and then to bed for me."

"Tired?" he asked, handing me a slice. I took a bite and was instantly lost in the boardwalk taste as memories of the delicacy returned. "Good, isn't it?"

"Damn," I answered, my mouth still full. "I forgot how amazing boardwalk pizza tasted."

"Help yourself to the kitchen," Ryan said, sitting down in front of a computer. "And if you need to use the computer, I can help with that. My dad? Not so much."

"Hey now," Jericho said, objecting. "I get around just enough on that thing."

I sensed the ongoing joke and appreciated the levity. "Afraid I'm in the same boat. I know enough to get by, but that's it. I still prefer reading words on paper when I can."

"Exactly," Jericho agreed, raising his pizza slice in a mock toast.

"Technology is lost on your generation," his son commented, turning his chair away.

By the time I'd finished eating, I was falling asleep where I stood, and all I could think to do was to lie down. After Jericho showed me to the guest room, I stripped what I had on, abandoning the day to a clothy heap on the floor, and retired in nothing but a thin T-shirt and my panties. I told myself to wash up, to brush my teeth and to floss, but my body said no. Giving in, I dropped onto the bed, spreading my arms and legs across the covers, the mattress sinking and hugging me. I closed my eyes, and the room was gone, the long day taking its toll.

In the darkness, there was starlight guiding me, the forest beneath my feet, leaves and branches blanketing the floor, rustling and snapping as I searched aimlessly, chasing the ghost of a baby's cry. An owl hooted an objection, stopping me dead, its golden eyes guiding me toward another path, insisting I go north instead. I followed my guide, trusting, but sensed the danger as the branches underfoot turned to bones and the forest became a grave.

A pinch came to my arm, a bite from a forest bug, attacking; then another pinch, another attack, more painful than the first. I opened my eyes alarmed, Jericho's frame above mine, his fingers wrapped around my arm, his face shadowed by the night.

"What the fuck?" I yelled with a start, shoving him away from me.

"I'm sorry," he began. "I tried knocking, and called your name, but you were out."

I covered my front and pulled a blanket across my bare legs. My feet in the open, the chilly air setting goosebumps on my skin.

"What? What is it?" I realized I was raising my voice and struggled to clear my head of the sleepy confusion and the nightmare.

As my eyes adjusted to the dark, I checked my phone and saw most of the night had already gone, and the sky outside my window had turned a brighter shade. It was already early in the morning. I could have sworn I'd only just closed my eyes. The nightmare aside, I couldn't remember the last time I'd slept straight through the night. It might have been years ago.

Jericho went to the other side of the room, putting a safe distance between us, his hand still raised.

"What is it?" I asked, a pang of guilt in my tone.

He shook his head. "Listen, I didn't mean to scare you."

"It's okay," I told him and tightened the blanket around my front, fighting the bedsheet's corners. "It's me. I live alone and I'm not used to being woken."

"We have another body," he said then, the words waking me instantly. "Some night fishermen discovered it. It's located in a backwater channel, so the marine patrol is already on site, but they need a detective to process the scene."

I began to understand the urgency. A body, the bay, the tide, seawater, sand critters, and no detectives on staff. Time. "Got it," I grumbled and combed my fingers through my hair. "I suppose the chief is looking for me to extend my favor?"

Jericho nodded. "Yeah, something like that."

"Give me ten minutes," I told him and motioned to my door. As he began to leave, I took hold of his hand, adding, "Listen, I am sorry, it's nothing personal. I didn't mean to react the way I did."

The touch was subtle, and his eyes were clear and large and seeing me. I might have been groggy, but I felt a gentle pass of affection.

"Not at all. It's perfectly understandable," he said. "The chief extends his apology too, he's sorry your vacation is, well, turning into a bit of work. We'll make it up to you. I promise."

"Was it another girl?" I asked, more awake now, thinking about the yacht, or the possibility of the baby. I wanted details.

"It's a man," he answered. "Reports so far tell me the body is male, naked, and found face down."

As Jericho left me alone to shower and dress, I tried to shake the guilt I felt for shouting at him. Now there was another body, another death. Given the location, murder was first to come to mind.

CHAPTER 20

It was still early, the sun just beginning to rise, the birds waking in song, their silhouettes perched against a hazy pink daybreak. The moon had already shrunk to the size of a walnut and had turned fuzzy and ghostly white.

Most of the broken glass in my car had been cleaned up and bagged, courtesy of Jericho and Ryan. The car was near spotless and filled with the smell of the ocean and burnt coffee, a much better mix. Coffee was my only insistence, a necessary stop at an all-night quick mart for caffeine. I was beginning to regret it. The coffee tasted as though it had been on a hotplate for more hours than I'd slept.

"Thanks again for the room," I said. I motioned to the rear seat, adding, "And for the help from you and your son."

"It was the least we could do," he answered.

"Any word on the girl from the yacht? Is she awake? How about the victim from the woods?"

Jericho shook his head. "Nothing yet. We should hear from Swales later this morning regarding cause of death for the girl on the boat."

I gripped the steering wheel, hesitating to ask about the baby, knowing the search had shifted to a recovery. "And the baby?"

"Nothing," he said glumly, steam from his coffee hiding his face.

"That's disappointing." I had hoped for news. The sound of the baby's haunting cry in my nightmare remained fresh in my mind. I needed to change the subject and asked, "We're going for a boat ride?"

"Just over there," Jericho answered, motioning to a parking spot. "That's my place, the marine-patrol station. We'll be driving south through Oregon Inlet."

"How far?" I asked, seeing the water, but not wanting to come across as afraid. "I mean, in reference to a road? For my report."

Jericho understood, answering, "The bridge we drove over, Route 64, the body was discovered south of there." I made a note of the location.

The inside of the station resembled most police stations, but this station had boats. From the entrance, the desks and offices were above the water, reminding me of a firehouse, with us standing on the loft and overlooking an indoor–outdoor boat ramp.

We walked briskly, Jericho putting on safety gear, handing me the same, telling me to tighten the front, and that the size would fit. I ditched my coffee as we hurried, and followed his lead, threading my arms through the lifejacket's holes.

"Ready?" Jericho asked, pulling his closed using a combination of his teeth and his free hand.

I searched around the patrol boat's sparse interior, expecting to find another officer, but we were alone. Without a word, an engineer gave us a send-off, the bottom of his rubber boot shoving the boat adrift.

"Casey?"

"Wait," I said. He thumbed a button on the dashboard, bringing two black motors to life behind us. The sudden thunder made me jump, and I waved my hands to him, asking, "You're okay to drive?"

"I'm fine," he answered, hooking the wheel with his hand. He tapped a silver bar to the left of him. "You'll want to hold this. We'll be there in a few minutes."

Before I could say another word, the motors roared and the front of the boat pitched up and blocked my view. My belly shot into my throat, and for a dreadful moment, I was certain we'd flip. Jericho shoved the throttle and toggled a switch labeled *trim*. The bow eased back into the water, bringing with it a fierce wind that pressed against my face and chest and turned my body to ice as though I were a lightning rod for the cold. He struck another switch and filled the darkness with electric blue, the overhead lights bouncing around us, letting me see other boats and black figures casting nets and standing with long poles while they worked fishing lines and crab pots.

We passed a larger boat that was traveling in the opposite direction and jumped its wake, filling the air with a fine mist of seawater, wetting my hair and face, putting the taste of salt in my mouth. The exuberance and the power of the drive was as thrilling as a carnival ride. At once, I felt giddy, the adrenaline pumping through me with a caffeine kick.

The drive steadied, the ocean opening in front of us, clear of the traffic, the shoreline hidden in the dim light. Jericho checked on me from time to time, spying my hands, my fingers clutching the metal bar, my knuckles whiter than the sea foam as we cut across the ocean's plane with the lively spryness of a jackrabbit fleeing the hungry mouth of a fox.

We slowed suddenly, the boat dropping out of the air and easing back into the sea, a flood of water rushing from behind us, raising and lowering the boat like a deep breath.

"What did you think? Not so bad?" he asked.

I tried to hide the exhilaration but blurted an abrupt laugh. "Way better than the coffee!"

He smiled. "Yeah, it's a lot more fun than a patrol car," he added. "Has it been a while since you've been on a boat?"

"Like this?" I asked, unable to stop smiling. "Truthfully, the biggest boat I've ever been on was a little rowboat. Crabbing and fishing only."

His eyes grew large with surprise. "Well, I hope it was okay then," he said. His face turned serious as he handed off the bow line.

"The body is over there," a patrol officer told us.

I shook from the cold and the adrenaline, but did my best to leave it behind. I scanned the surroundings. *Over there* could have been miles from anywhere. Three other boats were strung up against the shore like horses outside of a saloon, their bridle lines slung over a wooden hitching rail.

A freezing shock rifled up my legs, my feet instantly soaked with cold seawater. We made our way through the overgrowth of plants, the humidity stinging my brow as a halo of gnats swarmed around my head. The crowded growth opened and I saw a man and woman and their two boys in a boat, a floodlight above a small crowd of uniformed officers. I also saw the body and what nature had already done to it. As if on cue, a technician bent over and picked off a sand crab climbing aboard the meaty prize.

CHAPTER 21

I went to the body but struggled to get a solid step; the marshy ground stole my footing. Each step let out a burp and threatened to suck the shoes off my feet. The early light helped, the sun rising above a wall of seagrass, a breeze pushing and pulling it in a gentle sway. The ocean smell was powerful but paled in comparison to the marshy grounds where we stood—the algae and the muck pungent.

The body had not started to decompose. There were no signs of bloat or expelling of gases, which told me the death was recent. I wasn't sure if the Outer Banks was a party town, but from this vantage point, the dead man seemed to be college age, leaving me to wonder if he'd been out for a night of partying, got lost, stripped naked for whatever reason, collapsed, and then died from an overdose or exposure.

"Anyone find his clothes?" I asked the group. The officers and technicians searched each other's responses, their heads shaking, telling me my first theory was wrong. If partying was the cause, where were his clothes? Surely he didn't come all this way naked.

"I'd say that's a no," someone answered.

"Thank you," I said, lowering myself over the body. It wasn't until I was closer that the scent of death hit me, the breeze turning south, driving the wind over the corpse. An officer smeared a fingerful of salve beneath his nose, passing the small tin around. With the odor, my initial estimated time of death was off, and we'd have to rely on body temperature and other factors. "Who was first on the scene?"

"I was, ma'am," the officer with the salve answered.

"Has the family who found him been interviewed?"

"No, ma'am," he answered, glancing to the husband and wife.

I watched as the couple traded concerned looks, turning then to face their boys. They'd already seen more than any child their age should. We didn't need to prolong things.

"Let's get their statements, and their contact information so we can follow up," I said. "They shouldn't stay for this." I nodded my thanks at the parents.

The officer did as I asked, taking my instruction and leaving me with the body.

"A day?" Jericho said, asking. "Maybe less."

"Maybe longer," I said, pointing toward an arm and the crease of the man's shoulder, noting the deep blue and how the skin had gone taut.

"Eighty degrees," a technician announced, holding up a body thermometer. "Give or take."

"At a one-and-a-half degree drop for every hour following death," I began, checking my phone's calculator, and noting the air temperature at seventy-five degrees. "That's less than twenty hours or so. But not by much."

"With this humidity, the sunlight, it's not unusual to see the temperature off some," Jericho said, as he leaned over, and plucked another critter from the dead body. He held up a small crab and flicked it into the nearby grass. It landed with a plunk. "Definitely less than twenty-four hours. I'd say it's closer to eighteen. If the body had been here any longer, the *wildlife* would have had a lot more of him."

I took hold of the dead man's arm, moving it, noting the rigor mortis and the blood pooling. "It appears he died here. Face down."

Jericho shined his light on the body, creating a white spotlight between the shoulder blades and below the neck to reveal a pattern, an outline. The imprint was of a boot, the horizontal tread having dug grooves into the skin.

"This could be murder," he said.

"Is that a footprint?" someone asked from behind me. Seawater invaded my shoes as I sank into the muck. Surely there were bodily fluids mixing with the cold brine, wetting my socks and my skin and getting between my toes. The feel of it turned my stomach. I stood and repositioned myself.

"Put these on," a crime-scene technician offered. I looked into the sun, which was climbing fast, finding the dark shape of a woman, her hair blowing toward me. In her hands, two pairs of plastic booties. "These will keep your feet dry."

"Thanks," I said, handing a pair to Jericho. We helped each other, leaning as we hastily pushed and pulled the elasticated plastic around our feet, eager to continue with the body. "Someone get a picture of the boot print on the back—"

A technician's camera flashed as I spoke. The camera lens was ringed with a strobe-light circling the glass. The flash blinded me a moment, the boot print's shape burned in my eyes, appearing like a neon-green-and-blue painting.

"Flash get ya?" Jericho asked. "Gotta turn away when they use that thing."

"No kidding."

"The ribs," one of the crime-scene technicians said, lifting the other arm, the rigor mortis sounding a pop and snap like the reedy grass-stalks crunching beneath our feet. "There's a lot of bruising on this side."

"So he was beaten," Jericho stated flatly.

"I suppose that confirms this is a murder case and eliminates my theory."

"What's that?" he asked.

"Initially, I thought of partying. An overdose or wandering aimlessly, shedding clothes and then dying stupidly from exposure."

"Do you see that a lot?"

"I've seen my share in the city. How about around here?"

"Occasionally, but mostly they wash up on the beach after trying to out-swim the waves. The undertow or current gets them," he answered.

"There's that as well," I commented, and went to the victim's feet, the coloring around the heel and toes already a morbid purple, the skin shriveled, and the ankles showing every path of blood stopped when the man's heart died. "Look at his feet."

"What about them?" one of the technicians asked.

"If this was accidental, even if the victim had been in a fight, got baked, and somehow made his way out here, his feet would look very different," I explained.

Jericho and the technicians glanced around at all the white booties, lifting a knee, checking the undersides of their feet. I followed their gaze and saw the torn holes and the gouges puncturing the plastic. I saw the grime and stains too and imagined what a pair of bare feet running in the marsh would look like.

Jericho shined a beam of light to get a closer look. The soles of the man's feet were clean. Too clean. "The victim was carried," he offered.

"Stripped, then beaten, and transported. He was brought here," I said. "There is no knowing where the beginning of this crime took place."

"This isn't the original crime scene?" a technician asked.

"It's not. The question is, was he already dead?" I asked, knowing nobody could answer. Not yet anyway. "The autopsy will tell us. For now, the boot print on the back gives us a good indication that he was pushed into this stuff and—"

"Drowned?" someone suggested.

"Or suffocated," I added, walking around the other side of the body, my feet sweeping a thick puddle with a splash. I noticed the water and stopped. "What about the tide?"

"It's rising," Jericho said, his upturned face fixed in a grimace. "This whole area is tidal, so we have to consider the water being higher when the body was dumped. Any evidence left behind is gone."

"How high does the water get?" I asked.

Jericho stood, listened, cupping his ear. I did the same, and in the distance, I heard the breaking waves of the ocean's shoreline. "Not much higher, we're further in. It'll get harder to move the body soon," he said.

"We need to hurry before the water is too much," I said and waved two technicians toward the victim's shoulders.

Jericho followed, understanding what I wanted to do. "Let's flip him."

I snapped the latex around my wrists, pulling the glove until my fingers were wrapped. I did the same with my boots, tightening them before shoving my hands beneath the victim's torso. "On three," I said. "One. Two. And…"

Suction held the victim in place. We strained against the invisible force, fighting the earth. Air bubbles erupted around my wrapped feet, releasing a boggy gas that made me gag. The technician to my left did the same, jumping back as the body finally loosened and turned over.

For the first time in my career, I saw a death mask, the victim's facial expression frozen with terror, his final living moments captured forever by packed mud and gritty sand. The sight of it sent a chill through every cell in my body.

"Oh fuck!" Jericho yelled, jumping up as if he'd seen a ghost. The color drained from his face, turning it gray like the corpse. Jericho took hold of the victim again, and then gently lowered him.

I searched Jericho's face for a clue to his reaction, but he wouldn't look up, his eyes were fixed as he brushed a clump of caked sand away from the victim's hair.

"What is it?" I asked, trying to understand.

"Oh fuck," he repeated, his words breaking, his mouth hanging open.

I felt the emotion in his voice, felt it christen our morning and turn our good work into something horrible, a memory he'd never forget.

"It's Robert," he said, reaching for the man's face, but holding back, knowing we had to finish processing the scene. There were tears standing in his eyes. He swiped at them quickly, drying his face and clearing his throat. "It's Robert Stewart, Gladys's boy. The one I was helping."

"The waitress?" I asked, the name registering briefly.

Jericho gave me a nod, turning to hide his emotion. "He was just a boy."

CHAPTER 22

The drive to the morgue was a quiet one. Jericho made his phone calls, having identified the body in the field, and discussed how best to tell Gladys Stewart her son was dead. He'd asked if I would accompany him, and I'd agreed. It wasn't to satisfy any formal requirement or anything official. It was simply to be there. As an investigating detective, I wanted to see where Robert Stewart lived too, having learned he still lived at home. And if his death was a murder, I needed to find anything that might offer a glimpse into his last days.

As Jericho made his calls, I considered Robert Stewart having been employed at the juvenile detention center, right by the woods, and where I'd found the pregnant girl. I revisited my earlier idea, the conspiracy involving a detention-center guard and a pregnant inmate. What if the victim had discovered the illegal pregnancy? Protecting the secret was a possible motive. It was pure speculation, but sometimes speculation becomes the root of a working theory.

I mentioned the investigation, telling Jericho I'd ask for permission from Gladys before searching their home. He understood, his face perplexed as he argued on the phone about identifying the body.

"Understood. We'll visit with the victim's mother," he said, holding his phone like a microphone. "As for the positive identification, I already made one in the field, do we have to bring his mother to the morgue also?"

He hung up the phone, his gaze falling out the window. I wanted to tell him about the procedures back at our station, the necessity of having a family member make the identification. But I was certain he already knew the formalities, and that his arguing wasn't going to help anything. He was just trying to save the woman some grief.

"I'm sorry for your loss."

"I just wanted to make this less painful for Gladys."

"It doesn't have to be today," I offered, knowing his good intentions would do little to help. "A day will give us a chance to learn more and could help answer her questions."

But he shook his head. "We're just delaying her pain. As soon as we're ready, we'll go to her house and escort her to the morgue."

"So Robert worked at the girl's detention center?" I asked, my tone investigative.

"He did."

"Close to where I found the pregnant girl."

Jericho said nothing at first, picking at his phone case, mulling over the clear link I was trying to establish. "Connecting some dots?" he finally asked, his tone dismissive. "That's a lot of dots."

"Not really," I said, realizing he might be too close to this case. I should have kept the idea to myself, at least for now while initiating the investigation.

He held a pinched expression, his jaw clenching. "Look, I appreciate the work, but I also think you might be jumping ahead."

"Maybe," I said, agreeing verbally, but knowing I had a connection to follow.

"Let's wait until the girl is identified," he suggested, changing in his tone.

"Fair enough," I told him, deciding to keep the theories to myself.

"Fair enough," he repeated.

"I'll need to see his room," I said, trying not to sound callous or unfeeling.

"I expected so," he said. "I want a look as well. He was a good kid. I can't imagine he was into anything. But you never really know."

I looked over my shoulder, and to the broken window, seeing the hole Jericho's son had been kind enough to cover with clear packing tape. Some of my belongings remained piled to one side. I considered the space and if we were to taxi Robert's mother, and suggested, "We might need a patrol car—make it official and all."

He nodded. "We will," he agreed. "Turn in here, follow the wagon."

Robert Stewart's body was in front of us, a white wagon with official logos printed on the doors. We'd completed the processing and followed the delivery from the marshes to the morgue. As busy as I felt, I knew the morgue was equally busy, the medical examiner working overtime.

Word had come during the night that the medical examiner was ready to present the dead girl found on the yacht. I was finally getting the opportunity to see if it was Hannah. By now, I'd lost count of the bodies, the number of times I'd held a drawing of Hannah next to the face of a deceased girl, trying to decipher death and to see what life would have looked like in its place.

Buildings passed by the car's windows as we turned into the driveway. A flash of memories came to me, showing all the girls before now, along with the mixed feelings of sadness and relief, the search for Hannah continuing. I was certain this time would be the same. A refrigerated drawer, a frosty nip of cold, and the mortician pulling back the sheet.

Why would anyone subject themselves to such torture? My chest surged with a familiar angst as I pictured Hannah and remembered why I was in the Outer Banks. Like before, I prepared myself mentally, hardening my feelings, putting a guard in place to protect what was fragile.

The wagon with Robert Stewart slowed to turn into the receiving bay. My palms were sweaty, my fingers numb. I glanced over to Jericho, searching his eyes, and couldn't help but wonder if he was ready for this.

CHAPTER 23

We entered the building where we were met by the chief medical examiner, Dr. Terri Swales. She was shorter than I expected, an older woman with a frizzy ball of hair, which bounced as she shook my hand vigorously. She wore a navy-blue pantsuit along with a pair of faded green Crocs on her feet.

"Jericho," she said, her hand on his arm. She leaned in to embrace him, her voice somber, "I heard about Gladys Stewart's boy."

"It was terrible," he began.

She patted his arm to console him. "You need to bring me strangers, not somebody you know," she replied. "But of course, you know everyone."

Jericho said nothing more, sentiment stealing his words. He squeezed her arm, the two understanding each other.

"Detective White," she instructed. "If you will follow me, the body from the yacht is prepared."

I did as the doctor said, walking with her to an elevator as her Crocs made soft kissing sounds against the granite floors. She tapped the lowest button on the elevator's panel, shutting the folded doors and sending us into the guts of the building. The temperature dropped with each level, slices of metal and concrete passing, the air laden with the smell of refrigeration and death. It was a scent I'd never get used to. Nobody should.

We entered a cinder-block room with a row of lockers where we were offered a change of disposable fabric coveralls, and cloth booties to go over our shoes.

"I keep a clean house," Dr. Swales said in a steady southern twang. From the palm of her hand, a container of salve. I took the coveralls and booties, but passed on the salve, which also had a smell I'd never get used to.

"I understand your involvement began with a request to see the body from the yacht case," the doctor said.

"That's correct. I'm working another investigation." My face warmed and I side-eyed Jericho, wondering if he'd mentioned anything about my daughter's kidnapping. "Is that an issue?"

"Not at all," she answered politely. "I'm just struggling to keep up."

"Keep up?" I asked.

She hesitated and rubbed her forehead. "I'm not sure about where you're from, but the Outer Banks is generally a quiet town. A peaceful vacation town. Three bodies in less than forty-eight hours is highly unusual."

"I suppose it is," I answered, and slipped the coveralls over my feet.

As we changed, Dr. Swales gave the familiar warning of what to expect and what the body would look like after a day. I listened to her descriptions, respectfully keeping quiet, nodding with understanding. My thoughts were all about Hannah, a mental preparation, letting the other cases recess to the back of my mind. I held onto my folder, digging inside until I touched Hannah's picture.

"I've been told you are helping with the investigation of the girl from the woods as well."

"Correct," I answered. In my head, I saw images of my daughter. I also saw the pregnant girl, the grit on her face rutted by tears. My brain tried to bargain, tried to decide which was a less painful sight. They both hurt. "Is the girl's autopsy complete too?"

The doctor shook her head, answering, "Like I say, I don't usually see so much traffic. It'll be soon."

I wasn't sure how to respond to her, and answered, "I'll help where I can and while I'm in town."

"You mean you're not the new detective?" she asked.

Jericho shrugged, answering for me, "It's still in the works. Detective White has been kind enough to lend a hand."

"Three bodies," she went on to repeat, her accent stronger. She made *tsk-tsk-tsk* sound as she led us through a pair of thick rubber doors. They flapped behind us, the second room filled with cold storage. Dr. Swales urged us toward one of the drawers. "Detective White. If it hasn't been said, your help is greatly appreciated."

She opened the unit's door. I took in a breath. The metal handle clanked as a puff of cold air fell from the inside and revealed a pair of feet, a pale tag with black writing strung to one toe. The place where the name should be was blank. The girl's skin was nearly white, but with deep purple and blue puddling where her blood had settled. I glanced at the toe-tag again, and in my head, I saw Hannah's name, a morbid flicker of relief coming to me, the search for my daughter finally over. Metal scraped on metal, shrieking as Dr. Swales pulled the drawer clear of the storage locker.

"You okay?" Jericho asked.

"I'm okay," I said, unable to say more, my mouth suddenly dry, my breath vanishing. I waved my hand instead, then clutched the drawer's cold steel, bracing myself, my eyes fixed on the white sheet covering the body.

"Toxicology report came back—" Dr. Swales began.

"Can we just…" I said, interrupting.

Dr. Swales stopped, her hands on the sheet. She looked to Jericho and me, and asked, "Am I missing something?"

"The older case. It's a *missing* person case," Jericho said.

"Oh. I see," she answered. Her expression changed, sympathy shone from her eyes. "Do you have a picture?"

I opened my folder and leafed through the years of pictures and drawings, finding the most recent. "Here," I said, handing it to her. "It's a drawing. The missing person's appearance has been approximated using family photos."

"Allow me," Dr. Swales said, taking the drawing and cupping my hand in hers. "I can help with this."

"We can," Jericho added.

"Really, I'm fine." But I was lying, and they knew it.

Dr. Swales studied the drawing, her eyes darting from me to the picture, and then back to me. "She's a beautiful girl."

"She is," I said, my voice weak, unease stealing my strength.

"Like her mother?" Dr. Swales added with a question, her eyes on mine, staying there a moment. I answered with a short nod. "But this body is not the person in this picture."

"No?"

"No," she confirmed. She motioned to the sheet, asking without words. I gave another short nod. She revealed the girl's face, pulling the cover back with a flick of her wrist. At once I could see it wasn't Hannah, a mix of relief and ache coming to me. Dr. Swales traced the brow and nose, the skin beneath her gloved finger white like snow, the girl's features becoming lost along with life. "It's the bone structure. Can you see? It is very different. These cheekbones are high, and the eyes are much closer together."

"Cause of death?" Jericho asked, taking us back to the root of the case, the abandoned yacht, and our need to understand how two potentially underage girls could be on board.

"It wasn't the drugs," Dr. Swales said. "She was heavily impaired, though. Toxicology report came back with every party drug imaginable. But it was the injury to her skull that killed her."

"Blunt force trauma?" I asked, touching the girl's hair, brushing it back. She couldn't have been more than fourteen. "That's what the initial report stated."

"But whether it's from a fall, or an intentional blow to the head, is for you to determine," the doctor said.

"There was blood on the upper deck where she'd been found, a metal post fixed to the yacht," Jericho said.

"Yes, I saw the post," I said. "We'll get it cast, determine if it's a fit and identify if she fell and struck her head."

Dr. Swales nodded, and offered, "I'll get a technician out there."

The rubber doors swung open, an orderly entering with a gurney, the body of Robert Stewart beneath the sheet, his feet exposed like an uprooted tree.

"Robert Stewart," Jericho declared.

"As I've mentioned, it's busy. While I won't have an official autopsy for another day, I can offer a review, provide any preliminary findings while we're all here."

"I'd like that," I said, keen to establish as soon as possible any links between these tragic cases.

Jericho didn't reply but gave his approval with a nod.

"Over here, Derek," Dr. Swales told the orderly. The man rolled the gurney, turning it, and accidentally struck the corner of a table. The metal clashed, ringing the air, the hit jostling the body, causing Robert Stewart's arm to fall from beneath the cover.

"Sorry," the orderly told us, taking hold of Robert's arm.

"Wait!" I shouted. "Don't touch him."

"What is it?" Jericho asked, the grim sadness on his face abruptly changing. The orderly froze.

It was the victim's hand, clenched into a fist. Through his fingers, through the grime and filth, I saw colors that shouldn't have been there—sky blue with a deeper indigo like the feathers of a tropical bird.

Jericho knelt, putting on gloves, and pried open Robert's fingers. I placed an evidence bag beneath, positioning to catch whatever Robert had taken hold of before dying. His fingers snapped like twigs, flower petals emptying from his palm, their stems torn.

"What are those?" Dr. Swales asked.

"I don't know," Jericho answered. "But they're not from around here, and definitely not from where his body was discovered."

"Dahlias," the orderly said, kneeling next to Jericho, pointing to the flower, cautious not to touch it. "I help my grandma plant them every year. They started blooming a few weeks ago."

"Do they grow wild?" I asked.

"Nah," the orderly answered. "You have to plant tubers. I get them at a garden store. This time of the year, you can buy the whole plant too."

"Tubers?"

"They're like a bulb but look like brown baby carrots. With dahlias, you plant the tubers after the last spring frost, and then by end of summer, you've got flowers. All different colors. Fireworks from the ground, my gran calls them."

"How long do they bloom?" Jericho asked, motioning to Dr. Swales who knew immediately what he wanted. The doctor's Crocs squealed as she pivoted and produced a small evidence bag, a medical instrument in her other hand to help scrape the dirt from beneath Robert's fingernails. I carefully sealed the bag with the flowers, the first significant component to our murder investigation. Jericho held Robert's hand as Dr. Swales collected the dirt, which was dark and of a heavy consistency, similar to potting soil, and nothing like the ground where the body was discovered.

"At my gran's house, her garden will have the flowers blooming until the first autumn frost. They stand a few feet tall and I think the blooms might open and close like clockwork, but those could be another flower I'm thinking of. You'd have to check on it."

"Clockwork," I said, repeating the orderly's words. Jericho held up the bag. I looked to the largest of the blue flowers, its bud and torn stem, and tried to identify if a time could be determined from the flower's state. "Looks to be stuck at mid-bloom. Not sure what that means."

"Morning," Jericho suggested. "Or could be late afternoon."

I shrugged. "What we can say is the victim was near a garden when he was attacked. Early morning, or late evening. In the struggle, he snatched the flowers—" I began, and demonstrated, clutching the air. "The victim held them in his hand, hiding them, and then was taken to the marsh where he was held down and killed."

"How do you know he was killed?" Dr. Swales asked.

Jericho pulled the sheet to reveal Robert's face, the death mask stuck in place, stony like a statue's expression. "Help me out," he asked the orderly, showing he wanted to put Robert onto his side. As they rolled the body, a gurgling sound came from the back of Robert's throat, bubbles surfacing from between his swelled lips. "We identified this at the scene."

"Bruising," Dr. Swales began, inspecting the boot print between the shoulder blades. "It can be more prominent post-mortem. A size thirteen?"

"Give or take," Jericho answered.

"Hold this," the orderly said to me. I followed his lead, placing my hand on the victim's torso. "I'm a size thirteen." He offered his shoe to Dr. Swales. She eagerly took it, placing it above the bruising, fitting the outline like a puzzle piece.

"If the shoe fits," Jericho offered. The orderly's was the same size, a match, save for the width and the grooves and treads. We lowered the body, and I turned away when air spewed from between the lips. "Now we need a cause of death."

"Thanks to the boot mark, I have an idea of what to look for, but have to follow procedure and produce a complete report," Dr. Swales said, her accent thicker again as she handed the orderly his shoe.

"Wouldn't expect any less," Jericho told her.

"Are you going to see his mother?" she asked. "Bring her in for identification?"

"That's likely," I said.

As we left Dr. Swales with Robert Stewart, I held up the evidence bag with our first significant clue, blue dahlia flowers. And I couldn't help but wonder if there was any way Dr. Swales could change the boy's face, change his expression before Gladys arrived. No mother should ever see their child like that.

CHAPTER 24

The room's refrigeration had put an ache in my throat. I needed to get outside and into the sunlight. I pushed through the thick rubber doors, their weight swinging with a whoosh after Jericho followed me. The temperature on the other side had lifted some, but I still shook with a shiver. We were two steps from the stairs when I heard Dr. Swales calling out to us.

"Detective," she said. I could hear her crocs kissing the granite, her pace nearly in a run. The door swung open, the short woman breathing heavy with her hand against her chest. "Detective White, I thought you might want to see this."

In her hand she held a tablet, an email open with sentences highlighted regarding a set of recently submitted fingerprints, their findings and the nationwide results. There were no matches.

"Whose?" I asked.

"The fingerprints from the girl in the woods, there's no identification."

"Zero?" Jericho asked, whiskers scratching as he rubbed his chin.

"But her age…" I questioned. "Most children are fingerprinted, the records kept in the event of an Amber Alert."

"True, true," Dr. Swales replied, her brow creasing. "Even the private schools participate."

"Unless she'd never been fingerprinted," I said, believing the explanation might be simple, yet dreadful. I kept my voice low, knowing I had a tendency to get loud when working up an idea.

"Given her state, the possibility of captivity, and the attempt on her life. What if she's never been to school?"

Jericho shook his head. "You mean she's been living off the grid?" he asked. "We've got some recluse campers, but they've only cropped up the last few years."

"There's what she was wearing too, the old nightgown. What if she was forced to wear it?" I asked, thinking aloud. "What if she was kidnapped at a young age? Pre-school, maybe earlier."

Jericho shook his head again, but in Dr. Swales's big eyes, her glasses magnifying them, I saw my idea take root. "In my preliminary report," she began hastily, swiping the tablet's screen until her handwritten notes appeared. "I noted her age as roughly sixteen, as you'd surmised. Physical state? Growth oddly stunted. She was also extremely malnourished, particularly with her pregnancy nearly full-term. She had a surgical scar, right abdomen, which is likely from the removal of an appendix. I'd also identified previously broken bones, notably the left arm and three ribs."

"Jesus," Jericho said, the tablet's light reflecting in his eyes.

"There were also scars on her shoulder and her buttocks," Swales said, hesitating. "These appear to be bite marks."

"Human?" I asked, hating the sound of the question.

"That's just it," she said with a shrug. "They're a mix. The oldest scars are small, unrecognizable, almost like cigarette burns. But there are others, larger, human teeth, well formed."

"Escalation?" I suggested, believing there was significance. "Can you cast them? Create an impression set?"

"Already scheduled," she answered.

"May I?" I asked, holding my phone near the tablet to take a picture of her notes.

"Certainly," Dr. Swales answered, turning the brightness up and holding the tablet. "I don't suspect we'll find anything additional regarding death. The doctor's notes from the emergency room cited significant blood loss. Surely a contributing factor in her death."

"What's your idea?" Jericho asked, tipping his head toward my phone.

"Missing persons cases," I answered. His expression remained unchanged, leaving me to wonder if he agreed or not. "We need to rule out the possibility."

"Start eight... wait nine, ten," Dr. Swales said with southern enthusiasm, her lips moving as she counted her fingers. "Go back ten years."

"Why is that?"

"The appendix scar," she answered, a look of pride coming over her face. "It's dated. The surgery took place well before the Laparoscopic techniques became the standard."

"I'll go back fifteen years, and work my way forward," I said, my teeth chattering, but my mind filled with a twisted excitement that we finally had a lead. "There's no knowing where the girl came from, but we'll start local."

"Jericho, would you be a gentleman and please escort our guest detective to someplace warm," the doctor said in a mannerly twang. She squeezed my arm affectionately, adding, "It was nice to have met you. Though I wish it were under different circumstances. Of course, most who I meet in my line of work are a result of rather unfortunate circumstances."

"Thank you," I said, feeling a connection to the doctor. "Next time, then."

"I'll send you notice when the final autopsy is complete. And I'll do the same for Robert Stewart as well."

I made my way to the steps, an idea of researching missing persons fresh in my mind. I glanced over my shoulder in time to see the doctor's frizzy hair disappear behind the rubber doors. Jericho kept step with me, my feet hitting the granite, taking to the stairs with an eagerness to get warm.

But my time in the sun would have to wait, my bones remaining cold, a chill setting in them.

The morgue was a few levels below the main floor of the township building. We exited into a massive corridor, majestic, grandiose, but damp and stony, every inch of it lined with granite of black, gray, and ash white. Jericho explained how all the municipal buildings were built from the same quarry stone, including the courthouse, township building and the walls lining the morgue.

It wasn't the sightseeing that delayed my exit though. In the rich corridors next to the courthouse, we ran into District Attorney Ashtole and Mayor Jonathon Miller, their voices an echo, greeting me with arms extended and questions on their lips.

"I've already heard so much about you," the mayor said, his barrel chest filling like a machine as he sucked in air. The man stood a half-foot over me, and though he smiled, his face was fixed in a scowl, his bushy eyebrows stuck in a permanent slant. His shoulders were wide like a football player's and his hands were like clubs. I wasn't normally intimidated but he had a presence, and I suddenly found myself feeling nervous.

"It's nice to meet you," I answered, my hand disappearing in his.

Ashtole stood at his side, dwarfed, nearly hidden.

"What's the progress?" the district attorney asked, his voice annoyingly sharp, like the bark of an ankle-high dog. "Three bodies. We need something to tell the press. Heck, the timing is awful."

"Daniel," the mayor said in a foreboding tone. He looked down his nose, adding, "Remember what we talked about? I'm sure the dead did not intend to inconvenience any of us."

The district attorney sank into the shadow of the mayor and rephrased his question, "Is there progress or a status we can report?"

"Yes. And no," I answered, and tried to take my hand. The mayor tightened his grip, covering my fingers and wrist with his other hand. As Jericho and Ashtole exchanged case details, the mayor looked me up and down, his brown eyes shiny.

"Do you have any blockers, any impediments I can clear for you?" he asked, brushing my hand. "That's my job. It's what I'm good at."

I jerked my arm, the sudden motion briefly catching Jericho's attention. I cleared my throat saying, "We're waiting on Dr. Swales to furnish additional information as to the cause of death for each of the cases."

"And so the question we must ask: Are the cases related?" the mayor said, his lips curled in what would have been a warm smile but felt false. He moved closer, his chest near mine, asking, "What I mean, Detective White, in your professional opinion, is if the cases *were* linked, what might we be facing?"

I could smell him, a strangely clinical scent. Two days of clues bounced around my head like ping-pong balls, my gut telling me to share my thoughts about the detention center, about the girl in the woods and Robert Stewart's employment. I caught a look from Jericho and knew I didn't have anything concrete yet to share. I had nothing solid to connect the cases.

"It's too early to say," I told him, backing away.

"I understand you are here on vacation," the mayor said, changing the subject. "I want to thank you for stepping up and helping while we are re-staffing."

"It's not quite the vacation I'd expected, but I am seeing a lot more of the Outer Banks than most do."

"A sightseer? You must come to my estate," he said with sudden warmth in his voice. "It's the last of its kind in the Outer Banks."

"It does look grand. A visit is very tempting," I admitted. I motioned to Jericho. "We saw your estate from afar while processing a crime scene."

His nostrils flared with excitement. "Well, then you must accept my invitation, a dinner or brunch if that's more to your liking." The mayor straightened at the sound of doors opening and closing. "There's a century of history inside."

"I will," I said, feeling a true interest, but also thinking I could slip through the hedges, the backyard pools and tennis courts, and find my way onto the detention-center grounds. "Sir, if you'll excuse us?"

"Yes, work first," the mayor said, running his fingers through his hair, a rabble of news reporters entering the building, jockeying for position, the echo of footfalls like a stampede. The mayor swung around, but added, "You'll keep us informed? After all, we work for the public."

"I will," I told them, and turned to a side exit before the reporters reached Ashtole and the mayor.

As Jericho and I passed a grand stairway with figures carved into the speckled stone, camera shutters and questions came from all directions, the mayor and Ashtole fielding them, answering each without actually answering any, in what was perfectly appropriate political gibberish. I'd been unable to offer anything concrete and appreciated their ability to mask the true status of the cases from the press. We needed more time, and I was itching to review the missing persons cases.

CHAPTER 25

After half the morning in town, working multiple investigations, I finally saw the inside of the station where Jericho had once been the sheriff. Unlike my station's open-floor concept, something I loathed, his station was more suited to the purposes of law enforcement. Police desks and cubicles, fingerprint and photography stations, a reception desk with a waiting area, and offices lining the walls, some with titles embossed on the door's glass, others windowless and blank, the rooms meant for interrogations and interviews. Before Jericho went on to meet with Sheriff Petro he led me to the steps to cold storage, where evidence, paperwork, and every old case file was kept.

Descending the stairs, sliding my fingers along the banister, a lingering touch of the familiar tuned me to the work at hand. I was back in my element. While qualified to work a murder case, it was the kidnapping cases I'd always felt most at home with. Deep down, I knew what the feeling was really all about. I was fishing. On some deep level, I truly believed by reviewing old and new cases, I had a chance of coming across a missing child that might somehow be related to Hannah's kidnapping.

As I reached the bottom, floorboards above creaked and groaned, sending a shimmer of dust into the light. The storage area was like something out of an old mystery novel. Amber-colored wall lights cast moon shapes on the sandstone and plaster, water damage had stained the floors, and the evidence cage was pitted by the salt air. There was the smell too, a mix of damp sand and mildew. Thankfully, everything was stored in heavy plastic, guarded and properly labeled, and easy to navigate.

From what I could tell, decades of case files had been shelved in sturdy wax-coated boxes, the folders ordered by the date of the kidnappings, the plastic sleeves adorned with yellow labels to provide the victims' names. The count of missing persons cases was surprising, as the Outer Banks wasn't hugely populated. The labeling led me to find three years' worth of cases, dating back fifteen years from today. When I weeded out all but the children, I had ten to review. Ten children had disappeared in a span of three years. How was this not a national story? There'd been other serial kidnappers, the cases followed across America.

Three folders into my reading—the paper crisp, undamaged, but aged—I began to understand a pattern, to identify consistencies in the kidnappings. Nearly all the children were vacationing with their families. Could that have been the reason for the lack of press coverage? Maybe there was press, but local only? With the families remaining for a short time only, their hopes drained, before returning home to mourn and resume their lives, was it the lack of a network? My mind wandered through ideas as I tried to think like a predator. If the Outer Banks had one, they knew to pray on children outside of their community.

Another two cases and another two children, both on vacation. Their faces, smiling up at me from the old photographs, were unfamiliar, and there was nothing to lead me to think of the pregnant girl. But when I opened the sixth case file, I knew in an instant who it was I'd come across on the dirt road. The room became still and my breath stuck in my throat. I'd found Cheryl Parry.

It was her, the picture taken when she was six years old. Goosebumps rose on my arms. There was no mistaking her golden eyes, the color strikingly beautiful. I'd come to learn a true amber eye color was one of the rarest. I would recognize hers anywhere, and at any age. I flipped the case folder over, re-reading the labels. The case involved sisters, Cheryl and Ruby, fraternal twins, both kidnapped from the boardwalk nine years earlier. I scoured the pages, the court documents, witness reports, everything from cover to cover, including any mentions of identifying marks—an appendix scar for Cheryl Parry and a birthmark on Ruby Parry's leg.

"Twins," I said, my voice hollow in the closed space.

I went on to read about Ruby Parry. The twin sister had golden eyes too, a mirror of her sister's. A sour taste ticked the back of my throat when I came across a medical examiner's report, the pages folded and placed in an envelope with the printed municipal logo on the outside. The finding told me the twin sister did not survive. I bounced my knee restlessly and held my breath, preparing myself. This was the part of the job I hated most, the part I'd never stomach.

As feared, the child's death was gruesome in detail, her body discovered days after the kidnapping. I ran my finger down the page, skimming the morbidness, flipping the report's pages, spotting grisly keywords like *broken bones, sexual assault,* and *bite marks* on the child's torso. I found the line about cause of death: asphyxiation due to strangulation. A memory flashed to show the bruising around Cheryl Parry's neck, the bruised outline the shape of fingers, hands, the thumbprints clearly visible. And then I heard a voice, fading words about bite marks on Cheryl's shoulder and buttocks. At the bottom of the medical examiner's report, I read the signature line, Dr. Swales. I'd hoped my next visit with the doctor would be under more friendly circumstances, but that wasn't going be the case.

I brushed Cheryl's photo, seeing her face as I'd seen it on the road, and seeing the torture and the despair. A twinge of heartbreak pinched my insides, an unexpected connection to the girl I tried to help. I spent the next half hour recording every page in detail, clicking photo after photo on my phone. I replaced the case folders and boxes as I'd found them, and climbed the stairs, returning to the station's main floor. This was a case. So many questions flooded my mind, but one struck me hard and shone through the noise of the others like a bright neon sign blasting through the dead black of night.

Where had Cheryl Parry been the last nine years?

CHAPTER 26

HIM

There were hands on the cages, something he strictly forbade. A squeal came, palms rubbing the metal bars, grating his nerves, incessant and needling.

"Scrub!" he demanded and bit the end of a cigarette. The buckets empty, the evening chores finished. If they wanted to eat, they'd clean now. "Nothing until you're done! Every inch!"

Bristles rushed across skin, the abrasive noise giving him pause. Then came the soft cries, the whimpering, telling him they were doing it right. He smiled.

The television powered on, the rear of it casting light onto the wall, a shower of snow on the tube and static in his ears. The news appeared, the lead story about *her*. They'd found her.

He cursed his careless rush and his believing, at first, that she was dead. His secret was no longer his anymore. The news wouldn't change anything though. He couldn't stop. He'd never stop.

The face of District Attorney Ashtole appeared, a disdain coming to him like heartburn. The reception fading, he angled the television's rabbit ears, pinching the metal and spinning them until they faced west toward the larger television stations.

She was there! He leapt to his feet, and rushed to capture her, pressing record and play on the VCR, the buttons seated in unison, a red light blinking. The district attorney took a reporter's question.

More heartburn, the DA's face an aggravating sight. It was the new detective he wanted to see.

"There!" he said, finding her again, a hard beauty. He went to his knees, a grunt in his throat. She was so familiar. But why?

The question perplexed him, his nose nearly touching the television.

The press conference ended, the camera's view jostled as the reporters raced to ask questions. She filled the frame then, a reporter sticking a microphone in her face.

He could barely contain himself, his eyes darting from the screen to the VCR and back. He'd have her now. He recorded every second—her lips and nose and eyes saved on video tape like the brush strokes used to create the *Mona Lisa*.

When she was gone, he rewound the tape and played it back, over and over. He had her now, but it was temporary. He decided then, he had to have her forever.

CHAPTER 27

The station had become busier while I was reviewing old kidnapping cases. I checked the time and saw two hours had already passed. In my head, it felt like fifteen minutes. The mayor and Ashtole had arrived, bringing with them a parade of reporters. Word of Cheryl Parry's death must have been released by the hospital, the reporter picking up my patrol escort dispatch from a radio scan. I gripped the old case file, preserving the victim's identity until I could review it with Jericho and the chief.

As before, Ashtole eluded the questions while the reporters' voices rose and fell. With the mayor's lead, the questions ended abruptly as the two reached the safety of the sheriff's office. Packed with county officials, Sheriff Petro was seated behind his desk, his bald head bobbing back and forth while he tried to keep up with the heated conversations. Around him men and women in suits, their faces red, fingers wagging, the hollow echo of deep tones as heated words were spilled. I faced the other direction, knowing it best to get out of sight or risk getting sucked into their world.

Television monitors flashed news alerts overhead, the screens showing a recap of Ashtole and the mayor's earlier press conference, with pictures of the super yacht in the background. Another report came onto the screen, titled "Jane Doe". I slowed to listen and heard mention of a pregnancy and a search for a missing baby, confirming this information had been released as well. That could be a good thing: more volunteers and broader visibility. My arms tensed around the Parry sisters' case folder. I wanted to get back out to the woods, unable to give up hope just yet. They called it a recovery, but to me it was still a search. There are miracles, and there's no knowing when one is going to occur.

Jericho approached and swung open a wooden railing gate, holding it for me. "It's always busy during the vacation season, but this is a little above average," he said. "By the end of September, this place will be a ghost town. It's a break."

"I bet it is," I said, surprised by the chaos.

"Sometimes though, I think I kind of like the noise. The off season can be too quiet."

I sensed the disappointment of a summer season ending, but to me, the idea of an empty town sounded good. "Most places, it's like this all the time—the crazy chaos I see in Philly is a constant, sometimes endless."

"PK," Jericho said, speaking over the noise. "I need your help on this." We made our way into the heart of the station as uniformed and non-uniformed officers approached, patting Jericho on the shoulder, tapping his side affectionately, speaking close to him, whispering, and always referring to him as "Sheriff". I glanced over to his old office, the current sheriff continuing to wrangle the heated conversation. There was an odd dichotomy, having both the former and the current chiefs working so closely together, but it seemed to serve the community well. To me, it only added to the mystery of who Jericho really was.

"How's the wing?" the man Jericho called PK asked. He was lean and had brown skin and thinning dark hair, and spoke with a slight accent I couldn't place. PK took hold of Jericho's left hand with an awkward greeting. "Getting better?"

"Slow. But it's getting there," Jericho answered.

"Man… Dude, I'm so sorry," he said. "I had no idea about your partner, and your wife. All that time."

"Appreciate it," Jericho told him, turning to introduce me. "PK, Detective Casey White. She'll be helping with a few cases."

The man pushed his wispy hair into place and eagerly took my hand. "My name is PK, I'm the director of the station's IT department."

"He's the technical guru I mentioned," Jericho added. He leaned toward PK, adding, "I like the new title, so you're planning to add some staff? Maybe grow the IT department to two or more?"

"Shut up," PK answered, his face flushing as Jericho smirked. He faced me, asking in a single breath, "So you're new? A detective? Where are you sitting? Was it a transfer? Did'ya move close by? Have you been to the boardwalk?"

The questions rattled off his tongue like water splashing onto the floor.

"PK?"

The man acknowledged Jericho and caught his breath before quieting.

"Just here to help out. Temporary role while I work another case," I said.

"Oh, okay," PK said, minding his words, rocking onto his toes and then asking, "So what do you guys have for me?"

I motioned to the television, the news story about Jane Doe. "Her," I told him. "For starters."

"Jane Doe. The story that's been all over the news," he said, his focus shifting to a monitor and then back.

"I believe I know her identity."

"What's that?" Jericho asked, glancing at the case file from the basement. "I recognize the plastic sleeving, you found something?"

"I did."

I went to PK's cubicle, deciding the desk with the four monitors, three keyboards, and more mice and tablets than I could count, must be his. When he took to his chair, I asked, "Do you have the phone app that ages people?"

He snorted a laugh, answering, "Made me look like my nani."

"How about a child?" I asked, opening the Parry case folder, placing a picture of Cheryl Parry as a child atop one of the keyboards. Jericho came to my side, picking through the file, recollection registering on his face.

"Jesus, you think Jane Doe is the missing Parry sister?" he asked. Without waiting for me to answer, he added, "I remember them, remember her sister too. Horrible."

"First, we need to digitize—" PK said, more interested in the technical challenge than the history. He scanned the picture, the glass bed throwing a blade of blue light while passing over the old photograph.

"How many years are we adding?" PK asked, his monitor flickering until the pixels were bright with Cheryl Parry's face. When I confirmed eight to ten, we huddled around his desk, her golden eyes staring at the three of us. The IT technician worked the controls, shifting levels and adjustments, the age-accelerator application performing its magic. I'd done similar with Hannah, though I had enlisted an artist, using family photographs to approximate her age. What appeared on the monitor was as good as anything we'd ever come up with using charcoal and paper. When PK was done, the image on the screen was Jane Doe, the girl from the woods.

"That's her," I said, my heart swelling with pride and sadness. There was relief in having identified the girl, but putting a name to a face while knowing the tragedy of the case was also painful. Over the years, too many cases ended in similar tragedy, each murdered child a lash against my soul, killing me a little every time.

"It's her?" PK asked, raising his voice. "No shit! Did we just identify Jane Doe!"

"Hold on there," Jericho said, his hand clamped on PK's shoulder. "We'll want to get these pictures to Dr. Swales and to Ashtole, let them coordinate and communicate it across the leadership team. There're the Parrys too, the parents. They'll need to be notified."

"We also need to determine if there are any connections between the different cases," I reminded Jericho.

"Connections?" PK asked.

"Show him the girl from the yacht," Jericho said.

I did, swiping my phone's screen, turning it around to show the girl discovered in the yacht's galley lying in her hospital bed.

"We're trying to identify the survivor discovered on the yacht. She had nothing on her."

PK studied the picture a minute and then frowned. "I think I know where you guys are going with this, but with the tubes and the tape and her eyelids shut like that," he said, motioning to his face. "It'll be tough to match anything. Facial recognition is just so-so when it isn't a clear image. I mean, shit, put on a hat, some dark shades, make a funny face, and the algorithms vomit garbage. Know what I'm saying?"

"Just look at what you were able to accomplish," I told him, holding Cheryl Parry's photograph next to his monitor.

"Listen to Detective White. We know you can work some more magic," Jericho said. "We're at a flat zero on who and how any of this connects—but we think there is a connection—so anything you can give us is better than nothing."

He shook his head. "What I'm saying is, I don't think we'll get any matches. Not against any of the public galleries, anyway."

"Come on, PK, I've seen you do a lot more with less," Jericho countered, trying to feed the engineer's ego.

PK sighed, his eyes darting to his monitors and keyboards and back to us. "I can't make any promises," he said, taking my phone for a closer look. As he studied the photograph, he asked, "What of the fingerprints? Did'ya get any?"

"Still waiting on the girls' from the yacht," I told him.

"There's one more picture to add. Swipe again to the left," I told him. He did as I asked, the screen changing to show the second girl from the yacht, the picture of her from the morgue. "We need you to add her too. Three faces. At a minimum, we need to understand how the girls on the yacht knew each other."

"This girl is dead," PK said gruffly.

"Can't get anything past you," Jericho chided.

"I'm thinking connections online, social media, Snapchat, Instagram?"

PK rolled his eyes. "Guys, I can work with Cheryl Parry's aged picture. The girl in the hospital will be hard enough. But this one? Eyelids are shut, her face is dead. Wait! What if—?" PK stopped mid-sentence, his expression blanking.

"Yup, there he goes," Jericho said, straightening to leave. "Easier than I thought."

"What?" I asked, confused, scanning the area behind me, trying to understand what the man was staring at.

"He's cooking up some ideas," Jericho answered. "That's what he looks like when he's thinking."

"Okay," I said, easing my phone from between PK's fingers.

"I think I know what we can do," PK finally said. "I can't promise anything though."

"Understood," I said.

"Tell me, have I got approval to go dark on this one? I'll need to go there if my idea is going to work."

"Whatever it takes," I assured him, recognizing he meant the Dark Web, the use of darknet accesses. His request reminded me of an earlier consideration. I thought of the yacht, of international waters, adding, "We've discussed the possibility of trafficking being involved."

"Which is why I need to go dark. But, just to confirm, only the two girls were on the yacht. Correct?" PK asked. "The hospital girl and the girl in the morgue?"

"Correct," I said. "For Cheryl Parry, we still can't confirm anything except her identity."

"Nuff said guys, I'll get on it."

"I knew you would," Jericho said.

My gut told me there was no connection between the yacht and Cheryl Parry, but I couldn't confirm it yet, so every idea had to remain open.

"Listen, there's no reason to hang around," PK said, his chair squeaking as he spun around to face his computer equipment. "It'll be awhile. It could take a couple days."

But I had one more question and took a seat next to PK. "I get that you're good with tech…"

"Tech is what I do," he answered proudly. His gaze went to his desk, the mess of it, his eyes rolling. "Tech is all I do."

"Sometimes, it's the *all* you do that makes you stand out," I told him, recognizing the tone and thinking about my wall.

We locked eyes.

"What is it? How can I help?" he asked.

"I saw some public cameras, security or surveillance. Can we get access?"

PK opened a map of the Outer Banks on the screen where I could easily identify camera positions sprinkled across it, the icons sandwiched between the bay and the ocean.

"Pick one," PK said with a wave as if presenting a prize. "This happens to be my very first project here. I even installed one, got up there on the ladder, a leather toolbelt around—"

"That's great," I said, cutting him off, distracted by the activity in the sheriff's office. There was an urgency to discuss Cheryl Parry's case with the leadership team. "I need access to these, along with recordings." I pointed to the intersection of Bayberry Avenue and Elk Run Road, the smaller being an access road, the only way in or out of the girls' detention center.

"Easy enough," PK answered. "I can add up to thirty days video footage too."

"Yes please!" I said. "This is great. It could tell us if Cheryl Parry had ever been there."

I wouldn't say it aloud, but the conspiracy idea of a guard's involvement with Cheryl Parry was still strong in my mind.

"It's what I do." He then looked over his shoulder, asking, "Where are you headed in case I need to reach you?"

Jericho frowned, knowing the grim task that was ahead of us.

I straightened to check on the busy activity in the sheriff's office. "After we let the higher-ups over there know what's going on, we have to tell Gladys Stewart her son is dead."

CHAPTER 28

Before leaving the station, we met with Mayor Tuttle, Chief Pryce, Sheriff Petro and Ashtole. The office was tight, the air warm and thick and uncomfortable. There was sweat on my neck and dripping down my back. There was a tension too, a need to feed the press. This was the type of pressure I hated in the job, the manic rush to confirm details that warranted more time, deserved more time.

I presented my findings, Ashtole's expression fixed with one eyebrow higher than the other, and the others commenting, telling me they all remembered the Parry sisters. We had no fingerprints to confirm, but with Dr. Swales assistance, and with an expedited patrol escort to meet the parents, pictures of Cheryl Parry were presented. I could only imagine her parents' faces, surely a mirror of horror as any would be when learning the ill fate of their child. They made the confirmation and Jane Doe was officially identified as Cheryl Parry.

Another hour slipped, the clocks on the station walls advancing like armies marching across seized lands. There was no getting back the lost minutes and, for now, I had to play the official part of Detective, standing in the background as the station was turned into a stage for Ashtole and the mayor to take. On the other side of the small gate, the reporters and news crews stood up microphones and cameras, erecting metal stands like skeletons. The station disappeared behind a ceiling-high curtain of electronics. A new press conference had begun, and the reporters hung on every word. The political engine that drove the Outer Banks had to feed the sharks, had to give them something to negate the bad press scaring away the tourists and threatening the remaining days of the vacation season.

I'd never been one to like the camera and did my best to stay as far in the background as possible. Ashtole looked nervous, peering over his shoulder toward the mayor, the mayor giving him an encouraging nod, nudging him to take the lead and deliver the news.

Ashtole straightened his tie and announced, "This morning, Jane Doe's identification was made."

On word of the missing girl's discovery, the press rallied, a roar of questions rising. Ashtole flinched as the cameras flashed and brightened the podium in a wash of harsh light.

Ashtole continued, "Almost nine years ago, Ruby and Cheryl Parry went missing. They were six years of age at the time. Unfortunately, Ruby's body was discovered a short time later. And now, Cheryl Parry has been found."

Unlike the first time I'd met Ashtole, the press, the television cameras, and the studio lights stole much of his confidence. It could have been the context of the news too, a big case, unsolved, a girl suddenly reappearing after nine years. On his bald head, the lights gleamed, his skin shiny. Ashtole took hold of his wiry glasses, clearing his eyes, and then folded his arms in front of him.

"Sadly, Cheryl Parry had sustained injuries of which she did not survive."

"Have her parents been notified?" a reporter shouted.

Another yelled, "What were the nature of her injuries?"

One by one, Ashtole did his best to field the questions, answering each with a political prowess one needs to prove worthy of the position he sought.

"Does Cheryl Parry's return have anything to do with the mystery yacht's arrival?" a reporter asked. It was the same reporter I'd seen at the dock—fiery red hair and wearing half a suit.

"We have very limited knowledge relating to Cheryl Parry's sudden reappearance at this time," Ashtole began, taking a long pause to wipe his glasses.

"Oh shit," Jericho said quietly. "I think Ashtole is about to play detective and say something he shouldn't."

That's a lot of dots, I heard in my head.

"The yacht's arrival *is* particularly suspect, and there may be a connection, having received it with two young women on board, of which one is deceased and the other is currently in intensive care."

"Damn it," Jericho said sharply.

"He just linked the cases," I commented.

"Regarding Cheryl Parry's sister, is there reason to believe Ruby Parry's murderer was onboard the yacht as well?"

"And here goes the speculation," I said, questioning Ashtole, understanding Jericho's earlier reluctance to connect anything until we had more evidence to work with.

The mayor stepped forward then, his hand on Ashtole's shoulder and his other hand covering the microphone. He leaned in and whispered into the district attorney's ear.

"There's a reason why that guy's got elected so many times. He knows how to work the reporters," Jericho said.

Ashtole stepped back, letting the mayor continue with the questions.

We'd seen enough and exited the station with our focus on Gladys Stewart. I wasn't sure what would come of the press conference, but mostly I was thinking of the number of open kidnapping cases stored on the shelves beneath the station. How many more unsolved cases were there? I expected I'd find out soon.

CHAPTER 29

A swarm of angry bees had settled in my gut, anxiety gnawing with a relenting appetite. This wasn't the first time I'd delivered news of someone's death, but no matter how many times I'd done it, it was always gut-wrenching. We'd driven across Wright Memorial Bridge, staying on route 158 another few miles before turning into a housing development, the road sloping, the houses lined up like dominoes at the bottom of a shallow valley.

As we drove, I scanned the streets, noticing the steady changes in the neighborhood. By now, we were far from the ocean, far from the boardwalk and the rental properties and vacationers. This was where most of the year-round residents lived. We turned onto a second street, passing single-level houses—small, cozy, two to three bedrooms with single car driveways. There was nothing posh or expensive about them, but the streets were well tended and the yards nicely kept, with white picket fences, garden gnomes, hummingbird feeders and sun-covered patios.

I searched for a hive, an infestation, a drug corner or den, anything of the sort that was characteristic of spurring gang-related crimes, and murder. In my head, I saw Robert Stewart's face, the terror he experienced when held down to suffocate or drown. Could it have been a drug deal gone horribly wrong? An unpaid debt?

A gang-related murder would make sense, giving me something to kick around with the investigation. But from the looks of his street, his death had nothing to do with where he lived, which only helped elevate in my mind, my questions about his employment at the detention center and its close proximity to the woods and Cheryl Parry.

"Sheriff," I heard as we exited my car. A second patrol parked behind us, the officer tipping her chin, indicating she'd remain until instructed. We'd come prepared with a patrol car in the event Gladys Stewart wanted to go to the morgue and meet with Dr. Swales.

When Robert's mother answered the door, I knew I'd made a mistake. Gladys Stewart's face went sheet-white and she began to wobble, the watering jug in her hand slipping, the tin crashing. It was the patrol car. I should have had it arrive ten minutes after us.

Jericho saw Gladys's reaction and moved swiftly, taking hold of her just as she fell into a porch column. The clamoring of a wind chime echoed when the woman went to her knees, taking the chimes with her, the strung metal and glass tangled in her fingers. "It's about Robert, isn't it? It's about my boy."

"Let's get you inside," I said, coming to Jericho's aid, helping him help the woman to her feet.

"I know it's bad," she said, beginning to cry. "It's never good when the police arrive at your home."

Jericho gave me a look, his eyes darting to the patrol car with a shake of his head. Embarrassed, I shrugged with an apology. It was the smallest of overlooked details, but its impact was detrimental. We half carried the stout woman to a chair in her living room, her skin clammy.

I took off toward the rear of the house, finding the kitchen and filling a glass with ice and water. Everything was where it should be, clean, orderly, and as homey on the inside as her house was on the outside. From the shelves, with the intricate doilies and Hummel figurines, to the black-and-white cat-clock on the wall with the eyes shifting back and forth, there was nothing immediately suspect about where Robert Stewart lived.

"Gladys," Jericho said, taking the glass from my hand and putting it to the woman's lips. Color warmed her face some, ruddy blotches appearing on her cheeks, points of it almost crimson. There was sweat above her brow and across her lips, and her hands shook as she cradled the glass and tried to take a mouthful. "Gladys, it is about Robert."

"Please," she began, her head shaking, her eyelids half shut, tears springing from the corners. "No!"

I didn't hesitate and knew Jericho was hurting, his affection for the family making the delivery of such news almost impossible. I jumped in to take the lead, the obligation coming with the role I'd adopted.

"Ma'am, my name is—"

"White," she said. "My memory might have some holes like the cheese, but I remember you."

Her eyes met mine, her body tensing.

"Yes, ma'am, Detective Casey White," I said, ensuring she understood who I was.

"My boy?" she asked, bracing herself as though I'd raised my fist.

"Ma'am, your son was found in the marshes close to the ocean. I'm sorry to tell you, but he was unresponsive."

She belted a wheezing cry, her chest heaving. Tears ran freely, wetting her face. "My boy!"

Jericho's eyes glistened. He found a box of tissues and placed them on the woman's lap. He sat closer to her, his head down, hand on her back. She leaned against him and rested her head on his shoulder.

"The paramedics, Marine Patrol, and local officers responded, but your son had already passed," I continued.

"My Robert is dead?" she cried.

I'd recognized the behavior, the disbelief, the inability to accept the news. "Yes, ma'am," I answered with confirmation—the formal obligation complete.

"I want to see him," she said, shaking her head sternly and abruptly wiping her eyes. She turned to Jericho, clapped her hand on top of his with a slap. "Take me to see my Robert. Take me now!"

"We can take you soon," I said.

In a soft voice, without going into detail, Jericho imparted the cause of her son's death. "We'll find out what happened," he assured her.

Gladys lost focus, her expression slipping toward confusion and awe. I couldn't be certain she'd understood Jericho's words. She was breathing heavy and shifting back and forth as though readying herself for a run toward the front door. Jericho put his hand on her shoulder, nudging her. She flinched, startled, her glassy stare jumping between Jericho and me. A moment later, she was with us again.

"I'm sorry Gladys," Jericho said. "So very sorry."

She cried, taking to his shoulder again. Between the heavy sobs, the questions from Robert's mother surfaced like air bubbles. *How did this happen? Why him?* These were followed by, *Such a good boy, he never hurt anyone.* Jericho's chin trembled, his eyes watered as they consoled one another.

"I held his hand when he came into this world," Gladys Stewart said, straightening herself. She cleaned her face and did her best to contain the fluttery breath that came with the sobbing. Gladys eased herself toward the end of the chair and put her hand onto Jericho's shoulder and stood. She swayed briefly. "I'm going to get my bag. And then I'm going to see my son. I need to hold his hand so he knows I'm here." Her voice broke as she spoke, giving me a chill.

"We have a patrol car that can take you to him," I told her.

"I suppose you'll want to see his room?" she asked, surprising me. She caught my expression, adding, "Hon, I watch all the crime shows. I've got an idea of what comes next."

"Yes, ma'am, if that would be okay with you, I need to see his room."

She fixed her sight on the door, her face empty. "My boy was a good boy. Someone did this to him," she said. She clutched her bag, let out a rattling sigh and opened the front door. "It's down the hall, second door on the right. Stay as long as necessary."

CHAPTER 30

Robert Stewart's bedroom was about what I expected for someone his age, he was stuck between adolescence and adulthood. There were pinups of bathing-suit models and rock-n-roll bands covering his bedroom walls, while mail sat neatly piled in the corner of his desk, an indication he'd been actively paying his bills. His computer was turned on, its screen stuck with his name in spinning letters, waiting for someone to touch the keys or to move the mouse. His clothes near the front of his closet were more adult than for high school, and toward the rear there were four matching collared shirts, ironed slacks and the type of dress shoes made for standing on your feet all day—a work wardrobe. There were maroon logos embroidered on the shirtsleeves, the letters: CSJCF.

"What does CSJCF stand for?" I asked Jericho, taking one of the dress shirts, holding it up for him to see. Jericho leafed through the stack of mail on the desk, looking up briefly to see what I was holding.

"Currituck Sound Juvenile Correctional Facility," he said flatly. "It's a mouthful, 'detention center' is easier. I'd put in a word for Robert. He got a part-time position there, started as an orderly, but after he graduated and got some training, he worked his way up to become a guard."

"It's been a full-time job for a while?"

"It has," Jericho said with a nod as he worked the mouse on the desk, shaking it to bring up the password prompt on the computer's screen. He jabbed the keys, entering a short password, hitting enter, but the screen locked with a message to *Try Again*. "Last I spoke to him, he was considering this as a career. He really took to the job, even wanted to explore the administrative side and to start taking some business-management classes."

"We'll have to check the laundry basket," I said, noticing a shirt missing.

Jericho came to my side and ran his fingers along the sleeve of the shirt I was holding. "These don't go in the laundry. They've been cleaned and pressed by a dry cleaner. But that wouldn't explain the one missing shirt. Could be he was wearing it when he went missing."

"So he could have been at work?"

Jericho cocked his head. "Or he was on his way home. But, there's also the question of why his work never called the house, or notified his mother."

"Maybe they did," I suggested, hanging the shirt and moving to his bed. I jotted a note on my phone about the missing shirt, his work calling, and questioned what might have become of the boy's clothes—not a single stitch was found anywhere near his body. "Why take his clothes?" There was no way for Jericho to know why. I waved the question, and asked, "Any reason to believe Robert Stewart might have had enemies, someone out to get him?"

Jericho thought about my question, his focus toward the ceiling, and then answered, "Not that I've heard." He lowered himself to check beneath the bed. "But I suppose anything is possible," he continued, his voice muted. "Maybe it was girls who'd spent time at the detention center, their taking revenge on the place through Robert?"

I met Jericho on the floor, lifted the bed covers from the other side to him, and began to sift through a graveyard of neglected and forgotten teenage junk. A plume of dust rose and shimmered in the window's sunlight. I backed up, threatened by a sneeze. Jericho came up from the floor, a narrow purple bong in his hand. He plunked it on the bed to show me.

"Anything with it?" I asked, taking hold, bringing the end to my nose and smelling the faint scent of marijuana. While there was some residue, the bong was empty of water, dry and covered in dust. "This is old. Too old."

"I'd say years old," he added. "Not to mention, Currituck's drug-testing policy has employees peeing in a cup regularly. Strict. Nothing is allowed, especially if you're a guard."

"Because he's in contact with the inmates."

"Correct. It's likely Robert forgot it was even under his bed."

From Jericho, I felt the sadness and the gloom that comes with a loss. I had questions, but was hesitant to ask them. I fidgeted a moment, reconsidering, but went ahead.

"You said you helped Robert with the position at Currituck. So you knew him well?"

"All his life," Jericho answered. "His father and I were high-school friends, along with my wife and Gladys. They were a few years ahead of us, but we hung around together. There were a few others in our small group too, a few you've met, like the DA."

"Ashtole?" I asked, shocked.

Jericho answered with a laugh. "Yeah, there's some history."

"Small world," I said. "Your families got together a lot?"

"Something like that. Gladys's husband passed when Robert was just a boy. Her health went downhill soon after. My wife and I helped, we'd bring Robert over on weekends so he could hang out with my son. I'd take them hiking, fishing, the usual outdoor stuff," Jericho said, sentiment coming back into his voice. He waved at the dust in the air, annoyed, hiding his emotions in the activity. "He's a good kid. Was a good kid. He deserved better than this."

"I'm sorry," I said, not realizing how close they'd been. He shoved the bong beneath the bed as anger came from him like heat rippling above a road. When he stood, he dropped onto the bed. I joined him, sitting close enough to put my hand on his back. He relaxed to my touch. "Do you need to take a break?"

He looked at me, ready to answer, but said nothing. The blue and green in his eyes glistened, and I found myself staring. He moved close enough that I could smell him. I was struck with a sudden flutter of nerves. Jericho shifted again, the distance between us just inches, leaning, his lips near mine. I froze, uncertain of what to do—should I get up, or let him kiss me? But it wasn't a kiss he sought. His eyes were focused on what was behind me.

"Hello," he said, his warm breath touching my skin as heat flashed on my neck. I followed his gaze, standing with him, going to Robert's dresser, and to the rectangle mirror on the wall. Stuffed in the corners, and lining the sides, a collection of ticket stubs, photographs, scraps of paper with numbers and names. It was years of Robert's life, documented and displayed in one place. "Maybe we can find out where he's been? Find out who he's been with?"

But I barely heard Jericho as blood rushed into my head, blurring my thoughts, my heartbeat crushing my ears. I shoved past him, knocking him out of my way. I braced the dresser and pushed onto my toes, stretching to try to reach what I had found—photographs, strips of black and white, the kind spat out of old-fashioned photo-booth machines. They'd been shoved into the mirror's frame, seated between the pane of dirty glass and the chipped wood. "That can't be," I heard myself say, my insides trembling. "Jericho, tell me you see it too?"

"I see them," he said, his voice a whisper in my ear. "Could be there're a few of his friends we'll want to interview."

But Jericho didn't see what I saw. Robert Stewart was tall, I didn't realize just how tall until I was watching Jericho struggle to reach above me and take hold of the photographs. He pinched the corner of one, shook his fingers and caused them to fall atop the dresser, two landing face up and the third face down. Each strip had four photographs, four poses of Robert with his friends, smiling and making goofy faces. But it was what I couldn't see yet that held me still as if a criminal were holding me at gunpoint. I flipped the third strip over, my breath hot, my fingers moving from the first to the second and so on, tracing the girl sitting and posing with Robert. It was Hannah.

"It's her!" I said with a gasp, sucking in the dusty air.

I grabbed the latest drawing of my daughter, placing it on the dresser to compare them. They were as near a match as I'd ever seen in all my years of searching. I was hyperventilating and a strange unease hit me, sweaty and tingly, the room swaying sideways into a spin. Jericho put his hand on my arm to steady me and take me to the end of the bed. I couldn't let go of my drawing and the pictures. There were tears of relief and tears of joy, and a deep-seated feeling of intrigue as to how my girl could be here, how a photograph of her was in this room, in this house, the house of a dead man, and just hours from Philadelphia, the home she'd been kidnapped from all those years ago.

The mattress sagged as Jericho sat next to me, his good hand on mine, taking hold of the picture, setting it next to the drawing, studying the two, comparing them.

I wiped my face, and exclaimed, "Jericho, she is alive. I always knew she was. This is Hannah."

"I see the resemblance," Jericho said, his voice wavering, unconvinced. "But this is a drawing. I mean, I see the similarity, but the odds, the chances—"

I shook my head, interrupting him, "I know it seems impossible, but I know my baby's face, I know it's her."

"Then it's Hannah," he answered.

But there was a condescension in his voice. Heat returned, my cheeks on fire. He sounded like my ex-husband and the thousand similar comments I'd heard over the years. Anger filled me like steam in a boiling kettle. I knew that tone, had heard it too often. It was a naysayer's tone.

"You don't have to believe me," I said defensively. I shook off his hand, yanking the photograph from him. I held it up, adding, "As the lead investigating detective, this is a person of interest. Meaning, we'll need to interview her."

"I agree," he answered. "Absolutely agree, one-hundred percent. But listen, I didn't mean to sound—"

I raised my hand, trying to evade any confrontation, answering, "I get it. It's fine. If I were in your shoes, I'd think the same."

Jericho stood and offered his hand. He gave me a hard look, his eyes telling me he wanted to make things right but couldn't find the words.

I took his hand, stood, and repeated, "It's fine. Let's just go."

"Listen, I know a lot of people, a lot of the residents in the area," he said, shaking his head as he tried to explain. "But I don't recognize her."

"I'll run it by Robert's mother. At the diner, she mentioned there was a girl Robert had been seeing," I said softly, feeling awkward, a little embarrassed by my reaction. "She's a person of interest."

"Casey, you're right, we need to interview her. Hold it up," Jericho said, taking my hand with the photograph. "Like this."

I followed his motions, holding the photo strip so he could snap a picture with his phone. "Are you sending it to PK?" I asked.

He gave me a nod. "PK is the quickest at getting an identification when all we've got are pictures."

"How long?"

"Never can tell," he answered, hitting send and then reading his screen. His brow furrowed. "We've got to go."

"What is it?"

"It's a girl," he answered. "A pack of Boy Scouts hiking called in a report of a body."

"Another body," I heard myself say, a cold dread filling my stomach as I considered Ashtole's slip at the press conference. "Where?" I glanced at Robert's closet, at the embroidered letters: CSJCF.

"The woods," he told me, opening the front door. "The same woods where you found Cheryl Parry."

What if there had been someone else on the super yacht? What if they'd been released into a population of vacationers, walking amongst them, hunting and preying, and then dumping the bodies in the woods? *The traffic*, as Dr. Swales had put it. The sudden number of bodies unusual for the Outer Banks. And we were no closer to finding the killer.

Jericho headed toward my car, but before I followed, I had to look at the photographs again. Of the four, it was the last photograph that made my insides hurt—it was a picture of Hannah and Robert facing each other, their eyes locked in a deep stare. It was easy to see they were a couple. But more than that, I could see they were in love.

CHAPTER 31

I saw the bite marks first, my mind immediately telling me they had to be from an animal, that it was nature reacting to an opportunity. I lied to myself for as long as I could. I lied until I was close enough to see the truth, evident and raw. The bites were human.

I stepped around the body, scanning the woods, entertaining the dreadful thought that there could be more. A killer had settled in the Outer Banks and was using the woods as their dumping ground. Cheryl Parry may have been first. And this was the killer's second victim. But what of the girls on the yacht or Robert Stewart?

There were eyes on me, waiting, heads turned, looks traded, questions on the faces. There was Jericho and three of the crime-scene technicians I'd met on the super yacht. I knelt next to the body, a shard of sunlight sharply focused on the largest of bite marks, the skin ragged, the bone in the victim's shoulder exposed and horribly bright. Like Cheryl Parry, the girl's body was dressed in a similar nightgown, the style very old, rustic or Amish maybe.

The world stopped then, time standing still. Soft forest sounds drifted into my ears as I lowered my face until I found the victim's. Her eyes were open, the moment of death frozen in them. Her mouth lay open too, tongue dark and stuck between her teeth. I backed away, bowing my head, relief gushing as time resumed. The victim wasn't Hannah.

"Age, late teens," I began, standing again, the sting of a camera's flash illuminating the girl's torso. The crime-scene technician focused on the teeth marks near the shoulder, a thin yellow ruler adjacent to the bite mark's circumference, measuring size and providing scale. "White. Female. Approximately five foot and two inches."

"This is bad," Jericho said in a hollow voice, sitting on his heels, his chin resting in his hand as he surveyed the surroundings.

I considered his comment, regarded the gruesome act of biting someone, ripping their flesh. Jericho was right. "So much rage."

"Strangled?" Jericho asked. "Same as Parry?"

"Yes. It appears so."

"Two in the woods. Two on the yacht."

"We don't know if they're related," I reminded him, and carefully moved the girl's brown hair from around her neck. "Can you get this?" The crime-scene technician followed, the camera's flash throwing light on the bruises across the victim's neck and face.

The sound of leaves shuffling and branches breaking came from the road, where a team of technicians and patrol officers were marching toward us like geese flying in formation, with District Attorney Ashtole in the lead.

"I'm going to need some answers," Ashtole said, leaning over the crime-scene tape, his focus jumping around as he took in the scene. He straightened with a look of disgust. "Jesus."

"Body temperature is in the low nineties," a technician called out. "Dead approximately eight to twelve hours."

"Gathering notes for another news conference?" Jericho asked, standing. He took a deep breath, his annoyance evident by the glare on his face, carried over by what we'd seen at the press conference.

"We're providing a necessary service," the district attorney answered without looking up. "The people have a right to know."

"They have the right to be informed," Jericho barked, challenging him. "But that's it. Telling the public there's a link between the cases was irresponsible."

Ashtole stood firm, his arms crossed. "And how do you know they aren't?" When Jericho didn't answer, Ashtole raised his arms in a gesture that left him looking like a scarecrow.

"We don't," I said. "We don't have enough information to connect anything other than the Parry sisters and this victim."

"Let's start with that," Ashtole said, moving to the worst of the bite marks. "What did you see in the Parry case file? Ruby's. I remember there being bite marks."

I swiped my phone's screen, and then turned it around to face Ashtole and Jericho.

"Let me see that," he said, taking hold, zooming on the seven-year-old, her dead eyes gray and lifeless, her body showing the days of exposure to the elements, along with severe bruising around her slender neck, her ribs broken and protruding. But amidst the injuries and the signs of strangulation, there were bite marks as Dr. Swales had described, their location between the girl's shoulder and neck. At such a young age, and with the girl's small frame, the bites were gigantic, more hideous than I could have imagined.

"What a terrible case," Ashtole said, returning my phone. "Remember it like yesterday."

Daniel Ashtole knelt for a closer look at the latest victim. "Back then, after Ruby Parry's body was discovered, we brought all kinds of people in for questioning. Might have been a hundred." He took off his glasses and pinched his nose. "We never found anything."

"You knew the case?" I asked, not realizing how deep the history went.

"I knew her case. Shit, I still know Ruby's case," he said, wiping his eyeglasses, pushing them back onto his face. "It still keeps me up at night."

"Daniel, listen, I'm not disagreeing with you," Jericho said, his tone even, sympathetic.

"No?" Ashtole snapped, but then caught his frustration. "Well, sometimes it feels like you are."

Jericho shook his head, saying, "Not at all. In fact, I think you might be on to something. That is, the yacht showing up at the same time as the murders."

"Wait," I said, raising my voice. "Let's work with Dr. Swales. Get the autopsy completed, compare the bite marks. Let science do its job. Right?"

"Agreed," Jericho answered. "Let the science connect the murders. Until then, we have to keep the ideas open."

"Fair enough," Ashtole answered.

"But watch what you say on television," Jericho added.

"I can do that," Ashtole said. His demeanor changed then as he circled the crime-scene tape, his expression like that of a man at a funeral paying his respects. He put his hand to his neck, asking, "Strangled?"

"It appears so," I told him. "Dr. Swales will confirm a cause of death."

"Pregnant too?"

I shook my head, but was only guessing, a blanket of earth still covering the victims middle.

"It doesn't appear so," a technician answered, sifting through the dirt.

Ashtole continued, "And another shallow grave?"

"It's two to three feet deep. Same as the last one," the technician answered, her round face peering up at us. "But only some of the dirt was backfilled."

"The science. First, the Parry sisters, and now this," Ashtole said.

"The marks. The locations of them," I said. "It's a concrete connection."

"But the gap of nine years?" Jericho asked. "Why now?"

"You don't think there's anything in the appearance of the super yacht?" Ashtole said, repeating the idea of a killer returning to the Outer Banks.

"The wounds are completely different," I told him, stretching onto my toes to clarify my doubt. "One girl died from a fractured skull, what might be an accident. And the other, hospitalized, a drug overdose. There were no bite marks found on either of them. The only connection to that case is the unfortunate timing of its arrival."

"Why the shallow graves, and partial burying?" Ashtole mused, ignoring me, his toe pushing at the mound of backfill. "That must mean something."

"It means the killer was in a hurry," I explained. "But we don't know why. A serial killer usually doesn't stop what they're doing."

In the pause, laughter carried on a breeze and sifted through the trees. It was the detention center, the girls in the courtyard, their scheduled hour outside ticking the same minutes of the day as when it was Cheryl Parry's grave we'd investigated.

Ashtole cupped his hand behind his ear. "What is that?"

"It's the detention center," Jericho said and faced the sound. "It's where Gladys's boy worked."

"I heard about her son," Ashtole said, walking to Jericho. "I'm on my way to pay my condolences."

The men's words faded with the singing and laughter, my mind fixed on the murder. Why hadn't the killer, or killers, finished burying the victim? The grave had been deep enough. I listened to the woods, hoping to hear an answer. There was the single road leading in and out of the woods, and beneath the sound of the detention-center girls and the low drone of conversations around the body, I could hear a song playing on the radio while a car pulled to the road's edge and parked, loose asphalt and stone ticking as it tumbled down the embankment.

"They were interrupted!" I said, raising my voice. "What time was the body discovered by the Boy Scouts?"

Jericho checked his phone. "That would be around the time we headed over to Gladys Stewart's house."

"He was interrupted," I said again.

The technician overheard me, her gaze falling to the dirt she was removing from the victim's chest, an oddly shaped birthmark showing through the grit.

"Ol?" the technician blurted, her round cheeks pale, her freckles bright on her nose.

"What is it?" I asked.

"It... it can't be," she said, and then ran to her kit, her hands shuffling through the case and clutching a fine-haired brush. She came back and whisked the dirt from around the victim's eyes and nose and lips. The technician fell back with a sharp scream.

"What?"

"Oh my God!" she whispered with tears springing to her eyes. "It's Ol. Olivia Jones."

It didn't take any time to confirm the identification of Olivia Jones. With a name from the technician and the victim's fingerprints, no search was needed. The prints matched against a set from the girl's grade-school days. Her parents were called, the horrible news delivered. I couldn't help but think they felt an immeasurable weight had lifted, as sad as it was. I would have felt the same. There's been times I'd even wished the same.

Olivia Jones was seven when she went missing eight years earlier. Her parents owned a beach home, staying the summer months with their children. They'd employed Jennifer Simms as the children's babysitter, who'd later grow up to become a crime-scene technician. It was on Jennifer's watch that their daughter went missing. And it was Jennifer who would eventually discover the body of their daughter. In a single moment, eight years of guilt crushed the technician, her body ravaged as she crumpled to the ground in front of us, our words inconsolable as we helped to escort her from the crime scene.

CHAPTER 32

The day had gotten away from me, from us, with Jericho finally insisting we needed a break. It didn't happen often, but I felt I could go on all night—a clue-hunting motor inside me revving, firing the pistons, and moving my feet from one clue to the next. Hannah had been to the Outer Banks, and I had to know more, had to know if she was still here.

"Everything will be there in the morning," he insisted. "We'll start fresh."

With reluctance, I caved, and agreed to his request. I found my way to the room offered by Jericho and slept without interruption. I didn't dream, and I didn't wake before the sunrise.

It was late morning by the time we made our way back to the station, the case picking up at exactly the same pace we'd left it the night before. The crime scene had been processed, and the body of Olivia Jones was taken to the morgue. When we entered, I urged Ashtole and Jericho toward the station's basement, and the storage area for the old files.

"Those cases down there," I began, feeling nervous, the small of my back damp. "So far, we've got two of the girls, and Ruby Parry. We need to go deeper. We need to open the unsolved kidnapping cases from six, ten, fifteen years ago."

A look of foreboding blanketed Ashtole's face. He searched the stair's dark interior, asking, "You think more girls will show up, don't you?"

I cocked an eyebrow. "We have two already."

He began texting, shaking his head.

"When I reviewed the early cases, there was a high number of missing children, all girls, all in a small span of time. By national standards, the curve was grossly disproportionate."

Ashtole considered my words, pausing his typing. "Yeah, I remember there were a lot."

"That's right," Jericho added, sleep still in his eyes as he slurped a mouthful of coffee. "We went to the schools, talked to the kids about not going anywhere alone, especially at night."

"What are you thinking?" Ashtole asked, his focus returning to the phone's screen.

"What if the girls never left?"

Ashtole stopped texting again, his jaw slack. His face went pale, a cold grimness in his eyes. "You mean, you think they're still here? They've been here all along?"

"And so has the kidnapper," I said.

"Oh my God," Jericho said quietly, careful about who might be listening.

Silence swallowed time as the three of us stood unmoving, reading each other, reading the possibilities, and fearing the magnitude of what I'd suggested.

I flinched as a new text message buzzed. "That's me," I told them, showing my phone.

Jericho raised his phone with mine. "Seems PK worked late last night, might have something for us."

"About what you said," Ashtole began, texting again, his fingers moving rapidly. "It's solid. It's also enough for me to brief the mayor. You're good with that?"

"I'm good with that," I told him, but wished it wasn't so, wished anything other than the idea of the missing girls having been here all this time, held captive beneath the town's very nose. More so, I was bothered by the murders. Why now? What had triggered them?

PK had indeed found something during his evening efforts. Though his text was cryptic, a dire warning I didn't fully understand until seeing a parade of men and women enter the station, an endless stream of blue and yellow, their faces hard, unflinching as they marched in orderly fashion.

At once, the station was abuzz with activity, the vibe shifting. Whatever it was that PK had discovered had warranted a call to the FBI. A dozen agents wearing dark suits, their hair cropped short, gathered around a wall of computer screens. Them and other station monitors came alive and displayed a drab-looking room, curtained, empty, save for a metal folding chair at the center.

"What is this?" I asked Jericho.

He shook his head, his focus jumping from the FBI to the monitors. "I have no idea."

Sheriff Petro and the chief were huddled in the sheriff's office, their faces stoic as an older woman addressed them, writing on a whiteboard, orchestrating or coordinating, or both. Ashtole joined them, taking to the corner of the office, his pencil-thin lips pressed white.

"Damn, that looks bad," I commented.

"It does," Jericho agreed.

"This isn't about our case. It's something else."

PK approached, his face twisted as if he held a secret. Immediately I could sense disappointment from Jericho. *Jurisdiction*, I thought, wondering which of the cases must have been flagged and become a federal investigation.

"Did you do this?" Jericho's tone was harsh, but quiet.

The younger man shook his head. "It was Sheriff Petro," he said, his gaze in the direction of the sheriff's office. "It was the pictures of the yacht girls. I got a hit really quick and then—"

"And then?" Jericho asked, scanning the office. "This happened?"

"Sheriff Petro called the FBI?" I asked.

"Yeah. There was nothing I could do about it," he answered, his eyes apologetic. "He said he had to report it."

"You should have called me!" said Jericho.

"I did," PK protested.

"What about the other girls?" I asked, intervening, trying to give PK some breathing room.

"Nah. I only got hits on the girls from the yacht," he said. "Oh, and I have some videos to show you from the detention center."

"The Parry girls?"

He shook his head again. "I got plenty of hits with them, but they were all from publications, newspaper articles, stuff like that."

"So this is about the yacht. The FBI must be suspecting the crimes occurred in international waters?"

"Right," PK answered me eagerly. "It's the metadata in the pictures. Most photos contain metadata, unless it's been deliberately removed. The pics found in my search that matched still had their metadata intact. That's when the FBI got involved. Check these out," he began, displaying pictures of the girls from the yacht, both dressed in the string bikinis with the yacht's luxurious stateroom behind them. "I found these late last night. Time stamps show the pictures were posted from the night before the girls were discovered."

"Posted by who?" I asked.

He shrugged. "Not a single identifying person. Just the girls. But whoever posted them on social media—"

"It's the metadata that gave you the yacht's location?" Jericho asked.

"Damn right. Geo-tagged." PK shuffled through a folder, and then another, all with pictures from the yacht. "The yacht never moved, the latitude and longitude from the pictures were all the same."

"They were anchored in international waters," I said. "But what we don't know is how the girls got there."

"Whoever was on the yacht took the electronic records," Jericho commented, referring to our wheelhouse search. "Wouldn't they have known that we could trace them from the photos posted online?"

"And what about the camera they were taken on?" I asked, adding to Jericho's question. "Is there anything in the pictures to identify the hardware?"

PK shook his head. "We can try tracing the serial number, the MAC address, but it was probably a disposable phone, a pre-paid with a cheap camera. They could have thrown it overboard."

"Lucky for us, the photos were posted first," I said. "But it did bring the Feds here, and the case will transfer to them."

"So now we know the yacht *was* in international waters," Jericho said, taking to a seat and offering me the one next to him, but I preferred to stay standing.

"And what else?" I asked, watching the surrounding monitors and the crowd of agents. "It's got to do with what's on the monitors?"

"That is the real news," PK commented. He switched screens, juggling a few windows until the same image was displayed. "I took the new pictures of the yacht girls and added them to a search gallery. Once I lowered the matching threshold to compensate for the lower resolution, and broadened the detection across some dark-web branches, boom! Found this site, and found a lot of previous recordings from it too."

"Help me understand what it is we're looking at," Jericho said.

"We have video clips of an underground auction where there are people bidding and viewers watching. It's like some kind of wild reality show."

"An auction?" I asked.

"That feed the Feds are watching is a live video stream," he said. PK tilted the bigger of his monitors to face us. "However, I can show you recordings from a few days ago."

My stomach pinched, a dreadful understanding coming to me as text ran across the bottom of the screen. An empty chair with a lacy shawl hung over the back of it was at the center of the room, a white-and-gray curtain hanging in the background. In the upper corners of the screen there were countdown clocks, with one to the left set to zero, and the other set to five hours and thirty minutes. "It's the girls. They're being auctioned."

PK nodded grimly, adjusting the corner of his monitor. "Here's a clip posted from the other day."

The recording showed the same room, same countdown clocks, a flash of text running across the bottom. But in the video's playback, there were two seats, occupied by the girls from the yacht.

"It's them," I whispered, moving close enough to see the individual pixels on the screen.

Unlike the photographs PK had uncovered, there were no partying smiles, no string bikinis or makeup or paint on their nails. They were kids, dressed in their underwear, dark circles beneath their tired eyes as they followed someone's direction, the shadow of a person off camera, moving and telling them what to do.

The girl found on the yacht's deck was first to smile, but it was out of fear, her eyes glassy. The girl from the galley mimicked the motion, smiling briefly before her expression went empty again. Her motions were restless, jittery and scratching. "She's drug sick, or close to it," I said. "Explains the marks we found between her toes. They were probably forcing her to use before she boarded the yacht."

"The bidding," PK said, running his finger along the bottom. With the girl's smile, a rush of numbers and hashtags flooded the screen, bells ringing and confetti bombs exploding like a video game. "The highest bid wins the auction."

"This is sick," I said.

"Look at those numbers," PK said. "Jeez, that's more than I make in a year."

Jericho said, "It's more than most. But that might help us too. It's easier to follow big money."

When the video ended, PK swung his chair around, "That's the game show," he said. "Nasty stuff."

"Deadly too," Jericho said.

"You mentioned testing Cheryl Parry's picture? You placed her photo in your gallery and changed the matching threshold, all of that?" I asked. A notion was coming to me, an idea that might explain the sudden murders of girls who'd been missing for so many years. "How about the latest victim?"

"I did," he answered, his voice wavering. "Only, the last set of pictures you sent, those of the latest victim, that job is still running. I should have results in a few hours though."

"What is the oldest auction video you were able to find?" I asked, realizing the girls' kidnappers could be the same sex traffickers behind the auctions and the yacht. I'd read horror stories of girls and boys locked into trafficking rings for years. What if the woods killer had also found the auction site?

"A few weeks, maybe a month or so. The dates aren't entirely reliable. Not with the mirror sites and copies of copies available," he said with a shrug. "I don't have an original date."

"Keep the search going. If there's a hit on Cheryl Parry or Olivia Jones, it's possible the killer might have used the auction site."

PK nodded.

There was caution in Jericho's eyes. Was he considering my theory about the auction site and the victims from the woods? What I proposed was feasible. As sickening as it was, a website like this was a perfect place for a serial killer to shop for their next victim.

CHAPTER 33

HIM

Another news conference. Another opportunity to see her. He'd been near her already, had stood in the shadows, watching, close enough to catch her smell, to see the smooth skin on her neck pulse.

It was the news he'd have to watch. For now, anyway. Eventually he would touch her. And she'd clean for him too, just like the others. Like all the others.

The VCR buttons glowed against a black canvas, the room dark, the way he liked it, his prizes kept in their cages, a few in their rooms too. He was worried as he glanced toward the remaining girls, the necessity to finish conflicting with his desires to keep them. He had to bury them, like he'd always done.

CHAPTER 34

My stomach twisted as PK continued to busily click through screen after screen, his eyes glancing over cubical walls, the FBI activities gaining momentum. Agents had lined one side of the station, collecting desks, grouping them together like lunch tables, and adorning the surface with laptops like placemats.

There was one agent the others interacted with more than any other. She had reddish-brown hair, round green eyes, and full lips. She listened, and never answered immediately. Agent Rivera, I heard someone say, and I was certain we'd work with her soon.

"Here's the other video," PK said with a final mouse click.

"The intersection," I said, recognizing it. "Bayberry Avenue and Elk Run Road, the road to the detention center."

"It is. At thirty days, there was way too much video to put eyes on, so I scripted some Python code, a bit of video-frame grabbing with object detection, and added the face matching."

"Using the pictures?"

"At first, yeah," he said, his face filled with excitement, eager to tell us more.

"And then?" Jericho urged.

"I got nothing. I mean nothing on the girls from the yacht, except for maybe one frame, but not sure."

"Nothing." I frowned. "That doesn't sound promising."

He poised his finger in a *what-if* gesture and explained. "Rather than search for a particular face, I decided to perform a match on every face dating back the last thirty days."

"Matched to what?" I asked, confused.

"Each other," he answered, his smile broadening, his teeth glistening from the lights overhead. Jericho side-eyed me, and waited for my reaction. When we remained unenthused, PK's smile faded. "Don't you get it?"

Jericho shook his head. "Afraid not."

"By matching every face in a car at that intersection, I was able to produce a list of the detention center's most frequent visitors."

"Including Robert Stewart?" Jericho asked.

PK shook his head, answering, "Including everyone. Robert too. He showed up the average count, nothing out of the ordinary from other employees."

"Removing the detention center staff," I began, my phone in hand, my fingers bouncing across the screen with a new note. "Show me the top-five visitors."

PK raised his chin. "Now you're getting it." He opened the video app, the left column showing faces, and the right column showing their counts over the last thirty days.

Jericho shifted restlessly, asking, "How would this differ from us checking the sign-in sheet at the detention center's front desk?"

"Who's to say they signed in?" PK asked. "I mean, you might be right, but I thought it would be helpful to see the traffic of the people visiting regularly."

"It does," I said, leaning, my hand close to the screen. "Why do I know him?"

"That's Harlan Jacobs," Jericho answered, his brow furrowed. "You saw him at the super yacht. He owns the local marina."

"And he also visits the detention center," I said, and ran my finger to the count. "Every day, sometimes two to three times."

"I wouldn't have expected to see him there at all," Jericho replied, his mind at work. He turned to PK. "Are those numbers correct?

From your count, Harlan has been at the detention center forty times in the last month."

"They're right," PK said. "I even upped the match threshold to filter any false positives. But it gets better."

"Better?"

PK took to his mouse, clicking the button rapidly again and turning his monitors into a sort of colorful montage. He played back the thirty days, showing only vision of the selected driver, Harlan.

"Cool script, right? Had some bugs, but once I—"

"Cool, that's fine," Jericho interrupted, his hand raised as we watched the video snippets with Harlan coming and going, hands on a different steering wheel more times than I could count. He drove trucks, large and small. He drove cars, sedans and coupes and SUVs. He even drove a stretch limousine in one of the videos.

"He must be working part-time as an Uber driver. But the different cars?" Jericho said, though he sounded unconvinced. "And the trucks. What's he delivering? And why would he be delivering at three in the morning?"

"If he was driving for Uber, why is he always the only person in the car?" I asked.

"He's not always alone," PK exclaimed, rising in his seat, opening another window on the screen. "I got suspicious about the same thing. Check out the passenger and rear seats in these pictures. I had to clean them up some, use a contrast mask to highlight the—"

"That's good," I said, PK's voice drifting as I studied the still frames, a blanket covering the seats. Harlan had company with him. "He's hiding someone, and he knew the cameras were there."

"Maybe. Or, maybe Harlan kept them hidden while on the road," Jericho offered. "The street patrols are heavier during vacation season."

"You said you had a frame showing one of the girls?" I asked PK.

He rocked his head back and forth. "Not one of the yacht girls, but a girl. I'm thinking the guy snuck her out of the detention center." He double clicked, showing a blanket covering a passenger's neck and shoulders, the image grainy, the color crippled by a blur of green and blue, but her face fully exposed.

"Zoom in," I demanded, nearly biting my tongue. PK clicked, the girl's face enlarged, the image resembling Hannah. My hands were like clubs as I fumbled through my bag, a sickening stew rising into my mouth. I held the photo-booth picture next to the monitor, the images side by side.

"That's her," PK said, taking hold. "And isn't that Robert Stewart?"

"It is," Jericho said solemnly.

"Wait, Robert worked at the detention center. Did he know that girl? Do you think he was involved with the auctions too?"

"Auctions?" Jericho asked, raising his voice.

PK sank low in his seat.

"Why?" I asked, a wave of nausea hitting me. "What else do you have?"

"It's just—" PK began, and then stopped. In his face, I saw the hesitation.

I took the picture from him, asking, "Did you use that one in your search too? Did you add Harlan's passenger to your gallery?"

PK glanced at us, his earlier enthusiasm checked as he reluctantly answered, "I did."

"And?"

"There was an auction—"

I jumped to my feet, the legs of my chair scraping as I went to the monitor. "Show me!"

PK's face blanked as he played the footage showing the same dank room, the girl I believed to be Hannah sitting in the chair. I tried to breathe, a deep shudder in my chest squeezing my heart.

She wore only a bra and underwear, each the color of her skin. The girl nervously bit on a fingernail, and then abruptly stopped when the figure of a man appeared in shadow. She turned to face the camera with trepidation in her eyes.

I almost cried then, seeing who she'd become since she was taken from me. There was a hard look about her I hadn't seen in the photograph with Robert Stewart. It instantly made me sad. It wasn't just the piercings and tattoo on her neck I could now see, but she carried a hardness, a type that forms over time like a fossil. There was an insecurity too, a vulnerability. In my experience, it was some of the hardest looking that were the most fragile. Hannah's gaze shifted to the shadow figure, recognizing the motions, following instructions and lowering her arms to reveal her chest.

"Hannah?" I said as she combed her fingers through her hair, sweeping it away from her face. Her eyes remained locked on the person with the camera, their shadow bleeding onto the drop cloth behind her. She sat up and put on a fake smile, her dimples forced, her eyes wet. My voice was caught in my throat as I studied every detail.

"Who is Hannah?" I heard PK ask. "Do you guys know the girl?"

"It's part of another investigation Detective White is working."

I felt dazed by the horrible thoughts running through my head. I cleared my throat and asked, "How many times? How many videos?"

"I only found the one," PK answered. "I haven't found any others."

"Where are the recordings coming from?" Jericho asked. "I mean, the auctions are held, but why would any recordings stick around?"

"Because they're sick fucks," I said, disgusted. "Probably use it to beat off, or whatever it is they need to do."

PK gave a slight nod. "You're probably right. Once content is online, nothing gets tossed, nothing is ever truly erased. And even an audience of one is still an audience."

I couldn't take my eyes off the screen and the tally of bids flying across the bottom, each bid increasing like a lottery prize. I wanted to throw up.

"I suppose," Jericho said. He must have sensed my anger and jabbed PK's keyboard, stopping the video as the winning bid appeared at the top of the screen.

"Oh shit. Sorry," PK said, and turned off the monitor.

Jericho leaned back, a question forming. "Is there anything in the videos we could use to find the source?"

"I've already tried," PK said. "The videos were scrubbed. They're clean. There's nothing, no metadata, no source IP addresses, nothing."

"Robert Stewart is dead," I said in a flat tone. I held up the photograph of Robert and Hannah. "Somehow Robert Stewart is pictured with a girl from one of the auctions—"

Jericho shook his head, his posture straightening as he interrupted, "God no! Robert would never get involved in something so vile." His voice shook, his face was glum.

"Maybe not," I said. I gave him a look, locking eyes, trying to lessen the pain, the disappointment of learning a horrible truth about a loved one, no matter how sour it was. I held up the photo-booth picture. "But this is what we know, and this girl was in that video."

Jericho sat back with a thump, scratching his chin, bothered. He said nothing, the silence filled by the agents shuffling office furniture and Agent Rivera calling out commands.

"We also have the marina guy too," PK offered. "Harlan. We have a ton of video coverage, including the one with the girl from the auction."

"He needs to be questioned," Jericho said with a rasp.

It hit me then, seeing a girl I believed to be Hannah in a sex-trafficking video. A sudden emotion came that I couldn't hide. I backed away abruptly. PK and Jericho's stares following me. Tears wet my cheeks and I grabbed my mouth to keep it together. My skin turned hot as if hit by a summer wind. I spun around and sought the station's exit, sick with a million confusing questions.

CHAPTER 35

The FBI took the lead over the auction site PK discovered. They would also oversee the investigations relating to the super yacht and the girls discovered on board. There was the strong possibility of a trafficking ring in international waters with a national connection.

This was big. This was overwhelmingly big. Any help offered, was help we needed. It also involved my daughter, and no matter how big, I'd stay involved. What came next was an auction and with it a sting operation. I'd be involved in that too.

It was PK who deciphered the auction site and provided details to the FBI. With the station cleared, all the reporters finally gone, the cross-agency teams filed into the meeting area for a presentation of the evidence.

FBI Agent Rivera took to the front, her presence quieting the group as eyes focused on PK. Jericho's IT guru stood at the ready, his previous nerves now absent as he dove into the slides and the details needed for the teams to work the case.

"He's a natural," I whispered to Jericho.

"Yeah," Jericho answered, a frown forming. "That's unfortunate."

I leaned in, my lips near his ear, "What do you mean?"

He faced me, the projector's light shining in his eyes. "It means we're going to lose him. And I hate to see him go."

In the front row, Agent Rivera and her team traded comments, their questions to PK solidly answered, his confidence carrying the presentation, carrying the team. The FBI would do well to have him.

"I get it," I said. "Just think of all the good he'll do."

"Yeah, I suppose. He deserves it. He really does."

As the presentation progressed, questions about winning the auction and staging a sting were asked and answered. The technical questions about crypto currency and the darknet were handled by PK while Agent Rivera managed the financial challenges.

"Lights," Agent Rivera commanded. At once, the room went bright, the shine causing me to squint. Rivera stood and fanned her face, the air gently lifting her hair. "Can we get some air in here too?"

Agents along the far wall raised the shades and opened the windows, the smell of beach and ocean spilling inside.

"We also need a boat," an agent said to the group. "A big one."

Bodies twisted, their gaze falling on Jericho. As the senior marine-patrol officer, his involvement was required.

He shook his head. "I don't see how it would work," he began as agents stood, talked amongst themselves, and exchanged ideas. "Based on what we know, if there's a rendezvous, the traffickers will set the meeting in international waters. We'll need a big enough boat that doesn't have 'Marine Patrol' plastered along the hull."

"They'll be expecting a yacht," I blurted. And without fully understanding the jurisdiction issues, I asked, "What about the super yacht?"

"The yacht would work," Jericho agreed. "It takes a special license to captain, but we have that covered."

"Can we use it?" an FBI agent asked. "Is it still considered a crime scene?"

"It's already processed," I told them. Jurisdiction over the yacht, I realized, might actually mean me. "As far as investigative matters, the yacht is available."

"It's not like we're taking the thing for a ride around the block," another agent stated. Chuckles and laughs rolled through the group. "Kidding aside, the FBI would need to officially commandeer the vessel."

"Done," Agent Rivera said, her phone in hand, brow raised with authority. "It's available. We have the yacht. We also have the funds. Now we just need to win this thing."

With her statement, the room shifted back to PK. He swiped at his face, his forehead shiny, his thinning hair disheveled. With so much riding on the auction, his nerves finally surfaced. I felt for him too, but he should be nervous, he needed to be nervous. A girl's life depended on him succeeding.

When the presentation ended, the room's silence dried like a puddle in the sun, and the commotion gained as the teams set up equipment for the auction. Agent Alexa Rivera approached, her arm extended. Her hand was firm, but soft. Her eyes warm, but focused. Her demeanor reserved. I also sensed command and confidence and the respect of her position.

"Alexa Rivera," she said, formally greeting me, tucking a lock of hair behind her ear. "I understand you furnished some of the pictures, and also began the yacht's investigation?"

"I did," I answered, and picked up my bag, her gaze following the folder poking out of the top. "There are additional pictures from the previous auctions."

She took hold of my folder, asking, "May I?"

I handed Agent Rivera the picture of Harlan leaving the detention center. She studied the image.

"This is the one link we've established to the detention center. The individual's name is Harlan Jacobs."

"He owns the local marina," Jericho said.

"An APB has been issued?" she asked.

"Correct," I said. "A patrol was dispatched and swung by his place of residence and his business. No hits."

"A runner? That's about the fastest path to showing guilt," she said, and handed the picture off with instructions. She left my side to stand next to PK, his hands busily working two laptops. "Very impressive work. I understand you've been the technical lead on multiple cases?"

Jericho nudged my arm as PK answered, "For some time."

Agent Rivera made her way around the table, approval on her face. PK flashed a nervous smile in our direction.

"He is so loving this," Jericho whispered.

"The live auction is about to start," PK announced.

The room went silent. Attention focused on the large monitor and the image of the single chair as one of the clocks struck zero. I was nervous about what we were about to see. Keystrokes rattled from PK's laptop, his fingers already a blur, his selected handle *4ngel0fDeath* fixed at the bottom as he bid, and rebid, countering all other amounts.

"There," I said, the chair taken by a girl, fourteen or fifteen, her hair light red and her skin linen-white. She kept her wide eyes on the person behind the camera, following their lead, the shadow pantomiming a smile like we'd seen before, and then urging the girl to pinch her cheeks, bring color to them. The girl wore a bra and underwear, both black, a stark contrast to the color of her skin. Her cheeks warmed with a red flush, but her lips remained thin and firm and colorless. She was terrified.

"Make another bid," someone demanded. PK was losing, a flurry of giant bids crushing his. "You're not keeping up!"

"I'm trying," PK said, his fingertips grinding the keys with maddening speed.

"Don't lose this," I said, my mouth dry as I followed the bids, having lost sight of his *4ngel0fDeath* handle. Another flurry of bids sent the price up ten times the initial amount.

"Shit," PK grumbled, swiping at his eyes. "Fuck! I have to cap it. Bid it all!"

"No wait!" Rivera yelled, but PK slammed the enter key, sending a bid amount that eclipsed all others by more than three times. The room let out a gasp. The bidding slowed and then stopped, PK's monstrous amount standing alone in the top spot.

"The reserve," he assured the room. "But we won't need it. Nobody will touch—" A new bid bumped his. And then a second, and a third. The speaker sounded bells and whistles, confetti animations exploded on the screen with each amount knocking *4ngel0fDeath* out of the top spot. PK dropped below fifth place.

"You were saying?" someone asked.

I went to the monitor as if I could somehow comfort the girl, knowing she was about to be auctioned like property, shipped to international waters, where she'd be drugged and raped. A living nightmare, a horror show. My heart ached for her. Worst yet, what if it was the killer bidding, her nightmare ending in death?

I spoke up. "What's the reserve?"

PK crushed his energy drink, aluminum crumpling. He answered, "The reserve was set to triple the bid. But that's everything."

"Have you ever seen it higher?" Agent Rivera asked. She was measuring the possibility we'd lose, that we'd have to pull back on the sting operation. "Is it possible these numbers are a fluke?"

"A fluke?" PK asked, annoyed with not understanding the question. He entered a new bid, taking his handle into third place.

"What Agent Rivera is asking is how legitimate are those other bids," I said.

"You're asking if they're inflated," PK said, nodding his head, sweat gleaming.

"You mean, those are fake?!" another agent said.

"They could be," PK answered. "It's called gamification. It's a basic strategy, game logic used to get me to bid more money. That is, make me *want* to bid more money. The idea is to treat it like a game so I lose sight of the objective, my focus shifting to winning for the sake of winning."

"Fake or not, bid the reserve anyway," Rivera concluded and moved next to me as the girl on the screen began to cry, a haunting reminder this was not a game. "For her sake, we can't lose."

"Yes, ma'am," PK said, adding a zero to the end of his last bid.

"Oh my God! That's a lot of fucking money," an agent muttered.

"Keep your comments in check," Rivera commanded. "We're playing this one to win."

"Please, that has to do it," PK said, wiping his face. He leaned back into the chair and stretched his arms.

Not a single bid came after his. With a flash of celebratory animations, his bid rose into the number-one position and all bidding activity on the screen ceased. The girl continued to cry, the shadow urging her to smile. She swiped at her nose and reared back as the shadowy figure grew to a monstrous size, a threatening hand above her.

The auction ended a moment later, the dark figure shrinking back to normal size, the girl standing and moving off the screen, a lone hand in view snapping their fingers. Caucasian, no rings, black hair on the knuckles, pudgy, suggesting an overweight male. I jotted notes on my phone and saw two other agents doing the same. It was the only lead we got from the auction's live feed.

"What's next?" Rivera asked, punching her hips with her fists, turning to face the room.

As if on cue, PK raised a hand and said, "The money is exchanged, and I've got the time and the coordinates for the meeting."

Rivera and I exchanged a glance. "Now we ride," I said.

CHAPTER 36

The auction had ended with little fanfare. The room emptied silently, leaving me with Jericho and Agent Rivera to work the logistics and coordinate the rendezvous. We had the day to make the logistics work, and slammed headfirst into multiple bureaucratic *Go, No-Go* moments which snagged progress like a snare, our plans teetering on disaster.

The rendezvous was planned to occur at the gut of midnight, and a final inter-agency agreement was reached. No less than a hundred phone calls had been made, possibly more, the sting operation approved by ranks climbing into the Governor's office. When the dust settled, and the stirring commotions slowed, a team was decided—it would be a shared effort across agencies, the FBI, the Marine Patrol, local law enforcement, and we'd have PK working at the helm as the winner of the auction.

PK would join us on the yacht, maintaining a connection with the auctioneers. If everything went as planned, by the end of the evening we would put into custody the men and women running the site. But more than anything, we'd save a girl. While I felt comfortable with the plan, the killer played on my mind. There were the open cases, the missing children dating back years, and we had no confirming evidence the woods killer ever used the auction site. *The girl in the auction,* I decided, setting my mind on what I could do now. *Save the girl.*

With the sun hanging on the lip of the horizon, and the last scraps of daylight to guide us, we'd set a nautical course for the coordinates, the super yacht back in action. The assembled team commandeered the yacht, which was diligently fueled and cleaned. We put in place a yacht's captain using one of the Outer Bank's own, Officer Riddle. He was round and breathed heavily as he walked. He also held a license to captain the yacht and was a former police officer before making a move to the marine patrol and working for Jericho.

Riddle wasted no time in proving himself, taking command and directing the yacht's activities as we loaded a half dozen marine-patrol officers and an equal number of agents from the FBI. We departed after Riddle was assured that the *souls on board,* as he called us, were secure. He navigated the yacht through the shallow inlet, easily working the coast until the open sea was in sight.

I stayed on the deck for the ride to the meeting place. We passed beaches as they emptied, the day's beachgoers trudging through the sand, their bags in tow and towels slung over their shoulders. A shallow wake rippled on the ocean's surface and rapped against the yacht's hull. We passed fishing boats and rock jetties, teeming with people of all shapes and sizes, their arms stretched like the minute hand of a clock, casting lines into the sea in hopes of hitting a night bite. We were surrounded by beauty while gliding along the ocean, but I felt at odds with enjoying the tranquility when on a mission that was rife with tragedy.

The last stretches of the Outer Banks were miles of beach property that had died quietly over the years, consumed by rising seawaters, a cancer to the million-dollar vacation paradise. Waves flooded the shores, the surf pounding and running beneath the homes—some barely surviving while others had been beaten, leaning abandoned and in ruin.

"Sad, isn't it?" Jericho said.

"I bet it was beautiful once."

"Uh-huh. There was a time when the surf was more than a hundred yards from those houses," he said, pulling a cigarette from his jacket pocket, lighting it.

"No kidding. It happened fast?"

"It did," he said, squinting as smoke went into his eyes, the burn turning them watery red.

"Give me that," I said and crumpled the stick between my fingers, the paper and tobacco swept into the sea like confetti carried by the wind. "You're on duty, and it's bad for you."

His eyes followed the tobacco remains. "I've been wanting to quit, anyway."

The yacht turned to show giant machines on the beaches. "What are they?" I asked.

"Those are part of the beach replenishment project. They suck the sand from the ocean like giant vacuums and pour it like wet cement back onto the remains of the beach. It's supposed to add another five years."

"Sounds expensive," I said. The enormous green vacuums stood obscurely amidst the remaining houses. "Does it work?"

He gave me a shrug, answering, "It does, but the sand will get taken again in a year or two, anyway."

We approached the end of the islands, passing a beautiful cove glistening with fiery orange and red, reminding me of something on a postcard or a scene from *Gilligan's Island*. "Do you think all this will be gone one day?"

Jericho nodded. "At least this part will. Eventually, everything west of it too, the town and suburb, what remains will become beach front." I found myself moving closer to him, a cool breeze on my skin. I shook with a chill, my thin jacket not keeping off the sea breeze. His hand went to my back, rubbing to help warm me. "From Riddle's estimates, we should reach the site of the rendezvous in a few hours. Let's get inside and work the plans."

"You two okay down there," PK yelled from the upper deck, a tablet in hand.

"We're good," I shouted over the ocean noise.

The tech guru regarded us a moment and then ducked back into the wheelhouse.

"Yeah, I think you were right," I said.

"About what?"

"He's enjoying this."

"He is," Jericho answered. "And the bureau is showing a lot of interest."

With the sun gone, and the moon clouded over, the ocean and sky had morphed into a giant black pool, and we were blind. I couldn't see more than a foot from the edge of the yacht. Our order was to stay silent, stay dark, with only the wheelhouse lit for the traffickers to see. And in the wheelhouse with Riddle, PK waited, his laptop in hand—his role was to help secure the girl, and then the rest of us would take over. For now we remained on the deck, guns ready, squatting behind the railing.

"No lights," one of the agents said, yelling in a whisper. A few yards from this voice, a cell phone blinked and then went off. "We can't risk being seen."

The yacht lifted and dropped on a swell, swaying from side to side. Unable to see anything, the motion caused a stir in my belly, my mouth watering. I bit my upper lip until the sickness faded. "Damn," I whispered, cracking open a bottle of water.

"It's the darkness," Jericho said. "The rocking motion in the pitch-black plays with your brain."

"At least the waves aren't too bad," I said, closing my eyes, trying to imagine something innocuous like a field of tall grass, a breeze slightly bending the blades.

"When the nausea comes, breathe deeply through your nose. It'll help—"

But Jericho's words were cut short by the arrival of a boat. We heard a motor, small, the kind used on a raft or dinghy. We heard water lapping against its hull, and then a second and third motor, their locations coming from the sides. As instructed by Agent Rivera, PK exited the wheelhouse, showing himself in the cabin's light, his white shirt aglow in the dark as he waved toward the arriving parties.

Despite the chill in the air, nerves wet the back of my neck, my hand cramping on my gun. I was holding it too tight, the tension getting the better of me.

"Why are there three?" Jericho asked under his breath. He brought out his gun, and aimed it toward the deck, cocked and ready to fire. It was time. I lifted my gun too, the weight of it feeling heavy, alien. I couldn't remember the last time I'd discharged my weapon—the range maybe, as part of my annual certification.

"Over here," PK called into the darkness, clapping his hands. The motor closest cut off, snuffed like a fire extinguished. The second and third motors stopped too, leaving us in silence, waiting. "You'll need to come closer, so she can—"

The first bullet came like a bee buzzing by my head, hot metal singeing the air and opening a hole in the yacht. I didn't know what to make of it at first and peered over the railing in time to see the bright fireflies, three swarms, each twenty yards from us, flashes of blue and yellow light peppering the blackness and bellowing a roar like cannon fire. Pock marks appeared like a disease run rampant, enormous holes shredding the yacht's hull.

"Jesus! Get down!" Jericho screamed, just as one of the bullets bit my arm, its hot mouth chewing on my flesh. I let out a scream, but it was interrupted, my body tackled and slammed against the yacht's deck as more bullets flew overhead, hissing like feral animals, the air exploding.

"We've been setup. The whole fucking thing is a trap." Jericho braced himself against the deck rail, lifted his gun over the lip and fired aimlessly into the dark. Pain rifled into my shoulder, blood pouring down my arm and onto my hand, dressing my skin in a lacy red glove. I clenched my fist, finding function; the bullet had only grazed me.

The gunshots were impossibly deafening, but I followed the fireflies, using a sliver of open space in the railing, aimed directly into the swarms and fired into the assault. I emptied a clip and heard a splash amidst the thunderous barrage. At least one assailant was down, but the gunfire increased as if in retaliation, its anger an endless torrent.

I was screaming then, rage and terror feeding a stew of adrenaline and fright, my chest pounding with a thousand hammers, my muscles in motion like a hummingbird's wings flittering against a wind. My gun emptied again, but I kept smashing the trigger while I reached into my belt for a fresh clip, reloading and continuing where I'd left off. There were stars scattering from the sky, the images fleeting, my head spinning from the shock and mayhem. Another splash, a body floating face down, the darkness stealing it a moment later as I shifted and fired my weapon at the second boat.

Cloudy debris rained on us, the super yacht erupting, scattering its guts and glass, pieces gleaming in the wheelhouse light. Foam insulation and metal shrapnel flew as if thrown by a tornado. I choked on the smoke and glimpsed a look at the wheelhouse, the windows shattered and with no signs of Officer Riddle. And then I saw PK, his body slung over the side, his shirt bloodied. And for a brief moment, I thought he was still alive, convulsing, blood dripping in large streaks along the vessel. But the man I'd become fond of was dead, bullets continuing to enter his torso and causing his flesh to flinch and jump as the hot slugs macerated him. Agony came like mayhem, immense sadness touching the demand to fight. Jericho hadn't seen PK yet. He hadn't seen that his friend was dead.

The accompanying patrol boats did their best to guard and defend, swimming around the yacht like sharks, swirling the waters, always moving, returning fire into the darkness. The attack seemed to never end, but when I hammered my last clip into my gun, I heard the call for a ceasefire. And like the moon stealing the light, the gunfire abruptly ended.

The air was stiff with gunpowder, filling my nose with the smell of spent fireworks. But the scent of blood came to me too, sickening and morbid. My arm was sleeved in red, tacky and cold. Jericho did his best to wrap a torn cloth around the wound, talking to me, his voice stung by the ringing in my ears.

"I'm fine," I assured him, glancing at PK's body, unable to hear my own voice as the extent of death became clearer. "Jericho?"

The yacht's deck was covered with men and women cradling their torn limbs, holding their sides, yelling to anyone who'd listen. A woman I'd met at the station held her head in her hands while wandering in a circle, blood seeping from between her fingers as she argued senselessly with nobody. She found her FBI hat at her feet and tumbled onto her face as she tried to pick it up.

"Jesus!" Jericho cried.

"Listen to me!" I demanded, my voice hollow, barely recognizable. "It's PK."

He couldn't hear, but Jericho read my lips and peered over his shoulder. "Oh God!" he mouthed, his chin quivering. "Why didn't he get down!"

"Jericho, we can't help him, but we can help them," I said, standing.

But Jericho yanked my arm. I crashed to my knees. His eyes bulged with a piercing stare as he stuck to the railing and scanned the ocean, believing we might still be under attack. I put my hands to his face and checked his body for injury. When I found none, I held him and motioned for him to take deep breaths with me.

"It was a setup," he managed to say. "And now PK is dead."

"Listen. Stay low," I told him, raising my voice over the wails and cries of the injured. I crawled to the first of the wounded, finding she'd worn a vest, the front of it holding two bullets. But it was her head bleeding that was out of control. She'd been hit near her forehead, grazed like me, but sliced deep, causing her to bleed profusely.

"Use this," Agent Rivera instructed, holding a towel for me. Her arms were filled with more towels and bottles of water. "I grabbed what I could from inside."

"You okay?" I asked, my words still muffled.

"I can breathe," she mouthed, wincing, holding her side. "Broke a rib, but I'll be fine."

I moved to the next body, an agent with the FBI, his sandy hair matted flat against his head. He groaned and rolled to his side, trying to undo his vest. Like the first, he'd been saved too. "Can you stand?"

"I think so," he answered.

"Then you can help," I told him, giving him no time to wait. He cried out when I pulled him forward, my words an excuse to check behind him and make sure there were no other injuries. "You're good."

We did the same for the rest of the patrol, covering the deck before moving inside and to the wheelhouse. In all, PK was dead, and two of the agents. Four more were seriously injured, with one unresponsive and unlikely to survive. The patrol boats that came to our defense had minimal injuries, and were at the ready to help.

With the wheelhouse filling, it seemed everyone was screaming and yelling. There was talk of a helicopter and hollering about the timing and the critically wounded. And there was shouting about the plans, about how this should never have happened. And then there was talk about PK's body, and whether this was a crime scene, and if his body should remain where it was for processing, hung in the wind like wet clothes on a line.

"Take him down," Jericho demanded, dousing the fevered words with a single instruction. "There're enough witnesses here to address the investigation. We can be respectful. We can do that much."

PK's body was brought inside and placed on the floor. And from the grandest of staterooms, I tore a blanket from the oversized mattress and used it to cover his body.

"I'm sorry," I whispered while tucking the sheet beneath his arms. Rivera helped, doing the same on the other side.

"Almost have it," Riddle said, addressing the room, his thick fingers reworking the wiring beneath a control panel that had been decimated by the gunfire. "Just need to bypass this switch panel and relay and we'll have power. Now, if I can get this—"

The yacht rumbled and came alive, the deck vibrating, the cracked windows rattling, the remaining pieces breaking free and crashing to the floor. The large motors spat seawater as they came to life. Riddle jumped up and pushed a lever and then another, accelerating. We left him to his work, left PK's body, and took to the deck to check on the injured.

In the open, the air moved through my hair, the night's massacre spewing a deadly scent like a fisherman's bloody chum line. It wasn't long before the buzz of adrenaline and shock began to fade and open the flood gates. I wanted to cry, to scream, to raise my fists and yell. It was the blood that got to me the most, the pungent smell, stomach-turning, metallic. It was too much.

"Drink this," Jericho said, handing me some water.

I waved it off, bracing the deck rail, leaning over the side and dry-heaving, pinching my gut, my arm throbbing. "I can't keep anything down right now."

"Let's go up front," he suggested, taking my hand, leading us to the yacht's bow. "Fresh air. Try to stay up-wind until you feel better."

"I don't think that's possible," I answered flatly, looking at the carnage. "Not after this. Not anytime soon. I don't think any of us will feel better."

Without warning, I took him into my arms, my hands racing up and down his body, checking him again, making sure he wasn't hit. He held me, really held me, his heart pounding with mine, the both of us trembling.

"I've never seen anything like this. And PK, so young," he said, his eyes glazed wet. He sipped his water and looked hard at the bottle. "Now would be a good time for something stronger." He let out a muffled laugh.

"Maybe," I answered. "Jericho? How did this happen?"

"They knew we were coming."

"But how?"

We looked at each other, the silent suspicion lying between us. As much as we couldn't believe it, someone had leaked.

CHAPTER 37

It was early in the morning. The night was slipping into day, the sky a rich blue. The colors made me think of the blue dahlias in Robert Stewart's hand, his death, and his photo with Hannah, of course. The flowers were a clue into Robert Stewart's murder, but offered little, their popularity making it impossible to isolate a source. We were no closer to solving any of the crimes, and today we'd face questions about the evening's attack on the yacht, PK's death and the other officers and agents who'd fallen in the line of duty.

I crashed soon after we'd arrived back to shore, the rush of adrenaline draining and turning me off like a lightbulb. Most of us had spent the evening in the hospital, hooked up to bags of fluids, monitored as we recovered. I couldn't stay long though, and forced myself out of bed, out of the hospital gown and back into my clothes. I wanted to monitor the press crowd, knowing news about the yacht would bring them to the dock. I left Jericho behind, the hospital linen on his bed rising and falling with a steady snore.

Six hours had passed since the assault on the water. I could still feel the sting in my arm, the throb and pull of tissue-glue stitches; the gunpowder still burned in my nose and I still heard ringing in my ears. I'd survived, and I'd have the scar on my arm to remind me of the nightmare. In all, the attack may have been only minutes, but in my head, in my heart, it was an eternity. As for the yacht, seeing it in the early daylight slammed the horror into my brain. It was bad. It was worse than I could imagine. The once pristine white-and-black vessel had been cut into pieces, shredded like a sheet of paper.

News vans lined the dock, antennae extended, the satellite dishes swaying like flowers in a field. A steady gathering pressed the police barricade, a testament to the morbid sense of curiosity. Cameras with long lenses poked through the gawking faces, glassy muzzles focused on the super yacht. There was chatter like small talk at a funeral, the buzz coming with questions unanswered, speculations and theories spouting like gospel. And as expected, a hodgepodge of local police grew in number, with FBI agents, marine-patrol officers, and crime-scene technicians swarming the yacht and the area surrounding the dock. A few technicians hung from ropes, working the yacht's tortured side, taking pictures, digging for bullet slugs and measuring whatever it was that needed measuring.

Online, curious stories began to trend about the yacht again. There were new hashtags labeling it a death ship, and theories posted about how it was owned by a drug cartel, the hull equipped with hidden firepower like an old-time war ship made for canon battles. An even hotter twist was a chase across the sea with pirates boarding and taking control like something out of a wild adventure movie. There was even mention of Harlan Jacobs's marina playing host to the pirates.

The FBI guarded the actual details of what happened, curbing the speculations posted on the social-media sites, carefully working the questions by the press—some of which were touching close to what had actually happened. After all, every rumor has a sliver of truth, and we needed to hide as much of this one as possible.

A breeze cut my thoughts, the wind blowing tattered crime-scene tape like the tails of a kite in flight. A patrol officer ripped the faded line, and replaced it with a new string, marking most of the dock as a crime scene. I thought I'd laugh, but bit my tongue, the exhaustion feeding a poor sense of humor. This was no crime scene. This was carnage, the yacht was a dead body we'd dragged back.

"What a sight," District Attorney Ashtole said, his shoes scraping against the sandy pavement. "I heard about PK. Huge loss," he continued. My eyes remaining fixed on the yacht. "The yacht is drawing quite a few this morning, I think the FBI will be taking it soon."

"PK was a good kid," I heard myself say, a breeze whistling as seabirds hovered above, plumed breasts against the wind, their beady eyes searching for a meal. I turned to the DA, adding, "It'll be good to get the yacht out of here."

Ashtole drank from a steaming paper cup, one brow raised, answering, "There's some confusion about a location though, which is why the yacht is still with us." While his position on either case was none, he'd come to the dock to pay his respects and to offer any help his office could provide. There was also another news conference to prepare for. He meant well, but public visibility meant more pressure. He put his hand on my shoulder, it was gentle and soft like a child's, adding, "I am sorry for what happened. When you agreed to help, I never expected any of this. How's the arm?"

"Grazed. It's nothing," I said without expression. "A few stitches is all."

"Good," he answered, turning back to face the yacht. "What a mess."

"It is," Jericho agreed, showing up beside me, clean-shaven, his hair wet and slicked back. "PK's family has been notified. Hardest call I've ever made in—"

Jericho bowed his head, his palm pressed to his face, his words shortened by the loss of his friend. Ashtole went to him, consoling, his voice a whisper. Jericho nodded. In the distance, shutters clicked, reporters and photographers drawn to the emotional interaction.

"Chin up," Ashtole told him and cleared his throat, wrestling with a sudden show of affection. "We'll make it right. We will."

"But how did they know?" Jericho asked, a blank look on his face.

"I think the auction had to have been a setup," Ashtole offered, his idea telling me we'd been made well before boarding the yacht, before PK had placed the first bid.

"They knew," I said. "Somehow, they knew. What about Harlan Jacobs, the all-points bulletin issued, was it the timing of it?"

"Could be," Jericho answered. "If you're right, and Harlan is involved, the APB would have definitely raised some eyebrows."

My body tensed, fixing on the idea we might be responsible. I faced the yacht, throat tightening, and asked, "Did we do this?"

"Nonsense!" Ashtole said, his voice stern and raised. He locked his eyes with mine. "You guys followed protocol. Don't you try and shoulder what happened. Capeesh?"

"Capeesh," I told him, thankful for his words.

Our phones buzzed then, an alert from the station. "That can't be good," I said, flipping through the screen, one eye on the text, the other on Jericho. His face emptied with the news as I read the same words.

"Another body," he commented in a flat tone.

"The same place, too."

"Woman, a shallow grave, naked and possibly in her early twenties," Ashtole commented, holding his phone. He raised his arms in a wave, "What is going on here?"

I shook my head, unable to answer. The burn in my lungs tasted like gunpowder. The ringing in my ears, a steady constant. But none of these bothered me. My feet were ready to move. I needed to be in the woods. I *had* to be in the woods. I saw the basement of the station, the box full of sleeved case files, and the faces of missing children from half a decade ago. In my heart I believed the victim would be one of them.

"The missing children, the case files," I began, turning away from the cameras. "It's one of them. I'm sure of it."

"You have your cases," Ashtole said, nodding firmly, motioning for me to go. "You have full cooperation and priority."

"All of them?"

"All. If this latest victim has been missing too, I'll get more resources, scour every case we have going back fifteen years."

"God, I want to be wrong," I said, the idea of girls being held all these years, only to be murdered and dumped in the woods.

Ashtole's arms fell to his side, his chin down, a frown fixed. "Detective White, I don't think you are."

CHAPTER 38

The killer was taunting us. Their continued use of the woods a blatant way of saying they were smarter. I hated the idea, but with my feet next to another shallow grave, and the smell of blood and death in my nose, I began to think maybe they were. Word had come that forensics on the previous two graves produced no helpful leads. This was the third grave, and my hope the killer might make a mistake was dwindling. I carefully stepped around the site, avoiding eye contact with everyone, angry at myself, angry I'd failed to make a difference.

I pressed my knees against the forest floor, a twig digging into my leg as I spread my fingers and gripped the earth until it was beneath my fingernails. I had to see if the victim was Hannah. I had to, because that's what I did. That's what I always did.

I took a breath, held it, and lowered myself until my chin touched the dirt. The victim's hair was sandy brown, a mix of filth and grit riddled throughout it, leaving me to think she'd been dragged, perhaps killed elsewhere and brought to the woods. Her jaw hung slack, possibly broken, her tongue swelled profusely, deep purple and jutting like a tree root. And her eyes, the pupils black and floating in gray pools that were spotted red. It was a sign of petechia, the killer having strangled the victim.

It wasn't Hannah. My heart was struck with a brief wave of relief. I shook it off and checked my phone to compare this girl to the picture of the girl from the recent auction. The auction girl's snow-white skin was a stark contrast against red hair, which quickly showed this wasn't her. The picture stung though, a fresh reminder we'd failed to save her too.

I stood up when I heard leaves rustling, branches breaking, motion in nearby shrubs. My mind swung wildly with ideas the killer was behind a tree, watching, taunting, teasing in silence. They might even be taking pictures of our macabre camp—me at the grave, technicians at work, Jericho on his phone. If the killer posted them on the Dark Web, I bet PK could find them. But PK was dead too. Dead like this child. That's what she was. A child. My guess, fourteen or fifteen years of age.

"What is it?"

"The killer knows us," I told Jericho, searching the trees to be sure, spinning around with mounting paranoia. One of the technicians stood with me, feeding off my reaction, her hands up, guarding.

Jericho spied the forest's edge, searching it. When he was satisfied, he suggested, "Or maybe they're just stupidly brazen and clueless?"

"I doubt it," I said without expression, and faced the grave again.

"I've seen it before," he told me. "There's no discounting dumb or taking it for granted."

"Check out the gown." The victim was dressed in the same turn-of-the-century nightgown Cheryl Parry and Olivia Jones were found wearing. "Any chance there's a laundry service that's been in business a long time?"

"There're a few," he said, holding his phone, taking a picture of the nightgown. "They mostly service restaurants and hotels. I can get a list for you."

"Crop the photo around this part," I said, guiding with my hand, my interest in the nightgown's pattern, the weave of it. "I'm fairly sure it's the same from Cheryl Parry's nightgown."

"Got it."

"I think they're the real thing. I mean, genuine antiques and not something you'd pick up shopping online."

He shook his head, asking, "Are they a particular style? You know, like a negligee?"

"Far from it," I said, showing him my screen. "This is what Cheryl Parry was wearing."

Jericho went to the victim. "It's the same pattern," he confirmed. "I don't think I've ever seen a nightgown like it."

"I doubt many have."

"Except maybe someone who cleans garments for a living," he added, catching on to what I wanted. "I'll get started on contacting the businesses."

My phone erupted, notifications running up the screen. Annoyed, I quieted the speaker.

"Someone must really need to talk to you," one of the technicians said, a grin on her upturned face.

"Yeah, I suppose they do." My phone's screen listed one name over and over, the count of emails doubling and then tripling. District Attorney, Ashtole.

With Ashtole's help, I received pictures and case details from the unsolved kidnappings that fit our time period. Soon after leaving the dock he'd secured resources at the station, a small team thrown together to review every case file from the box of folders I'd compiled, picking though each, and sending those matching select criteria to my phone.

Without PK, I used an app to age the faces a few years. A technician studied the pictures with me, analyzing the latest victim against the aged photographs. It wasn't long before we had a relatively good indication who she was. Stephanie Marsh had disappeared twelve years earlier, nine at the time, walking alone on the boardwalk, the attendant at a concession stand selling corndogs on a stick being the last to have seen the child. She'd be twenty-one today, a number of years older than what I'd assessed when first arriving at the crime scene.

Dr. Swales made a rare appearance, joining us in the field, as she called it, her attendance urged by Ashtole and the mayor to provide us with an immediate assessment.

"This is out of control," she said, dressed in white coveralls, her face unmasked, her hair balled tightly in a bun that pulled the skin on her forehead. Without waiting for a reply, she focused on the victim, her gloved fingers beneath the girl's neck, a bothered expression on her face, her square glasses slipping to the end of her nose.

"Same M.O." I offered. She shook her head.

"Yes, and no." Her southern accent was faint. "So much rage. Much more than before."

"How do you mean?" I asked.

"The ligature marks are broader around the neck area." Like before in the morgue, Dr. Swales guided my hand beneath the victim's head and toward her neck. "Do you feel that?" she asked, her glasses magnifying her eyes.

The victim's neck was supple like Play-Doh. I shook my head, unsure. "I don't know what I'm supposed to feel."

"Asphyxiation from strangulation."

"Same as the other victims."

She held up her finger, adding, "The X-ray will also confirm two, maybe three vertebrae are fractured."

"You mean, the killer broke her neck?"

"They did." Dr. Swales motioned to the gown, asking a crime-scene technician for permission, "May I?"

"Yes, certainly. We're done with this area."

"Look here," she began. "There are signs of significant malnourishment, and years of abuse. Old bite marks too, horrible scarring."

"Her arm," I suggested, noting an awkward bend, previously broken, the bones stitched without having been set properly.

"Yes, a terrible break, torture really," she said, lifting the victim's arm, tracing the break.

"The victim is twenty-one years old," I said, trying to picture her alive. "But she doesn't look any older than a teen."

"Her growth was stunted perhaps." Swales easily lifted the victim onto their side. "And look at her spine, how it is hunched over as though she was confined to a small space for extended periods."

Dr. Swales frowned, dipping her head, her gaze fixed on the gown and following the pattern in the stitching. "That gown," she said. "It's the same as the first two girls?"

"Have you seen it before?"

Her eyes narrowed, almost closing, as she searched her memory. The silence was eclipsed by the song of a tree frog, the first of the evening, the day moving fast, our time in the woods proving long. "I've seen it, but I just can't recall when that was. Or even where."

CHAPTER 39

Of the kidnapping cases Ashtole had turned over to me, five were young girls dating back over eleven years. I leafed through every document, every photograph, every witness statement. I learned the girls' names, their height and weight, and their eye and hair colors. There was Julianna Brown and Amelia Sato, the two youngest, aged only six when they'd been taken. There was Shannon Gordon and Dianne Taylor, cousins, but they'd grown up together and were more like sisters. They were seven when last seen. And the last of the unsolved cases, Stephanie Marsh, whose body we may have just identified. All the victims had been vacationing with their families, all from out of state. I made them my own, *my* cases, and vested myself in them.

"You okay?" Jericho asked, handing me an energy bar. Eagerly, I took it, chewed a bite and handed it back.

With Stephanie Marsh's body removed from the shallow grave, and the crime-scene technicians finished, darkness had blanketed the woods.

"You know, this isn't quite the night on the town I'd had in mind," he said with a sheepish grin.

"What?" I joked. "It's a one-course meal and a walk beneath the stars." I stopped a moment to stretch my back, the hours working with Dr. Swales catching up to me.

"Does have its elements," he said, as tree frogs sang and a night owl called.

"I could get used to this."

"It's easy to make this place home," he commented warmly, his face shaded by dusky light.

The moon was already in the sky, hanging effortlessly above the forest. A blood-orange shale stone. It gave us some light, but I could get lost if I took my eyes off the path.

"We better get out of here before it gets too dark," Jericho said, clouds easing across the sky like a lumbering giant, the edge of it turning the woods black.

"Can you see anything?"

"Just enough," he answered. "We've got about fifteen minutes before complete darkness."

I shrunk down when a sudden flapping noise pushed air above my head. The woods went silent again, save for the tree frogs and a breeze scuttling leaves.

"Tell me about her," I said, feeling the moment was right, my shoulder bumping against him. "Your wife."

His breathing changed, becoming deeper as he considered the conversation's direction. The cloud passed, returning the light. "My wife?"

"Sure. I mean, if you want to."

"Tell you what. I'll share if you share," he challenged.

"You already know my story," I reminded him, nudging his arm playfully. "Okay, fine. I'll bite. I'll share and then you share."

"I want to know about the Burgess case."

I flinched at the name, leaning away, instinctive, guarding. My mouth went dry, the cozy moment between us turning uncomfortable.

"How do you know about that?" I asked, defensively. "It was my captain, wasn't it? The chief found out?"

"He was only checking on you," Jericho said, looking apologetic. "He happened to mention the Burgess case and wanted to see how you were doing."

I tried to speak, but a hot stone had set in the pit of my throat. What Jericho asked was significant, the memory returning like a knife splitting me open. A long silence came between us.

"I almost killed someone," I finally said, my voice shaky. "I almost killed another cop."

Jericho looked on, his face stony in a cast of gray light.

"What happened?" he asked, tilting his head as if awaiting a confession. This wasn't a confession though, but I felt he deserved to know.

"It was the Burgess case," I began. As I spoke, I stepped on a branch, the twig snapping in two and causing me to jump, my insides jittery with nerves. "When I arrived on scene, I saw the car. I mean, it was the same car. From my daughter's kidnapping. The one I was trying to find at Fitz's Garage."

"I recall you mentioning the type."

"Even the covered license plate and the kidnapper's eyes in the rearview window. All the same."

"What else?" he asked, brow raised with disbelief.

I hesitated, knowing how crazy it must have sounded. "I saw her bracelet."

"Bracelet?"

A drink, I needed a drink, the cotton in my mouth stealing my words. I opened a water bottle, gulping a mouthful before I could continue.

"When Hannah was taken from me, she'd been wearing a charm bracelet. It had the moon and stars and other pieces made of cheap plastic. I couldn't stand the thing, but she loved it. Wore it every day—you know, the way kids get attached to some things."

"My son wore a cape. Called it his superhero cape," Jericho said, lifting the mood. "Damn thing stunk to hell."

"When I identified the car and saw the kidnapper, I pulled my gun." A shudder rushed through me, the images so clear they continued to fool my brain. "And there was Hannah's bracelet. A patrol officer found it inside the car."

"Hey!" Jericho shouted, his voice startling me. We'd reached the edge of the road, my car's passenger door open, the frame of a man inside. The stranger's clothes were black, his head covered. He wasn't a cop, and he wasn't a crime-scene technician. "Hold it!" Jericho ordered.

The moon had disappeared behind another cloud, my story about the Burgess case quieted by the interruption as other patrol officers joined us, having heard Jericho's yell. The figure crawled out, standing to face us, his hands hidden.

"Arms in the air!" one of the officers yelled. "Identify yourself."

Silence fell over us, our guns at the ready, bracing, uncertain if the stranger was holding a weapon. Flashes of light played in my periphery, false images, a memory scalded by the shootout on the yacht. I turned off my gun's safety, raising my arms with a steady aim. My gunshot wound ached, the throb more of a reminder than real.

"For your safety and ours, raise your hands!" I demanded.

We heard a man's voice then, his humming a soft tune that might have been a children's rhyme. He dared another step, entering into a faint blade of light next to my car, his head and shoulders covered with black netting. The stranger was well over six feet. As he turned toward the woods, I also saw his pale fingers, Caucasian, his left hand visible, no rings, no tattoos, nothing familiar or similar to the image of the hand we'd seen in the auction video.

I could feel heartbeats thrumming, blood rushing through my veins, carrying adrenaline to every cell of my body. Easing onto the balls of my feet, I mirrored the stranger's movements, his easing out of the light and nearing the woods. I could tell he was trying to get a jump and leave nothing to chance.

The man's humming stopped and he twisted around in a run. I dug my shoe into the loose soil and took off after him with Jericho and the patrol officers pursuing close behind.

"Get down!" I screamed, my gun pointed at the figure. "Now!"

But the stranger was already further ahead, his figure a blur, vaulting over fallen trees, and dipping beneath branches. He was running a path I couldn't see. The chase came to a hill, a downhill momentum building, bodies moving faster than our legs could carry, the wind pressing my skin and tossing my hair.

"Jesus!" one of the officers screamed, his chest plowing into a branchy overhang, his lungs emptying in a wheezy gasp.

We were down to three, but only one was needed. I had the stranger in my sights, the air like fire in my lungs as I kept pace, dodging obstacles, turning tight corners, our speed increasing with huge strides. The stranger was trying to lose me, and for a moment, I thought he might, cutting through the trees and around boulders. It became clear, he knew the woods, he knew his dumping grounds. This was our suspect.

"Stop or I'll shoot," I yelled, deciding to fire into the air, cocking my gun, but then holding back and relieving the hammer. What if the bullet came down and hit an officer? I holstered my weapon, losing step with the suspect, the distance between us lengthening, his frame seeming to glide on air.

My lungs raged, my throat and neck burned, and my brow dripped. I couldn't keep up with him. A crash of broken branches and a scream came from behind us. I glanced over my shoulder to see the other officer somersaulting over bushes. And on the forest floor behind them, a stretch of a shadows chased us as the far side of the hill was thrown in darkness, the moon disappearing behind massive clouds.

"Can't—" Jericho yelled, and then I heard him tumble, his body slamming into the ground. I felt concern for him rising suddenly.

The blackness was teemed with bushes, the wiry branches striking my arms and legs and face, cutting and stinging as I struggled through a tangle of tall shrubbery. But suddenly, the forest was gone. The trees, the boulders, the suspect, there was nothing but space, and nothing beneath me. I'd run clear out of the woods, emptiness blanketing me. I began to fall and screamed, my arms swinging wildly, fingers splayed, hands clutching the air as it rushed upward, before finding something to grab hold of. It was a rope, the feel of it like wood. I held it, swinging until I struck solid earth, gravity urging me to let go.

But where was the suspect? My mind flashed with the last images of him, slowing to a near stop, briefly looking over his shoulder before turning sharply as the lights went out. I'd kept my path straight and ran off the side of a mountain.

In my blindness, I became aware of the predicament I was in, realizing I'd hit the side of a cliff, my feet dangling, a thick tree root in my hand— not a rope—a pebbly spill tumbling from its mouth. I searched the sky, the moon stuck behind clouds, cresting like a halo, preventing me from seeing the truth beneath my feet. I had no idea how high the cliff was. Maybe that was a good thing.

My brain throbbed. It pulsed with an ache inching through my arms and hands. I wouldn't be able to hold on long, and terror and fear rose like a wave approaching an unsuspecting beach. It was coming, and it was going to crash.

"Hold on!" I heard Jericho shout. His voice was tensed with grave concern. "Oh Jesus, Casey. Are you there?"

"Barely," I managed to say, understanding he was as blind as I was. The root slipped from between my fingers. I let out a scream and tried climbing.

The clouds finally moved, the landscape coming alive as if by a giant lightbulb. And then I wished it hadn't. I screamed, looking below me, seeing the tops of trees amidst a forest. "Oh God!"

"Don't look down!"

"Too late," I tried to laugh, but couldn't, my stomach twisting in my throat. There was sixty feet of nothing beneath my toes. "Shit! That's a long way down."

"Yeah, it is!" he yelled. "Whoever that was, they're gone too."

"Jericho, he knew these woods," I shouted up at him. "Before I lost the light, the guy stopped. He knew the cliff was here. He knew I'd fly off the side of it."

"Then we can charge him for attempted murder too," Jericho joked.

A ball of dirt hit my face, breaking into crumbs. "What are you doing!" I demanded, his face coloring, glazed in sweat as he hung over the cliff's edge. He surveyed the exposed tree roots and rocks, lowering his good arm, his fingers within reach.

"Come on, Casey, you've got to climb!" His voice was strained and his bad arm flopped against the cliff's dirt lip.

A single muscle twitch turned into two. There was another, and then three more, a dance I couldn't control starting beneath my skin. I was trembling and cramping and terrified to use Jericho as a ladder.

"What's holding you?" I asked, shedding a tear. I was afraid to touch him. Terrified he'd spill over me and plummet to his death.

"I'm secure, I've got my legs wrapped around a tree," he assured me, gravity inching him closer, veins popping on his forehead and neck.

I climbed. I dug into the wall, the packed dirt and stone enough to hoist me until I could take Jericho's hand. "Are you okay?" I asked, my muscles shaking profusely.

"I got you." His grip was like a vice, his body receding from the edge, lifting me with him. When his shoulders were secured, I could only see the side of his head. He yelled down, "Climb over me!"

There were other voices, the patrol officers searching for us. "Stay back," I warned.

"Don't come any closer," Jericho yelled.

Sweat dripped into my eyes as my strength faded. "I'm scared," I cried, my muscles suddenly frozen, leaving me unable to move.

Jericho rolled enough for me to see him. "You have to. Please, Casey."

I gripped his arm and then his shoulder, digging my fingers into his skin and clothes, scrambling until my cheek was next to his. A moment later, I grabbed his belt, and felt his arm between my legs, his muscles quivering as he held me while I caught my breath.

I continued when I could, finding myself on top of him, sliding over his body and then rolling off to the side in a cloud of dust.

"Casey?"

"Yeah," I answered, breathless, crawling away from the cliff's edge.

"That concludes the rock-climbing portion of the date I promised."

I began to laugh, pain in my ribs, cramps in every muscle. But my laughs turned to cries and emotion.

"Hey?" He put his arm around me so I could lay my head on his chest. "You're okay now."

"I know," I said, unable to stop the tears. Feelings seemed to come from nowhere as though years of reserves had been tapped.

"What is it?"

"I don't know," I said, lying to him. Maybe it was the closeness of dying. I couldn't say. But in that moment, I felt vulnerable and exposed. I felt raw. "I think it's everything."

"The Burgess case?" he asked. I cried harder. The shame of it. The embarrassment and humiliation. The idea I could have accidentally taken a man's life. Jericho held me closer, my body fitting his. "Was it your daughter's bracelet?"

I shook my head and cleared my eyes. "I thought it was though."

"What was it?"

"Candy," I revealed feeling overwhelmed with shame. "It was one of those candy bracelets."

"I used to see my wife," he told me, calmly sharing, my body rising and falling as he took a deep breath. "I mean, I used to see her *after* she was murdered."

"After?"

He nodded with moonlight brightening his face. "I saw her everywhere, especially in mirrors. I even heard her sometimes."

"Heard? What did she say?"

"They weren't words exactly. But some of the time, she was as clear to me as you are. And other times, I saw her as she'd been found, her voice a terrible noise, a frightening scream."

"That must have been horrible," I said, touching his face, the moon in his wet eyes.

"It's okay," he said, trying to comfort me. "You made a mistake."

"None of it was okay," I told him as flashes of red and blue struck the leafy canopy. Footfalls came then, as did voices and radios and squelching static. The woods were alive. If the stranger was the killer, we'd ruined our chance at catching him. But worse than that, he was in my car. He knew we were onto him. He knew me.

CHAPTER 40

HIM

Detective Casey White. He had her secrets, the case file open, the folder held flat against the floor, and also her picture on the television. Their eyes were on him, metal clacking with the slightest movements, their interests growing like his appetite.

"Scrub!" he demanded with a shout. He decided to share then, knowing their time was short. "I'll let you see her too. But only when you're clean."

The scrubbing began, the soft cries bringing him satisfaction, his need for control satiated.

"Your daughter," he said to the screen, barely able to contain his excitement. And as he leafed through the baby pictures, and the drawings, he began to understand who she was, a laugh rising. He saw why the detective's face was so familiar to him.

"You're not Hannah. That's not your name at all," he said, remembering her, remembering what he'd done and wondering if she'd lived. "Oh, what secrets we weave."

"Kidnapped," he said, flipping the pages and setting fire to the end of a cigarette. "Bested by a red car. What a shame."

He closed the folder, a satisfaction coming to him. He glanced at the doors along the wall; the padlocks, two open, the remaining closed. His woods were gone. She took them from him. It was a shattering loss, the heat of anger simmering with blood pulsing in his head. A child's tune came to his lips, soothing as the others joined in humming the nursery rhyme.

"You took my place," he said angrily, tracing Detective White's face, the television charging his fingers with static energy. He held up her case file, the folder firmly between his fingers. It was a payment for his loss, her taking his burying place. "So I took something from you."

CHAPTER 41

It was gone. Of all the belongings in my car, the only thing taken was the folder containing Hannah's case file. Nothing anyone said, or could say, comforted me. Years of notes and leads and the original police and investigation reports were taken. For the first time since Hannah's kidnapping, I felt alone, utterly alone, a massive emptiness in me, a hole I couldn't fill. With the case file, Hannah was always with me. Call it a kind of distorted obsession, my maintaining an album of my daughter, a drawing for each year in Hannah's life, but it kept her close. And now it was all gone.

I snatched a few hours' sleep, my mind racing in and out of nightmares. In one of them I saw Hannah dangling from a cliff, the tattoo on her neck alive, the head of a muscle car, the motor screaming, the grill snarling. In another, Jericho held the folder with Hannah's case file, having found it in the woods. He offered it to me, but the car spat a blade from under the hood, slicing through his arm, the end of it draining like a garden hose, his face pasty and turning grim with death.

I left the nightmares where I'd found them, and sought Dr. Swales, her southern drawl announcing she'd entered the station. Jericho was bleary-eyed as well, but between the two of us, I believe there was at least six hours of rest somewhere in the last twenty-four. I wondered about his dreams—were they nightmares too?

"Don't you two look a sight," Dr. Swales said, greeting us with a cardboard tray of coffees. "I heard about the adventures last evening and thought you could use a cup."

"You didn't have to," I said, appreciating the uptick in quality over the black acid sold at the Quick Mart.

"You'll need it," she continued. "I also heard there was a theft."

I tapped the side of my head. "I still have what's upstairs."

She squeezed my arm affectionately. "Good attitude."

"It's the drawings I want. The artist always kept the originals for her portfolio, so I might be able to get new copies."

Her brow raised. "Well that sounds promising," she commented.

Swales nudged her chin toward a station monitor as it flicked on, the screen filling with a familiar sight—it was another news conference, reporters clamoring about an uncaught serial killer, the potential death of businesses at the time of year the Outer Banks needed every vacation dollar.

"Feeding the press," I said, a taste of coffee warming me.

"Listen, I got a call last night. They mentioned the identification in the field, but requested confirmation."

"And—?" Jericho began.

"Stephanie Marsh, isn't it?" I asked, thinking of the app we used.

"Yes. I met with her parents just after sunrise," she answered, steam from her cup clouding her glasses. "Before this morning, they'd visited the morgue for every unidentified girl matching their daughter's age. Stephanie's mother insisted she knew her daughter was still here."

"She was right," I commented, wishing I had the same sense for Hannah. "The victim's neck. Was it fractured?"

Swales sipped the hot coffee, her eyes on the screen behind us. I glanced briefly to find Ashtole at the podium, accompanied by Sheriff Petro. The mayor was there too, but stayed in the back in the shadows and nearly out of the camera's view, leaving the chore to Petro and Ashtole.

"Three vertebrae broken," she answered, holding up three fingers. "If I didn't know any better, the killer continued squeezing after the victim was dead."

"Jesus!" Jericho replied, his face grim. "Who is this guy?"

"How about a pregnancy?" I asked. Cheryl Parry's baby was gone. Cheryl's baby was another victim. A forgotten victim. What if there was another pregnancy?

"One of the first things I checked," Swales said. "So far, it's only been Cheryl Parry."

"We're hitting a wall," I said, frustrated over the lost chance in the woods, the loss of Hannah's case file. I paced in front of Jericho and Dr. Swales, their eyes following me.

On the table was the stack of case files brought up from the station's storage, the plastic sleeving removed, four girls still missing, girls who I believed were still alive. For now, anyway. I lifted the folders, held them up and then placed each on the table, side by side, the girls' names printed on the face of each folder.

"This is who we have to protect. These girls were stolen from their families, and I'm convinced they're still alive, still in the Outer Banks."

Swales joined me at the table, reading each name, her voice silent, her lips moving. "Find them," she said, bowing her head. "I don't want to see any more of this."

"It's a priority," I assured her.

Dr. Swales spun around to face the exit, her crocs planting a familiar kiss against the floor. "As for me, I need to make the findings official for Stephanie Marsh. But I do have a gift for you."

"More than the coffee?"

"Stephanie Marsh fought back. We collected skin and blood from beneath her fingernails."

"She scratched her attacker?"

"It seems that way," she answered, her frizzy hair swaying with a bob. "The collected skin and blood were fresh, and substantial enough for DNA analysis."

"That's amazing news," I said, feeling as though a break in the case might be in reach.

Swales held her hands in the air in a *whoa* motion. She said softly, "Time. I need more time. Once we have a DNA profile, we can submit it for a search, enlist our bureau friends over there. And even then, we'll only get a hit if the killer's DNA profile was ever recorded."

I glanced toward Agent Rivera and her team, their work on the yacht case heavy, especially with the loss of PK. There was still no sign of Harlan, or enough evidence to legally search the detention center.

"Do keep us posted," Jericho said. A sheet of paper was handed to him. He read a few words and passed it to me. "As for us, with nothing immediate, I think I have a boat ride planned for today."

"Boat?" I asked, my hand going to the case files. "I was thinking of the boardwalk where some of the girls had disappeared."

"Rivera is looking for help. It's the yacht's dinghy. There could be evidence she'll need for a warrant. What do you say? Interested in another boat ride?"

I considered the auction video with Hannah as I listened to the news conference, the inaccuracy of a question answered. Sheriff Petro gave a nod to a reporter, telling them the victims from the woods had been positively identified. He grouped them with the other victims, including the girls from the yacht.

I shook my head at the TV but said to Jericho, "Yeah, I'll go."

"What's the matter?"

"We need to bring clarity to the cases and separate them," I said, motioning to the press conference. "Not just in here, but there too."

"Some of us are still on the fence. But let's see what we can find," he offered. "Rivera enlisted Marine Patrol, and I agreed."

*

We were at the patrol boat within the hour, the morning had burned off, the sun beating on us as clouds lumbered from the west.

"Storm clouds," Jericho said. But the billowing giants looked innocent enough to me, like enormous pillows. "See their height? It's the friction, they're going to open up fiercely."

I offered a hand, taking hold of the patrol boat's rope, throwing slack into the line as though I'd done it a million times. I watched Jericho's movements, mirroring him, rolling the loose line and tucking it for storage on the boat.

"And you believe this is the dinghy from the yacht?" I asked.

"Same make and model. It's also the only one we know to be missing. There's also the cove it's stuck in. From where the yacht was found that's the place it'd be. But it won't last if a harsh wind picks up, along with the next high tide. The dinghy will sink."

"Tell me what to do," I said, sounding impatient, feeling anxious.

Jericho caught my tone, saw me rushing. "Easy, we'll get there, maybe just grab a seat for a few minutes. I'll be back in ten and then we'll be on our way."

"Ten," I answered, repeating his words. I offered a half-smile, trying to make light of it, but sensed his concern. "Okay fine, I'll wait. I'm just a little on edge."

"A little?" he asked. "I'll try to be back in five."

"Five," I agreed and climbed aboard the patrol boat to wait.

Four missing girls, possibly held captive like animals. That's all I could think about as an image of Stephanie Marsh flashed when I closed my eyes—her curved spine and broken arm and bite marks. Missing the killer in the woods, and knowing he had the girls had put me on edge. I was losing my handle on this case. The entire world had suddenly gone into slow motion while I raced at a million miles per hour trying to contain it. And even then, it still felt as though I couldn't move fast enough.

"You've got to relax," I told myself, taking in the sight of the ocean and the beaches, trying to find some kind of calm as the surf lapped the side of the patrol boat like a metronome. I tuned into the soothing sound, hoping it would help.

The early afternoon was downright steamy, swampy even, the heat and humidity covering us in a muggy haze. I could smell the heat. I watched as Jericho crossed the station's parking lot, the asphalt a wavy mirage. *Five minutes,* he'd said. I checked my phone impatiently.

I fanned my face and dipped my hand over the side, splashing seawater onto the back of my neck. Jericho was right, there'd be a storm later. But for now, the clouds were only a threat. We had time.

Two minutes passed. I took out the picture of Hannah and Robert Stewart, a beam of sunlight skipping off the evidence bag. I stared at the last of the four pictures, certain they were in love. We needed to find her. Whoever killed Robert could also be after her. I shuddered at the thought; it was a grave concern, gnawing. The boardwalk was on my list. I had to retrace the kidnappings, and I'd also identified the only possible location the photographs of Hannah could have been taken, the arcade. With the help of Jericho's son, and some time on their computer, we were able to determine the make and model of the photo booth. It was known as the *little miss model 11*, and the booth was vintage. Still in service, it was also the only one of its kind in all of the Outer Banks.

I tucked the photograph safely into my bag and picked up the intersection picture of Harlan with Hannah, the single connection to the picture being the auction site and our only living victim, the girl from the yacht's galley. I'd started to call her Coma Girl. We'd been told her condition had finally leveled. No worse, and no better. The doctors kept her on rounds of dialysis, cleansing her blood, telling us time was what she needed. And if by some miracle she woke up, there was no knowing what damage she might be facing. The doctors warned us about that too.

"Mental deficits," one of them had said.

"Long term care, possibly a convalescence home," the other added.

I stayed hopeful for her, and for the work the FBI was doing to identify her. Until then, Coma Girl and her dead friend would remain ghosts.

"Ready?" Jericho asked, calling from across the parking lot. He jogged toward me, holding the boat's keys, his shoes scraping the ramp. "We're all signed out and ready to go."

"How far?" I asked as he climbed aboard and knelt down. For a moment, it seemed as though he were proposing, his position awkward and comical. I held his shoulder, adding a hand where he needed one. He paused, seeming to be waiting for me.

"What are you doing?" I asked.

"The locker," he answered, pointing beneath me. "You're sitting on it."

I got up, red-faced, telling him, "Listen, I'm sorry I was short with you, a bit anxious."

He said nothing as he knelt to open the locker and fished out boating gear—emergency life jackets and windbreakers with a padded lining. "Should fit. Here, put these on," he instructed, handing me the smaller pair. "We're going beyond the inlet, and the ocean can get rough this time of day."

"Can get?" I asked, peering into the bay and the endless whitecaps.

"The bay?" he asked, following my gaze. "Nah, those are tiny. One to three footers. We'll be shielded for most of the ride, but there's an open area after some islands that is going to feel like we've hit a wall."

"Jericho, about my daughter," I began, kneeling next to him with the picture of Harlan and Hannah. "She's my priority. She's my girl and I'm going to do whatever I have to."

"Regardless of the law?" he asked, his words sounding like a dare, but also telling me he understood the depth of what I'd do. He squinted against the sunlight, a slight grin appearing. "You sure do sound a lot like me."

"Is that so?"

"Casey, I understand," he answered, taking my hand as we stood. "God knows I've been there. To hell and back. It's very dangerous."

Thoughts of his wife's death came to me. "I'm sorry for your loss," I told him, giving his hand a squeeze, making sure he saw me, saw the sincerity without making him feel uncomfortable. "But we're talking about my daughter. She's alive. I'll do what I have to. Even if that means dying for her."

I put the picture away and secured my bag in a locker. Jericho showed me how to put on the emergency life jacket, his hand on mine guiding the ties on the front and then tightening the sides. When he stopped, I raised my head and found his eyes again.

"I know the nightmare," he said, his body warm. "So maybe you should try living for your daughter first. I wish I had."

I didn't know what to say, but thought of my wall, of the colored yarn, the tacked photos, the hundreds and maybe thousands of hours standing in one place, raveling and unraveling what I thought were leads and hopeful paths leading to Hannah.

I tugged on his shirt, asking, "What happened?"

He backed away, reluctant to share. There was more that happened after his wife's death, more than his hearing and seeing her ghost.

I grabbed his emergency jacket, wanting to know. "You can't just say that without telling me what I'm risking."

"It'll destroy you," he answered coldly. Then added, "I was so lost, I spent most of last year refusing to accept my wife's death. I wouldn't believe it, and I almost died because of it."

"That won't happen to me," I said defiantly.

Jericho checked the straps, slipping his finger beneath the fabric, jerking it hard enough to pull me close to him.

"I hope not," he said, his voice soft and intimate. "I like you, and I'd hate to see this consume you the way it did me."

A pang of emotion warmed me as I eased closer, my feet between his. He searched my eyes for understanding. His chest pressed against mine, rising and falling.

My voice broke as I repeated, "It won't."

"Be careful," he replied, his voice emotional. I wasn't sure if he was still talking about his dead wife, my daughter, or what was starting between us. My heart fluttered, the moment charged, electric.

"I will," I assured him, and leaned up onto my toes until my lips were on his, surprising him, surprising myself.

He returned my affection, harder, pulling me into him. The kiss was moving, and I wondered if I was the first woman to be with him since his wife's death. He was the first man I'd shown any affection toward since my husband disappeared from my life. I slid my arms around his middle, my fingers on the back of his neck, and stayed lost in the moment.

He ended it with a call from a gull, his breathing heavy as he handed me a windbreaker. "The size seems right, put this on too. You'll need it."

It took me a moment to catch my breath, but I picked up on his cue for us to get moving, the heat from his touch fading as I shoved my hands through the windbreaker's sleeves. "Jericho, it's an oven out here." I held my arms out like a scarecrow. "Why are we wearing these jackets?"

He let out a short laugh, answering, "Oh, you'll see."

CHAPTER 42

Jericho gripped the steering wheel, his knuckles white. I held onto the bar next to the console, the twin motors racing to a fevered pitch, vaulting us forward, pitching the front of the patrol boat out of the water, the bow climbing upward like a rocket escaping the surf's watery clutches.

My teeth began to chatter almost instantly. I closed the wind-breaker. Jericho motioned toward the sea, getting my attention, showing me the beauty that lay just beyond the beaches. It was another chance to see the Outer Banks. Jericho steered the patrol boat into the main channel, zigzagging the bow through the red-and-green buoy markers, steadying our path toward the inlet's mouth. A dozen dolphins raced with us—humps of steel-gray and blue jumping and diving, their bottle-shaped noses jutting from the water, followed by their entire bodies, a comical smile plastered on their faces. Jericho slowed so they could come along our side, a few choosing to jump the wake behind us.

"This is amazing," I screamed, smiling, the wind swallowing my words, a pang of guilt needling the moment's joy. I was here to work, to save Hannah, to save the missing girls. I thought of Jericho's words about living too. I let go for the moment, let myself see what it was Jericho wanted to show me. I realized then, his insistence to go after the dinghy wasn't just about helping the FBI, it was to help me.

He pointed over my shoulder where the ocean opened up into an endless blue carpet, the surface rippling with frothy whitecaps. A

flock of birds flew in unison like a team of ballet dancers, taking turns
in suicide dives—their gray-and-white feathered bodies tightening
into the shape of arrows as they disappeared headfirst into the ocean,
surfacing a moment later with fish filling their orange bills.

At once, the birds shot into the sky as we speared a nearby wave,
jolting me with a harsh thump, my spine tingling as if hit with an
electric shock. Jericho remained locked in place. He worked with
effortless motion, muscle memory, his shifting and turning the
wheel occurring in advance of the breaking waves, predicting their
paths like a fortune teller, keeping the boat nestled between them
and surfing the troughs.

The roughest of the seas faded as we steered toward the last of
the Outer Banks, and what I expected must be the southernmost tip
of the vacation hotspot. I felt the motors slow, the vibrations in my
feet fading like an amusement ride coming to an end. We'd arrived.
A part of me was glad, believing I might have a limit to the rough
water, my stomach having found its way into my throat and leaving
me feeling a little green.

The winds shifted to our backs as Jericho pitched the wheel to
the right, aiming toward the coast. There wasn't much to look at,
but in the distance I saw the edge of land, a short beach in the shape
of a giant fish hook, along with a single dirt road with some solitary
trees. And there was something in the water—boulders the size of
houses, their earth-colored rooftops breaking the surface. Jericho
carefully steered clear of the danger.

"Do you see it?" I asked.

"Over there, caught up on the shore," he answered. I followed his
stare, finding the dinghy. "It fits the description of what is standard
for the yacht."

There were no identifying marks, no numbers or registration.
The small outboard motor was askew like a broken neck, the bottom

of it likely hung up on the boulders, or maybe buried in the sand. Reluctantly, I searched for a body, my instincts telling me that whoever took the dingy could not have survived the rough seas. The beaches were bare, the crashing waves likely to have carried them away. The side of the vessel was partially deflated, the gray rubber drooping in a pout. The inside was empty, a bright-yellow rope tied to a forward boat cleat, taut and without slack.

"It looks anchored," I said, pointing out the rope.

"Maybe," Jericho said, stripping off his vest and windbreaker. He slipped off his shoes, kicking them aside, and unbuckled his pants too. "Hope you don't mind getting wet."

"Wet?"

He flicked his fingers, drops of seawater landing on my legs.

"Might want to strip some of that." Jericho jumped behind the bench seat and dropped an anchor into the water. The patrol boat's line went slack almost at once as the echo of metal striking stone rang like a submerged bell. As he sat to remove his socks, he looked at me and waited. "Are you coming?"

I lifted a lid to one of the lockers, searching the gear, and asked, "Any kind of wetsuit?"

"Nothing on this rig," he said. "Plus, it's shallow, waist deep is all."

"Okay, give me a minute," I told him, undressing, deciding there was no point in being shy. Down to my underwear, I approached the boat's side, Jericho splashing into the ocean ahead of me.

He wiped his face. "It's safe and warm like bath water." Jericho waved his arm, coaxing me. "Jump."

I did as he said, taking the leap. The water was ice cold and hit me with an exhilarating shock. My feet hit the boulder Jericho stood on, sliding against the soft algae, sending me off its edge and into deeper water, the surface swallowing me in a single gulp.

"Shit, that is slippery!" I hollered with a cough, a breeze cooling my wet face.

"I should've warned you," he laughed, squinting against the beaming sunlight. "There's no slippery-when-wet signs around here." He laughed again.

I swept the water, sending a splash, drenching him. "Who you laughing at?" I joked and gave him a playful jab. "That's for lying about the warm bath water too."

"Yeah, give it a minute."

"Now what?" I asked and swam alongside the dinghy, taking hold of the anchor rope.

"Well, since you're already wet—"

"What?" I interrupted.

"We'll need to push the dinghy on shore, but to do that, we have to free up that anchor line."

I waded past him, deeper, the water taking the heat from my legs and bottom and inviting me to drop to my shoulders. It was easier to swim, easier to use my arms and paddle until I floated by the other end of the dinghy. The side of it had been completely torn open, the rubber showing a large cavity, as though it had been bitten. My mind immediately went to sharks and the memory of the horror movies I'd watched every year in a sick pre-vacation ritual before going to the shore.

"Shark bite?" I asked, half-joking.

Jericho nodded, his grin turning serious. "Yeah, that'd be my guess." His gaze shifted, searching the surrounding water.

"Seriously?"

He nodded, but answered, "Nope. Not at all."

"Aren't you the jokester," I said, annoyed, remembering how the movie *Jaws* ruined my ocean swims for an entire summer.

"But this cove is filled with boulders sharp enough to slice through steel," he explained. He pointed to the beach, adding, "See the shape of the peninsula, how it hooks into the ocean? We see a lot of junk get caught up in here."

"That's how you knew the dinghy would end up here?" I asked, following the tail ends of the beach and rocks, the crooked finger extending into the ocean in a *come-hither* shape.

"A yacht that size had to have a dinghy, or two. Best guess since it was missing, it'd be here. If not, it'd been sunk or lost forever," he answered. "We call this place 'the hook' for a reason. And since it's here, that tells me whoever was on the yacht with the girls must have used it, boarded another boat and then set this adrift."

"I don't follow," I said. I made my way around the other side and grabbed the anchor rope, the nylon stretching as the dinghy lifted with the swell.

"With the yacht malfunctioned, the electronics burned out, rather than get caught with the girls, they abandoned them, and took the dinghy to get picked up somewhere else."

"Jericho," I began, and then waited for him to face me. "You're finally starting to think the cases are unrelated. Aren't you?"

"I am," he answered. "The press conferences are wrong. I was wrong."

"What was it that changed your mind?"

"The old kidnapping cases you had us pull. And then Stephanie Marsh. That's what did it for me."

"Well, related or not, we still have two girls with no identification for either of them, the auctions, and my daughter."

"And PK," he added.

I pulled on the anchor line, plucking it like a guitar string, following its yellow blur beneath the surface, the sight of it dimming and ending with the shape of a metal butterfly. "Does the anchor have wings?"

Jericho chuckled. "Yeah, something like that." Beads of water on his chin shined, reflecting like diamonds.

But with the anchor, there was a bag stuck to it, dark and white, and big. "I think I see something else."

"Probably sea garbage. It might have got snagged on the way here."

"I think it's a duffle bag," I told him.

Jericho frowned, his complexion changing as he waded around the front to join me, the surf lapping against his chest. He held his bad arm high as he tried to keep it dry. "What's the matter?"

"Well, in my experience, I hear the words duffle bag and my insides get knotty."

I took hold of his shoulder when he gripped the slack nylon and tugged it. The anchor stayed fixed. "I don't follow what you mean."

"We had a really bad time of it with my last case," he said, his hand gliding down my side, holding my waist as he pulled himself to the shallower water. "It was a terrible murder. A young girl. I can still see her face as clear as I'm seeing you. Crab pot and a duffle bag, not far from here either."

"Hard to tell, but it's definitely big enough to hold a body."

Jericho remained bothered, his eyes narrowing. "What if there was another death?"

"You think another girl from the yacht?" I asked with a crushing thought of Hannah. "But why not the other two?"

"I dunno." The frown disappeared. "Just a hypothesis, thinking aloud."

"Do you want me to get it?" I asked. The breeze picked up and sent a ripple of waves splashing against my chest and face. I was vaguely aware my bra might be see-through when wet, but was afraid to look down, afraid to draw attention to it. "I'm about as wet as I can get and think we should retrieve it."

Jericho eyed his arm, the gauzy wrap, the shell of it becoming soft where there were splash marks. "Can you swim? I mean, are you comfortable swimming in the ocean? It's not like a pool."

"I can swim," I assured him. "With as many summers as I've spent on the shores in Jersey. Plus, you've got the rope. That anchor isn't moving. It'll be a guideline."

"We need that bag," he said, agreeing, his gaze falling to my chest briefly and then back to me.

Bashfulness pushed a smile onto my lips. I ducked beneath the water to wet my head. I wasn't sure if I minded his taking a look. I also wondered if I'd mind if he hadn't. When I was beneath the water, I set my sights on the end of the rope, the anchor and the bag.

I came up and dried my face. Jericho helped, combing my hair behind my ears, his eyes searching mine.

"What?" I asked, my arm around his middle. "What's the matter?"

"Saltwater. Your eyes are red."

"I'll be quick," I assured him, anxious to get this done. I wanted to see what was in the bag too. "You'll be my eyes. I'll pull myself to the anchor, and only open my eyes when I get there. Anything happens, snap the line, or bang on it or anything to let me know."

"Ready?" he asked, his bad arm safely in the dinghy, holding the side of the small boat while he held the anchor line.

I wasn't ready, wasn't sure I could be ready, but if there was the possibility of a body in the duffle bag, I'd brace for the cold descent and make the dive.

CHAPTER 43

Before my dive, I retrieved gloves from the boat, following Jericho's direction, finding a box of the standard issue in a locker. We needed protection from whatever was inside the duffle bag. Who knew where the yacht had been, or what other drug paraphernalia, possibly containing blood-borne pathogens, might be involved. We also needed to preserve the evidence, protecting it from us too.

"You've got plenty of investigation gloves, but no scuba gear, no wetsuits?" I asked sarcastically, dropping the box of gloves in the dinghy.

We slipped a pair into place, helping each other.

"Wrong boat," he repeated with a tilt of his head.

Heat climbed my neck as I dipped beneath the surface to hide an unavoidable smile. When I surfaced, I went to his side, our bodies touching, my smile gone, shyness replaced with a bravery I hadn't felt in years.

Jericho blushed, his eyes shifting to the water and then to the rope. "Let's get a move on, Detective White."

"One, two, and," I counted, skipping the third with a deep breath and plunging from the stony platform into deeper water. I held onto the rope, felt the nylon on my skin, my fingers sliding along, gripping and pulling, and then repeating, descending toward the lodged anchor. With Jericho keeping his hold strong and tight, the rope never budged. Though my eyes were closed, the light shining through faded as I descended deeper into the colder murky water.

I went through a patch of kelp—slithering seagrass brushing my sides and sliding along my legs. I tensed and moved carefully, fearing I'd tangle in them. When my fingers hit a nylon knot and the metal butterfly wings, I chanced a look, opening my eyes to stinging seawater. It was dark and blurry and the water pressure pushed on me, but the shadowy outline of the duffle bag was enough for me to take the fabric handle into my grasp. It was heavy, dangerously heavy, and would weigh me down when I started back for the surface.

My ears were clogged, the pressure threatening to burst them. I gave Jericho a wave as the first cramp hit my chest. It was a warning to get back, and I hastily gripped the anchor's metal wings, rocking the blades up and down like a playground seesaw. The duffle bag came free almost at once, its handles tangling in the rope; a chance happening perhaps, which could mean it was merely junk picked up at sea, as Jericho had suggested.

A fire started inside me. The burn crept from my belly and into my lungs and then my throat, begging me to open my mouth and take a breath. I knew I only had a few seconds more with the anchor before I'd have to turn back, but I was desperate not to disappoint Jericho. I had the duffle bag, and maybe that was enough.

The burning intensity forced me to turn away, my foot accidentally kicking the metal. I had leverage and kicked again, jarring the blades free. It was a lucky break, but I thought little of it as my chest threatened to burst like a balloon.

There was a moment of eerie calm as a shiver of glowing fish swam around me, their interest waning and then interrupted by the anchor's movement. Jericho must have sensed something was wrong, maybe he saw I'd slowed my climb. He yanked the anchor's line in huge strides, its ascension methodical, but quickening. I could only imagine his struggles with one arm, and then considered he must have gone into the water with both, forgoing the bandaging, the upcoming surgery.

My mind raced, threatening. Desperate, I looped the bag's handle around the anchor. Losing the extra weight freed me to use the little strength I had and reach the surface. I broke through the water with a splash, gasping, sucking the sea air in gulps, coughing and heaving. I let out a cry, but the world dimmed. My arms and legs were dead. I rolled onto my back in a dead man's float, like I'd been taught as a child, using my hands to wade me toward the dinghy. An arm came across my ribcage, gripping my side, holding me. A misty spray of water splashed around me and I heard the low tones of Jericho yelling.

"I got you," he shouted.

"The bag," I said, the exhaustion slipping as I gained strength.

"You should've let it go," he said with anger in his voice.

"I had it," I told him, my hand canvasing behind me, landing on Jericho and then the dinghy. "I thought I had both, but it was too heavy."

"Can you stand?"

I found the algae-covered stone, pinching my toes until the mossy feel squished between them. "I'll be okay," I told him and turned around, hugging him as he helped me lay my arms over the side of the dinghy.

"Got to give you a top score for the effort," he said, dropping the anchor into the dinghy, the metal clanking, the sunlight showing the scrape marks where I'd freed it. The duffle bag was next, the weight of it making Jericho groan. I peered up into his face, and then saw the covering on his arm, drenched and hanging loose, revealing a torture of bruised skin and the stitched puzzle pieces poking through.

"Oh, Jericho," I exclaimed, finding the strength to go to his attention.

He didn't shy away or try to hide the injuries. He let me in. He let me see what had happened to him. My eyes were locked on the damage, the wonder of what could have caused such destruction. The pain of what he went through must have been unbearable and hit me in the heart with a deep care to want to fix it for him. I didn't know what would help though and searched around for anything we could use to wrap and protect it. He needed a hospital to get the wounds cleaned. I did my best to work with the tattered bandages, stealing some of the investigation gloves to rewrap his arm.

"We have to get back," I said.

"I know, but I have to know what's in the duffle first."

I knew how he felt and picked up the handle with my gloved hand, pinching the zipper and tugging to slide it open. Jericho put his hand on mine, forcing me to wait.

"What's the matter?"

"One second," he said, feeling the outside of the bag. "Just want to make sure it isn't a body."

I pulled the zipper and revealed the inside. My gut told me the anchor had picked up a lost bag, the tide's surf surprising a beach goer who'd parked their blanket too close to the ocean. But inside were clothes. Orange. I unraveled the cloth, discovering a jumpsuit, the kind issued to inmates in prison. There was another inside. My thoughts immediately went to the detention center. I found a pouch of makeup next, the colors matching what I'd seen on Coma Girl, as did the nail polish.

"It's the girl's stuff," I said. I held it up for Jericho to see, for him to confirm.

"They hold the auction, the girls are dropped off. One dies—could be accidental. And the other overdoses."

"And to most, the overdose looked like she died. With both girls underage, the men or women—"

"Or both," he offered.

"—abandon the yacht, taking the dinghy and all the girls' belongings."

Jericho added, "They expected the yacht to sink, and they wanted to ditch the evidence. They wanted to leave the belongings in another location. Ocean currents could easily put a continent between the bag and the yacht. What they didn't count on was the yacht staying afloat or the dinghy hanging up with the anchor and bag."

"What's this?" I said, my fingers digging deeper and landing on hard plastic. Identification badges. I brought them into the sunlight, the yacht girls' pictures and names squarely at the center. "Jericho, we know who they are."

"CSJCF," Jericho mouthed, holding up one of the jumpsuits, then he said louder. "Currituck Sound Juvenile Correctional Facility."

Jericho's stare went cold, staying fixed on the identification badges, seawater dripping from his hand.

I held up the first badge for him to see, and said, "We have Bobbi Thule. Deceased. She was only fourteen." I exclaimed, "This is the evidence Rivera needs. This is more than enough for a warrant."

"It is," he said, his face grim. I could sense he was angry. He picked up the second ID, adding, "And the overdose case, the girl who might end up never speaking again, her name is Stacie Wu. She's fifteen."

"But?" I asked, expecting him to share in the excitement of the find opening the door for us.

"Robert," he answered. "I don't understand how he fits into all this."

I took his hand. "We'll find out," I assured him.

I fished out two weights—ten-pound plates from a gym—remembering one of the yacht's staterooms having exercise equipment. "Looks like they used these to weigh the bag down, dropping the duffle overboard."

"But they had no idea the bag had caught onto the anchor. These people probably never worked a small boat like a dinghy. I'm surprised we're not finding their bodies too."

I shoved the makeup and clothes aside, digging through the duffle bag for another identification badge, wondering if it was possible Hannah was an inmate too.

"Please…"

"What are you looking for?"

"I'm checking for more," I said, my voice cracking.

"We need to call this in, tell the FBI, tell them to work up whatever paperwork is needed to do a detention center site visit."

I'd emptied the duffle bag before finally giving up, Jericho's words floating on a breeze, something I heard, but nothing I'd registered.

"Okay," I said, disappointed.

"We'll find her." He handed me the girls' identifications and motioned to the bag. "We also need to get Dr. Swales involved so she can notify the girls' parents."

"Still on the fence?" I asked, believing this was hard proof the auctions and girls on the yacht had nothing to do with the missing girls, with the woods killer.

"Not anymore," Jericho answered, knowing exactly what I was referring to.

"And we have to take care of that," I added, pointing at his arm. Without giving it a second thought, I re-wrapped the loose bandaging, careful not to do more harm to his injury. Jericho lifted his hand, grateful. I tied the wet gauzy remains with the latex gloves as best I could, hoping it would hold together on the return.

CHAPTER 44

The boat ride to the patrol station was an experience of cold I'd never felt before. When we hit dry land, I took to the sun like a sponge and soaked in every drop. Immediately, I sent pictures of the identification badges to Agent Rivera. She replied about cueing her team to take on the detention center.

"You'll warm up soon," Jericho assured me, taking the duffle bag. "I've got a locker, and some gear here."

"I'll change at the house," I said, eager to jump in my car, knowing the inside was toasty warm. I motioned to the duffle bag. "The station, but then we're going to take care of that arm."

Jericho retreated into the patrol station, a small gathering of uniformed officers following him. I went to my car, my hands shaking, the car keys jangling, and my teeth chattering hard enough to make my jaw hurt.

I'd driven a mile or two from the station when the storm was on top of me. Jericho had said thunderstorms would hit by late afternoon, and they did, blowing in with a force I'd never experienced. It was as if someone had flicked a switch, lightning sliced open the clouds to spill rain like a waterfall. I faced a wall as high as the heavens, the color as black as midnight. Thunder rattled my car and shook the broken rear window. Drivers put their hazards on, some slowing or pulling off to the side of the road. Others held their paths, defiant.

I followed the latter, eager to reach Jericho's house, switching on my hazards and throwing on the windshield wipers to their highest setting. Rain mixed with hail stones, pelting the windshield. I cursed the old wipers I'd never fixed, a strand of torn rubber dangling as the metal scraped the glass. I shot a look at my rearview mirror and at the hole in the window. The tape Jericho's son had used held tight and kept the rear seat dry. It'd be another day before the new window could be installed.

A horn blared, filling my car with a raucous sound.

"What the—?" I yelled, annoyed. I rolled through a green light and then drove past a blinking yellow, pressing the accelerator, trying to pick up speed. A large truck rode my bumper, their grill in my rear window, its black-and-chrome upright slats looking like teeth. The motor was as deafening as the horn, the window's tape vibrating and doing little to dampen the noise. I slowed to a stop at the next light.

A bump.

"Are you kidding me!" I hollered, irritated. The streetlight flicked green, and I thumped the pedal, accelerating to get out of the way and let the truck pass.

A second bump.

Growing concern invaded my thoughts, but I dismissed it as paranoia. I shifted lanes, speeding up, and slid on the wet pavement, losing control of my car briefly enough to give me a start and put my nerves on edge.

"Go around me!" I yelled, waving my hand. I rolled my window open, doubting they could see through the patched glass. Rain blew into the car and ran down my arm, drenching my shirt as I waved and avoided the temptation to give them the finger. My gesture was ignored and invited another bump, the toothy grill chewing on my bumper.

I floored the gas pedal and the motor screamed with a surprising lurch. The truck shifted, speeding up, following, its bumper touching mine again, the shiny grill sneering at me through my side mirror.

"Fucking hick!" I hollered, certain a bunch of kids were playing around. A joy ride perhaps—boys tempting the adolescent driver with a dare. The next strike jerked my car hard enough for my rear tires to swing, sweeping into a fishtail. I straightened my wheel and regained control, but it left my hands shaking, afraid, my insides fluttery like jelly.

I'd had enough and took the first right turn, entering onto a narrow bridge that bordered the back-channel waters and the island marshes. But the truck turned with me, staying close, keeping the space between us only inches apart, careful to never reveal a license plate or the face of the driver. My chest tightened and my knuckles strained as I held the steering wheel. This wasn't the act of some stupid teenagers out for a joy ride. This was someone who knew who I was, knew I was doing more than vacationing at the Outer Banks.

"Maybe you knew Robert Stewart? Or one of the girls?" I said, speaking to myself, trying to reason and steady my nerves. But my legs shook, muscles quivering horribly as the adrenaline took hold like a drug. I considered Hannah's stolen case file, the woods killer in my car, dread rolling my stomach. "Or is that you?"

The truck bumped harder this time, my steering wheel jerking out of my grasp, the front of my car taking a wild sharp turn, the front tire digging into the bridge's pavement like a dull spade to drought-ridden earth. I grabbed for the wheel before my car barreled into the railing. It was then I saw we were completely alone. There was rushing water on both sides, the railing made up of wood posts with metal cross rails. I'd trapped myself with nowhere to go. There was nothing ahead but water and no room to turn around.

The truck barreled into me then, no bump this time, no mercy. The crushing blow caved in my bumper and slammed my body against the seat's headrest, bouncing me forward into the steering wheel. My head and chest struck the deploying airbag, a gunshot detonating in my ears, powder filling my nose and mouth, choking me. The crash stole the air from my lungs as my car veered hard to the left, coming to a stop with the motor sputtering and threatening to die. Dazed, I hooked the wheel, pressed the gas pedal and jerked down to the right. It was another mistake, a poor move, like a rookie chess player exposing their King to checkmate. I knew it as soon as my car ended in a skid. My heart dropped.

The truck's next assault slammed into the right-side bumper, the corner, academic—the position we'd been taught to use when pursuing another car. But this strike wasn't meant to turn me around, it was meant to destroy me. I felt myself take flight, all four wheels leaving the safety of the pavement, the inside of my car suddenly as quiet as a church mass.

I tensed as blood rushed into my eyes and head. There was no relief though, only silence. I lost hold of the steering wheel, my body rising, suspended, the safety belt digging into my shoulder and across my lap. My car flipped, crashing in a violent blow, crumpling like a tin can, caving in the roof, the windows exploding, the broken glass shooting into the car as if launched by shotguns, cutting and stinging like a tantrum of bees. The outside spun into view, turning sideways, and then flipping over and over. Dizzying blackness crept in and out of focus as I struggled for air and tasted blood instead.

Then there was quiet, a sense of calm, glass pebbles ticking against the pavement like raindrops. I was upside down, my front bumper fettered into the bridge's railing and posts, wedged like a shim, the metal bent, the posts' timber split and gripping my car.

I gagged and spat the taste of old pennies, blood pouring from my nose and into my throat. My heart stopped when I heard tires peeling against the wet pavement. I saw the truck, saw the lone driver behind the wheel, saw them both barreling toward me to finish what was started.

I wasn't going to survive. I was going to die on this bridge, die without knowing if my girl was safe. The truck lunged, and in my mind I saw Hannah, saw her loving eyes as she held the attention of Robert Stewart. I hoped she'd found happiness with him, even if it was brief. If I knew the truth, I could die with peace. I closed my eyes, bracing for the impact. Skidding noises came then, the truck stopping abruptly. A door opened and slammed shut as boots hit the pavement. I dared a look, fright filling me like a trapped animal about to meet its hunter.

The driver walked around the front of the truck, their body and face staying hidden from me. But I could see boots, a man's work boots with a rigid tread, like the kind we'd found imprinted onto Robert Stewart's back. Desperation set in, my arms flailing, my shoulders pinned as I scanned my car for something to defend myself with. But everything was out of reach. Blackness crept, vision blinking in and out, my arms becoming heavy and numb. The man came to the side of my car, slowing, turning, his boots biting into the road, the sound grating.

He did nothing, leaving me to wonder if this was a warning as he ran back to his truck, grunting curses under his breath, jumping in and flooring the accelerator. The truck raced past the remains of my car while blaring its horn in what I thought would have been the final moments of my life. The horn faded, warbling and singing praise for a job well done as it ran from the scene. I'd been spared.

I saw another car, heard its horn, saw their lights flashing, a man on his phone and a woman behind the wheel. The truck driver had been interrupted, saving me. The scent of spilled oil and antifreeze were the last things I remembered, along with the darkness, the foggy view of the bridge, upside down and fading.

"Hannah?" I said, and then I remembered nothing.

CHAPTER 45

A black abyss. I was gone. No smell. No sound. No pain. Nothing. Just an empty span of time. It was long enough to see Hannah again, a familiar wound opening, angst tipping my heart with the overwhelming hope for it to be over. But Hannah faded to kaleidoscope colors when a light beamed into my eyes, the shine flying from side to side like some kind of galactic comet.

Fingers touched my neck and a voice spoke in my ears. My hands were heavy like clubs. My fingers tingled, warm and itchy and swollen. There was blood—the taste of it anyway—on my tongue and the sticky-dry feel of it around my mouth. I was upside down, my eyes throbbing, pulsing with my heartbeat.

"Ma'am, can you tell me your name?" I heard, as chunks of glass clinked against my car's metal carcass.

"Hannah," I groaned, thinking of my girl.

"Okay, Hannah, I want you to listen to me—"

"No. No, my name is Casey," I corrected the woman, coughing. It was hard to breathe, the seatbelt's strap digging into me like a dull blade. "Hannah is my daughter."

There was a commotion then, urgency as the woman poked her head through the broken window, scanning the inside of my car from corner to corner.

"Ma'am? Was your daughter with you?"

I shook my head and winced, a sharp pinch at the top of my spine. "No. I'm alone."

"Do you remember what happened?" she asked, the heat of her breath on my skin while she worked to wrap my neck in a pillowy collar.

Blue-and-red lights shimmered against the car's broken windshield, as my alertness returned. "Listen, I'm fine."

She let out a sigh, a smirk forming. "I'm sure you are, but play along so we're convinced of it too."

"Okay," I told her, understanding she had a role in what was happening just as I had a role in being the victim, the truck driver's attack a clear attempt to end me. Our investigations had touched a nerve—struck it with a hammer. I just didn't know which case—the yacht, the girls in the woods, or maybe Robert Stewart. "I'm a cop, a detective, and I'm working with Jericho Flynn. Have someone call dispatch and ask to have him meet us here."

"The sheriff?" the woman asked with flirty animation in her eyes.

I almost laughed, but could only chuckle. "Yes, the one and only," I answered lightly.

"What a looker. *Vote Flynn to win*," she commented and then caught herself. "I liked his campaigns."

"Handsome, yes," I said, agreeing with the small talk, though a tick of agitation made me restless. "Are we almost done?"

"Just trying to assess if we need to use a backboard."

I saw images of a bright-yellow backboard and straps of thick hospital tape crisscrossing my body. My patience had worn thin. Without asking, I released the seatbelt and tumbled onto the car's ceiling. Pain knifed the back of my skull, the padded donut doing little to cushion the fall. But I could breathe fully again, a prize for my freedom.

"Can I get some hands!" the paramedic yelled, her fingers digging into my armpits, helping me slide through the window. "And someone get in contact with the sheriff. Flynn, that is."

I managed to get to my feet, but the view spun mercilessly, and for a moment I thought I was going to puke. I eagerly sucked in the cool air, the taste of it fresh with the passing rainstorm.

"My head is a little fuzzy, but other than that, I'm fine," I exclaimed, swaying and then catching myself.

The paramedic looked troubled, her hand clutching my forearm, holding me in place as she assessed how I was doing. "We'll still need to take you to the hospital. Let a doctor evaluate your injuries."

"Two aspirin," I said. "And a ride."

Like most storms, there's a clearing that comes after. Sometimes it's breathtaking—the sunlight glinting through raindrops, a wispy steam hugging the pavement, and rainbows arching overhead. And then there are storms that send debris into the path of everything, throwing tree limbs, garbage pales, even street signs, like a child having a fit.

For as far as I could see, the bridge and the road had fared the latter, debris covering the pavement, road signs bent or toppled entirely, weakened trees leaning precariously and threatening power lines. The creek was still swollen and running fast like a river, but the stained color had started to clear. I sat on the edge of the ambulance's bay, a towel around my shoulders, pale skin bleeding through my wet clothes, and exposed where the fabric had been torn and shredded. My head ached as I gazed at my feet, a shoe on one foot, the other bare. I wiggled my wrinkled toes and then peeked downstream, wondering how long it would take before my other shoe reached the ocean.

"How do you feel?" the paramedic asked. Her face was in mine again, the bright light flying from side to side and burning after-images into the back of my eyeballs. "Any dizziness? Nausea?"

"Well, when you do that—" I began with my voice raised, but then caught my tone and answered, "—tired, maybe? But I feel better."

"That could be the adrenaline, but could also be a sign of a concussion," she speculated and ran her hands through my hair, her blue-covered fingers gently probing my scalp in search of an injury. "You have a decent bump up there. We'll ice it."

"Well, ain't that a sorry sight." I heard Jericho's voice, and then a car door closing. I felt a stir in my chest, fluttery like before. He paused to assess what remained of my car. "Damn, I guess we won't need that rear window after all."

"Your blood pressure is slightly elevated, but that could also be from the—" the paramedic started saying.

I shoved the blood-pressure cuff from my arm in a swift motion as Jericho came around the back of the ambulance. The paramedic did her best to hide her smile, clearing the cuff and handing me an ice pack.

"Thank you," I said. "I'll be fine." I tried to hold the ice pack, but my hand shook as though it had a mind of its own.

Jericho touched me briefly, the paramedic noticing. He took the ice pack, holding it for me. He motioned to my face, to where I struck the airbag, and said, "That's going to leave a mark. Are you going to get checked at the hospital?" Before I could answer, he faced the paramedic asking, "Are we taking a ride?"

The woman shook her head, her green eyes wide, answering, "Minor cuts, a few abrasions, a bump. Most of it typical of what we'd see when an airbag deploys. I'm not a doctor though. And we don't usually offer an option."

"But in my case," I began, jumping to my feet, the wooziness leaving me weak. I held onto Jericho's shoulder, bracing myself, my barefoot against the wet pavement, the surface still warm from the afternoon sun. "You'll make an exception?"

She shook her head, answering, "I can only make a recommendation. Stay close to someone for the evening. And if there are any signs of trouble, go to the emergency room."

The ambulance moved on, weaving around the debris, the lights and sirens turned off, leaving me alone with Jericho. A marine-patrol vehicle was parked behind us, its blue-and-red lights continuing to skip and bounce against the remains of my broken car. Maybe it was the hit on my head, the wooziness, but I let my guard down, tears welling in my eyes, the terror of what had happened resonating like a song that was stuck in my head.

"I was scared," I confessed to Jericho. "Terrified."

"Of course you were," he said, moving close enough for me to lean into him, his arm around me, my head on his shoulder.

"Can I share something with you?"

"Anything."

"I always thought if I faced death, I wouldn't fight it. I always thought I'd go, relieved to have it over with."

I waited for a response, his chest rising with a sigh.

"But that's not what happened, is it?" he asked. "And it surprised you."

I found his eyes, asking, "Have you had the same thing happen?"

"There was a moment," he said and motioned to his arm, freshly bandaged. "The crash. I was certain it was the end, and thought I'd go easily. But I wasn't ready."

"Yeah. I guess I'm not ready either," I told him, his head turning toward an arriving truck.

The tow truck stopped. It was the flatbed kind, with the steel cables made to drag monsters from the deep. Only, my monster happened to be the very last of what remained from a life I once had.

I'd bought the car with my husband soon after we sold the minivan, a few months shy of a year following Hannah's kidnapping. It was the last thing we ever purchased together. He left me two weeks later.

"Sad to see it go?" Jericho asked, sensing where my thoughts were.

"A little," I confessed, bracing his shoulder again, my head still in a fog. "It wasn't much, but I'd had the car for a long time."

"I'll take care of the accident report, get the details from you and send it over. Should save you some time."

"Jericho, it wasn't an accident," I said, my voice flat as metal scraped against the road with a shrilling noise, the tow truck dragging my car onto its wheels. The front bumper peeled like the rind of an orange, groaning a soft, mushy sound before snapping like a tree's branch, the mangled plastic and metal freeing from the bridge's railing. "A truck ran me off the road. You can't see it, but the driver struck the rear a few times, hard enough to flip me."

I felt Jericho's whole body grow tense, his hand opening and closing in a fist as he considered what I said. He left me and went to the car, telling the driver to stop. He knelt and pressed against the corner of the rear bumper, felt the crack before standing and inspecting the skid marks, the truck's tires wider than my small car's.

"Definitely a truck," he said. "Do you think you could identify the driver?"

A blurry face came to my mind, the rain sweeping over the truck's windshield and stealing the details. "Uh-uh. The storm was too thick." And then I remembered the last moments before passing out. I remembered the boots. "But I'm almost certain that whoever it was also killed Robert Stewart."

CHAPTER 46

The smell of fresh sheets hit me as I fell onto the bed. Jericho did his best to remove my wet shoe, his hand rubbing my toes, gently drying them with a towel.

I pulled my foot away with a laugh. "Sorry, I'm a little ticklish."

He chuckled at my reaction. "So that's your kryptonite."

"Yeah, that's my kryptonite. Everyone has their weakness." Without thought, I unbuttoned my jeans and began sliding them down my legs.

"I'll bring you another towel," he said, averting his eyes.

I shook my head, comfortable enough around him, or maybe just too tired to care. I did my best to take off the wet denim. When I got stuck, I motioned to my legs, saying, "I could use a hand."

"How about a hot shower?" he offered, tugging on one pant leg, and then peeling off the other. "I can make you some tea or coffee too."

I was shivering again, my bare legs wet and cold. "Hot shower and tea," I answered, noticing his gaze lingering. And then asked, "Or a hot chocolate?"

"Sure," he answered, laying the towel across my lap. "I might even have some of those mini marshmallows."

"Marshmallows would be amazing."

He left me alone. I closed my eyes and listened to the house speak. I heard the stir of saucers and cups coming from the kitchen. I heard the opening of a cabinet and then water filling a kettle. I stripped the rest of my wet clothes and did as Jericho suggested, taking to the bathroom to clean off the briny smell and the scratchy feel from my skin.

The shower warmed my body, and the hot chocolate warmed my soul. I'd all but forgotten about the truck driver by the time moonlight shone through the bedroom window. In the distance, I heard a clothes dryer, I heard the buttons on my jeans clanking against the spinning metal drum. The soft noise urged me to sleep, telling me to close my eyes and leave the day.

"How are you doing?" Jericho asked, the shape of his body showing in the door. "Can I get you anything else?"

"I think I'm set," I said to him, lifting my arm in the dark, holding out my hand, hoping he'd accept my invitation.

He came to the bed and put his hand in mine. "Forget about everything," he said in a gentle voice. "Forget about the work and get some rest. You've done more than most."

"Thank you for the help." I was nervous and uncertain of what to say next. I wasn't sure what I wanted, but I knew I didn't want him to leave, my thoughts going to the kiss we'd shared. "Could…"

He'd shifted as if to stand, but then waited. "What is it?"

"Would you stay with me?" I asked, a flit of nerves in my voice. At once, I realized how it must have sounded, but his expression never betrayed what he thought. I quickly added, "I mean, just stay with me. I don't want to be alone."

"I understand," he said. He held up his hand, saying, "One minute." Jericho left the room. I could hardly believe my words, or the strange feelings that had found a place in my head and in my heart.

A closet door opened and then closed. Jericho returned with a pillow tucked beneath his arm and a heavy blanket slung over his shoulder. He flattened the comforter, spreading it across the floor, and climbing beneath it as best as he could with one arm and then lay down. When he'd settled, his hand emerged on my bed, finding mine with a squeeze.

"I'm a light sleeper," he told me. "I'll check on you tonight. Make sure you're okay."

I said nothing, but returned the gesture, our fingers woven together. The sounds of rustling tree branches and crickets seeped into the room, the house itself nearly silent save for the tumbling clothes drying. It wasn't long before Jericho's breathing deepened and grew heavy and his hand slipped from mine.

I rolled onto my side, my eyes adjusting to the room's light. Finding my bravery, I left the comfort of the bed, my toes gripping the carpet as I carefully knelt beside him. And like a robber opening a safe, I silently lifted the comforter and tucked myself beneath it, my legs touching his. At once, I could feel the heat of his body. He moved then, waking. I froze.

"Is this okay?" I asked, whispering and sharing his pillow. "I didn't want to be alone."

He reached around, finding my waist and helped me lay closer to him. "Of course," he said.

I wrapped my arm around him and fit my body with his, pairing us, his heart beating next to mine as we fell asleep together.

CHAPTER 47

I woke twice in the night. The first, in Jericho's arms, in his embrace, and then with him in mine. At one point we'd slipped out of our clothes, easily losing them, our legs and arms intertwined, Jericho finding me and then me finding him. Lost treasures remembered, we made love by the shallow light coming into his guest room, our misfortunes abandoned, our hearts touching.

With our evening together, the gentleness, I'd all but forgotten about the truck driver and the pain from the day. And after, I'd slept, dreamless and sound, but it was morning now and my body ached and felt stiff from the crash. I felt swelling around my cheek and eye, which I hoped could be hidden with makeup. And my left ear had an unforgiving ring muffling what I could hear.

I'd survived whatever threat the truck driver had in mind. I pressed my hand against the pillow, the cool side of it inviting, along with a breeze lifting the curtains. The ocean sounds and smells carried into the room. *I could live here*, I thought, taking a breath, tasting the sea. After all, I'd had no plans, no destination, just an idea of leaving my old life and starting new.

I heard a shower running, Jericho's place next to me cold. He'd gone to his room to start the day. Reluctantly, I got up, but felt I could sleep another hour. Hannah needed me though. And so did Robert Stewart. And so did the girls in the woods and Stacie Wu, Coma Girl. I closed my eyes and saw an image of the truck driver's boot, and then an image of the boot print on Robert's back. They were the same. I was convinced of it. I had to find the bastard who'd run me off the road.

I gasped when I looked in the bathroom mirror, the face in the glass frightful. Contusions pooled around my right eye and cheek, colors swirled like yesterday's storm clouds. The bump on my forehead had thankfully gotten smaller, but the scrapes and scabbing would be with me the next week. I splashed cold water into my eyes and ran my fingers through my hair before poking around my bag for the little makeup I'd brought. With luck, I could make it work.

"Good morning to you," Jericho said, his voice coming from the guest room. "Coffee?"

"Please," I answered, brushing my hair back, the excitement of his company hastening the cover-up application. I didn't want him to see my face like this. "I'll be down in a few minutes."

"The chief gave an okay for a car. It's yours if you need it."

I thought of the station, the boardwalk, the woods, the yacht, and even considered revisiting where Robert's body had been discovered. I answered, "I think I'll need it."

"Are you up for a ride?" Jericho asked.

I stretched around the door frame, showing only my good side, and asked hesitantly, "Land or sea?"

"Land," he answered with a crooked smile. "The station first, and then it's time to visit the detention center."

Agent Rivera had the paperwork, the discovered identification badges enough for the court to issue all the necessary warrants. It also meant the bureau had given approvals for a search of the detention center and to pursue an investigation. It meant I'd find out how it could be that my daughter was involved.

*

The station was stuffed with reporters, easily outnumbering the visiting FBI and the local police. Even at the early hour, every seat and table had a body, eagerly awaiting a news update. The crowded station had nothing to do with Robert Stewart or the girls in the woods, though. And it wasn't about the dead girl or her friend in a coma. It was about the death ship, the super yacht.

Like the smallest of snowballs, the yacht's story kept growing, the mystery becoming an avalanche. There was no stopping the popularity of it. In the days since the auction and the shootout, *Pirates of the Outer Banks* had become one of the leading headlines. It had reached a national stage, with federal officials showing up on talk shows to promise patrolling of the oceans and protecting the voting public.

The station monitors showed Sheriff Petro and District Attorney Ashtole, their faces flooded with bright camera lights as they held a brief news conference outside the sheriff's office. The questions and bantering went back and forth a few minutes before the sheriff called for an end to it, his face red with anger, the reporters scattering like mice fleeing the onset of lights.

While the lead story continued to work for us, masking the truth of what actually happened, I could see the frustration on Sheriff Petro's face. Jericho saw it too. The door to his office shut with force, a gathering of public officials behind the glass, and all of them talking at the same time while Petro nodded to nobody in particular.

"Care to comment?" a reporter asked Jericho. "Has Harlan Jacobs been brought in for questioning? Is he connected to the pirates?"

Jericho dismissed him as we went through the gate separating the station's heart from the rabble.

"What the heck did I miss?" I asked Agent Rivera. Her usual kept look was off, bags carrying her eyes, her neatly combed hair mussed. She held a tablet in one hand and the largest paper cup of coffee I'd ever seen.

"A lot, actually. With what you recovered yesterday, we've turned this place upside down," she answered. Rivera looked closely then, her hand motioning around her face, asking, "What the hell happened to you?"

"I had some car trouble," I answered flatly.

"Car trouble?"

"Yeah, well, something like that," I told her. "So you're going in on the detention center?"

Agent Rivera led us deeper into the station, out of earshot from the reporters. We settled behind one of the cubicles, the opening to PK's desk within a few feet, the space just as it had been days earlier. Jericho stood a moment, eyes glazed, unmoving.

"It's okay if you want to move," I said, offering the place next to me. He joined us, turning his back with a sigh.

"Those identification badges are our passes to the front door of the detention center," Agent Rivera said. "This is getting a lot of attention from the top. See the older gentleman talking to the mayor and Sheriff Petro? That's my supervisor's boss's boss," she said, eyes wide, brow raised.

"They're here?" I asked, spying a man in Petro's office, his white curls and red face resembling my captain's.

"When arrests are made, and charges filed, they'll go for the death penalty."

"Not surprised," I added, thinking of the officers killed.

"And the reporters?" Jericho asked. "They still think it was a hijacking? International pirates?"

"Pirates of the Outer Banks," Rivera answered. "Which is good for us."

"They know about us, but they don't suspect we know about them."

"Correct," Rivera answered.

"The pirate story wasn't expected, but it'll give us good cover," Jericho commented.

"What about Harlan?" I asked with a rush of concern. He was the single possible connection I had to Hannah. If the press blew up any attention around Harlan, we could lose him as a suspect in the yacht case. "On our way in, a reporter asked about a pirate, asked if Harlan Jacobs was connected."

"It was the timing, wasn't it?" Jericho asked.

"A few reporters caught on to the APB issued. Very unfortunate timing for Mr. Harlan Jacobs. Now folks think he's some kind of pirate, or that he's working with them, feeding them his customers' GPS coordinates so their yachts get looted."

"Well there goes his business," Jericho said without emotion. "It's going to be impossible to find him now."

"We need Harlan," I said sharply. "He's the only connection to the auction site, to Hannah."

"Hannah?" Agent Rivera asked. "I didn't know there was a name."

I froze, ideas rolling around my head like marbles. "An older case," I began, and wet my lips. I reached for my folder, Hannah's case file, deciding to show it to Rivera, reveal the truth of what brought me to the Outer Banks. I opened my bag, but it was gone. I'd forgotten. A hole in place of where it should be. Resigned, my chin low, I found Rivera's eyes and told her, "I believe the girl in the photograph with Harlan Jacobs is Hannah White, my daughter. She was kidnapped fourteen years ago and I've been searching for her since then."

I held my breath, a pressure behind my eyes strained as I waited for Rivera to say something.

She began with a shake of her head, mouth agape, uncertainty and wonder in her eyes. "I don't know what to say, I had no idea—"

"There's nothing to say," Jericho said, his shoulders square and his eyes shifting between us. "There's nothing to prevent Detective White from continuing to support this case."

"Correct. Not with this case, there isn't," Rivera said, her eyes warming. She closed the distance between us, her hand on mine. "If there is anything at all I can do to help."

"Thank you," I began, but was interrupted by a sudden commotion from the front of the station. At once we stopped talking, our attentions caught.

A man entered the station, swinging the gate with a kick of his foot while staring down one of the reporters who'd attempted to ask a question. It was Harlan, his face ragged and worn, his skin had an oily shine and his bald head gleamed from the overhead lights. He'd been crying, his cheeks wet and eyes red. He wore the same soiled dungarees and shirt with sweat stains and motor grease I'd seen the other day.

Sheriff Petro and the lead of the FBI exited Petro's office with their hands to their side. We still had no idea the depths of Harlan's involvement.

It was his expression that gave me concern and ticked a notion about the possibility he wasn't here to turn himself in. Moving to the center of the room, Harlan hitched up onto his toes, scanning the station, searching over the cubical walls and desks while nervously shuffling a toothpick in his mouth.

He was looking for someone and immediately I sensed the growing danger as officers and FBI agents circled around him, their guns in hand, and their stances in the advance position with one foot forward and the other behind. Instinctively, I reached for my weapon, cupping the butt of my gun in my palm, securing it with a firm grip. I didn't draw it though, looking to Harlan's hands instead, needing to see if he was a threat. The eerie hush over the station must have triggered the perilous situation in which he'd put himself. Harlan slowed, his feet dragging against the floor as he shuffled back a step. He stopped and raised his hands with his head bowed. He found us then, his focus on Jericho.

"Sheriff, I need to see you," Harlan called out, his words in a yell as spit ran from his lips. "I need to see you before someone puts a bullet in me."

CHAPTER 48

Harlan Jacobs might have been the most exhausted person I'd ever seen. Then again, it isn't often I stopped to look in the mirror. I rushed to his side, guarding him as a mountain of reporters closed around us, ignoring the wooden gate, encroaching where they weren't permitted. Jericho intervened, shouldering them out of the way, taking Harlan's arm as Sheriff Petro cleared a path to an interview room.

"Are you Harlan Jacobs?" a reporter asked, already knowing the answer. "Is it true you released customer information to the pirates? Did you know they were associated with terrorists?"

"Terrorists?" Harlan asked, a gruff sound coming with a grunt. "I—"

"Not here," I told him, squeezing his arm. He kept quiet and lowered his head. His clothes smelled like sour sweat and motor oil.

"Why did you do it?" another reporter yelled, her voice a shrill cackle. "How long have you been working with pirates?"

"I don't know any pirates!" Harlan hollered. I squeezed harder, forcing him into the hallway. He muttered something to himself then, his voice soft, but enough to send a chill through me. "Pirates would be nicer."

Jericho and Agent Rivera followed me into the interrogation room, a tape recorder at the center of the table, a microphone sitting in wait. The FBI had jurisdiction over the interview, and Agent Rivera requested we attend. With the possibility of this man having known Hannah, I needed to be there.

Harlan fell into the chair, dropping his arms to his sides, and leaned back as if he were letting all his worries spill onto the floor. He was getting comfortable.

I flopped my bag hard on top of the table. Harlan's eyes sprang open. I didn't want him to be comfortable.

"What can we do for you?" I asked.

Harlan sat up abruptly, a questioning look on his face. "You guys want me to answer questions. Right?"

"You came to us," Jericho answered, catching on to my approach. We needed Harlan to open up to us. I wanted him to talk first, to spill whatever might be most pressing on his mind. In my experience, it was the fastest way to the truth, and we had no time to spare by teasing anything out of him.

Harlan swept his arm across the metal table, asking, "How about some coffee? Please?"

"Before we get started, do you require representation?" I asked. With the interview being recorded, I had to ensure every word was usable.

"A lawyer?" he asked.

"Yes. A lawyer."

He shook his head. "No lawyer is going to help me now."

"Interview subject has refused representation," I said for the tape. "Tell us what can we do for you."

A patrol officer came to the room, and stood in the door, his neck craning to see over Jericho's shoulder, curious about the questioning, as he was asked to bring a coffee. Harlan waited until the man was gone. "I didn't have anything to do with it."

"Specifically?" Agent Rivera asked.

"You know what I'm talking about," he answered snidely.

"Enlighten us," she said.

"The exchange," he said. The room remained quiet. He added, "The yacht, the shooting!"

Agent Rivera took the seat across from Harlan, her hands flat against the table's surface. "I understand you know a lot about it though, about the location and the time of the attack."

The patrol officer returned, carrying a cup of coffee and handed it to Harlan. The smell filled the room, the steam floating above the Styrofoam lip like a secret for only Harlan to enjoy.

"Sure. I mean, I captained yachts from time to time, but I didn't have anything to do with that one."

"And that's why you're here?" I asked, trying to both contain my disgust for the man and wanting to devour every word he offered—he'd been with Hannah.

"No, it's because I'm not a pirate... or a freaking terrorist," he answered, taking a sip and cringing.

"What does that matter to us?" Rivera asked.

"The press has it wrong. There are no pirates," he began to explain, and leaned against the chair again. Only this time, I thought I could actually see the life draining out of him. "I'm here because I need federal protection."

"Protection from who?" Jericho asked.

"The people who shot up the yacht. The people who killed those men and women," he said. He tried to swallow but his mouth was too dry. His focus shifted to the table. "They'll kill me the first chance they get."

"And why is that?"

Tears puddled in his eyes. "Because I helped them. Because I've been helping them."

"Two FBI agents were killed," Agent Rivera said in a low voice. "Justice must be served."

Harlan slumped forward, his head shaking. "They said they were just going to scare you guys! So you'd back the fuck off!"

"What happened was a capital offense," Rivera continued calmly. "And North Carolina is a death-penalty state."

"No, no, no!" Harlan rambled, his face white like a sheet, his chest shaking with a deep sob. "I can't do time! No fucking way!"

"Then help us help you."

Harlan sat up unexpectedly, the chair legs scratching, his expression blanking. "Fuck! Who am I kidding anyway? Like I said, I'm dead. They'll get to me before I ever get inside."

"Who are *they*?" Jericho asked, his voice sounding concerned. We had to hear him say it, record him revealing the detention center so as to eliminate any ambiguity or leading questions a smart-aleck defense attorney might tease apart later.

"I need protection," he repeated, tears dripping, his neck pink, his color returning. "They're an army. And ain't nobody can hide from them."

"Who?" I asked, but Harlan was gone, his face in his hands, sobbing again.

I took the opportunity and spread pictures across the table. I wanted him to see the dead girls from the woods. His reaction would help confirm the cases were unrelated, that the detention center had nothing to do with the area of woods near the property. The pictures slid over the metal, pictures of Cheryl Parry, Olivia Jones, and Stephanie Marsh, their faces grim, their eyelids closed, pale and lifeless and eerie like a statue's blank stare.

"Look at these," I said, but Harlan kept his face covered. I picked the worst of them, shoving them beneath his face and demanded, "Look at these!"

Harlan peered through his fingers and shook his head, answering, "Get them the fuck away from me!"

"Did you have any involvement with their deaths?" I asked. Harlan continued to shake his head. "The people you want protection from, did they have any involvement?"

"No!" he cried, swiping his hand over the table. I collected the pictures. He sobbed, blubbering, "I don't know."

Jericho put the detention-center identification badges onto the table next and snapped his fingers, continuing until Harlan quieted. His eyes bloodshot, he focused on the badges and the pictures of Bobbi Thule and Stacie Wu. He tapped his finger on Stacie Wu's picture. "Did she live?"

"She did," I answered. "You were there?"

Harlan shook his head. "I couldn't get back to the yacht in time. Rough seas. But I heard there'd been an accident, one girl dead. The other overdosed. If she's alive, she's in danger too."

"Why?"

"I've seen a lot of kids go into that place and never come out."

Jericho looked at Rivera.

"Already on it," she answered him, referring to getting protection placed at the hospital.

"They're everywhere," Harlan told us. "Ain't just what you see. They've got people waiting in the dark too."

Harlan's cries turned to moans, louder this time. The man was losing it and I feared we'd get nothing from him. Jericho took to the chair, pushed the coffee in front of Harlan and produced a bent cigarette from his pocket.

"Smoke?" he asked.

"Yeah."

Harlan's hand shook as he tried to hold the cigarette. I helped him, his hands in mine, bile rising in the pit of my throat, disgusted by him, by who he was, and who he'd been to my daughter. Jericho lit the end of the cigarette as Harlan's sobs abated, replaced by guttural shudders.

"Thank you," he managed to say. He glanced at each of us, adding, "I swear to you, nobody was supposed to get hurt."

"Let us help you," Rivera offered, her voice soft. "But you're going to have to clear up the details for us."

Jericho straightened the identification badges, and asked, "Tell us how you know them."

Harlan sipped his coffee and took a drag of the cigarette, smoke rising from his mouth and nose as if his insides were on fire. He let out a crackly cough, the cigarette satisfying his craving, and answered, "I drove them out to their appointments. That's what we called them, appointments. That's all I did. I drove."

"Okay then," I said. "Tell us about the appointments."

"Four hours. That's what they pay for, so that's what they get. That gives me the hour driving them out to sea, and then another hour to get back to land. Then there's still time enough to get the girls back to the detention center."

He'd said it. He'd mentioned the detention center. "Currituck Sound Juvenile Correctional Facility?" I asked, wanting the clarification recorded.

Harlan looked to Jericho, confused, and then to me. "Of course, it's the only detention center around here."

There was an edge of confidence in his tone now. That was a good sign. It was enough to tell me he was ready. I took a chance and placed the pictures of Hannah with Robert Stewart onto the table. "And them too?"

Harlan studied the strip of photo-booth pictures as Rivera traded glances with Jericho. Harlan looked at me, a slow nod forming as he poked at the strip.

"Yeah, I saw her a few times."

The bile returned, rising in my mouth. For a moment I thought I might vomit all over Harlan, the man who escorted my daughter to a yacht in the middle of the ocean to be used as a sex slave. My knees went weak. I was afraid for Harlan, and afraid for me—a demon inside wanted to emerge and rip the man's head off and beat him until there was nothing but a bloody pulp.

"And this one?" I placed the intersection picture showing him with Hannah. "How about this time?"

"Damn," he said, picking it up, nostrils flared, smoke drifting from them. "I wondered about that night. Fucking cameras. It's the only road in and out of the detention center."

"You remember taking her?"

He nodded slowly, his eyes closing as the picture fell from between his fingers. "She's the one that got away. Disappeared. They've been looking for her ever since."

Immediately, I saw Jericho and Rivera look in my direction, gauging my emotions, my reaction to hearing about the danger Hannah might be in. I did nothing to show it, but I was consumed by dread for my daughter. I gave Jericho a nod for him to continue.

"And him?" he asked, pointing back to Robert Stewart, veins showing in his neck. "Was he involved?"

Harlan took a closer look and shook his head. "I can't say. I think I've seen him around the detention center. But, I mean, they all look the same to me. Like I said, they're an army."

"How many girls from the detention center have been involved?" Agent Rivera asked, her phone in her hand, texting as feet shuffled on the other side of the door. This case was growing.

"You're gonna have to narrow the question for me," he answered, smoking his cigarette, the tears gone, an odd calm in his expression as though he was accepting his fate, a fate none of us really knew or understood. But he understood it, and that scared me.

"I don't follow," Rivera said.

"Which part?" Harlan asked. "There're multiple legs in the transport. There're the appointments, and then everything else."

"You tell us," I said, intrigued, beginning to believe we'd only scratched the surface.

He shook his head again. "I warned them about using the local girls, and that fucking stupid auction site. But it was the gravy. A lot of fucking money in their pocket with none of the royalties going to the north."

"The gravy?" Rivera questioned. "Royalties?"

Harlan sipped his coffee, cringing, and added, "The auction site, that was just a small part. Take young, American girls, and put them online. Once word got around, rich fucks lined up and down the coast and paid top dollar for a few hours with them. *The appointments*."

"And you will confirm transporting them?" I asked, wanting to record him saying it.

He gave me a nod, answering, "Yeah. It was great money."

"Girls can't just come and go from a detention center," Jericho countered. "And with girls missing, there'd have been an investigation."

"Girls went missing from there all the time," Harlan said. "They called it a work release or some shit like that. They even have falsified forms with signatures."

"But the detention center wouldn't be able to explain the identification badges turning up the way they did."

"Are you serious?" Harlan asked, confounded and glancing at each of us. "Listen to me. Who's to say the girls didn't run off? They get a work release, and then they're gone—the chain of custody broken. But you're missing the point, nobody is looking for these girls."

"We're looking," I said, raising the picture of Hannah.

"It doesn't matter, anyway. She can't run forever. Their reach is more than any cop shop or the FBI." There were tears in his eyes again. "And that's why I'm a dead man."

"And you think she's in danger too?" I asked, the firmness in my voice breaking with motherly concern.

"Don't you get it, we're all in danger." He shifted onto his elbows, his focus wandering up and down, finding the bruises though the makeup on my face. "The attack on the yacht, and whatever else happened to you. Seems they've already taken some shots."

"What you're describing is trafficking, sex crimes, rape," Rivera said, her voice lowering.

"It's fucking hot in here," Harlan said. Beads of sweat cradled his brow. A moment passed, the tears returning. "This is so much deeper. I wish I never got fucking involved."

"Tell us about the north?" Jericho asked. "The royalties."

"Like I said, the auctions were just the gravy, no royalties for those."

"Gravy," Jericho said and tossed a pack of cigarettes in front of Harlan. "Go on. We've got all the time you need."

Harlan snuffed the butt into the ashtray, the ember wheezing a final breath. He took Jericho's pack and fished out another, wiping his sweaty face and exclaimed, "The meat and potatoes, that's the real stuff."

"And you used your customers' yachts?"

"For the meat and potatoes? I used everything I could find. Fishing boats, salvage boats, yachts, anything I had in my marina. The work was all about transportation."

"Transportation?" Rivera asked, her fingers tapping feverishly onto her phone, shadows stirring beneath the door.

"Who else were you transporting?" I asked, believing we were tapping into the vein of the crime. I cringed, adding, "I mean, who were the meat and potatoes."

"The kids," he answered, cigarette smoke clouding his face. "Shit, over the years, I've brought what's gotta be close to a thousand by now."

"Brought?" Rivera asked, blinking, trying to hide her surprise. "Brought from where?"

Harlan sat up, perched his elbow on the table and cradled his face in his palm. "The sea. Like I was some kind of fisherman," he answered. "These kids came from around the world, all ages too, some were really young, though. That bothered me a bit."

"A bit!" I said, my voice cracking. "And you delivered these kids to the detention center?"

"I did," Harlan answered, lowering his head, tears falling to the table like raindrops.

CHAPTER 49

Our principal witness talked for two more hours, telling us when the trafficking had started, the payments, the money laundering, and who was involved. He told us everything. And he was right, it was bigger than any of us. This case stretched from the western shores to the east, north and south, and then overseas where it touched the borders of other countries, importing children for work, illegal adoptions, factories, and as mules and sex slaves. The crimes were hideous and daunting.

At one point we'd even brought in a whiteboard and filled the room with Ashtole, Mayor Miller, Sheriff Petro, and the FBI leads, as Harlan Jacobs diagrammed the operation—girls and boys from other countries (poor, desolate, most not knowing a word of English), a couple dozen at a time, brought in by sea and transported by truck in the dead of night, then housed in the detention center. Some were immediately dispatched, their destinations unknown, never to be seen again. Others stayed in the detention center and were provided bunks and food and then forced into drugs. A light trickle at first. That was the rule, but over time they were given more, enough to make them pliable and eager to trade services once reaching their destinations. It was sickening. All of this happened within miles of the law, miles of one of the most popular vacation spots in the country. And nobody knew.

He went on to tell us about a gang in Philadelphia known as the Wilts. They owned the girls and paid handsomely to the detention center and to Harlan. I knew of the gang. A vicious bunch. And until now, I'd no idea the extent of their reach. But I knew what they could do, and the idea that Hannah was in their sights made me terrified for her.

By the time Harlan had grown tired of showing us his world, the FBI had already secured a small army to take on the detention center, mitigating any risk of additional casualties. Jericho and I could only stand there in wonder and awe, taking in the details on the whiteboard, the massiveness of the operation and organization behind it.

The auctions we'd found were the gravy, as Harlan had put it. Good old greed; there's nothing more dependable. The detention-center guards wanted the money and borrowed on the Wilts name, inspired by them, and the operations of the crime family. They saw an opportunity with the girls in their custody, and seized it. The auctions had been conducted without the knowledge of the Wilts gang. But with the super yacht and Bobbi Thule and Stacie Wu, the auctions were exposed, the *gravy* jeopardizing the main operation. They held one last auction, the one we'd bid on, but the Wilts were already onto it, shutting it down, and nearly shutting us down too.

Harlan couldn't tell us for certain who was in the boats that night—the Wilts, the guards, or a team of both. With word of the Wilts involvement, Agent Rivera phoned in support from the FBI's Philadelphia offices, their team joining ours, coordinating a strike that'd turn over every rock. We couldn't risk jeopardizing the safety of the victims still housed in the detention center.

From Harlan, one thing we learned was clear, the girls in the woods had never been involved in any of the auctions. As far as we could determine, they'd never been at the detention center either. I'd showed Harlan the pictures again, including earlier pictures from years before when they girls were kidnapped. He couldn't identify them and mentioned the news conferences and his seeing their faces on the television.

"It's the money," he went on to explain. "The Wilts family is about making money. They're not going to take product into the woods and kill it. Not unless they've been crossed."

His words were vile, but at the same time, he made sense.

While we had a lead on the mystery yacht and the auctions, I feared the serial killer we lost in the woods was going to strike again. The open cases weighed heavy on me. He was going to strike soon.

"A word?" Agent Rivera asked when we'd finished. We stepped aside, taking to a corner outside the interview room. "It's about Stacie Wu—"

"Shit," I said, anticipating the worst. "Did she pass?"

"No," Rivera answered, shaking her head. "In fact, she's awake. And she's talking."

CHAPTER 50

While the FBI worked to secure an overthrow of the detention center, Jericho and I went to speak with Stacie Wu, to take her statement, expecting she'd be able to confirm Harlan's story. Another officer could have gone, but I'd insisted, feeling close to the girl and wanting to see her. The hallway leading to her hospital room was absent of traffic, save for two officers placed there, guarding her as per Agent Rivera's earlier request. With the reporters sighting Harlan at the station, there was no telling what news had been leaked, or what dangers any of us were in.

"Sheriff," the officers said, acknowledging Jericho from his previous life.

"Officers," he answered warmly. "How is she?"

"We just got here," one guard answered.

The other adding, "The doctor is with her."

As we opened the door, a tall man pushed past us, his lab coat flailing behind him.

"How is she, Doc?" Jericho asked.

Without turning, the doctor gave a wave, his voice trailing, "Strong girl. She'll make a full recovery."

"What's the recovery time look like?" Jericho asked.

But the doctor was nearing the end of the hallway, his shoes clopping against the granite floor.

"Wonder what's with him," one of the officers said.

Boots, I thought, stealing a glimpse of his shoes. "Did you check his credentials?" I quickly asked.

The officers traded a look. "He had one of those—" one began nervously, her fingers on her chest.

"A stethoscope?" I asked.

"Yeah," she agreed. "A stethoscope."

Alarms rang from Stacie Wu's room. We opened the door to see the machines flashing with alerts, the girl's small body convulsing, arching with horrid disfiguration as if possessed by a hundred demons. Her eyes were open wide, but completely void of life and sunken into her skull, her cheekbones protruding through her skin as she spat and vomited pink foam.

"Fuck!" Jericho yelled. A team of nurses and doctors rushed toward the room, a stampede echoing from the hallway walls. "That guy did something!"

I ran, taking off in the direction of the man, his square frame disappearing around the corner, the tail of his white coat following. I was quick on my feet and reached the end of the hall just as he opened a door to the stairwell.

Boots, I confirmed, seeing them again, the thick sole and heavy work canvas. They were the same as those I'd seen on the bridge. I slammed against the stairwell's metal door, entered the landing and gripped the railing. He had to have stopped mid-step, hiding.

I whispered nervously to myself, "Up or down?" Knowing the wrong decision would give him a lead I could never make up.

Above me, I saw the stairs spiral two more floors toward the roof, the metal railing clean of any hands. And below me, there was nothing but the same, the rail running the length of steps before turning and repeating. I followed the details, searched for a clue, and tried to recall if there was a garage exit at the bottom. There must have been. A shadow caught my eye then—distinct, the slightest bit of movement telling me it was him. I flew down the stairs, careful to catch each step's tread so I wouldn't fall.

When I hit the next landing, I eased over the rail, seeing if I could spy any movements. The narrow space exploded with white light, a gunshot in the closed space piercing my ears as a bullet whizzed by my head. I fell backward to safety and pulled my gun. Footsteps came rapidly and bounced off the walls as I got to the next landing, my shoulder against the brickwork, descending, protected. A door opened below, the exit to the garage. He was getting away.

My chest thumped in rhythm to the stairs passing beneath my feet. I reached the bottom and kicked open the metal door, my shoe landing squarely on the steel bar, releasing the latch and showing me the garage. It was just the one floor, a pad of concrete the size of a small field, with an exit leading to the main road. There were parking spots marked for doctors on one side, administrators and visitors on the other. And it was empty, save for the musty sea smell. There wasn't a sound or sign of the man, or that he'd been here. I holstered my gun and considered the door to my left, the possibility he'd been bold enough to enter the first floor of the hospital.

When I stepped back, letting go of the garage door, it swung suddenly with a whoosh, the metal corner grazing my eye, the force of the bar clipping my hip and throwing me into the stairs. My lungs emptied and I let out a groan. The man with the doctor's coat stood in the doorway, his boots the same as the ones I'd seen on the bridge.

The first-floor door opened then, a nurse and doctor entering the stairwell, a clipboard in the doctor's hand, reviewing instructions, the nurse nodding and repeating them back to her. A gust of wind rushed out of the hospital and sent the man's white coat into the air like a ghost taking flight. And like a ghost, he disappeared a moment later, leaving me alone with the doctor and nurse.

"Are you okay?" the nurse yelled, his voice rising with concern. "Can you tell us what happened?"

His hands were warm as he inspected the side of my face. I gripped his shoulder to get back on my feet.

"Go back inside," I instructed. The doctor shook her head, perplexed. "I'm a cop, do it! It's for your safety."

They followed my instruction as I eased the door to the garage open. The doctor and nurse went back the way they came, opening the door to the hospital, sending a fresh puff of air to rush over me. A moment later, I was alone.

I returned to Stacie Wu's room, while the patrol officers guarding the door were busy talking on their radios and two additional officers were arriving. It was a sign something bad had happened inside the hospital room. When I opened the door, the nurses had already started turning off the machines. She was dead.

An older nurse, stout, with dark skin and hair an odd shade of gray-blue, began to remove the tubes running down Stacie's arms, the bags of fluid and intravenous injections.

"Ma'am," I began, raising my hand. "We're treating this as a crime scene."

The nurse retreated, taking a step back. "Oh, I see, I'll ask before I touch."

"Thank you. The technicians will be here shortly," I said, somberly. "Dr. Swales was notified too."

"I can't confirm it," the nurse said. "But I think the patient suffered an overdose."

She flipped a switch, quieting a machine. The nurse went on to work around Stacie, careful with what she touched, humming as she worked, the song reminding me of a hymn. The doctor and other nurses exited, leaving Stacie alone with the three of us.

The nurse gave me a look and said, "Honey, you might want us to take a look at that."

Jericho took my chin in his fingers, nudging so I'd turn my head to face him. He grimaced, and asked, "Does the other guy look worse?"

"Funny," I answered. "I haven't had this many bruises since training."

"Some vacation," he tried to joke.

"I'll get you an ice pack," the nurse offered. I shook my head, but she ignored me. "It'll keep down the inflammation and stop the blood from rising into a shiner."

"You'll have a pair," Jericho exclaimed, motioning to both eyes. "But seriously, no more going it alone. It's too dangerous."

"You're right," I told him. "He got away, but I can tell you who I think it is."

He shrugged, but then guessed, "Your truck driver?"

"He wore the same style boots."

Jericho's attention shifted to our latest victim. "What's that in her hand?" He went to Stacie's side, her fingers making a fist, holding a pen like a dagger.

"That's odd," the nurse said. "I must have left it in here."

"Yours?"

"Mm hmm."

"Maybe the victim recognized the guy," Jericho suggested. "If he was from the detention center, then maybe she knew she was in danger and tried to defend herself."

"I doubt that," the nurse said, chiming in. "The girl wouldn't have had the strength. Could barely move her arms."

"Or maybe she was writing something down?" I suggested.

Instinctively, we began to search the bed, taking care around the crime scene and to be respectful as we lifted Stacie's arms and her pillow, and searched around her legs and the crack between the bed frame and the end of the mattress.

"I found it," the nurse called out, picking up a note from the floor. "Well I'll be, you were right. She wrote something and it must have fallen off the bed."

The nurse held up a paper napkin for me to see, her fingers wrapped in latex, the color matching her hair. There was a single word written in the pen's gobby blue ink, the napkin torn in parts.

I read it out for them, "She wrote the letters G-A-R, and I think what might be the letter D."

"Guard?" Jericho guessed. "A guard from the detention center?"

"She knew she was in danger," I added, producing an evidence bag to hold Stacie Wu's final statement.

"The poor thing," the nurse said.

"Did you talk to her at all?" Jericho asked.

"Prayed with her every day," she answered, her blueish hair moving like stiff Jell-O. "Pray with everybody I take care of."

"When she woke from her coma, did she say anything to you?" I asked.

The nurse pondered, her eyes focusing on Stacie as she went back to work.

"Anything about a yacht or where she'd been?"

The nurse shook her head. "Girl didn't say much of anything except to call the police. Which we did. She hummed a bit when I'd sing for her."

"Thank you for your time," I said, then held up the evidence bag. "And for the help to find this."

CHAPTER 51

It was nearly a full day before we had our people assembled and were prepared to storm Currituck Sound Juvenile Correctional Facility. Additional paperwork had been filed, complete with judges' signatures at the local and federal levels. Agent Rivera had secured staff from the bureau's Philadelphia branch, who had quite a lot to say about the Wilts gang. Unfortunately, the detention center had not been on their radar. It hadn't been on anyone's.

Feeling banged up, I took the advice of Agent Rivera and stayed back in the loaner car parked outside the center. I'd go in after the first wave was initiated. While an early-morning surprise was the plan, there was no telling what kind of firepower the guards had. And if this was the group responsible for the attack on the yacht, I'd already seen enough.

Jericho stayed back too, but I suspected it had more to do with his arm than anything else. It was bothering him. He wouldn't tell me anything specific, but another night in his home, showering together and tending to the bandages, I could see what retrieving the duffle bag from the ocean had done.

"In a few," he assured me when I pestered about his trip to the doctor. "We're almost done. I can feel it."

"Promise?" I asked, fussing over the bandaging. "You have to promise me."

"I promise," he answered, his eyes catching mine. I couldn't look away and eased into his arms, my hands on his face, bringing his lips to mine. It wasn't a short kiss either, but the kind to tell him how I felt. He held me the way I wanted to be held and kissed me too. There was something more between us than curiosity and satisfying a carnal need. I wanted to feel more—*yearned* might be a better word. And I sensed the same from him.

"We're ready for you." I heard Agent Rivera's voice, my eyes on a jumbo jet as it crawled along the horizon. "Come on up the hill."

"That was too easy," Jericho said to me, and then put his mouth to the radio. "We're coming up."

As we climbed the road, the entrance on a long hill, I saw the overhang of a cliff and a steeper hill to the left of it. Just beyond, I saw the woods where Jericho and I had stood when searching for Cheryl Parry's baby.

"Jericho, over there," I said, taking his arm and motioning to the woods. The proximity was closer than expected, the change of angle giving me a different perspective, another vantage to consider other possibilities. "What if the baby is still alive? What if the baby was here all along?"

"That would mean Cheryl Parry would have to have been here," he answered, our shoes scraping the asphalt as we trudged the incline. Sweat beaded above his lip and over his brow, the sun making him squint as his eyes tracked the path from the detention center to the hill and then the woods. "I mean, it's possible. We'll know for certain once we have a list of inmate records. Shit, anything is possible."

"The records," I said, thinking wishfully, a faint hope Cheryl Parry's baby had survived.

We had almost made it to the top of the hill when an explosion shook the ground; a detonation from the campus. The rumble reached my feet, rising into my legs. Instinctively, we dropped to the ground.

"Rivera!" Jericho yelled into the radio as a plume of black smoke appeared above the trees. "Agent Rivera?"

I didn't wait for an answer and raced up the drive, my gun drawn, the smell of smoke filling my nose. There was rapid firing, the sound of an assault rifle followed by screams and hollering and demands to get down onto the ground.

I was breathing hard when I reached the center. At once I found the source of the explosion; smoke billowed from a charred structure, a single guard on his knees in front of the fire, a rifle next to him as FBI agents held him at gunpoint.

Behind this scene the grounds opened up to the campus—a single building, long, red-brick, with a small parking lot in front of it, and a rectangular sign with the name, Currituck Sound Juvenile Correctional Facility, in a bold lettering. Beyond the parking lot, twenty men and women dressed in army fatigues were on their knees with their ankles crossed and their hands behind their heads. On the other side of the detention center, dozens of girls, all of them dressed in dark-yellow or orange jumpsuits, some gawking at the fire, others yipping and hollering and screaming.

It was the quiet ones I noticed, though; the girls with their heads down, finding a place to stand alone, disinterested in seeing the fire or the guards. Those were the girls we'd want to talk to.

"We almost had everything ready," Agent Rivera exclaimed as she approached, her face sweaty, her breathing rapid.

Jericho arrived behind me, his hand on his hip and panting from the run up the hill.

"Who caused that?" he asked, coughing, trying to catch his breath.

"Stupid yokel guard," Rivera answered. "I'm guessing he's hiding something in there."

"Do you think he's in charge?"

"Not him," she answered.

I scanned the guards, finding one who stood out from the rest. Even when kneeling, I could see he was taller than the others. His hair red like fire, his skin pale, almost white, with freckles across his nose and cheeks. He held a grin and quietly laughed as if all of this was a joke. But what caught my attention more than anything was the stare he'd fixed on me. He knew me, and I suspected I knew him too.

"The yokel isn't your guy," I said. "That one is."

Rivera and Jericho glanced over to the man just as he let out another laugh.

"Something funny?" Rivera asked. "Got a joke you want to share?"

"I'm good," he answered, his stare never breaking.

"The boots," I told Jericho.

Every one of the guards wore the same style boots. Better yet, I could see the treads. I wasn't an expert, but they looked damn close to the markings carved into Robert Stewart's skin.

"I think we've got a shot at finding the boot that fits the print from Robert's body," he said.

As we turned the corner around a building, out of sight of the guards, Rivera faced us.

"By the way. That one," Rivera said, "he's a Wilts."

"Come again?" I asked.

"Jimmy Wilts," Rivera answered. "It was the first name we saw when we pulled the employment records for the judge's orders. Our Philadelphia office confirmed who he was too."

"As in the Wilts gang Harlan referred to?" Jericho asked.

"One and the same," she answered with a nod.

"That means this," Jericho began, his gaze going to the girls and the buildings. "All of this. It wasn't some random occurrence. It wasn't a bunch of guards who saw an opportunity and built the auction site."

"Correct. This wasn't random at all."

"This was planned. Orchestrated," Jericho said. "The Wilts infiltrated the detention center through employment—"

"—and then took it over," I said, finishing for him.

We approached the girls, their unruliness proving to be a lot to handle for the officers and FBI agents. The agents had strung their arms side to side, trying to form a makeshift pen and keep the girls in one place. But this only inspired a few of the inmates to test the boundaries and push the line.

"Girls, down!" Rivera yelled abruptly, giving me a start. "On the ground now! Legs crossed. Hands in your lap!"

To our surprise, the girls did as they were told. There were a few stragglers, but they all finally quieted and took to the pavement as instructed.

"Did you learn that at the academy?" I asked, impressed.

"Nope," she answered. "Eight years of Catholic school."

I heard a roar and rumble from beyond the hill, the bellow shaking the ground like a passing train. A trailer climbed the steep incline, puffing gray smoke, its motor wheezing before reaching the landing and parking along the lawn. Two more followed, close behind it, with a fire engine coming up the rear to extinguish the burning shed. The first two trailers would be used to interview the girls while the third was to help with the site. Currituck Sound Juvenile Correctional Facility was officially shut down, and the girls, their custody, had to be transferred to other facilities.

Another bus climbed the hill, sputtering, the motor's belts whining. Coal gray, cages on its windows, slow and rattling with armed guards inside. It was the bus that would carry the detention-center guards to jail. As if knowing what they were looking at, the girls were back on their feet cheering, yellow and orange jumping up and down, blending in a colorful mural.

"Girls!" Rivera yelled. Silence came over the group as they took to sitting again. "You'll have time, I promise. But first, we need your help."

The doors of the trailers opened and spilled out a handful of FBI agents who met the girls and escorted them inside, some with reluctance on their faces, others with smiles plastered from ear to ear, unable to contain their excitement.

"Them," I told Rivera, pointing out the few girls who'd tried to sit alone, their backs turned away from the guards. "You'll want to interview them. My bet is they know everything there is to know about the auction site."

"Yeah, I see them," she told me, frowning as she glared at the guards. She spoke into her radio and tugged my arm to show me a woman who looked to be a rookie and was dressed more like a camp counselor than an FBI agent. The woman gave us a nod and approached the girls.

"They'll be taken care of?" I asked, my words breaking with an unexpected rush of emotion. "Don't care what they did before, but they deserve better than what they got."

"I'm with you, sister," Rivera agreed. She motioned toward the rear of the building, and said, "This is just the start. Follow me, I've got something to show you."

"Are the buildings empty?" I asked before we continued. "Was there a baby inside, or any signs of a baby having been there?"

Rivera shook her head, answering, "Nothing like that reported, not even a crib." She continued on, waving her arm, encouraging me to follow. "You'll definitely need to see what's back here."

CHAPTER 52

We followed Rivera around the detention center's main building, passing a row of generators. When we reached the back, I thought there would be more girls, but then I worked out what Rivera wanted to show us. And then I saw.

"Oh my God," I whispered, my eyes finding fifty girls and boys, every color, every age, and all of them with frightful saucer eyes, the kind I'd seen on the news. The sight reminded me of a refugee camp, the children wearing lime-green jumpsuits, sitting quietly, their legs crossed and hands in their laps as though Rivera had already given the command. But I suspected nobody had said anything, their silence coming out of fear.

"How many?" Jericho asked, emotion in his voice.

"Four dozen," Rivera said, kneeling and giving a girl a smile. She returned the smile, cautiously. "They were all housed in this building. Kept separate. As far as we can tell, the center's inmates had no idea what was going on back here."

"Just like Harlan said," I confirmed. "Do we know where they came from?"

Rivera put her hands to her hips and shook her head, answering, "All over. We've counted six nationalities already. We're using our phones as translators."

"The cold cases?" I asked. "The missing girls?"

Jericho added, "Any girls in their teens—late teens—matching a description of the missing girls?"

"None," Rivera answered. "I distributed the pictures you gave us. Nothing."

"How long has this place been here?"

"Eight years," Jericho answered. "Why?"

"Might just be a coincidence," I said, taking a step closer to the girls and boys, their round eyes following me as I paced. I pointed toward the woods, finding the edge of the cliff where I'd almost fallen. "With the dumping ground for the girls' bodies so close, I can't help but think the guards, or a guard, is involved, but the years don't work."

"Sometimes it's easy to connect what you can't see," Rivera commented. "And then it's a struggle to make sense of it when the picture becomes clear."

"How's their health?" Jericho asked, his voice timid, expecting the worst.

"Well, that's the good news," she answered. "They're clean, well fed, and the rooms, the beds, all good, better than some summer camps."

"But?" he asked.

"The drugs," she answered. "Quite a few are sick and have a long road ahead of them."

"This isn't any—" I started to say, my words cut short, stuck in my throat. I patted Jericho's shoulder, urging him to turn around. "Guys?"

"What is it?" Rivera asked, her words following me as I went to the center of the courtyard and to an area that had been nursed and tended to for probably as long as the detention center had been around.

"Wait," Jericho called after me, but I couldn't slow down, wouldn't slow down.

I reached it then, my hands on the stems, the skin prickly with fine hairs giving life to the bud; a blue dahlia, its flower open, drinking the sunlight, the petals soft like velvet, the perfume strong.

Jericho came to my side and gently took hold of one of the flowers, saying, "Robert."

"Robert Stewart?" Rivera asked. "The victim in your other case? I understand he worked here. I also understand he was a guard."

"That's right," Jericho said, his expression dazed by the sight of the large garden. "But he wasn't with them, any of them. He wasn't a part of this."

"How do you know?" she asked.

Jericho crumpled the flower, turning the beauty into pulp before dropping it to the ground.

"I don't. But I knew Robert, even got him the job," Jericho said, anger in his voice. "We found these flowers in his hand."

I picked up the flower Jericho tossed aside and closed my fingers around it, and showed her. "Like this, post-mortem." I opened my fist, showing the crushed petals in my palm.

"And you think he was here? That he grabbed the flowers before he died."

"Before he was murdered," Jericho corrected her.

"Gard!" I said, raising my voice. I started searching every corner, finding the small shed, a clipboard hanging from a hook, a pen dangling from the bottom of a string.

"What is it?"

"G-A-R-D-E-N," I spelled out. "Stacie Wu wasn't misspelling the word *guard*. I think she was trying to spell the word *garden*."

Jericho poked a pile of mulch and top soil, shoving it with the tip of his foot.

"Garden," he said to himself. He didn't sound convinced, but took the blue dahlia from my hand and held it as if summoning Robert Stewart to help him see the link.

"You think there's a connection?" Rivera asked. "I mean, between Stacie Wu and Robert Stewart?"

"G-A-R-D. It fits," Jericho answered for me. He slowly shook his head, adding, "Damn, I think they were both trying to tell us something."

"What was it Harlan said?" I asked.

"Sometimes he'd seen kids go in and never seen them again."

Rivera turned away from us, her mouth on the radio, her finger on the button as it belched static. She instructed, "We're going to need a small backhoe and some recovery teams behind the detention center's main building."

Almost within the hour, much of the garden was infiltrated by FBI agents and crime-scene technicians—some carrying long metal rods, shoving them into the soil, probing the earth, searching for bodies. Others worked with cadaver dogs, specially trained to pick up the scent of a corpse, able to sniff one out in as much as six feet of dirt.

"Got something!" an agent yelled.

A technician was yanking her prodding rod, another was with a cadaver dog, its face eager to please and yelping in agreement. I followed a small team, but stopped when my feet reached the garden's boundary, deciding to wait while two technicians pushed through the vegetation until they reached the agent. I heard the earth being cut open, a shovel slicing the flower bed, the metal blade scraping the rocks, followed by the loose ground being cast aside. From the furthest corner, a cadaver dog whined in a fit.

"This one is close to the surface... Oh my God!" There was an upheaval, a person stumbling and the garden plants being trampled.

"What is it?" another agent asked, her voice pitching into a yell. The activities in the garden ceased while sickening moans erupted and the cadaver dog barked and whimpered.

"Getting sick," he told her, before exiting the garden entirely, his knees plunking into the soft earth as he heaved. His dog whined and licked his ear and neck with concern. "I'm sorry. A body, a hand, right near the surface."

"Get a hold of yourself," his commanding officer ordered, but then knelt by the man's side, her composure shifting, her hand on his back in a compassionate gesture. "I know the first time is rough."

"It seems we have a body, possibly more," Rivera said coldly.

"Stacie and Robert. They *were* trying to tell us something," Jericho added, his face gray. "Robert must have found out what was going on, and they killed him."

"Female, I think," a voice called from the shallow grave. "It's a few days, maybe. With all these flowers, the garden must have covered up the smell."

"Like flowers at a funeral," a voice suggested. "There was a time before embalming when they used large floral arrangements to mask the smell."

Rivera double-tapped the receiver button on her radio until there was a static belch. "Sir. I think you need to come to the site."

"What is it?" a froggy voice answered.

"Sir, we have the entire center in custody and have discovered multiple bodies."

"Hey, guys," the voice from the shallow grave called to us. "Might want to take a look at this. And could someone bring over some evidence bags?"

"Green rookie," Rivera mumbled, annoyed.

"I have some," I offered and followed the technician's voice, pushing through tall sunflowers, their stalks scratching my arms, the floral scent mixing with death. Jericho put his hand on my shoulder, using me to help guide him along a path to the scene. When we reached the technician, a flash scalded my eyes, a camera whining as the batteries recharged.

"Looks like the victim is holding something," the technician said. "I didn't want to continue until I got it bagged and tagged."

Another technician joined us. I handed her an evidence bag and watched the two work together as they carefully pried the dead girl's fingers to catch what was inside her fist—the sight reminding me of Robert Stewart and the blue petals.

"Maybe we should wait till we get to Dr. Swales?" Jericho suggested, the smell hitting him. But it was already too late, the girl's fingers opened, her knuckles cracking, a stringy bundle falling into the evidence bag. "What is that?"

The technicians stood as we gathered around for a closer look, their gloved fingers pinching the prize, untangling it as they cleaned the grime and dirt.

"Is that a bracelet?" one of them asked.

"What did you say?" But I didn't wait for an answer. Sunlight slipped through the dirt and filth and struck one of the bracelet's charms, a plastic charm. I dropped to my knees, the gleam piercing my heart with the power of a bullet.

"Oh yeah, like a kid's charm bracelet," another voice answered.

"No!" I cried. "No. Don't you say that! It can't be!"

But it was. Inside the evidence bag was Hannah's charm bracelet. I shoved my hands into the ground and felt Jericho's body pressing against mine, his hand on my arm, his chest against my back. I jerked myself free of him, and dove into the earth again, clawing the garden, eager to see my baby.

"What are you doing?" one of the technicians yelled.

But I ignored her and took hold of my girl's hand, clutching her pale fingers, begging for this to be a dream.

"You're disturbing the evidence!"

Handfuls of dirt and stone flew from my fists. I dug faster and deeper, one of my fingers smashing a rock, my fingernail peeling away entirely.

"Officer White, stop!" Agent Rivera demanded, her voice shaking with confusion, her hands on my shoulders.

I couldn't listen to their voices and scooped bigger handfuls. I needed to free my girl from her garden grave.

"Casey, please!"

I felt the top of Hannah's head, the touch surreal, a tangle of her hair in my fingers. The mix of flowers and death defined what was happening in my mind, defined my devotion to one thing, finding Hannah.

I screamed, "It's my daughter's! It's my daughter!"

"Casey, you can't know that!" Jericho pleaded in a yell, trying to reason, coaxing me away from the grave.

"We found her!" I yelled, falling backward, falling into a hundred hands, their fingers gripping and holding me.

"Secure her," Rivera demanded.

"They killed Hannah," I cried, my voice hoarse. "They got to her like Harlan said they would. And they killed my girl!"

CHAPTER 53

HIM

They should never have been, those people at the detention center.

His eyes were inches from the old television, stinging, watering, tears standing with his refusal to blink. On the screen, pictures of the detention center, the ruins of it.

"You did this," he spat, his belly warming with the idea of her, the sense she'd be with him soon. "You made this happen. But did you find her?"

He smashed the rewind button and then pressed play, watching the video footage again, the shadow of a news helicopter, the sound of the whirring blades. It was everyone's news now, the secrets no more.

He stood, and glanced at the doors, the padlocks in place, the cages opposite empty. His secrets remained safe, even if the guards at the detention center had revealed theirs.

The door handle was cold to the touch, the new padlock too, the room empty, the linens cleaned, a new wash basin and scrub brush poised in wait. He went to the narrow bed and lifted the nightgown, the old embroidered pattern a memory from when he was a child.

"You'll wear this," he said definitively, and looked over his shoulder in time to see Detective White's face. "You'll be my new addition, like your daughter almost was."

CHAPTER 54

For twelve hours I believed Hannah was dead. I believed my baby had perished at the hands of the men and women trafficking children. I was convinced she'd been captured by the Wilts gang, killed and then buried in the detention center's flower garden. And deep inside, I'd believed my life of searching for Hannah was over. But I know now that it wasn't my girl. The shock of learning the news sat cold in my gut.

The FBI worked fast to recover the bodies in the gardens, seven in all. Four of the dead were girls serving time in the detention center. The other three bodies were thought to have been children brought in by Harlan. None of the girls were from the open kidnapping cases. Their causes of death wouldn't be known until Dr. Swales completed the autopsies. However, preliminary reviews suggested a number of causes, including overdoses, which told us the garden had been used to hide remains rather than for ritual or for motivated killings.

When the parents of the dead girls we could identify had been notified, we'd learned the detention-center staff had informed them their daughters had been on work release and not returned. And since each of the girls had recently turned eighteen when that had happened, the detention center's custody had ended. For the parents who questioned the detention center, they were met with unanswered phone calls and emails.

I met Nichelle Wilkinson, a new-hire PK had made soon before his death. A tall and attractive woman, she was fresh out of school and had unexpectedly needed to step into PK's role. Her first task was to access the detention center's infrastructure. With approval from the bureau, Nichelle gained access to the center's IT systems and learned the dead girls had been processed as if their custody was released, the detention center's guardianship technically ending. We verified the dead girls had been involved in the auctions, our speculation leading to the guards eliminating the risk of the girls telling anyone on the outside what was going on inside. With no legal reasons to hold the girls, the guards killed them.

It was easy, I thought, with a sickening stir in me. *Too easy.* The men and women who did this had played every card perfectly, victimizing the girls for profit, getting rich in the process, and then murdering them to hide their crimes. How many more would have reached eighteen or neared their release date, only to be killed and buried in the garden? The thought gave me a shudder.

Of the bodies discovered, Kelli Tate was the girl holding Hannah's charm bracelet. She was also identified as the girl who'd been in the final auction, the one that never completed, but had ended in a shootout on the super yacht. I had no idea how Hannah's bracelet came to be in her possession, or how the girl died. Dr. Swales would give us the answer to the latter. But as to the first question, I only knew that Hannah could still be alive. We'd have a chance to learn more soon, a chance to sit with the remaining inmates, to interview them. I could only hope they'd know something about my daughter.

We had one of the Wilts in custody. But I knew of the crime family, knew of their history and how dangerous they were. Hannah was safe for now, but if the Wilts wanted to find her, they would.

"Drink this," Jericho said, offering me a paper cup, steam rolling over the lip. He gave me a half-smile, but with a slight cringe. "Hot chocolate. The sticker on the station's machine said it was the *World's Best*. Might be some false advertising, but it does smell okay."

"Thank you," I told him, taking the cup, wincing when the heat touched my finger, the bandaging around the missing fingernail turning tacky. Though it had been hours, my hands shook terribly, but that wasn't what had me worried. I'd lost it. I'd lost it entirely, and it had happened in front of everyone who mattered. Jericho sat next to me, his hand on my shoulder, squeezing with encouragement, his eyes consoling.

"How are you holding up?"

"I'm fine," I told him, distracted by the noises behind us, the clamor of reporters, and the constant parade of FBI agents as they piled evidence bags against Nichelle's cubical wall. I locked in on the heap of boots, each pair bagged and tagged. "How many of those?"

"A lot," he answered. "We've got some crime-scene technicians who'll be working them most of the night, possibly tomorrow, and the next day too."

"The tread is the same," I said, blowing the steam from my cup.

Jericho held up his phone, showing me a picture of the pattern on Robert Stewart's back. The photograph had been adjusted, the contrast raised, and the color channels separated so there were distinct points for comparison. Each of the finished images looked like a gravestone rubbing. And each brought the details we needed. It wasn't just the boot's size and tread, but every nick in the thick rubber, every cut, and even the person's gait, their wear on the shoe unique like a fingerprint.

"We'll find the shoe," Jericho said.

"Like Cinderella's slipper."

"I have something for you," a voice said from behind us, the accent welcome. I turned around to find Dr. Swales, her hair pushed to one side. "What a nightmare it was getting in here."

The station had stayed packed. And there were double, maybe triple the reporters now—if that was even possible. The story about the detention center hadn't just gone national, it was viral, and it was leading on every channel, every newspaper and every social-media site.

The front of the station fared worse than what I'd seen at the yacht scenes—camera vans lined the street with antennae and satellite dishes telescoping into the sky. News crews with microphones and celebrity reporters, and the incessant barrage of questions was a constant. It was orderly, yet chaotic, and it was likely to become the biggest case reported this summer.

"I'm surprised you made it past the peanut gallery," Jericho said, referring to the crowd of reporters.

"Oh, I have my ways," Swales told him, turning briefly to show us her hood. She laughed adding, "They probably thought I was a delivery boy."

"Are you here about the boots?" I asked.

She nodded. "It doesn't help that so many are size thirteens. Sir, you received the picture of the boot print?"

"I did," Jericho answered, holding up his phone.

"If there's a match, we'll find it," she said, repeating our earlier sentiment. "I just released Robert Stewart's body, his mother's arrangements for burial are this coming Saturday."

"What's the final cause?" I asked.

"Robert Stewart died of asphyxiation. We found sand and seawater in his mouth and lungs, matching the samples you provided from where his body was recovered."

"They held him down." I shook my head.

"But why there?" Jericho asked, his knee bouncing. "They'd obviously used the flower garden before—"

"For at least the last year," Swales said, interrupting. "Of the bodies in my morgue, one has been dead just a few days. The state of decomposition on the others tells me some had been buried in the garden for more than a year."

"So why didn't they bury Robert in the garden?" Jericho asked. "They used it specifically to hide the bodies."

Dr. Swales shrugged and primped her hair, pushing the frizzy pile into place. She turned to me, asking, "What's your thought?"

"I don't think they wanted to kill him," I told them, my words met with surprise. "I mean, I think his death might have been an accident."

"An accident? What about the flowers? The dahlias?" Jericho asked, sounding hurt. "Robert found out what they were doing and the fucking monsters killed him."

"Don't get me wrong, I understand," I answered as Dr. Swales pulled up a chair and sat down. I pointed at the boots, adding, "Hear me out. We have fifteen men and women in custody. That's fifteen involved in a massive trafficking ring. That's a huge number. Think about how hard it is to get just two criminals to work together. How many cases have you worked in your career where there were so many involved in murder, trafficking, sex crimes, and for such an extended time?"

"None that size," Jericho answered.

"With a Wilts family member running the detention center, maybe he brought some of his extended family with him, and then went on to adopt the rest."

"But Robert was a local," Jericho said, bothered.

"So maybe it was an invitation," Dr. Swales suggested. "Like hazing."

"An initiation?" Jericho asked. "To join them? As if they *were* a crime family?"

"To them, they are a crime family," I answered. "They likely thought of themselves as the Wilts' Outer Banks chapter."

"But Robert's hand, the flower petals," Swales said.

"I think Robert knew what was coming and was scared of what would happen if he refused," I said. "The initiation, or whatever it was, must have started in the garden. He'd grabbed the flowers and kept hold of them, even when they took him out to that place, stripped and beat him."

"They murdered him."

"They did," I said, agreeing, trying not to discount the crime. "But I don't think that was the plan… they held him down too long."

Dr. Swales picked up a bagged pair of boots, adding, "If it was an accident, the charges for the owner of the boot will change. Second-degree murder is my guess."

"An army, Harlan said. An army needs to grow," Jericho mused, his gaze wandering.

"You said you had something for me?" I asked Dr. Swales.

She put her hands on mine, enclosing the cup of hot chocolate, which had cooled. Her fingers were bony and cold, but smooth like silk. She crouched forward, her face near mine, her eyes huge behind her square glasses, an odd smile pasted on her lips.

"Open your hand," she instructed, southern accent lilting.

I did as she told me, and for my effort, she gave me an evidence bag, Hannah's bracelet inside, cleaned of the grave's death and grime.

"I thought you would want to see this."

"To keep?" I asked, knowing the answer already.

She cocked her head. "Eventually it will have to go into evidence, but I did my homework and I know your daughter's case."

"You do?" I asked, surprised and warmed by the care she took in understanding.

"I do," she said. "And I wanted you to see these, to confirm if it's at all possible this could be your daughter's."

"Or not," Jericho added, his gaze serious, his voice surprisingly cold. But sometimes the truth is cold. "Right now, you've only got a girl that resembles the drawings of your daughter."

I brought the bag close to my eyes, knowing exactly what to look for, but couldn't keep my hands still.

"Here, let me," Dr. Swales offered.

I returned the evidence bag. "Sorry."

"You don't have to be sorry," she said, bringing the bracelet close to her face as her glasses slid down her nose. "Tell me what to look for."

"The yellow star," I told her. I picked up the hot chocolate and drank a mouthful, trying to wet my throat. "My husband. My ex-husband that is. He bought Hannah the bracelet. But Hannah wasn't old enough yet, she chewed on everything. We couldn't keep anything out of her mouth." I shifted uncomfortably, realizing suddenly, the bracelet might not be Hannah's. "He insisted it was safe, and then it happened. She bit a piece off the yellow star. It scared me enough to take it away until she was older, a toddler."

"I don't see a yellow star," Dr. Swales told me, her eyes squinting, focusing, my heart dipping. "Wait. Of course, with a piece broken, I wouldn't be looking for a star now. I'm looking for—"

She held up the bag, bringing it to the center for me and Jericho to see. Jericho flattened the plastic, and finished for Dr. Swales, "You're looking for half a star."

Tears rolled down my cheeks, their words leaving me unable to speak.

"Oh dear," Swales began, her voice choked. She put a hand to her chest, and said, "I do believe this could be your daughter's."

CHAPTER 55

I held the charm bracelet, unable to speak, unable to breathe, knowing I was right, the validation seeping into every part of me. Jericho rubbed my arm and Dr. Swales held my hand, both of them believing. Jericho stood and went to Nichelle's cubical, leaving us alone.

"I knew it was her," I said, fixing my eyes on the charm bracelet, turning each piece through the evidence bag, pinching the yellow star, confirming the two missing points. "There are times when it seems like it happened a few hours ago, the memories as if it were yesterday. In my head I can still smell her and hear her voice."

Swales gave a nod, but I could tell she was unsure of what I meant. "Your story, it's like something I'd see on the news. A case solved after all these years. Call it a miracle if that's your thing. These days, they're about the only good stories I ever see on the news."

"A miracle," I said with a sad smile. "But, we have to find her first."

"Never in my sixty years would I think to have been a part of one."

"But where is she now?"

"Nichelle may have something," Jericho interjected on his return.

"A lead?"

Nichelle appeared from her cubical, waving a sheet of paper, announcing, "Hot off the press. The detention center's identification badges. All of them. With access to their systems, I have everything."

"Is Hannah's in there?"

She handed me the paper, a color printout of an identification badge. The sheet was still warm to the touch, the smell of print toner in the air. It was Hannah, her piercings removed. She wore a grim expression, the kind I'd seen a million times while leafing through suspect books filled with mugshots. Grim or not, it was her, it was the girl in my pictures.

"Patricia Fitzgerald," I said, reading the name. "Her name is Patricia now."

"Look below the ID," Jericho said. "Arson. It's why she was in the detention center. And look at the address."

"Arson?" I asked. Then on reading the house number and street name, I slowly began to understand with a sickening blow where Hannah had been all this time. Electricity ran through my body with a sudden shake as anger took hold.

"Casey?" Dr. Swales asked, taking my hands. "What is it?"

I waved the sheet and shook my head. "Are you certain about this address?"

"What?" Swales asked, tipping her head to see. I handed her the sheet. She eagerly took hold and read the address, her lips moving in silence. "This is a good thing. No? You have her home address. And it's so close."

I jumped to my feet and faced the door, answering over my shoulder, "Yeah. It's a good thing."

The smell of ash and soot lingered, and probably would until the remains of the burnt house was torn down. I forced a breath through my mouth, the humid air carrying the smell for miles like that from an animal carcass.

Anger brewed in me, deep and sickening. There was sadness and regret there too, but they paled by comparison. How long had the Fitz's Garage clue been on my wall? Where would Hannah be today if I'd been more diligent, more thorough? I'd failed her on the lawn when she was taken from me. And I'd failed her again when I tacked a clue over the top of the Fitz's Garage phone number, never following up on the lead, burying what would have taken me to my daughter.

I eased the car door closed, the latch clicking quietly enough. I didn't want the woman we'd encountered last time to hear us coming; I wanted to be in a position of surprise. And yet, I had no earthly idea what I was going to do when I saw her. Hannah wasn't here, but I needed answers. I needed to know why this place was listed as her home address. What if the woman from before was the woman I'd been searching for, who'd lured Hannah into the car? I checked my gun, checked the safety, and questioned if I should wear it at all.

"That's her artwork," Jericho said, pointing to the tinder remains of the home. "It's what landed her at the detention center."

"She burned down the house?" I said, still in disbelief. I felt as if I should come to Hannah's defense. I didn't know the girl, though I still added, "Maybe it was an accident."

Jericho hesitated, uncertain how to answer. He held the report. "That doesn't happen by accident."

"No," I said, agreeing. "No, it doesn't."

"Doesn't look like anyone is home," Jericho said, closing his door without care for the noise he made.

"Easy!" I said, forcing my voice, a ragged whisper.

"Nobody is home," he repeated. "No car. The trailer lights are off. Front door is shut."

He was right. The trailer tucked in behind the house's shell was locked up, windows dark, empty. There wasn't a sign of life on the property.

"Can we put a warrant out, an APB, anything?" I asked, feeling desperate.

Jericho considered the request, and said, "You know, I believe we can." His words surprised me. "We have the identification badge matching the pictures of your daughter. And we have you and Dr. Swales confirming the charm bracelet. That's more than enough to suggest questioning the woman."

"Do it," I said without emotion, kicking at the gravel, a hot wave of disappointment coming over me as I scanned the property. It was the same empty feeling I'd get when stringing yarn on my wall, only to take it down hours later when the new clue hadn't panned out as expected. "Let's see what's in the barn."

"You sure?" Jericho asked.

"Humor me," I said, staring at the old building. It was tall, dilapidated, with long threads of barn-red paint peeling off, the breeze catching the loose strands.

Jericho climbed the drive, following me, his feet digging into the gravel. "What do you want to see in there?"

"Remember how the woman acted when we were here?"

"Sure. Crazy."

I shook my head. "Crazy is one way. I'm thinking she was also hiding something. So let's find out what it was." Guilt had me shifting about, my chin quivering. "I just wish I'd followed up sooner."

"You've got to stop that," Jericho warned. He came to my side. "Remember what we talked about."

"Yeah," I said. "I guess I have a lot of practice is all."

"We don't have a warrant here," he pointed out.

I cleared my throat, shaking the tension out of my hands. "When suspecting hidden evidence, we have the legal right to engage a search."

We stopped at the house, the wood frame charred severely enough to leave me wondering how it remained standing at all. I dared a touch, just one, my fingers on the scalloped wood, touching what Hannah had done and questioning why she would have done something so destructive.

Jericho warned, "Watch out for them yellow-jackets. Nasty this time of year."

We slowed and walked softly around a stout apple tree, the ground littered with fruit, the air sweet. I nudged an apple with my foot, turning it over to see the rot, a yellow-jacket hovering above it and waiting for a taste.

"Late in the season," I said, continuing on as the bugs buzzed around us. I took hold of the barn door, and said, "Let's hope it's unlocked."

"No locks that I can see," Jericho said, helping, yanking on the handle until the heavy door swung freely and opened. A gust of stale air rushed past us, lifting my hair as if we'd opened an ancient tomb. It was too dark to see inside.

I took hold of the other door. "Let's get this one too."

We opened up the barn, spilling light inside in what might have been the first time in years. I smelled horses and hay, the aroma sweet and warm the way I'd remembered a petting zoo when I'd taken Hannah.

At one time, the barn might have been used for horses, but that had ended with the adoption of car parts and garage tools. In the doorway's light I saw shelves lining the walls, carrying the type of tools mechanics used. An old lift-jack sat propped against one corner, and an air compressor in another, its round belly pitted with rust. And next to it, an antique gas pump, the glass covered with dusty filth, the rubber hose cracked with dry rot. At the center of the barn, the remains of an old car, canvas covering it, dingy and threadbare in spots, hiding what was beneath from the elements, preserving whatever work the owners had put into it.

"Husband was definitely a garage monkey," Jericho said, finding a light switch and flicking it. Long tubes on the ceiling blinked and hummed, spitting amber colors and setting fire to the fluorescent lights. They crackled with an electric spark and then came to life. "That's better."

"Tommy Fitzgerald," I said, eyeing another shelf of car parts. "The man sells his garage and then what? He retires? He maybe does some side work?"

"He wasn't ready to retire," Jericho offered. "My guess is he's on disability or some other program. When I looked up his address, there was nothing on him. No records, nothing criminal. Not even a speeding ticket."

"And his wife?"

"Nothing on her either."

With the lights on, I could see all the barn. There was no sign a girl had ever been here. No toys or doll houses. No leftover pet supplies like a rabbit cage or a hamster wheel.

"Jericho, I may have been wrong," I told him, disappointed by my assessment. I made my way deeper inside, the tickle of cobwebs spreading across my forehead, the threat of a spider imminent. I swiped at the webbing, chasing the creepiness with a shiver. "There's nothing here."

"Patience," he suggested, working his way along the south wall, picking through the tools on a workbench. "We're here now, so let's give the place a look."

"I'm looking, but one more spider, and—"

"Hello. And you must be Tommy," Jericho said, lifting a picture frame from the wall. "Wife, husband, and a child."

"Child?" I said, coming to his side. I let out a shaky laugh, relief, confirmation that came with knowing the girl in the photograph. "Look at her!"

"What?" Jericho asked. I leaned against him, the weight of the truth hitting me. "Casey?"

"That clue, the index card, it was the one all along," I told him, guilt revisiting with crushing force. "All these years she's been here."

"I'm not sure," he told me, holding the picture in the light. "The age makes it hard to see a resemblance."

"Wait," I demanded, swiping the glass clear of barn dust. "This will help."

I felt the tears prick my eyes and tried to hold them back as I fished through my bag to find my wallet with a picture of Hannah I'd taken days before she was abducted. Grief filled my chest and made me dizzy, but I managed to place my girl's picture on the glass. We studied them side by side. Jericho looked at every detail, his focus bouncing between the pictures.

"It really does look like her," he admitted, his voice wavering.

"Look at her hand," I demanded. "Her wrist." I pointed to each picture, showing him the charm bracelet.

"Oh my God," he said. "Casey…"

I went to the center of the barn, Jericho's words lost to me as I understood why Tommy Fitzgerald sold his garage, and what it was the woman was hiding. I tore into the old canvas like a lion ripping into the flesh of its prey. And like the spilling of blood, I saw the color red, encouraging me to shred the aged fabric, sending me into an almost manic state.

"Wait!" Jericho yelled over me, seeing it too and grabbing the opposite corner. "On three okay—one, two, three!"

And together we pulled away the cover like magicians revealing their secret, the barn filling with shimmering dust and torn canvas, pieces of it drifting in the light. When the air cleared, I saw what was hidden beneath, and it revealed the truth I'd been chasing. I dropped to my knees, tears springing, my fingers clutching the bumper of the car that had stolen my baby.

CHAPTER 56

The barn floor's nails dug into my knees as I pounded my fists on the red car. Jericho took hold of my arms and tried to stop me, tried to lift me up and away from what I'd known to be a monster—dormant all these years. I shoved his arm away, pushing him, and stayed where I was, intent on destroying the car.

"It's the car," I cried. "Jericho, this is the one. This is the car that took Hannah."

"We'll get to the bottom of this," he said, kneeling with me, trying to comfort my emotions as they gushed out of control.

"I'm sorry for what we done," a steady voice came from outside.

Without hesitation, I shot upward, my gun drawn and leveling on the source of the voice. Tommy Fitzgerald and his wife stood at the barn doors, their hands filled with groceries, the crumpling sound of shopping bags sounding as they reared back from the sight of me.

"Detective White!" Jericho demanded, a reproachful look in his eyes. "Casey, please! Lower your weapon."

"Tommy. She's the woman I told you about," the lady said. Her eyes were clear, and in them I saw the woman in the rearview mirror, the same grim smirk I'd seen when I tumbled onto the hot pavement chasing after Hannah. "She shouldn't be here."

"Stow it, Sheila," Tommy Fitzgerald demanded. He focused on me then. "Please put the gun down. I'll tell you everything."

I glanced at the picture from the wall, trying to recognize Tommy Fitzgerald holding my daughter. The man had aged a hundred years since then and looked old enough to be Sheila's father.

"Tommy?" Sheila asked, her voice pitching high in a maniacal song. "She ain't listening, Tommy."

"I said stow it!"

From the corner of my eye I saw Jericho thumbing his phone, whispering into it, telling the radio dispatch to send cars. "Police are on their way," he called.

My skin was hot, the barn suddenly like an oven, my pulse racing, a stampede of horses trampling my brain. I ran around the car, my gun aimed at them. "Bags down and get on your knees."

"Tommy!" she screamed, but her cries quickly grew into laughter. "I told you, Tommy, we should have moved away from here."

"Don't you want to know?" Tommy Fitzgerald asked, imploring. "Don't you want to know what happened to your daughter?"

"Get down!" I screamed.

Tommy Fitzgerald went to his knees with a grunt, the groceries dropping, scattering, canned peaches rolling beneath the car.

"Sheila, get down," Tommy pleaded.

"On your knees!" I demanded, wanting to strike the woman, but holding back. She eased down, slow and soundless, all the while keeping her eyes on mine.

Sheila's stare was glassy as she said, "She's my girl. Always. No changing it!"

Her words turned my stomach. "Why? Why did you take my baby?"

"She was mine!"

"It was my fault," Tommy Fitzgerald cried, his face waxy and red. "All of it—"

"Shut the fuck up, Tommy!" his wife screamed. Her husband shrank in the throes of her command. "You said you would take care of it. You promised me!"

"I will, Sheila," he told her. "I'll take care of it for you."

"You can start by answering some questions," Jericho said, lifting the picture frame.

Sheila looked over her shoulder, the distant sound of a siren reaching us. The police were coming.

I needed answers. Desperate to drive the truth out of them, I approached, wanting to punish, but reasoned instead.

"You've already confessed to taking my daughter. That's prison. Could be the rest of your life. But if you cooperate, if you tell us—"

"I killed her!" Tommy Fitzgerald screamed.

"What?"

His words zapped my strength. I stood down, my gun at my side. His wife burst into tears.

"No, no, Tommy," she blubbered. "Patty is alive. Patty is with us. God bless, she is with us!"

"Tell us who you killed, sir?" Jericho asked, his tone shifting to investigative, questioning the man.

I felt weak, and eased myself against the hood of the old car, releasing my gun's trigger, knowing it was an empty threat.

"Who?" I asked, a chill running through me. I'd heard the guilt in his voice and cursed him for making me feel any compassion for him, for the distant understanding in my heart.

"She was your girl's age," he began, his face turning purple and wet, his eyes bulging.

The sight of him had me scared for a moment and I raised my hand, instructing, "Breathe, and start from the beginning." I tried to contain my emotions, tried to sound like Jericho, like we were questioning a suspect, but I was too close, too eager.

"She's my girl," his wife insisted, carrying on. "God gave her to me!"

"Sir?" Jericho insisted.

"My car," he answered. "It was me and my father-in-law, we'd jacked up the front like we'd done a hundred times. But we needed a gasket before we could get started."

I searched the corner of the barn, finding the lift-jack I'd seen earlier, asking, "Your daughter? You were watching her?"

"I was. I shouldn't have kept the car up on the jack. I mean, we hadn't even taken a wrench to it yet. My father-in-law went to town for the part, and I went outside for a smoke. I thought... I thought Patty was with me, swore my daughter was right next to me. God! It was only a minute."

"Oh, Tommy!" Sheila cried with a scream. "No, no, no! Patty is fine, just a troubled spirit is all. We'll fix the house, she didn't mean to burn it. I'll get some paint—" The man's wife rambled on, her words filled with disillusioned plans about making things right.

"Go on," Jericho said. Car tires crunched on gravel outside the barn. He raised his hand for the officers to see him, to tell them to stay.

Tommy Fitzgerald's face was beyond any safe color, his lips pinched and purple with white froth at the corners of his mouth. "There was a terrible crash," he said, shaking his head back and forth. "I felt the ground shudder and rushed back inside, and found... I found the car on top of my little girl."

"You're wrong!" Sheila yelled defiantly, her gaze falling on me, her eyes as alive as the day I'd seen them in the rearview mirror. My mouth went dry, the sight frightening and filling me with a chill. "I found her Tommy! Just like I told you before. Patty likes to wander, but I found her on that woman's lawn."

"She died, Sheila. Her body was broken," Tommy cried. "We were grieving when my wife took the car. But my father-in-law and I never expected her to return with another child."

"My child!" I screamed at him. "And you let your wife just take her?"

"I had no idea who the girl was," he cried, blubbering. "But it was so easy. They looked so much alike. Same hair, same eyes, they could have been sisters. A few months alone, no contact with anyone, and nobody would ever know. They grow so fast at that age."

"We couldn't keep the car here," Sheila muttered clearly. She was composed, her manner focused, her faculties surfacing. "I couldn't keep the car here, not after what it had done. I drove for hours, the windows down, the radio off, looking for the perfect spot for me to destroy it like it had destroyed my child."

"And you saw Hannah?" I asked, knowing what happened next.

"I saw Patty," she answered, her expression slipping. She laughed to herself then, adding, "When I saw Patty again, I knew it had all been a terrible mistake, a big misunderstanding. My baby wandered is all. She likes to wander. I offered her a toy, a teddy bear, her favorite, you know, and then she was with me again. Tommy understood. But my father, he didn't understand, couldn't understand. And he left us."

The years caught up to me then and I went to her, threatening to swing, my mind bargaining between what I wanted to do and knowing what I had to do. Red-and-blue patrol lights skipped into my eyes and I staggered backward.

"You did this!" I cried soulfully. I went to her husband, "And you let her!"

"She's my wife," he said, his face like a tomato. "It was all my fault. And I couldn't let her go to jail, not to prison, not for something I'd done."

"You don't know what you're saying!" his wife snapped, sitting up, a laugh spilling from her lips.

"After a while, I made myself believe what I wanted to believe. It was like it never happened," Tommy said. There was pain in his eyes from the sting of confessing. "And over time, I convinced myself the girl was Patty, that she was my daughter."

"Sir," Jericho interrupted. "What did you do with your daughter's remains?"

"The apple tree," he answered, glumly. I stepped into the light coming through the barn doors and found the small apple tree, sadness squeezing my heart as I understood what it truly was. Beneath the tree and the fallen fruit, the tiny broken body of a girl resembling Hannah was buried, her memory betrayed, her spirit replaced and then forgotten. "You'll find my daughter there."

Patricia Anne Fitzgerald died the day before my daughter was kidnapped. Her body was recovered from a shallow grave beneath the apple tree and sent to Dr. Swales, as Jericho and I finished questioning the girl's mother and father. We could have taken them into custody immediately, could have removed them from the barn as the recovery team dug up the bones. But something in me wanted them to see the truth for themselves, to see what they'd intentionally forgotten all these years. And they did, the husband's weeping a punishing noise as the girl's body was lifted out of the ground.

"I'm so sorry, Patricia," he'd cried. His wife's mouth hung open, stuck in a silent scream. "I'm so, so sorry!"

There are many words for betrayal, many emotions and subsequent desires—and I know, if given the absence of conscience, I could have easily plucked the woman's eyes from her skull and shoved them down her husband's throat.

Instead, I pushed the anger aside, curbing it for now, curbing it for the sake of closing this case. I needed to concentrate on the girls found in the woods, their killer, and continue my search for Hannah. After all, Hannah needed to learn the truth about who she was.

That afternoon, standing in the barn, a scatter of dry dust in the air, breathing in the stale smell of motor oil and hay, I decided I wouldn't leave the Outer Banks until Hannah knew everything.

CHAPTER 57

The station pandemonium had all but disappeared since the trip to the barn, the monitors tuned into a new press conference. The reporters followed Mayor Miller, Ashtole, and Sheriff Petro like lemmings to the courthouse steps. Ashtole fielded questions from reporters, his confidence the best I'd seen, as he cited the criminal activities of the detention center, the seizure of the property, the guards in custody, the safety of the children, and the conclusion of the *ghost* yacht case, including the murder victims found in the woods.

But the press conference was misleading the public. The woods victims' case was yet to be solved. We knew it, but couldn't stop the train that was politics and their answering to the voting public—all in the name of saving the remaining summer vacation days.

As with every case like this, we had to account for the souls at the detention center and had the morbid task of identifying the bodies that had been buried in the garden. With a completed count of the detention center inmates, three girls remained missing, including Hannah, under her name, Patty Fitzgerald.

The center's records indicated the missing girls had been signed out for work releases. Lily's record showed the work release dated back more than a year: she'd be eighteen now, and free of the detention center. Michelle had only been signed out in recent months, but she would also be eighteen now, and free. Hannah's record, however, showed a work release signed in the last week, the date corresponding to Robert Stewart's death.

"Any progress?" I asked Dr. Swales as she and her staff worked an assembly line, reviewing the tread on each of the guards' boots, their hands gloved, lights on their foreheads beaming spotlights like a laser show.

"A work in progress," she answered. "Lend a hand?"

"Maybe in a few," Jericho answered from behind me.

"Hey, I thought you were with your son?" I asked. I had not expected to see him.

"Ryan is busy," he said, a fragile smile appearing, a hint of disappointment showing. "Seems the busier he gets, the less I see of him."

I took his arm, a gentle touch. "Maybe next time, tell him not to make plans."

Dr. Swales saw our interaction, an approving grin on her face.

"I brought some company," he said as I let him go. He motioned to the front.

From the station's entrance, Agent Rivera entered with two of the girls from the detention center, no longer dressed in the jumpsuits. I recognized one: a taller girl with a slender figure, a wing of golden hair covering her face. She'd been in the courtyard, alone during the takedown. What interested me was the way she'd faced the garden as if trying to tell us what to look for. The other girl was shorter with an oval face, her dark hair disheveled in the front, but pulled into a bun in the back, her eyes wide and filled with excitement as she took in everyone and everything around her.

"Girls," I said greeting them. "My name is Detective White."

"Detective," the taller girl said, taking my hand, fingers like pencils and an eye peering from behind her hair. "I'm Geraldine Lloyd."

"My name is Samantha Dawson," the other girl followed, her handshake firm, animated. "Everyone calls me Sammie."

"Take a seat, I'll get you the sodas and chips I promised," Rivera said.

"Ah. Barter system," Jericho joked. Rivera gave him a wink. "Come on, I'll show you to the vending machines."

"Kick the side, you'll get two," someone yelled from over a cubical wall.

"Great influence," Rivera chided. But as she passed, she asked, "Two, you said?"

"Two," came the voice.

I studied the girls' faces, curious what they wanted to talk about. "What brings you girls here?"

"Agent Rivera," Geraldine answered, finding a station monitor, the reporters still calling out questions to Sheriff Petro and Ashtole while the mayor stood in the shadows. An inset window showed a helicopter view of the detention center, its shadow flying across the ground like a great raptor hunting for prey. "Sammie, look, we're on television."

I lost them both to the news report, the inset picture growing to occupy the entire screen. Text scrolled along the bottom, the news crew reporting an explosion at Currituck Sound Juvenile Correctional Facility.

"There you are!" Sammie blurted, pointing to the screen.

"Nah, you can't tell," Geraldine replied.

The newsfeed showed the inmates lining up around the busses, the immigrant children brought there by Harlan sitting on the ground. There were crime-scene technicians, officers, and cadaver dogs sifting through the garden in a body-recovery effort, another gathering of officers around one who'd been taken to the side of a building. That was me. I cursed the news for showing the footage, but was thankful my face was blocked, and hopefully unrecognizable. The video footage should never have been televised, but the operation had been leaked and the coverage had gone viral almost instantly.

"Are those the guards' boots?" Geraldine said, her attention returning, her gaze fixed on Dr. Swales and the small team processing the shoe tread.

"They are."

"Will... will they ever get out?" Sammie asked. Her excitement vanished along with her color. She was scared. "I mean, can they ever get to us again?"

"We won't let that happen," Rivera answered, returning with the soda pop and potato chips. The girls dug in, ripping open the bags, snapping the plastic caps on the bottles. "Tell us about your friend, the one you mentioned was missing."

"Kelli?"

At once, I knew why Rivera brought the girls to see us. They knew Kelli Tate.

I asked, "When did you last see her?"

"She's dead, isn't she?" Sammie asked, moving a thick lock of hair so we could see her face.

Dr. Swales came to the table, having overheard the discussion, and took to the task of delivering news about their friend. "Yes. I'm afraid she is," Swales began. "Were you close?"

"Sorta," Geraldine answered flatly, eager to fish a chip out of the bag. "I mean, when you're inside, you need people. It's safer that way. You can't do the time alone."

"And she was 'people'?" I asked, understanding, but surprised how much the girls sounded like adult inmates I'd interviewed, men and women who'd already served years in prison.

"She was our people," Sammie answered, her mouth full, traces of oil and crumbs on her chin. "We stuck together."

"And her?" I asked nervously, placing the sheet of paper with a copy of Hannah's ID badge in front of them.

"Patty," Geraldine said with a firm nod. She exchanged a look with Sammie then, adding, "Don't know anything else though."

I recognized the girl knew more. I told them, "You won't get in trouble here. We're just trying to understand some things."

"Patty was next," Sammie said, slurping soda, returning a burp and giggling with Geraldine the way girls do. They may have stuck together for the sake of safety, but if there was any sadness for Kelli Tate, I didn't see it.

"Next?"

"To go."

"And this guard?" Jericho asked, placing a picture of Robert Stewart on the table.

They nodded in agreement.

"Good dude. He helped Patty a lot," Geraldine began. "They were together before—"

Sammie finished for her, "Before Patty blew up her house. He got her out of the center, but then Kelli got picked."

"He helped her escape?" Rivera asked, seeking clarification.

Sammie shrugged while Geraldine shook her head.

"Patty said they were going to take off together. Go west or south. I don't remember," Sammie said.

"Are they dead?" Geraldine asked, her chewing having stopped.

"He is," Jericho answered.

"Oh shit," Sammie exclaimed, straightening his picture. "He was always nice."

"And this?" I asked, placing Hannah's charm bracelet in front of them, the evidence bag crinkling as I flattened it on the table.

"That's Patty's," Geraldine said.

"She'd snuck it inside when she got sentenced," confirmed Sammie.

"Was she friends with Kelli too?"

The girls nodded together, but I was losing their attention, the press conference on screen stealing them from me, citing the magnificent work by the FBI and the local officials to end the horrible nightmares at the detention center.

I saw the girls exchange a look, their interest in the soda pop and chips gone.

"That's him," Sammie said to Geraldine. "He's like someone famous or something."

"He looks different on TV," Geraldine answered Sammie, their conversation private, excluding us. "Look how he's dressed."

"Who?" Jericho asked, going to the monitor. "Girls, do you recognize one of these men?"

"He comes to the detention center, and he—" Sammie stopped, her body tensing, reluctant to say more.

"You're safe girls," Rivera assured them.

Geraldine wet her lips, wiping the crumbs off, and continued for Sammie, "He used to visit. But then he started hurting the girls he picked."

"He picked?" Swales asked, recoiling with disgust. "Hurt them?"

"He hurt me, and he told me they'd kill me if I ever said anything," Sammie answered, her voice breaking.

"Who?" Jericho asked again, raising his voice.

The girl sank into her chair.

"Show them," Geraldine said, urging her friend. "Someone needs to know."

Sammie wiped her glassy eyes and stood, opening her shirt collar enough so we could see her shoulder. I recognized the scar at once, as did Dr. Swales. It was a bite mark resembling those found on the girls in the woods.

"Who did that to you?" I asked, a rise in my voice.

"He did," Sammie said, fear returning to her face.

"Often?" Dr. Swales asked, fingers on her lips and shock in her eyes. The girls nodded as one.

"How often?" I asked, seeing a connection forming between the woods' killer and the detention center after all.

"Every couple of weeks," Geraldine answered. She put her hands around her neck, adding, "But then he got rough, biting and other stuff. They wouldn't let him around us anymore."

"One of the guards?" I asked, confused, seeing Jericho shake his head as he listened.

"Not a guard," Sammie said, then pointed to the monitor, to the men answering questions. "It's him. The one next to the microphone."

Jericho stood wide-eyed, asking, "Are you sure?" He pressed his finger on the screen, as the mayor took to the podium. He was about to ask another question but stepped back when the mayor turned to face a reporter. On the side of his neck, a large gauzy bandage covered a wound. He repositioned the microphone, a similar bandage on his right hand, the position indicative of defensive wounds. "Casey, do you see that?"

"Blood and tissue found beneath the fingernails," I said softly, my heartbeat increasing, thinking of Stephanie Marsh. "We'll be able to get a match."

"Yeah, that's him," Geraldine confirmed.

"How many girls?" Rivera asked.

"There were five of us he liked the most, but when he got rough, we never saw him again. Not till today," Geraldine said.

"Dr. Swales?" I asked.

"I'm already on it," she answered, inspecting the bite mark. "It's older, scarring over. I'll try to get an impression, test it for a match."

"An impression?" Sammie asked, retreating, her hand up and guarding as she covered herself.

Dr. Swales coaxed Sammie back to her chair and knelt in front of her. "It's okay. It's not at all painful."

"And Patty?" I asked the girls, afraid to hear what they might say about my daughter.

Sammie nodded. "She got hurt real bad."

"We thought he killed her," Geraldine continued. "That's when they stopped letting him come around."

Their words spun in my head. I sat back in my chair with heartache clouding my mind.

"Girls," Rivera said, her eyes glistening. "I am so sorry this happened to you. And I promise, there will be justice."

I turned to Jericho, clearing my head and remembering the view from over the valley. To one side, I'd seen the detention center. To the other, the estate grounds. It was a short walk across the property line. "The mayor's estate…"

He nodded in understanding, and then repeated what he'd told me before, "The land was donated by the mayor, and then he helped fund the girls' juvenile detention center."

"Makes you wonder what his real motives were," Rivera said, her comment in line with my thinking as she sent a flurry of texts, likely setting up all the necessary warrants we'd need.

"It does make you wonder," I added, stifling the rage that came with learning what happened to my daughter. If I dwelled on what the mayor did, even for a moment, I'd react. We couldn't afford for that to happen. "Over the years, how many girls have been victimized?"

Rivera added, "It could be the mayor didn't count on the Wilts and the guards messing with his backyard playground, changing things with the auction site."

The station was silent a moment as the mayor answered a reporter's question about the bandage on his neck. He laughed it off with a comment, implying he had a small procedure to remove a suspicious growth on his neck. "Always wear your sunblock," he said. "Especially when visiting our beautiful Outer Banks, our beaches and our boardwalks."

"We're still missing something," Jericho said. We all faced him as he paused to examine the figure on the television. "The kidnapped girls from the woods, where have they been?"

"The estate," I said, realizing the ramifications of what we were about to do. There were still girls missing, still the chance they could be alive. "We have to go there."

CHAPTER 58

We had enough for a warrant, enough to search the mayor's estate, and to question his activities relating to the detention center. There was the bite mark on Sammie Dawson, along with her statement, and the statement from Geraldine Lloyd. But Agent Rivera had to secure the warrant first, which meant reviews and phone calls and signatures. Girls were missing, possibly imprisoned, and the clock was ticking.

In the commotion to prepare, Jericho had also received a vague follow-up about the antique nightgowns, answering a feeler he'd placed a day earlier. It was from one of the oldest cleaning services in the Outer Banks, and if they identified the mayor's estate, it could make the case.

I thought I'd die when I heard of the attack on Hannah, to know the mayor did that to her, that he was inside her, and to know she could have been one of the girls discovered in the woods. There was a level of rage that scared me, and made me question if I should leave my badge and gun behind in the car. I was alone, having slipped away, leaving everyone behind to do their tasks. We needed the paperwork, but there was nothing that said I couldn't venture to the mayor's estate and ask questions. After all, the mayor had invited me. To anyone who'd query it, I was following up on the mayor's invitation. With the evidence collected from Stephanie's body, I was sure we'd get an arrest and a conviction. But I needed to see him face to face.

As I stood in front of the estate doors, their height towering over me, I thought of the missing girls, my mind set on the possibility of finding them inside. I saw their innocence staring back at me from the old case-file pictures, and I imagined what they might look like today, believing strongly they were still alive. Setting aside warrants and the nightgowns, it was the mayor who'd kidnapped them.

"This way, ma'am," a portly woman said to me in broken English. She'd eagerly swung the door open when I'd flashed my badge. I'd decided to wear my gun too, but kept the holster secured.

I followed her inside, answering, "Gracias."

The woman was dressed in a housekeeper's uniform, a style that was fifty years removed of anything modern. The cloth had a paisley design and was long enough to cover her knees. A white apron hung from her front with straps winding around her waist. Her shoes caught my eyes too—they were like something my grandmother would have worn—white leather, short heels, an oxford style made for work, but uncomfortable.

The housekeeper's outfit complemented the style of the mansion. The estate retained a formal look, but was decades old, unchanged, and more like a museum than a home. The woman showed me to a room and left me alone. I crinkled my nose, the air thick with a damp must.

Stained windows stood twelve-feet high, a cover of heavy drapes drawn in front of them, casting bands of daylight into the receiving room. There were red-velvet chairs with gold trim, and an enormous leather sofa in the middle of the floor, plus a fireplace on the far wall big enough to fit my car inside. A white bearskin rug lay in front of the sofa, complete with the bear's head, its black eyes like marbles. And in the corners of the room, there stood statues, stone gods and goddesses, their eyes pale and lifeless.

The walls were covered in portraits and paintings, where I saw the history of the Outer Banks, the ownership of the land, the selling of properties, all the transactions by a single family. Standing in this room, I understood what Jericho had meant when he said the family was an institution.

Turning to the sofa, my heart skipped when I saw a baby's blanket on it. I picked it up and brought it my nose, the smell like sweet breath, a memory of when Hannah was only a few months old.

Cheryl Parry's baby, I thought, realizing where her baby had been born, knowing the child had never been in the woods. A cry came next. A soft baby's cry. I clutched the blanket.

"Oh this is unfortunate," the mayor said, entering the room, his gaze fixed on my hands and what was in them. Seeing him again, seeing how he towered over me, his size easily matched the man we'd chased in the woods. "Señorita Belleza was not to have let anyone inside without my escort."

"Sir," I began, but the mayor waved his hand. The baby's cry grew louder, bouncing along the stone walls. "Sir, can you explain the baby?"

"I'm keeping company," he answered plainly, roaming the greeting room with a slow gait, and then picking the swaddling blanket from my hands with a pinch of his fingers. The gauze bandage on his neck was crusty and yellow in the middle, the injury weeping. "I have company from out of state, distant cousins."

"Would you mind having them join us?" I asked.

"Join us?" he asked, repeating my words. "Well, I'm afraid I can't do that."

"Why?"

"You see, they've left for the weekend. They went north to Virginia's wine country for some tasting and sightseeing."

"And they left their baby?" I asked, challenging his story.

He raised his brow, "Why not?" he asked, one brow raised. "I'm quite capable."

I continued, "It would help if you would allow me to see the baby."

"No," he said, his brow narrowing in a frown as he went to the window and peered outside. A moment's silence ended with his asking, "You came alone?"

The hair on my arms and neck rose, a tremble in my gut. I considered my gun, but held still, insisting, "My colleagues are on their way."

"I think not," he said, removing his jacket and stepping around the couch. "Even if they are, they'll find nothing here."

"I'm going to need to see the baby."

The mayor cupped his ear, silence coming from the halls and the rooms of his mansion. "What baby?" he asked, playing games. Another cry. He raised his hands with a smile.

I rushed to exit the room, to follow the cries, the mayor side-stepping until he was in front of me, his arms stretched wide, his body eclipsing mine.

"It seems we're not going anywhere," he said, his hot breath in my ear. Fear squeezed my heart. He sensed it and let out a laugh. I jumped to the side, but was caught as he clapped my shoulder and held me, sliding his other hand behind my neck. My skin crawled beneath his groping touch. "Am I frightening you?"

"I need to see the baby," I insisted, my voice like a whimper, my legs shaking.

"I am frightening you," he exclaimed. He sniffed the air like a dog. "Yes."

I took hold of my gun, my thumb slipping to the safety snap. "You need to let me go."

He shoved his hand onto mine, locking my grip. "Oh, I don't think so," he answered, his expression changing as he licked his lips, his eyes cold and still. Before I could say another word, he was on me like a spider on its prey, gripping and spinning me around until we were out of the room and I was facing a spiraling stairwell, the steps leading down from the hall, the first turn entering darkness like a dungeon. From below, the crying began again. The baby was down there.

I raised my arms, trying to slip from his suffocating grasp, but the mayor was fast and laughed at the attempt as he easily hoisted me into the air, my toes striking the tiled walls, leaving me unable to catch my footing.

"You'll make a beautiful addition," he said, handling me as I let out a scream. His words stuck me raw as I understood his intentions.

Coming alone was a mistake. I had one chance, my gun's safety buckle released. I pulled my weapon and targeted the top of his head. With everything I had, I struck, the butt of my gun opening his scalp with a sickening thwack. He grunted once, his breath wheezy, his eyes rolling into his skull as we tumbled into a pile. The crash onto the granite floor stole my air briefly, his body on top of mine, my lungs pinched.

Daylight spinning, I followed the baby's wails, listened as it begged for me to get up, to stand, to run. I made it to my feet, my hands on my phone, dialing 9-1-1. I glanced at the bars on the screen, the signal weak, but kept the line open, knowing if the call went through, they'd send help.

I followed the crying, my feet like lead balloons. The mayor groaned as I escaped the room and came to the winding set of granite stairs, the baby's cries coming up from the darkness. I took to them, the heels of my shoes clapping each step, leading me into a larger room. It was more modern than the upstairs—dusky-blue carpet, drywall with simple sconces. There were empty playpens in one corner, changing tables next to them. And a crib with a colorful mobile dangling above it. The walls were covered with painted characters from *Sesame Street* and other childhood cartoon delights. I stepped around a litter of toys meant for toddlers, too old for a baby.

Another child, I considered, and then corrected myself, realizing the room looked like a daycare center. *Other children?*

On the opposite wall there were cages, the kind used for dogs and other animals. Inside, there were metal pans holding small buckets and a scouring brush. But there were no pets, no animals anywhere. I thought of Dr. Swales explaining how some of the victims' growth had been stunted, their spine curved. The victims had been held in the cages. But for how long? How long does it take to do that to a person?

I found an old television and a row of doors on the closest wall, each of them with a padlock, solid, heavy, a four-number dial combination on the bottom. There were crayon drawings tacked to the doors, child drawings with stick figures. The first drawing was ancient, a decade old, the masking tape having yellowed, and a single name, Dianne.

"Dianne Taylor," I whispered, one of the last girls on the list of cold cases. I knocked gently, my hands pressed against the door-panel. "Dianne?"

There was a commotion on the other side, a young girl's voice, and then a woman's, shadows appeared beneath the door, two pairs, standing inches from me.

"Who are you?"

"My name is Detective White," I told her, lightness in my chest from the excitement. "Are you Dianne Taylor?"

"I'm Dianne," she said. She mumbled some words, sounding annoyed, and then answered, "But I don't remember my last name. It might be Taylor."

"That's okay," I told her, trying to work the lock, my hands shaking badly as my pulse raced. "Do you know the lock's combination?"

"The lock?" she asked.

I heard another voice then, the child's. "Momma, who that?"

"She's going to help us," Dianne answered. It was good to hear Dianne recognizing I was there to help. Maybe she understood she'd been kidnapped, that she was being held. In cases like this, there was always a risk of a captive siding with their captor, even defending them.

I scanned the other doors. There were six in all; the last two open, their lights turned off. He had four girls, and possibly more children. The baby's cry grew stronger, it was likely coming from behind one of the locked doors.

When's your birthday? I thought wildly, then remembered it from Dianne's case file. I rolled the metal wheels, dialing in the four digits, and jerked the cold lump of metal. The lock remained fixed in place.

"When is your girl's birthday?" I called out.

"My girl, Gina?"

"Gina, that's a lovely name," I told her, trying to establish a trust. "What is Gina's birthday?"

"He let me name her," Dianne said, her voice slow, groggy. "I think it was March twelve? But I don't know, it's just what I remember them saying when she came out of me."

"Zero, three, one, two," I said, dialing the combination, jerking as hard as I could. The lock remained.

Footsteps on the tile steps echoed against stone walls, the pace quickening. I reached for my gun, but then remembered another date from Dianne's case file. He wouldn't have used their birthdays, he would have used the day of the kidnapping. I dialed in the date—zero, six, one and one. The lock broke free, and I sleeved the metal rod though the plate, releasing the door. "I got it—"

There was a crash then, an enormous weight on top of me, squeezing the air from my body and pinning my arms beneath me. My head was slammed into the carpeted floor with a spray of stars punching my sight, their shine swinging wildly in suffocating darkness, threatening to steal the life from my mind.

"I'm glad you weren't killed on that bridge," a voice spoke into my ear, his breath humid with the smell of cigarettes. "I've been watching you, Detective White. You're older than I like, but a very fine addition indeed. Your daughter was wonderful."

Repulsed, I dared to move. There came another strike, and his words, his presence, faded in and out, my consciousness crippled by the blow. Somewhere I heard cloth tearing, and felt a strange tugging on my shoulders and arms. There was the touch of cool air on my exposed skin. The odd sensation struck a dire fear in my soul, a fear of what he was going to do.

I could barely move as the mayor's body tensed and hardened, keeping me pinned to the ground. His breathing turned heavy, his hand on the back of my head, pressing my face into the floor. My mind began to clear when I felt him loosen my pants, wrenching my belt, the denim fighting to stay in place. There was cold around my middle where he'd torn away my clothing.

He cursed as he struggled and I strained to turn my head to see him, his body lifting above mine, his head poised like a coiling snake, his round face red, his lips shiny with spit as he shifted into position and struck me again.

In that moment, I felt what the other girls had felt. I felt the power of his teeth, felt them dig into my skin, sink into my flesh, his head wriggling back and forth. I screamed, it was blood-curdling, tears springing from my eyes, my legs kicking to buck his weight off me. He reared up again, blood running from his mouth and onto his chin. The pain was vicious, the agony sweeping. I jerked and spun violently to try to get away.

There were feet. In the dim view of consciousness, I saw what had to have been Dianne's feet, her child's beside hers, their skin like ivory, the tips of their toes pink, their shadows cast onto the wall along with the cartoon figures. In Dianne's hand I saw the lock. She raised it high above her as the mayor licked the blood on his lips with a satisfied grunt coming from the back of his throat. Dianne lifted up onto her toes and swung her arms, striking with enough force to send his head crashing into mine, the room exploding with a flash of light.

"I hit him," she shrieked, jumping up and down in celebration.

Dianne's girl knelt in front of me, her face turned sideways, auburn-colored hair falling to the carpet, dimples appearing with a shy smile, her blue eyes shiny. Her tiny finger came next, pressing the tip of my nose, with a word, "Beep." She giggled. I tried to smile with her, but struggled to stay conscious.

"Hi," I told her, pushing up onto my arms enough to roll the mayor's dead weight from me. I struggled to take a shallow breath and then pushed again, freeing my hips and legs. I was able to breathe deeper, but the stars returned to my eyes, zipping from one side to the next, comically chasing the dark.

Dianne knelt next to her daughter, her fingers near the bite mark on my shoulder. Although the woman was no longer the child from the pictures in her case file, I could see who she was once. She found my eyes and added, "He took others. But some are gone."

"I know." She let me hold her hand. But before I could say more, I heard the trample of feet and voices and shouting. It was Agent Rivera and Jericho and so many more, the chaos becoming indecipherable.

"Call for an ambulance!" Rivera yelled. I smelled her body wash, a mix of orange and bergamot, and felt her touch my back, gentle, caring. "Casey, help is on the way."

"They're here," I told her, fighting to stay awake. "The girls. They're here."

"We know," she said. "We have help on the way."

"Jericho?"

"I'm here," he said, his face near mine, his eyes red. He swiped at them. "Damn you for coming alone."

"A match?" I asked, my words slurred. "The nightgowns?"

"They were," he told me, his face fading.

"Oh that's good," I answered, drifting, an image of the antique nightgowns coming to me.

There were more footfalls. Many more. We'd saved someone today, saved a child from a future nightmare. More than anything though, I needed to close my eyes—my mind needed to go to some other place. The pain in my shoulder faded. The ache in my head became little more than a thing I remembered happening. The room disappeared as a baby's cry returned. I closed my eyes and listened. It was a good cry.

CHAPTER 59

I survived. The mayor died a day later. The blow to his head wasn't the cause of death though. He'd suffered a heart attack while being treated, his head being stitched where Dianne Taylor had opened it, his lawyers surrounding his hospital bed and fending off District Attorney Ashtole as charges were brought against him. The charges were historic, pitting Mayor Jonathon Miller as one of the country's worst serial killers.

Cheryl Parry's baby was found, fourth door from the end. Cheryl and Ruby's parents got to meet their grandchild, a baby boy. Dianne Taylor was also reunited with her parents, a news report seen across the country with Dianne introducing her daughter Gina to her tearful family.

There were two other survivors found in the basement. Lily Bennet was the first, she'd disappeared from the detention center more than a year before, the week of her eighteenth birthday. The detention-center paperwork had her listed as having gone on a work release, and then never returning. Similarly, Michelle Clarke had disappeared a month before her eighteenth birthday, the paperwork showing the same note. The other girls, those the mayor took from the detention center, and those he'd kidnapped years earlier, had all died by his hand, their remains buried on the estate grounds.

When the searching began, the expectation was to find the bodies we'd accounted for. To our horror, to the nation's horror, bodies were discovered everywhere, their deaths dating back decades. It would be weeks before every victim was found, some remaining unidentified.

During the recovery, a map was created to show where the bodies were buried. With the house at the center, the burials fanned outward like a spider's web. The FBI believed Jonathan Miller had run out of places to bury his victims, which is what led to his using the woods.

Of the recovered victims, one would say more than any other. It was the body of a young girl, her bones discovered closest to the main house. Her clothes, and the state of her corpse, indicated her death occurred forty years earlier. Dr. Swales found the old case: she was Sherri Foster, the missing daughter of the Miller family's old housekeeper. The investigator at the time concluded the girl had wandered into the neighboring woods, become lost, and had succumbed to the elements. It was believed Sherri Foster may have been the mayor's first victim. He was a teenager at the time and, for all we knew, his parents may have helped cover up the gory details.

We wouldn't know everything until well into the fall. Justice for what Jonathon Miller had done came too swiftly with his death. What justice could be served though? A single life for the dozens of women and children he'd murdered?

In one ironic twist, Jonathon Miller's family estate and fortune would go to his only living relatives, his children—Dianne Taylor's daughter Gina and Cheryl Parry's baby. It would require DNA testing to prove the mayor had fathered the children, but this would be a minor technicality.

Tommy Fitzgerald and his wife were arrested too. While the charges of kidnapping my daughter were clear, the death of their daughter was different. The story of the lift-jack and the tragic accident with Tommy's car was found to be the truth. Through some consumer investigation, Nichelle was able to identify a defect in the jack that had been reported, and that a manufacturer's recall was issued at one time.

Tommy Fitzgerald could never have known what would happen when they'd hoisted the front of the car into the air. District Attorney Ashtole told us there were only minor charges filed for the death of their daughter Patricia, but the two would face a lot of time for Hannah's kidnapping, as well as for the cover-up that followed. I trusted Ashtole would work everything out, the details of jurisdiction, and extradition, and all that went into whichever court had to be involved with any final rulings.

Robert Stewart's murderer was found too. And it was the finer details in the boot's tread and the print that pointed the FBI to the guard who'd held him down and suffocated him. As much as everyone suspected Jimmy Wilts to be the murderer, it was his third in command who'd done the deed—the same man who'd blown up the shed on the detention-center grounds and attempted to crush my car and drive me off a bridge.

An hour after confessing to his crimes, he'd surprised everyone and turned state's evidence on Jimmy Wilts, including giving evidence that went to the heart of the criminal organization. In protective custody along with Harlan, and their testimony given, it was unlikely the two would ever be seen again.

After the attack by Jonathan Miller, I'd stayed the night in the hospital, my head injury exacerbating issues from the car wreck on the bridge. The momentum of the first concussion had suddenly fed into the second blow, the two broiling into one and knocking me out of sorts until the next day. Even then, I stayed close to Jericho, my arm constantly with his, intertwined, the two of us holding each other up as the sad day of Robert Stewart's funeral came to be.

We gathered with Gladys Stewart and her family, along with Robert's friends, a steady rain turning the late-summer day gray and cold. Attendees gathered around Robert's grave, dressed in black, rain dripping from a sea of umbrellas, the sight of them tearful.

The funeral ended quietly, my hopes of seeing Hannah doused as the last of Robert's friends and family went to their cars, Gladys eagerly inviting everyone to the diner where she'd reserved the rear dining room.

"Thank you for coming with me," Jericho said as I undid his collar button and loosened his tie. "I'm not good with funerals. Usually avoid them, but this one, for Robert—"

"I know," I interrupted, standing up on my toes, tugging on his jacket and bringing him close enough to kiss. I didn't hold back either, moving into his body, embracing him. I wanted to comfort him, knowing the funeral would be difficult. "You did okay."

He returned my kiss, pressing hard, and then asked, "Does this mean you'll be staying?"

"It does," I told him, having held off on telling him my plans. I wanted to see the mayor's case through to the end, helping until the last victim was recovered. And there was my daughter. My heart ached at the sight of Robert Stewart's grave, and Hannah's not showing scared me. "If Hannah is here, then I want to be here."

"And?" he asked, raising his brow.

I gushed, recognizing the look on his face, and letting myself enjoy what I was feeling for him, the newness of it, the flirting and the excitement. "And, Mr. Jericho Flynn, I'd like to get to know you better too. A lot better."

"I'd like that." He turned around briefly, his gaze falling onto Robert Stewart's casket, the gravediggers folding a green tarp, uncovering a mound of dirt, their shovels at the ready to finish the man's burial. As though the clouds had wept with us, they had now stopped and parted, a ray of sunlight appearing. Songbirds flittered from tree to tree, the leaves turning over, their edges showing the end of summer.

"It's a sad day, but it's turning out beautiful."

"I thought she'd be here," I said, disappointed.

"Let's give it another ten and then head to the reception."

"Won't have to," I told him, squeezing his arm, urging him to look past the graveyard toward the trees behind the headstones. "Over there."

Hannah stood alone. I saw the tattoo and sunlight glinting from her piercings. She was too far to run after, and a single step would lead her to somewhere hidden beyond the trees.

"That's her," he said, surprise in his voice. "I think she saw us."

"Yeah, but she's a safe distance," I told him, every part of me wanting to run to her and take her into my arms.

"What do you want to do?" he asked.

I began to answer, but then stopped when Hannah raised her arm as if to wave. A moment later, she was gone, her swift motion taking my breath with her, and leaving me with a disappointment so massive there were no words to say.

CHAPTER 60

In my absence, my wall hadn't changed, save for the fresh collection of dust on the strung yarn and the picture I'd pinned up the day I left. Hannah's photo remained at the center, red yarn extending in every direction. And in return, the yellow threads bloomed low toward the floor and rose as high as the ceiling where it often changed to blue, the clues fading eventually to nothing.

But today was different. I had Jericho by my side. The drive to my old apartment was a quiet one, winter turning the outside drab and colorless, my mind occupied, nerves flipping, concerns rising as the destination neared. How would he react when seeing the person I used to be?

"This isn't who I am anymore," I told him. Jericho put his hand on my back, the bandaging gone, the wounds on his arm healing. "It's who I was."

"Are you ready to do this?" he asked, intending to help me dismantle years of work. His eyes were wandering, seeing the history of my daughter's kidnapping, the investigations, its entirety, complete, and in one place. Until now, he'd only had his imagination and what I'd told him about the wall.

"Yeah," I told him, pinching a thumbtack and yanking it out of the plaster.

"Let's do this," Jericho exclaimed, reaching above us with both hands, unraveling long spans of yarn, the pictures and notes drifting around us like snow. "Let me know when to box or bag?"

I gazed at the cardboard boxes on the floor, the crumpled plastic trash bags next to them. The boxes were to finish my packing. I'd be taking them back to the Outer Banks, along with my gun and shield, which also had a new home. Once the dust had settled on the detention center and Jonathon Miller's case, Chief Peter Pryce made me an offer to stay on full-time.

Around here, there's nothing more permanent than something temporary, he'd jokingly told me. I shook his hand and gladly accepted the job, having resigned my position at my old station.

"Bag," I sighed. "There's nothing to save here."

Having Jericho stand with me softened the scars on my heart. And in time, I believed it would help me find Hannah, and maybe soften hers too, help her heal and leave the past in the past.

Time takes time, Jericho had told me when he woke up after his surgery. At first, I didn't understand what he meant by the comment. But watching him rehab his arm and do the hard work to regain what was lost, I finally understood.

"Thank you," I said, my voice breaking as I put my arm around him. I borrowed his words then, telling him, "Time takes time."

When the wall was gone, the original color showing fully like a painter's empty canvas, I expected a pang of remorse or even some sadness, but I felt none of it. Instead, I only wanted to get on the road and to go home.

This chapter of my life was over. My next chapter waited for me in the Outer Banks. A mother's love is about suffering. It's also about hope and belief. I had my daughter to search for, and if Hannah was there, I would never leave.

A LETTER FROM
B.R. SPANGLER

I want to say a huge thank you for choosing to read *Where Lost Girls Go*. If you enjoyed it, and want to keep up to date with all my latest releases, just sign up at the following link. Your email address will never be shared and you can unsubscribe at any time.

www.bookouture.com/br-spangler

I hope you loved *Where Lost Girls Go*, and if you did, I would be very grateful if you could write a review. I'd love to hear what you think, and it makes such a difference helping new readers to discover one of my books for the first time.

I love hearing from my readers—you can get in touch on my Facebook page, through Twitter, Goodreads, or my website.

Thanks,
B.R. Spangler

authorbrianspangler

@BR_Spangler

brspangler.com

ACKNOWLEDGMENTS

While working on this novel, I was aided by several individuals to whom I wish to offer my immense gratitude and appreciation. Thank you for reading early drafts of book one, and for offering critiques and encouragement. As always, your feedback has helped to shape the story.

To Chris Cornely Razzi, Monica Spangler, Chris Patchell, Ann Spangler, and so many others for providing invaluable feedback, and helping me recognize the potential of this book.

Also, a thank you to Ellen Gleeson, Peta Nightingale, Kim Nash, and the wonderful team at Bookouture. I am fortunate to work with each of you and grateful for the help with this book.

A special thanks to my editor Ellen Gleeson, for all the amazing feedback and contributions and plot challenges which helped to elevate this story.

Made in the USA
Monee, IL
26 July 2024